MW01077510

BROKEN
SOULS
AND
BONES

BROKEN SOULS AND BONES

LJ ANDREWS

ACE
NEW YORK

ACE
Published by Berkley
An imprint of Penguin Random House LLC
1745 Broadway, New York, NY 10019
penguinrandomhouse.com

Book design by Daniel Brount
Map illustration by Alexis Seabrook

Export edition ISBN: 9780593954188

Library of Congress Cataloging-in-Publication Data

Names: Andrews, LJ, author.
Title: Broken souls and bones / LJ Andrews.
Description: New York: Ace, 2025. | Series: The Stonegate series; 1
Identifiers: LCCN 2024041236 (print) | LCCN 2024041237 (ebook) |
ISBN 9780593818671 (hardcover) | ISBN 9780593818695 (ebook)
Subjects: LCGFT: Fantasy fiction. | Romance fiction. | Novels.
Classification: LCC PS3601.N55268 B76 2025 (print) |
LCC PS3601.N55268 (ebook) | DDC 813/.6—dc23/eng/20241018
LC record available at https://lccn.loc.gov/2024041236
LC ebook record available at https://lccn.loc.gov/2024041237

Printed in the United States of America
1st Printing

The authorized representative in the EU for product safety and compliance is
Penguin Random House Ireland, Morrison Chambers, 32 Nassau Street,
Dublin D02 YH68, Ireland, https://eu-contact.penguin.ie.

To those who won't admit they wish the love interest was the villain every time. I see you.

Broken Souls and Bones contains dark themes and topics that might not be suitable for all readers. Your mental health matters.

This book contains mentions of the following: enslavement, attempted sexual assault, threats of assault, mutilation, torture, past abuse of a child, family abandonment, explicit sexual content, gore, murder, and violence.

PROLOGUE

THE FERAL BAY OF THE KING'S HOUNDS STIRRED HER FROM the nothing. Mists tangled around knobby branches and the sting of lingering heat from the flames still burned in her eyes.

"Keep those closed." Leather-wrapped fingers brushed over her lashes. "Don't let anyone see the silver in those eyes, girl. Hear me?"

The voice was hoarse and rough, older than hers but not as deep as her pap's.

"We get snatched, then we're dead. Maybe we shouldn't have done it." A new voice, a boy's that was young enough it cracked and squeaked, uncertain if it was yet a man's tone or still a child's.

"Quiet. We're here now, and we're seeing it through," snapped the first. "Get yourself into the damn shadows and stay down. Go. *Go.*"

A petulant protest from the second followed, but in the end the scrape of boots faded into the briars of the wood and was lost in the mists. The girl shifted and whimpered, muscles aching from running. Her mother told her to run—screamed at her to do it—and not look back.

Ropes held her tightly when she shifted, trying to break free, all at once desperate to find her family.

Through the haze in her mind she recalled the cruel sound of the door cracking against the wall, the iron and bronze blades cutting through the air, seeking flesh to split. She recalled the screams and blood.

So much blood.

"Stop fidgeting, godsdammit."

She froze. Those ropes keeping her bound were arms. And her cheek was pressed to cold leather that reeked of ash and sweat and the bite of forest mist.

Buried beneath a dark cowl she could make out a stubbled chin. Not bearded in long double braids and bone beads like her pap's, but a ghost of a beard was there.

She wanted to cry out, to plead with the man to let her be. There were straps of leather for knives and weapons over his shoulders, much the same as the raiders who burned her village. Fear choked off her pleas into nothing but jagged whimpers.

"Not a word, girl," he whispered, and she felt her weak body lower to the chilled forest floor. Brambles and little pebbles jabbed into her ribs. She tried to shift, but those leather-wrapped fingers curled around her chin, tilting her head back. "This'll sting, but it won't last long. Don't make a sound."

A hiss slid through the girl's teeth when a sharp bite of pain lanced across her throat. Through hooded lashes, she watched the faceless man pull back a knife. He mumbled strange words and brushed his fingers through something wet and hot on her neck.

She trembled, keeping still, terrified he might use the edge of his blade to finish her off.

In the next breath, her eyes fluttered, heavy with fatigue, and his sturdy arms scooped her up once again.

The fear burning in her veins faded to something gentler, something calm. Enough, the girl thought she might fall into a deep sleep.

Until her body shifted and she was handed over to new arms, thicker and smellier.

"She going to talk?" A smoke-burned rasp of a new voice broke the darkness.

"I've made certain she won't recall much of anything about this night. See that she's forgotten from others' memories."

"With what you be payin', I'll bury her in the realm of souls if you want. Won't be found, this one. You've my word."

Her pulse raced, her mind grew frantic, but her body kept still when heavy steps thudded across wood, and somewhere beneath it all was the lap of the tides and the smell of brine and rotting scales.

With a grunt and a breath of smoking spices in her face, the girl was nestled beside rigging and damp linens.

"Blessed little barnon, you are." The man spoke in common tongue, a dialect known throughout the three kingdoms and over the Night Ledges where feral folk claimed no king. Doubtless he was a tide wanderer, a soul without a land to call his own. "They coulda torn out your skinny little throat."

His thumping steps plodded away over wooden boards—a longship—she was on a boat.

No, she couldn't leave. There were people she was leaving behind. But . . . who?

As though the thick mists of the wood dug into her skull, the girl could not recall the fading faces in her mind. It was merely a feeling, a sense there was something—someone—she was forgetting.

Before the weight of exhaustion drew her into a murky sleep, the girl saw a darkly clad figure on the water's edge, a glow of flames at his back.

Across the breast of his leather jerkin was a double-headed raven. The emblem of Dravenmoor—the enemy kingdom. The land behind the raiders.

By the gods, they'd found her and the curse in her eyes had finally destroyed her entire world.

ROARK

THE BOY'S DEATH WAS MY FAULT.

Uther was found facedown in the river near the stone walls of the royal fortress before dawn. A new Stav Guard in the unit assigned to my watch, a mere boy of eighteen. The body was rent down the middle, chest flayed, ribs torn apart like a cracked goose egg.

He was sent to the hall of the gods in Salur too soon.

The flat cart holding the young guard's corpse rolled past a line of stoic Stav. The palace healer attempted to cover his pulpy face, tinted blue from a night in the water, but when the wheel struck a stone in the path, the linen pulled back.

My fists curled, digging into the callused flesh of my palms.

Uther's pale eyes were left open, too stiff to close, staring lifelessly at the noon sun in a wash of fright. Splatters of blood coated his neck, his lips, his shredded black tunic of the Stav.

"Dravens," a lanky Stav Guard murmured to another. "Had to be. Uther was a bone crafter."

I closed my eyes, despising the truth of it.

Tales of the different crafts of magic were written in the sagas of the first king, the Wanderer, who rescued a daughter of the gods. As a reward, the Wanderer was given pieces of the three mediums of the gods' power—bone, blood, and soul—to strengthen his fledgling kingdom.

Most within the realms of Stìgandr believed the tales were mere fables, but magical craft was real enough.

Bone craft manipulated bone into blades that were nigh unbreakable. It crafted healing tonics from bone powders, and poisons from boiled marrow. Blood craft used blood for spell casts and rune work. Soul craft took power from the dead, and was the common gift of Dravenmoor, the kingdom across the ravines.

Dravens despised King Damir of House Oleg, the king of Jorvandal, insisting he used craft to strengthen his warriors and armories through corrupt and forbidden ways.

I would not say they were wrong, but it did not lessen the rage in my blood that a boy was slaughtered for merely doing his duty.

"If I could, I'd burn every damn Draven on a pike," the guard went on.

His fellow Stav hissed at him to be silent, his gaze finding me—their superior and a Draven.

My blood belonged to the enemy kingdom, but fealty belonged to Jorvandal after being left for dead at the gates of the fortress a dozen winters ago.

But to some, even my own men, I would always be their enemy.

The heel of my boot cracked over the pebbles when I spun into the arched doorway of the Stav quarters, a longhouse built to fit dozens of men.

In the great hall, flames in the inglenook were dying to embers, and drinking horns of thin honey mead were toppled from recent nights of debauchery. Stav trainees had spent the cold months at Stonegate, but after the revelry, they were all now returned to their families and villages across the kingdom to await orders from the king.

A few younger Stav staggered to their feet, readying to greet me. I could reprimand them for not standing by for their fallen brother, but at the sight of the green tinge to their faces, the red in their eyes, perhaps they simply couldn't bear it.

I ignored their murmured salutes and strode into the larger chambers meant for Stav officers. My chamber was more a wing than anything. A library and study, a bedchamber, and a washroom. I bolted the door behind me and crossed the woven rug to the washroom in ten long strides.

Along the jagged scar that carved across my chest, throat, to the hinge of my jaw, was a roaring ache, like I'd swallowed the howling rage of the sea.

Bile rose in my chest, a harrowing sort of shadow coated my gaze.

I gripped the clay washbasin, breaths sharp and deep.

Violence was no stranger to me, but it grew harder to keep the lust for blood tamed. I was the Sentry of Stonegate, and the Sentry was meant to be the stoic measure of restraint.

In this moment, I wanted to be more of a monster than those who'd slaughtered Uther.

Heat slowly faded, the storm in my head lessened. I cupped the frigid water in the basin and splashed it over my face, then returned to the room.

"You, my friend, have the most pitiful stomach. The sight of death and blood has you spewing? Honestly, what sort of royal guardian have I shackled upon myself?"

Startled as I was that another voice was in my chamber, I did not show it.

Sprawled out on my bed, ankles crossed, Prince Thane the Bold smirked back at me, likely aware I'd been berating myself. In my haste to reach the washroom, I'd foolishly left my chamber unchecked.

I frowned and it only widened his grin.

You are an ass and belong in one of the hells. My fingers moved swiftly in response, but Thane could follow even my most frenzied gestures since he'd found me outside the keep, bloodied and broken, my voice carved out the same as my place in my own clan.

"Really?" The prince chuckled. "Which one, the molten or frosted?"

Both. What if I'd had a knife in my hand?

"Roark, my oldest, dearest, most frightening friend, the better question is, Why *didn't* you have your knife in your hand? Growing careless, Sentry."

I shook my head and went to a personal cart topped with a wide ewer of aged wine and a horn. I filled only one horn when Thane waved a palm, refusing my offer.

"Jests aside," Thane said, kicking his legs over the edge of the bed, "you're taking this death too hard."

He was my charge.

"Roark." Thane sighed. "Don't blame yourself for the actions of those bastards. It is not your fault."

It was. In so many ways the death of the young Stav was entirely my fault.

We don't know why he was killed, I told him.

"We'll find out, and when we do, whoever is responsible will pay."

I used one hand to respond. *Why are you here? Isn't your mother forcing you to plan your own wedding?*

"There likely won't be a wedding if Stav Guard are getting slaughtered." Thane winced. "Apologies, I'm careless with my words in your state of distress, allow me to try again. Yes, I've managed to slip my mother, flee the palace like a frightened child, and come to see you instead."

I let out a breath of air, a soft laugh.

Thane was a warrior prince from the golden ridge of hair braided down the center of his head to the bones pierced in his ear. He stood just taller than me, and I was no small man. But bony Queen Ingir and her endless revelry was enough to frighten away any man lest he be tossed into the madness of imported satins, silks, and different flavors of fillings for iced cakes.

"I've come for a purpose." Thane reached into the pocket of his trousers and removed a tattered, folded parchment. "You have heard of Jarl Jakobson, yes?"

The jarl obsessed with finding favor from the king?

Thane jabbed the folded parchment in the air between us. "The very one. He's made quite an interesting discovery."

The prince handed me the missive. I read it through once, then once more. Thane was no longer smiling.

My fingers gestured swiftly. *Jakobson is certain of this?*

"Seems my father's blood casts have finally worked."

King Damir couldn't claim the blood-tracking spells as his since the queen was the blood crafter in the fortress. Not that it mattered.

Seasons ago, King Damir took spilled blood from the house of the lost crafter. If any soul from the same bloodline came near, blood crafters would know it. The king's spells forced every village to have a royally decreed blood crafter within the borders.

All of it was done to find the child who'd disappeared. A child whose magical craft brought three kingdoms against a small village in the knolls.

There was nothing left of it now.

"But there's trouble." Thane interrupted my thoughts, pacing in front of my doorway. "Jarl Jakobson's blood crafter has sold the woman out to Draven Dark Watch scouts."

So the missives speak of a woman? The child who escaped was said to be a girl, more reason for greed and bloodlust from kings and queens to seek her out. *Any house sigil?*

It was common in the kingdoms to ink a brand below the left ear of a child by their first summer, a mark of bloodlines and heraldry for houses and clans.

One of Thane's brows arched. "Said to be manipulated. Some of the runes were added later to make a brand of the nameless. Curious, don't you think?"

If one wanted to hide rare craft, adding ink to a house sigil until it looked like a waif-and-wanderer symbol—folk without clans or house bloodlines—would be the wisest action to take.

"The jarl found the correspondence between the blood crafter and the scout," Thane explained. "Of course, Jakobson now wants some sort of reward for being the township to unearth the lost craft."

The prince went to the tall arched window, looking out at the distant wood over the walls. "My father always suspected the reported death of the girl was a ruse. You know that's why he forced each jarldom to have a blood crafter casting their spells. After all this time, he was right. A melder has been hidden from the king. A woman." Thane shook his head. "The first in five hundred winters, Roark. You know what this'll bring."

War, was all I gave in a one-handed reply.

If this report was even true, there would be new battles from the Red Ravines of Dravenmoor to the small seas of the kingdom of Myrda.

Damir would not allow anyone to take his prize again, and the queen of Dravenmoor would return for retribution for what she lost during those raids so long ago.

A melder's craft was only found perhaps once a generation, and rarely in a woman's blood. It was a collision of all three crafts—dangerous, coveted, and owned by Jorvan kings through treaties made long ago.

"War is certainly a risk. Which is why you're to go to this Skalfirth village." Thane chuckled when my mouth tightened. "The king has already arranged for Baldur to go with you. What a fortunate bastard you are."

A soft groan breathed from my throat. Baldur the Fox was as cunning as his name, brutal but a damn skilled Stav.

We'd trained together since boyhood, but when I surpassed him in skill with the blade, he built up resentment toward me. My rank in the Stav Guard as Thane's Sentry made me the prince's blade, his protection; it required me to do anything to keep the royal blood in his veins from spilling, even becoming a killer in the shadows.

The Sentry was not a true leader in the king's Stav, more assassin and brute when needed. Still, my position kept me under Thane's word and not the king's.

Baldur spent the night after my ranking by drunkenly mocking me, as though I ought to be disappointed.

As though I had not been placed exactly where I wanted to be.

"I wish I could be there," Thane said. "But with the attacks, I doubt I will ever be permitted to leave Stonegate again. Not unless my father sires another son, but alas, my mother would need to allow her husband into her bed if that were to happen."

As soon as the words were out of his mouth, the prince paused and shuddered.

What does the king wish us to do if it is confirmed the lost melder is alive? I gestured the question slowly, already anticipating the reply.

"Deal with the traitor who sold her out first, then use your methods to bring the melder home. Roark." Thane's voice lowered. "I know you don't always care for the craft of melders, but you must admit it has its uses to keep our people safer."

Debatable. My jaw pulsed.

Thane chuckled and rested a hand on my shoulder. "The king plans to increase patrols and move his ceremonies to more private locations. In fact, that is the other piece of this. Only select Stav will join you, guards who are sworn to secrecy. They will not speak of what you find in this village."

It wouldn't matter how the king tried to keep craft hidden behind the walls of the fortress. Blood and death always found melders.

The magic that ran in the veins of a melder crafted abominations that left souls and bodies corrupted, altered, and vicious.

Last harvest, the king's personal melder had been slaughtered. I felt nothing but relief with Melder Fadey's death. I thought, for once, there might be peace if melding craft were not here.

Gods, I'd almost allowed myself to forget the past wars, to forget lives had been lost trying to reach a small girl with silver in her eyes. Perhaps, I hoped, the Norns of fate had already cut her threads of life and sent her to Salur.

Maybe to one of the two hells to burn or freeze.

No mistake, now blood would spill again.

"We do this discreetly for as long as we can. We don't want another raid," Thane said, soft and low.

I closed my eyes against memories of distant screams, of smoke and burning flesh.

No kingdom escaped without loss. Thane lost his uncles. The smaller kingdom of Myrda lost its loyal seneschal and the queen's nephews.

Me—I lost my homeland and voice.

"You're to leave at first light," Thane said, clapping a hand on my shoulder. "Be careful, my friend. This woman will not be Fadey. I'd hate for her to bespell that dark heart of yours."

I scoffed. *I'd slit her throat if she tried. I have no love for melders, and that will never change.*

LYRA

I WAS ONCE TOLD WE NEVER TRULY KNEW ANOTHER SOUL until we saw the darkness they kept inside.

In this moment, I was looking into the eyes of evil.

I blinked, hoping the bastard could see a bit of the silver scar bending the dark center of my eyes, a warning he ought to choose his next moves with care. Pukki did nothing but gnaw on the clod of grass, wholly unbothered by my disdain.

"*Move.*" I tugged on the rope around the goat's neck.

A lethargic bleat followed, and the creature dipped his head to continue his graze of the meadow. I held out a palm, as though Pukki would understand the threat, and whispered, "I could break you, you stupid beast."

More gnawing, more snorting.

I let my head fall back and cursed the sky. "Fine. Stay there, you damn devil, but don't go anywhere until I finish."

I trudged up the narrow path to the small orchard of star

plums. The pale outer flesh gleamed in the sunrise, but when eaten, the centers were a crimson deeper than blood.

There, a cart stacked in wicker baskets remained, goat-less.

I glared at Pukki. His jaw rotated lazily, and he flicked his ears, slightly curious why I'd gone away, but not enough to move.

I dug a vial from the pocket of my burlap smock. I'd rinsed my eyes with the intent to intimidate a stupid creature with my scars, but he had no sense of self-preservation. Head tilted, I dropped some of the inky fluid into each eye, wincing against the bite of heat.

Thorn blossoms were lovely flowers that grew by the coast and were often used to dye tunics and wool. For me, the pressed blossoms hid the silver scars in my eyes behind a dark violet lie.

Beautiful, but the blossom dye stung like hot ash tossed in the face.

Time before the scars appeared was lost to a fog in my mind, a life I could not quite recall.

There were weak, vague memories of laughter and warm arms and a thick beard split into two braids. Sometimes I would dream of a woman's gentle voice singing me a folk song of lost souls.

Whenever I dreamed of the night of smoke and screams, I always saw eyes like a sunrise break through the shadows just before I woke.

The first memories I knew to be real for a certainty began in the cold walls of a youth house meant for abandoned or orphaned young ones. Wood laths overtaken by golden moss and silken webs in the corners gave me a roof and bed. There, I learned the silver dividing the black of my eyes was a cruel curse.

Gammal, the wizened maid whose spine arched like a

rounded hill, was the first to take note. I would never forget her knobby, crooked fingers working in a frenzy, teaching me to crush the petals of the blossoms, and forcing the dye over my lashes.

She had beautiful, coiled ink tattoos across her wrists that had faded from sun and seasons.

"Unfettered Folk marks," she told me. "Our young ones are given their marks to begin the sagas of their accomplishments. My clan was often covered in them by the time they were ready to fall into the realm of souls. A bit like your house runes."

On instinct, I brushed a hand over the tattoo beneath my ear where Gammal had helped alter the rune marks of what once was a sigil of a House named Bien.

The clans of the Unfettered were people beyond the cliffs of the Night Ledges in the North. People without a king, a queen, and no magical craft. They lived in huts and hunted with spears and stone axes. Some said the Unfettered shaved their teeth into sharp points.

Gammal's teeth had looked like mine.

The woman let me draw my own designs on her wrinkled skin whenever we finished chores, and she taught me how to hide the silver scars.

"Take the sting or take death, elskan," Gammal always whispered when I whimpered about the ache of the dyes. "Folk here kill for those scars."

Three veins of magical craft lived in the soil of the realms, all brutal and lovely on their own. But silver in the eyes was proof the Wanderer King's curse burned in the blood with the power of all. Power coveted enough it stirred wars.

Twice I'd witnessed the king's melder when the royal caravans entered the village, almost as though searching for something, yet never finding it. Folk always said he was so well guarded because he was also the king's consort, not only a crafter.

No one really understood why melding craft was coveted so fiercely, only that melders were never truly free.

Gammal led me to thick tomes where I could read the histories of wars in which our small seaside kingdom of Jorvandal allied with the lands of Myrda for nearly a century, before rising victorious over Dravenmoor.

For Jorvandal's aid, through treaties and sanctions, not only did Myrdan daughters always wed Jorvan kings, but melder craft would always belong to Stonegate, the royal keep.

I didn't remember the last raid hunting a new melder, only that it was during my tenth summer, and House Bien was the heart of the bloodshed. I wasn't a fool. I had the manipulated sigil runes, scars in my eyes, and nightmares aplenty of dark words, flames, and screams.

Always screams in the dark.

I dabbed at a few drops of the dye that slithered down my cheeks. Stav Guard would arrive soon, and their presence always set my nerves on jagged edges.

I shook out my hands. In the past, the Stav never noticed the simple woman with dirty fingernails and messy braids.

This time would be no different.

I set off for the final tree. The stout trunks of star plum trees made them the simplest fruit to reach in the orchard, but each thin whip of a branch tangled with the others like a spider's web, making it a battle to pluck the pome without a few bloody scrapes.

Cold fog sliced through the towering aspens like a misty river.

It was difficult to see much of anything beyond the towering wooden gates of the village, but I could taste the storm brewing—brine and smoke collided with a bit of fearful sweat.

The Fernwood held the water of the sea too tightly, thick and heavy, so a constant damp hung in the air no matter the season.

Prince Thane the Bold was preparing to wed the princess and heir of Myrda. Stav Guard had traipsed the petty kingdoms and villages for weeks to secure borders for the ceremony.

Skalfirth was their final stop.

The idea of it put Selena, the head cook in the jarl's household, into a fit of chants and blessings. Before dawn, she tossed a whittled talisman etched in runes of protection around my neck, convinced with the guard on the roads, Draven Dark Watch warriors would be hiding in the wood.

I plucked another plum, inspecting the skin for wormholes or bird bites. A twig snapped in the trees, lifting the hair on my arms. The sound of canvas rustling shifted to the scrape of reed baskets over the wood laths of my cart.

There, rummaging through all the baskets in my once-goat-pulled cart was a man, hooded in a thick, wool cloak.

My jaw set until my teeth ached. He was no ravager, of the clan who followed the feared Skul Drek, a Draven assassin.

Some suspected Skul Drek was behind the death of Melder Fadey.

But this sod didn't move with the shadows, or perch in the trees to spear his victim like a ravager. He wore a frayed hood, scuffed boots, and loud, feckless rummaging gave him up as a common thief.

Forced to hide the secret in my eyes since childhood, I'd learned how to handle a blade well enough.

From a loop on my belt, I yanked free a small paring knife and let it fly. A heavy *thunk* startled the thief when the blade dug into the side of the cart. Even Pukki lifted his greedy head to investigate.

In haste, I plucked a discarded plum from the ground and threw it. "Think you can thieve from us?"

A raspy grunt broke from beneath the cowl when the plum struck the side of his hood.

In a delirious sort of frenzy, I picked plum after soggy plum from the grass, and flung them one after the other, drawing closer to the cart with each step. Bruised pomes struck his shoulders, his hips, his legs, leaving cloying streaks of juices and thin flesh across his cloak.

The thief shielded his head with his arms. When he turned, readying to bolt back into the trees, one final plum collided with his brow. A low hiss slid through his teeth.

I yanked on the hilt of my knife, ripping it from the side of the cart, and prepared to slash against the bastard. By the time I whirled around, he'd rushed into the trees.

For a breath, the thief paused by a moss-soaked aspen, watching me. I could not see his eyes beneath his full cowl, but his gaze sliced through my chest like a burning torch held too close until he retreated into the thick of the Fernwood.

With a narrowed glare at Pukki—who did nothing but gnaw on his cud of wildflowers—I made quick work of inspecting the baskets. The steward of House Jakobson was not a man who feared using the rod for mistakes.

There'd been wardens at the young house who thought similarly, but Gammal had always looked out for me, and I was spared a great many lashings by her warnings. Each jarl in differing townships was like a king of their own village. They could decide how their servants were treated, and Jarl Jakobson often turned his gaze from the use of pain, thinking it made stronger folk.

With a few tugs on the twine to secure the baskets, I draped the leather harness over one shoulder and started to bring the cart to the aggravating creature myself until a wheel collided with something in the weeds.

"Damn this day to the hells." The curse slipped over my tongue as I knelt to clear away the foliage around the wheel.

A smooth, round stone with a weathered notch cracked through the center trapped the cart. I gingerly traced the sigil of a burning ax carved into the rock. An old totem where someone prayed to the Wanderer King.

I feared my curse of craft, but had always reveled in the saga of the first king.

Once a wandering Skald, he stumbled upon a lost maiden. For giving her shelter and his last strip of roasted herring, she revealed herself to be one of the beloved daughters of the god of wisdom.

As gratitude, the wanderer was given the maiden to wed and offered one medium to hold a piece of the gods' magic that he could use to build up his new kingdom.

The Wanderer King first chose bone, for bones were in no short supply, and soon held the grandest army with bone blades that could not break and armor that fitted like a dozen shields.

There was more to the tale, darker days that followed and brought different veins of magic.

With the violence and madness behind the final tales of the Wanderer, fewer folk still worshipped the first king, but here, in small sea towns or forest villages, totems were plentiful.

As though the soul of the Wanderer King even cared about any of the small, simple lives in the realms of Stìgandr.

I righted one of the baskets, catching sight of a symbol written in water that was fading swiftly.

A simple word the thief left behind, but the sharp sting of fear dug into my bones.

Liar.

3

LYRA

MY HANDS WOULDN'T CEASE SHAKING AS I GATHERED
what was left of the plums and began the battle of tethering Pukki to the cart. Already, the damp symbol faded into the
threads of the basket, but blood pounded in my skull.

"Súlka Bien." A man, a little breathless from the trek up the
slope, swiped a woolen hood off his pale, untamed curls.

I chuckled with relief. "Such formal greetings, *Ser* Darkwin."

Kael grinned. "I've been sent to find you, and I'll have you
know, Sel is convinced you've been taken by Dravens or perhaps
a wild hulda."

I snorted and shook my head.

Kael was my brother in every way but blood, and had only
returned mere days before from the mandatory training every
son of Jorvandal completed with the Stav Guard.

As a bone crafter, there was no mistaking Kael would receive
a missive soon enough, securing him an officer rank in the guard.

He would be handed a bone blade with an onyx pommel and leave again.

If he chose to join, of course.

Why wouldn't he? Kael deserved more than Skalfirth, and I held the wretched suspicion he remained here for my sake.

He paused a few paces away, brow furrowed. "Something's worrying you."

I cast a glance over my shoulder. "There was a scavenger here."

"A scavenger?" Kael tilted my chin with one knuckle. "All right?"

"I chased him off."

"Of course you did."

I glanced at the basket, no longer marked. "He wrote that I was a liar."

"Lyra, you always get like this when the Stav are nearby. Let me inspect you." With a bit of dramatics he tipped my head this way and that. "As I thought, your lies are well hidden."

Kael was the only soul beyond gentle Gammal who knew the truth. As a boy of twelve, when he'd first discovered my curse, he made a vow with a drop of his blood never to utter a word.

He never had.

I pinched the back of Kael's arm. "I know what I saw, you ass."

"What would you like to do, then? Flee into the wood? Go after this scavenger and take his eyes? I've been tempted to try a few more brutal things with my craft."

I laughed softly. Bone craft could crack spines if manipulated well enough, but Kael was too good in the heart. "Let's just get this damn creature back before Selena truly believes we've been kidnapped by trolls. I thought when you returned, you'd draw some of her attention away from me. But you, Kael Darkwin, have been intentionally taking tasks that keep you away from the cooking rooms."

"I can't help it if I'm so revered that folk are always asking to see me."

I shoved his shoulder. "You think too much of yourself."

"That's not what Märta said through her gasps earlier."

"Ah, still bedding a woman who has painted your name across her bedpost like a shrine?"

Kael winked and strode to the cart, propping one elbow on the edge. "She might have a slight obsession, but she is a delight in my bed."

"Bed." I blew out my lips. "You've never taken her anywhere other than the Fernwood."

"I resent that. I'll have it be known, I was between her thighs in the stables."

"Ass."

Kael was added to the servants of the jarl's household the winter after the youth house sent me. For a lonely boy and a lonely girl, we grew close, we shared our secrets, we protected each other.

If others held my stare too long, Kael would distract them. When anyone tried to learn of a past I hardly knew, Kael would bark at them to mind their own lives.

He was my only family.

"What do you need help with to get us back before the village is overturned?"

I jabbed a finger toward Pukki. "That foul beast needs to return to his duty and pull the damn cart."

Kael stroked Pukki's crooked horns, clicking his tongue, and the traitorous goat followed him without pause.

"I hate you." My smile faded and I spoke in a voice softer than before. "If you are taken into the guard today, I hope you know I am proud of you, but I cannot help feeling like it will change us. I will be a risk to you."

"Ly, I swore an oath. Those scars in your eyes are safe with me. My loyalty is not divided between you and the kingdom. All I hope is to use my craft and sword to keep you safe."

Kael bore his craft with pride while helping me conceal mine. I offered a weary smile. "You're much better than me, you pest."

"I know, you fool."

With Kael's help, I managed to tie Pukki to the cart.

"Have you heard anything about the murder of Melder Fadey?" I asked.

Despite the coldness I saw every time King Damir's melder stepped into a village, his sudden death lifted the hair on my neck.

"The killer has yet to be found," Kael said.

"You were in Stonegate, how did King Damir respond to losing his prized consort?"

"I did not see much of the king, but I'm certain he is filled with rage and vengeance." A muscle pulsed in Kael's jaw. "Fadey's death is unfortunate, and I know you like to think this, but that life is not in your future, Ly."

"Ah, are you one of the Norns of fate now?" I shoved his shoulder.

Kael chuckled. "Your fate is to live a long life free of stone walls."

A ram's horn blew from the distant gates, stalling Kael and me on the slope. My pulse thudded in my skull.

We didn't move, simply stared, frozen in fright, as canvas sails of two longships beat in the sea wind at the docks.

"The Stav." My teeth were on edge. "They're here."

4

LYRA

WE MANAGED TO BRIBE PUKKI DOWN THE HILLSIDE without toppling the baskets of herbs, roots, and berries much at all, and stepped through an opening in the crooked gates at the back of the longhouse.

Smoke billowed through the hole in the sod roof and through it I could make out the bustle of watchmen across the village towers.

I made quick work of untethering Pukki from his cart and took hold of one of the plum baskets, while Kael slung a canvas pack of thistle roots over his shoulder and took a basket of dewberries in his arms.

The jarl's longhouse was nearest to the outer gates. There, Thorian, an elder of the groundskeepers, greeted us.

Thorian kept a wooden pipe pinched between his teeth. His body was made of more bone than meat, but his aged, knobby fingers worked swiftly as he secured every pen for hogs and hens around the jarl's farm.

The old man lifted his head at the clatter of wheels approaching. "Been a while since you've left us, *isdotter.* Seems our lost boy found you just in time."

I grinned when the old man plucked his pipe from his lips and pecked my cheek as always. Thorian called me a daughter of ice since I came to the longhouse in winter.

Kael was the lost boy for what was done to him when he was discarded.

Loyal as the old man was to House Jakobson, Thorian shared my feelings that Kael had been wronged grievously by the jarl and his household.

Thorian drew in a long pull of his pipe, then freed the smoke in a cloud. "Be on watch, sweet ones. Selena is convinced the pond has been invaded by a fossegrim and is ready to sacrifice old Pukki to see the water spirit gone."

"Pukki would not be an adequate sacrifice." I schooled a glare on the old goat already gnawing on his grass. "He's too stupid."

Thorian waved me into the longhouse and turned his talk to Kael as they unloaded the spades and shears from the cart.

A door to the cooking side of the longhouse clattered open. "Lyra. Where have you been? Girl, *hurry.* Do you not hear the horn?"

Selena, hands on her rounded hips, leveled me in her most grisly stare. Try as she did, it was never enough to hide the tenderness in her soul.

Selena was a widow who believed in every vein of lore, and spent her days filling the table of the jarl with savory feasts and blessing each corner and rafter to keep the house free of haunts and trickster creatures.

Beyond Kael, Selena and Thorian were my favorite souls. Kindhearted and strong-willed. They looked after the both of us like an odd pair of makeshift parents.

When we needed guidance, Thorian would guide.

When we were ill, Selena would fill our stomachs with her teas and herbs until fevers faded.

"Thorian told us you're fretting over a fossegrim."

"I told that old fool I can hear the creature plucking those strings trying to lure us in."

I laughed, but let it fade when more than one servant hurried into the rooms to salt meat or slice bread.

On instinct, I kept my face turned away and placed my basket on the oak table. "I've brought you thistles. Thought you could make one of those herb tonics to sell at the harvest trade."

Selena patted my cheek and inspected the basket. "Many thanks, my girl. You know, some would say the gods did not see fit to bless me with children, but I see it as they merely saw fit to send me a beautiful girl and mischievous boy in another way. Now, get dressed. We've a great deal to prepare. I'll be needing your touch with the honey cakes."

Selena slipped through the ropes threaded with bone beads that divided areas of the cooking rooms from the great hall of the longhouse. She recited a few soft chants under her breath as she went to ward away the unheard fossegrim fiddle.

My chest burned with affection. Cruel as life could be, everywhere my fate led me, I found a few souls to love. I lived with a lie, heavy and terrible at times, but I could not hate how my path brought me Kael and a few kind folk in this house.

Selfish of me. I should not be glad Kael was a servant in the house of his birth. The house of which he should be the heir.

For the first twelve summers, Kael lived as Jarl Jakobson's first son. Born to the first wife who went to Salur after the heir was born.

When the second wife grew envious that her husband's son

was blessed with bone craft but her children were not, she threatened to take the jarl's new family away from Skalfirth to her father's house lest Kael be cast out, disowned, and the jarldom left to be inherited by her firstborn son.

It was a spineless act, but Kael was stripped of his inheritance, his house name, and left to serve his own blood as a stable boy— no family, no title.

Jakobson saw it as a mercy to allow his son to remain in the house at all.

All the folk living along the shores of the Green Fjord knew his birth house.

No one mentioned it.

Kael was given the name Darkwin, a title from a Skald saga of a prince who fell from his throne to the dark roots of the gods' tree and lived out his days in shadows.

"It is the way of things, Ly," Kael told me once when we were tasked with watching a line of fishing nets. Jakobson and Mikkal, his second son, had ridden past without a glance our way. "He hardly spoke to me anyway. Thorian said I remind him too much of my mother, and it pains him."

"That is nothing but weakness," I spat.

Kael nudged my shoulder. "Let it be and don't harbor such ill will toward the man. It'll pinch your face."

I did not speak of it again, but I never was the first to bow the head to Jarl Jakobson.

Inside a narrow alcove in the back rooms shared by the servants, I ripped off my dirty tunic, next my trousers and boots, tossing them on top of the narrow cot where I slept.

From a small wooden crate, I scrounged through my meager belongings, snatching up a plain woolen dress.

Simple. Dull. Invisible.

With trembling fingers, I stroked my braid free and knotted my dark hair behind my neck. Another horn blared from the watchtowers.

"*Shit.*" By now the jarl would be greeting the Stav Guard, and the rest of us would be expected to do the same.

I hopped on one leg, trying to shove my toes inside thin leather shoes.

On this side of the longhouse, I could see a portion of the main road. Like a pestilence, Stav Guard entered the inner market, spilling their blight across our dirt roads and blotting out any peace that lived here moments ago.

Doors on homes opened and people staggered into the streets. Others wore bemused expressions or carried platters of offerings and ewers of honey mead for their arrival.

Once dressed, I added more stinging dye to my eyes, wrapped the knife I'd thrown at the scavenger in a linen cloth, and used a thin leather belt to secure the blade to the side of my calf. Kael would roll his eyes, but the notion of remaining unarmed near Stav Guard rushed a noxious sort of panic through my veins.

Outside, sunlight spliced through the mists of early morning, dewdrops sweated off bubbled glass windows, and the damp, briny air dug into my lungs with each breath. As if Skalfirth wanted me to always remember its taste, its scent.

As if it knew this day would change everything.

Already, Kael and Selena took up their places near the back gates with the rest of the household.

I scooped up a handful of berries from a basket on the back stoop and rolled them around in my palm until some of the iridescent juice dribbled through my fingers. A ruse, a distraction, I'd learned well over time.

Keep the Stav looking elsewhere and they rarely cared to look such a common woman in the eye.

"A great many have come," Selena muttered.

Kael nodded. "Captain Baldur's unit. I'm surprised. They're the fiercest. Threats against the prince's betrothal must've increased."

It was no secret, Dravenmoor would not want a true royal match between kingdoms. Jorvan royals wed Myrdan nobles, but this was the first union in nearly a hundred winters where a Myrdan princess was of age and title to wed a Jorvan prince.

I'd seen the prince only once before, during my fourteenth winter when I was tasked with aiding Thorian with the fishing trade in a nearby township. While there, the king's caravan arrived to recruit a bone crafter into the Stav.

Thorian led me to the docks once our business was done, and as we'd pulled away from the shore, I caught a glimpse of the prince. Only a few seasons older than myself, Prince Thane had been draped in fine white fox furs, surrounded by Stav Guard, tossing pebbles into the tides.

He'd seemed so utterly bored.

Thane had caught my gaze as our ship peeled out to sea, and shouted, "Watch me skip it, my lady."

Without knowing me, the prince addressed me like noble blood ran in my veins. Then like all boys my age, rife with arrogance, the prince tossed a pebble, bowing with a flourish when the stone skipped four times before sinking into the tides.

I blew out a breath and stepped closer to Kael. The prince had been kind as a boy, but the Stav today looked nothing of the sort.

Each man was dressed as though he might be meeting the front lines of battle in his dark tunic embroidered with the white wolf head of Stonegate. Scattered throughout were servants and attendants who carried satchels and stuffed leather packs for gathering any weapons we traded.

"There's Baldur." Kael used his chin to point out the man at the head of the line.

Baldur the Fox was broad and stern. His beard was not yet to his chest, but he kept it knotted in a single plait secured with bone beads.

The captain was known for his fealty and ferocity, both in battle and in life. Young for a Stav officer, but he moved like a man who'd lived for centuries and had no patience for people around him.

Baldur stopped to greet Jarl Jakobson. Kael's unclaimed father was a handsome man, strong and skilled with the ax. His peppered beard was trimmed, his hair sleek and tame around his shoulders.

But even standing half a head taller than the captain, Jakobson seemed to shrink beneath Baldur's sneer.

"Come," I said, urging Kael to help me finish the cakes and saffron buns for the feast. "We don't need to watch men puff out their chests to compensate for lack in other areas."

Kael flicked my ear. "No one will want to take you as a wife if you speak so boldly."

"Perhaps I will not want to take on a husband if he cannot meet the challenge."

"Fair enough."

A few gasps and murmurs drew me to a pause.

"By the gods, the Sentry is here. Why?" Kael spoke with a touch of delight. "Ashwood is incredible with the blade, Ly. *Incredible.*"

Next to Baldur, another man shoved his way through.

All along his hood and shoulders were crimson stains. I recognized the cowl, the very stride of the scavenger from the wood. My stomach lurched. No. By the gods, no. The thief was no thief at all.

To some, Roark Ashwood was named Death Bringer. He and his blades were infamous. Known as the Sentry, Roark rose in power in Jorvandal from boyhood for his unique talent with the sword. Adopted as a child from Dravenmoor, some believed he was less the silent guard for Prince Thane and more the assassin for the throne.

I'd never seen him, not personally, only heard the whispers of how brutally he would kill to protect his royals. But watching him shove to the front of the line, there was almost a familiarity about the man, a sense of his power that peeled back my ribs and settled into my soul.

And the truth was, I'd assaulted the most dangerous man in the kingdom.

LYRA

THOUGHTS PUMMELED THROUGH MY SKULL IN QUICK SUC-
cession.

Kael's storm cloud eyes found me. He tilted his head as though breaking apart the sudden tension in my features. I needed to warn him, needed to tell him the scavenger had undoubtedly been Ashwood.

If I were punished, Kael and his temper would be pushed to the brink to keep from intervening.

The man laughed a great deal, but was protective to a fault, and boiled hot in his blood when he saw what he perceived to be injustice.

Vella, the jarl's new seer provided to him by Stonegate, stepped forward. The woman was indifferent to folk like me and, after he was disowned, even Kael. As a visionary, she was a prize for the jarl to ask and plead what the Norns might reveal of his fate through her runes and premonitions.

I found her overwrought and pretentious.

Vella faced Ashwood and his blades. Her icy-pale braids were thick and heavy, stacked on her head like a nest. Cracked white paint decorated her slender features and added more mystery than age. Black runes descended from the peak of her hairline to the undercurve of her chin and each nostril was pierced with a gold hoop.

"We bid welcome to the honorable Stav Guard of House Oleg at Stonegate," Vella said with an airy voice. "A feast has been ordered for your men. Let us sit together and celebrate the future union of kingdoms."

Baldur faced the elder. A clasp of silver raven wings kept his fur cloak fastened around his shoulder, a mark of his rank. Pale scars littered the edges of his face, and one front tooth was chipped. "After you, Seer."

Ashwood shifted on his feet, but never pulled back his hood. I remained frozen, locked in a bit of fear and curiosity.

The Sentry's hand twitched. No—his fingers moved in a deliberate pattern. Gods, did he speak with his hands? The man was known as a silent guard. I'd always taken it to mean he merely did not chatter much with others, but . . . perhaps he could *not* speak.

Baldur nodded, watching the Sentry's gesture, then faced Jarl Jakobson again. "Our guard will take up posts at the gates during our stay. They will be scanning for weak points or potential threats."

Jakobson opened his arms. "We are here to serve. Do as you must."

Ashwood pulled back his hood. Wind-tossed dark hair—braided on the sides to keep the wild strands out of his eyes—fluttered around his brow where a clear welt had reddened just above his left eye.

I dug my fingers into my palms, silently pleading he wouldn't . . .

He faced me, head tilted to one side, like he could hear my damn thoughts.

The wash of gold in his eyes was shockingly vibrant. Molten pools of ore that would burn should one draw too close.

They pierced through me, holding me entranced, almost like I'd seen such eyes before and merely forgot them.

But no one would forget the face of the Sentry.

Roark Ashwood was quite possibly the most captivating man I had ever seen. Tall, not overly broad, dark brows, sun-toasted skin, and a bit of dark stubble covered the straight lines of his face. A ridged scar ran from the left hinge of his jaw, over his throat, and ended across the right edge of his collarbone.

Harsh features, yet beneath it all was an imperfect beauty.

Roark narrowed his eyes into something hateful, almost violent. He knew—he had to know—I was the woman he'd faced in the Fernwood.

I held my breath, chest burning, and waited for him to look away. He didn't. If anything, the Sentry took a step closer, a flare to his gaze, like he might see someone else besides the woman throwing bruised plums.

The way his eyes burned in disdain was almost like he'd caught sight of something else—silver in the eyes and deadly craft in the blood.

THE FEAST WAS HELD AT TWILIGHT. ASTRA, THE YOUNGEST child of the jarl, leaned close to Baldur, reveling in the captain's hungry attentions.

Kael's jaw pulsed in annoyance from where we huddled in the doorway leading to the back corridors of the longhouse. Disowned, unclaimed, and forgotten as he was, his goodness would still see Astra as a sister.

She'd been small when he'd left the family, but as little as they knew of each other, Kael cared deeply about her. And what brother would want a sister who shone like a bright sun to be seduced by a man like Baldur?

"She's too young," he said, voice tight.

"Agreed," I said. "But there is nothing much we can do."

He grunted, then took up one of the ewers of mead from my hand. "Head down out there, Ly."

It was what he always said, a sort of promise between us. Alone, Kael told me to keep my shoulders back, to lift my chin. Around so many, especially Stav Guard, he would tell me to disappear.

If it were not my duty to serve the household, Kael would've insisted I remain in the back entirely.

Tonight, everyone was expected to keep the Stav comfortable with full bellies and drinking horns and portray House Jakobson as the most hospitable of hosts.

Together, we carried ewers and platters of Selena's cakes and sugared rolls into the great hall.

I knew this day was loathsome for Kael, knew how much he detested stepping foot into the hall of his childhood as though he had not sat on his father's left-hand side for a dozen summers.

"Avoid Ashwood," he whispered.

"You believe me, then?"

Kael scoffed. "No. I think you are uneasy and have convinced yourself your scavenger was the Sentry, but he has a way of sensing craft in the blood. I don't know how he does it, but keep a distance."

"You're saying this now?" My knuckles turned white as I gripped the handle of the wooden ewer tighter.

"I did not expect Sentry Ashwood to be here, or I would've made mention of it." Kael offered a nod to one of the noblemen of Skalfirth, who returned a pitiful smile.

I closed my eyes, blowing out a long stream of air. "Fine. I'll keep to the young Stav and survive their wandering hands."

Kael's eyes darkened. "I trained with the lot of them for six months, Lyra. They touch you, I'll cut off their fingers."

"Unless Ashwood cuts out my throat first." I was being child-ish, but fear and frustration tangled like barbed vines, leaving me stepping about like a rabid hound about to bite.

Kael filled another horn, then faced me, voice low. "Why would Ashwood be rummaging through a goat cart? Better yet, why would he call you a liar, then leave you be?"

"You're the one who knows him, so tell me."

"He wouldn't, that *is* what I'm telling you. If Roark Ashwood knew about you, trust me, he would not hesitate to haul you off."

"I saw the mark on his face where I struck him."

"Lyra, he would've acted by now and I'd be feeding you through bars near the rack."

My mouth pinched. I used the edge of my smock to scrub spilled ale off the corner of a table. "You never mentioned he does not speak."

"He does speak."

"I saw him, he uses gestures."

"Still speaking, simply in a way that is not the same as us." Kael lowered his tone. "You must swear you'll let this go. Don't draw his attention, Ly. Roark . . . he's fiercely protective of Prince Thane. They treat each other like brothers, not guard and royal."

"Like us." I forced a smile, a pitiful attempt to lighten the tone, but feared it more or less shone like a grimace.

"Exactly." Kael frowned. "Swear to me you'll let this die."

My shoulders slumped, but I nodded and made my way toward the back of the great hall where the youngest, rowdiest of Stav Guard were placed.

Laughter and chatter echoed over tables alongside the beat of rawhide drums. Sweet hickory smoke floated from a wide inglenook in the corner, hiding the scent of sweat and leather from too many bodies in one space.

Painted clay bowls and plates were set along the numerous tables, and fine horns foamed with honey mead and sweet wines. Vella sat at the right hand of Jarl Jakobson near the head of the long oak table, her silver braids coiled around a headdress of bone and briars. Kohl lined her eyes and lips, but her wool robes were replaced with blue satin.

The jarl was lost in his cups earlier than was typical.

I counted over a dozen Stav seated beside other Skalfirth lawmakers. The Sentry was placed next to Baldur. Without the cloak over his shoulders, Roark's formidable form was easy to make out.

Before the Sentry could spot me again, I twisted away toward a table stacked in roasted meats, cheeses, and herbs. Through the feast, I kept busy, serving, cleaning, avoiding bawdy offers of Stav who promised to cause me to cry out in pleasure, and for a time worries over plums and deadly scavengers were nearly forgotten.

Selena chattered on with Hilda, a young wife of the local carpenter. Hilda; her brother, Edvin; and Kael were the only known bone crafters in the small village, but the siblings earned a proper living by using bone manipulation to craft whale and boar ribs into some of the sturdiest Stav breastplates and longbows.

Kael, if he did not find a place with the Stav, had already been offered a place in their shop should he desire it.

Again, I had to wonder if Kael would ever allow himself to live a better life knowing I remained here.

Vella rose from her seat, mead lifted. "We are honored with the Stav Guard, and as tradition demands for royal vows, we send with you boons for our prince and his new household."

Two men approached, arms heavy with furs. Vella gingerly unraveled the fur trappings on bone daggers that would break only if struck with a rare steel, swords made from the ribs of the same whale that would not draw blood should an enemy take it, silver rings, armbands, and crops from the harvest. By the end, Baldur wore an easy grin as he studied the fletching of one arrow. They were pleased, and soon the Stav Guard—and Ashwood— would be gone from our shores.

Baldur leaned into Roark for a breath, watching the Sentry's fingers move over the tabletop. The captain faced Vella with a sneer. "We accept your offerings. I am certain our king will be most pleased. Of course, it may take more than a few bone blades to keep his wrath from *you* after your betrayal."

Jarl Jakobson closed his eyes and took another long drink from his horn.

I halted the ewer, tipped halfway over a drinking horn of the pelt merchant, and felt heat prickle over my skin.

Vella's smile faded. "Betrayal?"

Baldur rose from his chair. "I am certain you all have heard the king's melder is dead, murdered by traitors to the crown who despise the gift of the gods."

"Fadey's death was troubling," Vella said, gently. "But I serve King Damir loyally. Ask Jarl Jakobson: I have not left Skalfirth in ages, not since the Norns told our king to place me within these borders."

"The Norns?" The captain's teeth flashed in the candlelight. "You want to give those tricksters the credit? The king sent you here because of your blood craft."

A few gasps filtered through the hall. Vella was a . . . seer. It was what we'd all been told. A blood crafter used runes and totems and spells to track weakness in blood.

Or . . . to find other craft in the blood for the king to recruit.

My insides overturned. No.

Baldur leaned onto his fingertips over the tabletop. "You, like all the other blood crafters the king placed in his townships, were here for one purpose—to find the lost bloodline. And you did, didn't you?"

Vella's painted lips tightened until the black edges cracked. "I do not understand what you mean, Captain Baldur."

The Fox drummed his fingers against the knotted wood, then slammed the silver wolf ring on his center knuckle over the boards. "You are nothing but a traitorous bitch. You found the craft in her blood, but instead of turning to your king, you turned to our enemies!"

More gasps. By now, Kael's pale eyes locked with mine across the hall. He jerked his head, a silent signal for me to duck into the back rooms.

I took another step, but my heart bottomed out. Every damn doorway was all at once filled with a Stav Guard, blades out.

My fingers trembled, and a storm, sharp and dangerous, filled Kael's eyes. He knew as well as I—we were trapped.

Baldur rounded the corner of the table, stalking Vella like the sly creature of his name. "But it goes deeper, doesn't it, woman? You were the one who sent word to Fadey that melder blood was sensed at the Red Ravines. Your word lured him out of the gates, and nearly over Draven borders. Tell me, did you stand by as the Dark Watch tore him apart?"

The inked runes on Vella's fingers distorted when she flexed and clenched her fists, once, twice. "Captain, I do not know—"

"Clever of you to wait some time before turning over the next melder to Dravenmoor," Baldur interjected, taking a step closer to the woman. "It would've been foolish to act too swiftly, but you've known for some time, haven't you? That the melder was in your gates."

Mead in the ewer sloshed when my grip trembled. No one, not even Vella, knew of me.

I was . . . I was certain of it.

Blood drained from my face when Ashwood, in all his dark silence, lifted his gaze to me. My pulse pounded in my skull, loud enough I was certain he could hear it.

"Your own jarl sold you out when he found one of your correspondences." Baldur canted his head, sneering down at Vella. "Anything to say?"

The woman didn't look away. "I did nothing but protect our people from tyrants. You misuse the craft of the gods, and the melder was your way to do it. I will not let it happen again."

"We'll see." Baldur snapped his fingers.

From the shadowed corners, Stav Guard shot into the hall.

Hilda screamed when a guard tore her away from Gisli, her new husband. A blade leveled at the man's throat when he tried to reach his wife. Edvin was tossed into the center of the hall next, his three young ones clinging to his wife's skirt, sobbing as they watched their father forced onto his knees.

The moment Kael was approached, it was clear the Stav Guard was claiming the bone crafters. In another breath, I was yanked away from the table, forcefully enough the ewer clattered on the floorboards, spilling mead across the boots of startled folk.

With the other crafters, I was shoved onto my knees. Kael's shoulder knocked against mine. When I met his gaze, his eyes were black with fear. He shook his head in a gentle warning to keep quiet, keep my head down.

"The gifted of this rotted little town." Baldur chuckled and slowly clapped his hands, mocking the lot of us.

"We only have three crafters," Lady Jakobson said from her place beside her husband.

"Or so you thought."

A feverish heat rippled up my neck when the captain's scuffed leather boots paused in front of me. Baldur said nothing, merely stood there for five, ten, a dozen heartbeats. I refused to look, refused to show my eyes lest terror reveal the truth beneath the dye.

"I offered you the traitor and melder if it is true," Jarl Jakobson shouted. "In return you were to leave our other crafters in peace."

I almost thought the jarl sounded uneasy, perhaps worried for his son placed at my side.

Baldur ignored the jarl and reached inside a pocket on his jerkin, removing a handful of shavings like crimson bark. He glanced briefly at Sentry Ashwood, then turned toward Vella.

"The king corrupts and destroys with his melder," Vella gritted out, now held between two Stav Guard. "It would be better for the craft to fall into extinction than be given to Stonegate."

"Yet you saw no trouble handing the craft to our enemies." Baldur's lip curled.

"At least the Draven folk understand where such a curse belongs." She whirled her head with enough force her pale braids whipped her chin, and narrowed her gaze on me. "In the darkest pits of the frosted hell to rot."

My lips parted. The woman knew and despised my very existence. Her indifference and coldness had not been from my station, it was all from the curse in my blood.

Tears and pleas for mercy rose from the people scattered throughout the hall. *Run, elskan! Run!* A faint memory of different pleas scraped against my thoughts. Like I'd been in a moment such as this before.

My pulse quickened with the urge to flee, to battle my way from these walls until I was free or dead.

Dark, scuffed boots shifted into my sights. Roark, silent and fierce, drew closer. His very presence radiated like a threat, one absorbed until it infected every heartbeat, every sharp draw of air.

Roark stood near me, but never looked away from Vella. The Sentry simply rested a hand on the hilt of a short blade with a crescent pommel. A symbol of inner court ranks. The sort of symbol that meant this man was present in the most important circles in Stonegate.

My skin felt too hot, too tight. Every pulse of my heart seemed to pump molten ore in my veins.

"What a waste," Baldur murmured. In the next breath, the captain shoved the red flakes into Vella's mouth.

One, maybe two heartbeats, and her breaths turned to ragged pants.

A scream rattled the hall when Vella dropped. Blood bubbled over her lips in foamy pink. She shuddered and convulsed, desperately reaching for the captain's leg.

The Sentry glanced over his shoulder, scrutinizing my every move.

If I was to die, he would know of my disdain. Eyes narrow and sharp, I held his gaze.

Ashwood had the gall to smirk, as though utterly pleased with the pain in this hall.

Another breath slid from Vella, but once it was spent, there was not another.

Tears blurred my sight. I didn't want to see the truth, but like a rope tugged against my face, I looked.

Foamy blood painted her lips. Vella was flat on her back.

Dead. She was dead.

LYRA

ROSEWOOD BARK WAS HARMLESS UNLESS IT WAS BOILED down to the green center. There was a pale berry in the Fernwood Kael and I nicknamed as venom fruit after we realized the juices caused blisters on our skin. Fire vine, a red-leafed ivy, reacted fiercely with whatever differences divided craft in the blood from folk without magic.

The red flakes in the captain's palm could be any combination of toxic herbs.

Hatred filled me like flames. I wanted to drive the knife tethered to my calf through the softest point of the captain's throat. I wanted to watch blood fountain over his lips the same as it had flowed from Vella.

I could hardly draw in a deep enough breath to fill my lungs.

Ashwood never looked away. The swirling gold of his eyes was harsh, like a rogue flame looking for a bit of skin to scorch.

He was the true fiend here. Whatever signal Ashwood gave, the captain merely reacted.

"See to them." Baldur waved a hand toward nearby guards, and they scattered through the hall.

The Stav were swift as snakes in the grass and blocked anyone in the hall from reaching the four of us, bent and hunched on the floorboards.

Baldur took slow, deliberate steps in front of the hall. "Craft has been revered as a true gift of the gods. The choice to use it in the service of your king has always been yours. So, to be met with such indifference, such deceit, it is a slight in these tumultuous times our king cannot ignore."

Edvin's jaw ticked. "You say we are revered, yet now we must submit"—he glanced at Vella's unmoving form—"or we die?"

Baldur chuckled. "The blood crafter was not truly one of you and brought her own fate. More than her lies, it is believed she used blood spells to weaken patrols, to bring disease to our Stav."

"You murdered her." The jagged words rolled over my lips before I could think better of it.

"Ly," Kael rasped through his teeth, a flare of desperation in his eyes. "Shut up."

"No, let her speak. I'm most interested in this one. You call me a murderer?" The captain hummed, then held out his hand toward a Stav. A stack of folded parchment tied in rough twine was placed in Baldur's palm. Baldur flipped one edge of the stack and clicked his teeth. "Do not take my word for it. See her betrayal for yourself, then tell me if you think differently of her, woman."

I jolted when the parchment slapped against the floor in front of me.

Baldur perched one hip on the edge of a table, taking a slow gulp from a horn.

My fingers trembled, but I opened one folded parchment and scanned the simple words. Locations of river routes, guard rotations, and bone crafters. A knot thickened in my throat like bile. Vella's name was signed in blood.

"Look at that last one," Baldur said, tilting his chin.

I didn't look at the captain; I lifted my attention to Roark. The Sentry was as stalwart as stone save the small curl to his lip when I picked up the last missive.

I saw the scars in her eyes. When the patrols leave Skalfirth, I will see to it that you have her and corruption will die at long last.

I shook my head. "No. This is wrong—"

"The woman was here to find the missing melder."

"A bloodline that is dead," Edvin bit out through his teeth. No mistake, the cries of his young ones were grating down his spine, and soon enough the man would snap.

"Yes, the child was supposedly slaughtered when the Draven armies raided," Baldur said. "Yet there never was a corpse laid at the feet of our king. There was enough reason to believe she was taken and hidden that your king placed blood crafters throughout the realm, searching for a glimpse of melder blood." The captain lowered to a crouch in front of me, teeth bared. "It is fortunate we intervened, or you would have been turned over to the ravagers of Skul Drek, perhaps the assassin himself. I hear the Draven queen gives the bastard agency to torture as he pleases."

"Lyra is no melder." Kael twisted against the guards holding him.

Roark's face contorted in disgust when he looked down at us.

Baldur took his Sentry's lead and faced Kael with a bite of controlled rage in his every word. "You, Darkwin, shall have to answer for the secrets you've kept."

I let out a shriek of horror when a Stav kicked Kael in the ribs. He coughed and curled over his knees, spitting bile.

"Stop this!" I made a move to reach for Kael, but my blood grew cold when Baldur's long fingers curled around my jaw, forcing my gaze to his.

"I can almost see the silver in these eyes." Baldur chuckled cruelly, then crumbled one of the missives in my face. "To me, you are as disloyal as the blood crafter. Gods, what might've been accomplished by now if you had not been such a coward and accepted your fate."

I tried to wrench free of his grip, but the captain merely tightened his hold until I was certain my teeth would slice through my cheeks.

Only when Ashwood clapped his hands did Baldur release me. The Sentry wore a look of dark anger and moved his fingers swiftly, sharply. I did not need to hear his voice to sense the fury in his tone.

Baldur yanked me to my feet. His lips dragged over my ear, his breath hot on my skin. "Seems our Sentry does not care for me damaging your face. By the by, he wonders if you took note of his message. Something about a liar?"

Kael coughed, his shoulders rising in rough breaths, the truth of it a cruel lash.

Ashwood knew me. He'd been sent ahead of the guard to sniff me out like a hound on the hunt.

Like a blow to the back of the head, I understood—the Stav were here for me, not to secure borders for a royal wedding.

Jarl Jakobson knew it; his unease was clear. He'd planned to sell me to Stonegate, and now because of his offering, his blood son was at risk of the blade for keeping my secrets.

Tears stung when I let my trembling gaze fall on the jarl. His jaw pulsed and the coward did not have the spine to meet my glare.

I clenched my jaw and looked back to the captain. "You are mistaken about me. I am merely a servant."

"No." Baldur dragged one callused fingertip down the curve of my cheek. "You're so much more. The time is long gone for you to submit your craft to Stonegate."

"I've no craft to submit."

Baldur laughed softly, a touch of venom buried in the sound. "This is how you desire our meet to go? Fine."

With the snap of the captain's fingers, Stav Guard moved like a storm rolling over the shore—fierce and unstoppable. In mere heartbeats, three guards had blades leveled at Kael.

"No!" I made a move to rush to their sides but a nearby Stav Guard gripped my wrist.

Kael paid little mind to the blade at his throat and looked at me. "No tears for me. We'll meet in Salur, where there are no fare-wells."

The sob burned in my chest, pain waiting to break free.

"You want to scream." Baldur's deep, slimy voice heated the curve of my ear. With slow steps, a true fox cornering a hare, the captain stepped around to face me. This close, it was simple enough to make out the sun-worn calluses of his skin, the slight freckles beneath the coarse hairs of his beard. "Tell us your story, how you came to be here, and perhaps he will greet the sunrise, Melder."

Sweat beaded between my fingers as I curled my fists. The longer I insisted I was not the melder they sought, the more Kael would be put at risk of harm.

"If it is blood you seek," I began, voice low and dark, "take it from me. Clearly, that is your aim. Leave the innocent alone."

"Innocent? I see no innocent here. Darkwin has known about your craft, a man I thought was made of honor."

Kael had never been one to recoil from a battle. Even as a child, unwanted and alone, he would stand firmly against drunkards in the hall who tried to harass servants, me, or Astra. He was unafraid to strike the jaw of cruel boys from nearby farms who'd taunt me for the nervous way I twitched my fingers, or the small gap between my teeth.

I'd always admired Kael Darkwin for his boldness, until this moment. My friend, my damn brother, sat back against his heels, spine straight, and a flare of rebellion in his eyes. "What do you want me to say, *my lord*? As Lyra told you, if you've come for blood, get on with it."

"Do you confess you know this woman is a melder and you willingly concealed her from Stonegate?"

"I see no silver in her eyes." Kael wore a smug sort of look. "And if I did, I certainly would not admit such a thing to you."

"*Kael.*" Panic tightened my throat.

His pale eyes flicked my way, too swiftly for anyone to notice. He was afraid.

Two Stav took hold of Kael's arms and pinned him facedown on the floorboards. They cut through his tunic, exposing the strong planes of his back. By the gods, they were going to flay him here; they'd peel the flesh off his bones, leave him to bleed out or rot with infection.

Jakobson looked pale, but did not protest. I could not say the same for Mikkal. Kael's half brother shot to his feet, shouting loud enough his mother commanded the very Stav Guard invading her damn home to remove her son from the room.

Kael was stalwart. Calm as the morning sea. He did not cry out, he did not move.

The ability to hold steady was lost on me. When I fought to keep still, my knees bounced. When I forced my legs to lock, I cracked one knuckle, then two, by my sides. After I curled my fingers into tight fists, my teeth clenched and shifted until I gnawed on my bottom lip.

Ashwood tilted his head like he might whisper something to Baldur. Instead, two of his fingers pointed to the floorboards, followed by a closed fist, then a quick flick of his thumb and first finger.

My limbs twitched as though my body yearned to run from the great hall, while a darker part wanted to reach for the knife in my boot again and ram it through as many Stav bellies as possible before they sliced through my heart.

The captain prowled around Kael. "A noble bastard, revered by the Stav Guard, and a bone crafter by blood. They named you Bare-Hands in your training."

The sting of tears collided with the heat of the dye in my eyes. In his missives while he was at Stonegate, Kael had sounded so damn proud to earn a name. Bare-Hands, all for his prowess for fighting without a blade, for taking down man after man with only his hands.

Baldur huffed when Kael said nothing. "Your father no longer claims you. A pity, for there is such potential in you. I assume you take after your mother's line. A respected house, am I right? Wasn't your mother the daughter of a warrior who slaughtered no less than two dozen Dravens before the gods took him to Salur?"

"Yes," Kael said, voice rough. "My every strength will always be credited to the woman who gave me life. No one else."

Jakobson dipped his chin, a wash of shame on his features.

Baldur's teeth gleamed like the fangs of a beast searching for the best way to sink into flesh. "You are bonded with the melder, but I wonder how much you truly matter to her."

The brawny Stav Guard holding me shoved a hand between my shoulders, nearly knocking me to the floorboards.

"Leave her alone!" Kael made a lunge for me, but was pinned facedown by two Stav.

"I'm beginning to think this village breeds liars." Baldur stroked his braided beard. "We've no use for such folk in Jorvandal. Burn it all."

Shouts bled to screams when the Stav moved as one, like their limbs were connected by a rod, and gathered torches from hanging lanterns and sconces on the walls.

"Captain Baldur," Jarl Jakobson shouted, gathering a sobbing Astra into his arms. "This was not our agreement."

"Plans change."

Before the guard at my back could touch me again, I rushed for Ashwood, gripping his arm. "Leave them, gods, I beg of you. I confess. I-I submit my craft, but beg of you to stop."

Roark looked at me with potent hatred; I could practically taste the sour burn of it. He stepped closer until our chests brushed. For a breath, two, I was frozen, locked in a spell.

"Stop this," I whispered. "Take me."

Ashwood pulled me into him. Shoulders to hips, I was pressed against the bastard who'd caused this. I thrashed and tried to pry myself free, but where I stepped, so did the Sentry, as though he were my broader reflection on a glass pond.

Ashwood's eyes held a new fire, a touch of warning, and gooseflesh lifted on my arms beneath his grip.

Women hugged their children to their breasts, sobbing. Men had gone for anything they could swing—stokers, carving knives, platters. Mead stained the floors, and breads and iced cakes were crumbled and smashed along tables.

Roark held up a fist and the Stav ceased their fight, wrestling the last of their opponents to the floor until the commotion faded into eerie quiet.

"Ly," Kael shouted. "Don't you dare."

Roark adjusted his hold, so my back was against his chest.

"You want them to live?" Baldur smirked. "Then impress us, and we leave Skalfirth with no more blood."

"How?" My breaths were heavy against the Sentry's body.

A woman materialized from the crowd. Clad in a fur cloak hemmed in red, the attire of Stonegate bone crafters. Her golden braids were styled in a crown around her head, and her mouth set in a taut line as she paused ten paces away. The flicker of lanterns in the hall glared over the shocking blue in her eyes.

She was Draven.

There were distinct markers of the Draven people—eyes in rich shades, so bright they practically glowed, and with her hair tied back I could make out a design of a double-headed raven on her neck, a ceremonial mark I'd once read was given to every Draven child by their third summer. For each household in Dravenmoor, different symbols might be added, much like the runes inked behind my ear.

Doubtless if Ashwood tossed back his hair, I would see his.

"You do not want your so-called brother to die, right?" Baldur tilted his head toward Kael.

Kael glared at me. I could nearly hear him demanding I shut my mouth and let him take the consequences. He was a stubborn bastard, but I could be even worse.

"I don't want him to be killed," I said firmly.

"Then save his life in a way only a melder can, and he'll receive his wish to join the Stav Guard." The captain unsheathed a dagger on his belt. "Fail to save him and we'll be short another crafter, and the people of this village will have nothing but stars overhead tonight. Those who survive."

The woman from Stonegate pressed her palms over Kael's chest. She blinked, a look of remorse on her face as she whispered, "Hold steady, Darkwin. It will be swift, I swear to you."

Gods, they knew each other.

A moment later and the hall filled with the cracks and snaps of bone.

LYRA

BONE CRAFTERS SHIFTED AND ALTERED BONES, BE IT CRAFT-ing a blade or armor, or snapping necks.

Beneath the woman's hands, Kael's body bent and twisted. His skin split with broken shards like jagged nails shredding his flesh.

She was *ripping* him open.

Time seemed to slow. Stav held people back. Thorian's shouts for Kael were muffled when four guards forced the old man to the ground.

"Time is being wasted," Baldur said, voice rough.

It took five heartbeats to realize he was speaking to me. Head in a fog, I dropped to my knees at Kael's side.

"Ly." Blood bubbled over his bottom lip. "Don't."

A simple word and I hated him for it. He did not want me to risk myself, but I would not lose him. Even if I didn't know how to save him.

One palm on his bloody chest, and the need—the *obsession*—to mend it all was as though a fist curled around the back of my neck, holding me in place. Be it instinct or something else, I knew there was a way to fix this.

As though the magic in my veins craved the opportunity to try.

By my side came the sound of leather stretching as a body crouched. Ashwood.

Roark did nothing but hold a hateful stare. No twitch of his lip, no flash of emotion. He was as stone until he removed a parcel wrapped in linen.

Once the flaps of the cloth were peeled back, all that was left was another jagged shard of bone.

A furrow gathered between my brows when the Sentry held out the piece.

"What?" I spat out the word, panicked and laced in disdain.

Roark held up one hand, curling and shaping his words like I would understand.

"Our Sentry is telling you a tale," Baldur said with a sneer.

"I've no time for tales." I leaned closer to Roark. "Hear this— you let him die, and I will slit my throat, for I serve no king who *slaughters* the innocent."

A rough sound, like the cut of a dry rasp, rose from Roark's chest. Almost a laugh.

"Sentry Ashwood is telling you a tale of bone," Baldur repeated. "He is telling you there are some pieces that can heal the gravest of wounds when melded into living bones."

Roark nudged his palm and the wrapped bone closer. He used his chin to gesture at Kael, then tilted his head to one side.

"He says—"

"I understand what he is saying," I gritted out through my teeth. In a swipe of my hand, I snatched up the bone. "But I don't understand how. What am I to do? Place it on him? Give a bit of my own flesh? Tell me and I will do it."

There would be no words shared between us, but Roark leaned forward like he might murmur the answer, his brow a mere finger's width from mine. I stilled when he used one knuckle to tap the place over my heart, then with the same finger, gestured at Kael.

Roark gave no further instructions. He rose and took three backward steps.

Through a blur of tears, with Kael's wet, thick breaths filling my head, I studied the bone. Ashwood's demands were clear enough—he believed I could find a way to make the healing bone save Kael's life by placing it—I assumed—against him.

When the heat of my palm touched the bone, something inside me fell away. Like gates sweeping open in my mind, a strange glow bled from Kael's shattered ribs and breastbone. Patterns of gilded stitches crossed this way and that over his battered wounds.

It took but a moment for my mind, perhaps an instinct, to note the glow revealed a possibility of how to include the new piece of bone, a way to seal the cracks and holes left behind.

I reeled over his body. "Kael, I-I know how. I see it."

His lashes fluttered. A weak smile crossed his lips as he whispered, "Let it be. I will greet you with the gods with a . . . curved horn, Ly."

"No." Nausea tossed through my middle for what needed to be done. "Salur can wait."

There was no time to scorch a blade in a flame. Infection we could face if he lived. He *would* live.

I took the knife Roark handed me, placed it at the open wound in Kael's chest, and began slicing it wider, deeper.

Screams of our people boiled in my brain with each cut of Kael's flesh. His eyes rolled into his head, no doubt with the pain so fierce his body was giving up.

I swallowed back the thrum of panic when he went limp.

Once the wound was wide enough for three fingers, I took up Ashwood's strange bone and maneuvered the edge into the bloodied flesh.

But there was more.

Intricate golden patterns honeycombed across Kael's front and Ashwood's healing shard. Heat prickled on the ends of my fingers, a need to reach out and follow the golden threads.

Baldur let out a groan of frustration at my back. "Hasten your damn hands, woman, or—"

Roark held up a closed fist. The man did not utter a sound, but one simple gesture sliced through the Stav unit like the lash of a whip. Spines straightened, jaws tightened. What sort of cruelty was given by those hands to demand such abrupt discipline?

Kael's chest was soaked in blood. He was no longer lucid and his sun-toasted skin had gone pallid and sickly, but through the gore, a soft hum of light pulsed with each weak beat of his heart.

With trembling hands, I maneuvered the shard into the bloodied flesh, bile burning my throat when my fingers brushed along the pulpy edges.

Beneath my palm, the new piece shifted, sinking into Kael's chest, as though an unseen force absorbed it into his body. Craft brightened like a silken web around his body.

No one gasped, no one uttered a sound at the sight of the gilded filaments, and it was frighteningly clear no one could see what was unraveling before my eyes. Unorganized and chaotic, the glow of fibrous magic flitted across the bone, desperate for a purpose, for a command.

I gingerly touched one thread. Heat teased the tip of my finger, and where my hand shifted, so, too, did the glimmering strand. The threads rearranged like Kael's bloody body and the bone inside were a spool with wool yarn, my hands the needle. With each movement, the strings of gold sutured the new shard into the broken edges of his wound.

My eyes fluttered closed.

The air grew colder. Where candlelight from sconces and chandeliers in the great hall had brightened the room, now the space was doused to misty gray. Shadows stretched up the walls and doorways like creatures so black they seemed to draw whatever was left of the light toward them.

When I lowered my gaze, a scream split from my chest.

Kael had been beneath my palms, but now only a soft glow of his shape remained. Each bone, each divot of his jaw, his spine, his ribs, was outlined in a golden sheen.

I spun around. Village folk, Stav Guard, all stood like radiant starlight beams. Flesh was gone, and it was as though I were witnessing the burn of their souls.

In the eerie silence came a laugh. Low, dark, like fear on the wind.

My scalp prickled with a sense of watchful eyes. I turned again and the blood froze in my veins. Clad all in shadows from cowl to boots to the skeins of inky black flowing off his shoulders, a figure—a creature—stood over Kael's vibrant form.

Tethered around his body was a thick, golden strand. Like the heavy ropes we used to lift the stuffed fishing nets onto the longships. The opposite end of the strand disappeared into the shadows, like a line to find his way through the darkness.

A vicious grin split from beneath his hood, followed by the slice of wicked copper eyes.

"Melder." The voice was as cold as the fiercest frosts and sliced across my heart. A sound heard somewhere within, as though part of my soul. "At long last, you're found." The shadow made a sound, like it was drawing in a long breath. "Your soul is familiar. Why?"

"Who are you?"

The click, click of his tongue, his claws, *something*, scraped down my spine. "I am he, and we are we."

"I-I-I want to save him." My hand fell to the glow of Kael's unmoving form. "Help me, please."

"How is it you've come here?"

"I don't know. I was handed a bone—"

Another laugh, deep and rough, rose from the phantom's chest. "Come to steal the souls in the bones? Come to corrupt the fallen for your own greed?"

"I don't want any of that. I want to save him."

"You take a soul from its rest." The shadow reached out a hand. Billows of smoky black rolled off his pointed finger. His attention was aimed at the new piece of bone I'd sewn into Kael's body. "Then I will take one to fill its place. A soul for a soul."

"Who are you?"

The spectral didn't respond, merely pulled back its cloak of shadows, revealing a thrashing shape on the murky ground. Add flesh and it might've been a small man, curled and skeletal.

Screams rattled the darkness. Cries of pain from the convulsing creature filled my ears until I clapped my palms to the sides of my head, desperate to muffle the agony of the sounds.

The more Kael's body melded with the new bone shard, the more the screeching figure broke apart, like embers in the wind. Golden ashes drifted over Kael's body, falling into the ghostly light of his bone.

All at once, the agony ended.

The wretched figure was gone and absorbed into Kael's heart.

In the silence, the shadow peered out from his misty cowl. The heat of its eyes like molten knives, reaching the marrow of my deepest fears, my dreariest thoughts.

"You destroy them"—a dark, wicked rasp scraped over my brain—"and they will destroy you."

I had no time to even scream before the shadow rushed toward me and its horrid coldness slashed into my chest.

8

ROARK

THE MELDER FLUNG BACKWARD, HER TRANCE BROKEN.
Sprawled out on the blood-soaked floor, she blinked.

Murmurs of Stav filtered across the hall. Folk of Skalfirth fell
under a harrowing silence, watching as the woman lifted her
bloody fingers with a bit of stun.

There was little time and patience to deal with hysterics if her
mind fell into panic.

I shifted a step nearer when she propped onto one elbow.
Breath caught in my chest, and I cursed my feckless reaction
when her eyes fell to me first. I'd anticipated frenzy and cries and
confusion, but she pinned me in place, as though she were peeling back my skin and glimpsing the darker edges of my soul.

There was a discomfiting peace in those eyes, like returning
home after a long frost.

I knew no other melder but Fadey. Being raised for half my
life in the Stonegate fortress, I had witnessed firsthand the brutality of melder craft. The lust for more, the corruption.

Still, for a moment, my hatred for melders dulled when her gaze found mine.

The woman was tall, clearly understood how to work, but still delicate in a way. Innocent. Not the sort I expected when we sailed here. Fadey had been a powerfully built man, as had the melders before him.

But she was stronger.

One touch and the bone shifted into place beneath Darkwin's ribs, melding the power of the soul bone into his broken wounds.

Fadey had worked slowly, with more blood and gore. When she started melding, the woman's hands worked as though she had used her craft from her earliest memories.

She was the melder who spurred deadly raids. So many lives were lost.

For her.

Because of her.

My jaw worked through the spark of disdain rising again. I shook out my hands, turned from her, and dragged three fingers over my chest, arching them out until I clapped them into my opposite palm. A gesture for the Stav to gather, for them to move to the boats.

Stav Guard chanted and pounded fists over their chests. Baldur stepped beside me. The damn grin on his face lifted the hair on my neck.

He reveled in the pain that he brought into this house.

With a sneer, the captain looked at the woman. "Prepare to sail. Bring the crafters. We take the new melder to our king."

Baldur wrenched her off the ground, too rough, and an odd resentment tightened my chest.

Something about her dug into my sympathies, and it was aggravating.

Moments after Lyra was on her feet, Darkwin drew in a new, deep breath.

A sob broke from her chest and tears filled her dark eyes, dripping rich blue drops onto her cheeks. I scoffed. Clever woman. When she peered at me again, the dyes had stained her skin and a thin, silver scar dug through the black centers of her eyes. Dyes, that was how she'd kept herself hidden for so damn long.

The honor given to a melder's household was enough even a mother would deliver her child to the gates of the royal keep upon the first glimpse of silver.

Except the fallen House Bien.

They kept their girl hidden until they paid with blood.

I'd barely met my twelfth summer when word filtered into Dravenmoor that the house of a new melder had been found. Distant memories of my folk strapping their longbows and seax blades to their shoulders still haunted my nights.

That raid was when I made a deadly misstep and lives were lost. Not long after, for my mistake, my folk left me for dead outside the walls of Stonegate, and the unexpected mercy of a young prince kept me breathing.

This woman—Lyra—had no sense of how soon her craft would be exploited.

"Sentry." A young Stav clicked his heels, drawing to stiff attention at my side. "Do we take them all with their households?"

The great hall fell into chaos and cries of folk pleading for the bone crafters to be left in peace. Darkwin was breathing, but bloody and still. Lyra called his name, each time her voice cracking a little more. On the opposite side of her, the two spare crafters reached for their families.

Perhaps they were innocent and knew nothing, but the laws of Stonegate gave Damir the power to take from traitors as he pleased, and the king always demanded every drop of magical blood be claimed.

I made a swift gesture. *Leave them. Only crafters.*

The Stav swallowed, then dipped his head and aided his fellow guards in tearing the man and woman away from their families.

"No!" The melder tugged against the guards, but her eyes found me.

A muscle flexed in my jaw, but I ignored her pleas and pushed my way through the chaos.

All at once, Darkwin thrashed in his own blood on the floorboards. Blood from the wound had stopped flowing, but his body kept convulsing.

"Help him!" Lyra twisted in Baldur's hold. "Remember, Sentry Ashwood, if he dies, then you have nothing. I swear it."

The blaze in her eyes sealed her threat. She'd send herself to Salur, no doubt.

When Baldur signaled for Emi—the bone crafter who tore Darkwin apart—I gripped his shoulder, shaking my head.

Emi's face had gone paler than it already was, and she was unsteady on her feet. Her damn craft had a bite to it. For bone crafters, the cost of manipulating in such a way caused phantom pains to burn in their own bodies.

No doubt, Emi's limbs and ribs were lined in discomfort, but I knew her—this unsteadiness rose from something else.

When we were alone, she would spew her rage for what I'd made her do.

Baldur shook me off and shouted at a young Stav. "Seal the wound tight enough he makes it to Stonegate to face the king."

The guard knelt beside Darkwin, wrapping clean linens over the split skin.

Already the soul bone was bolstering his broken ribs, and his chest appeared more intact. Soul bones healed and strengthened the living by absorbing pieces of the soul from the dead. The trouble was it was impossible to know if a healing body would take on the honor of the dead, or the darker desires.

When the melder shoved against Baldur's chest, the captain yanked her hair to reclaim his control.

Unbidden, the touch of his hands on her skin, the wince of pain on her features, brought another shock of rage to my blood.

I forced my steps to a halt, gathering my damn senses. What was I planning to do? Take her from Baldur and . . . what? Protect her? Shield her?

The sight of me so near brought her panic to a pause. Her silver-scarred gaze locked with mine, as though she could see every vicious thought in my head. Until a flash of something darker burned through and her lips curved into a sly sort of grin.

Dammit.

I lunged to stop her, but wasn't fast enough.

Lyra dropped as though her legs went boneless, managing to slip Baldur's grip. Before he could take hold of her wrist, she snagged a slender knife from the side of her calf.

Baldur recoiled when she slashed at his face. Lyra scrambled to her feet, swiping the blade at any Stav who approached, then pressed the edge of the knife to her throat.

I held up a fist to stop the men approaching her from every side. The melder and I would speak in our own way.

Her eyes were wild, the scars like falling stars in the velvet night.

"Leave them," she spat at me. "Leave my people. Take me, but you leave the rest."

A grin—for the first time since arriving—cut over my mouth. I'd been wrong. I thought her delicate; there was nothing delicate about this one.

She would not understand my words, but I asked the question all the same. *Meaning?*

"Lord Ashwood asks for your clarification," Baldur grumbled, no doubt irritable he'd been bested. "Who, exactly, are we to leave behind?"

"All the crafters."

My grin widened. *Treason has been found here and we cannot ignore it.*

"Treason can't be ignored," Baldur translated with effort. He was too haughty to take the time to learn how to deeply communicate with me.

I was glad for it and cared to speak with him as infrequently as possible.

I tilted my head to one side. *Because of the actions here, craft of this land now belongs to Stonegate.*

When Baldur finished the broken reply, defiance blazed in her features, and I wanted to keep the fury she hid beneath the simplicity of her station and appearance, burning like a wildfire in the wood.

When she stepped one way, I stepped the other. We circled each other like the sun chased the moon at dawn. Lyra didn't speak, merely pressed the knife into her skin, drawing a stream of blood that dripped down her slender throat.

I stopped my prowl, grin fading. *Spill another drop, woman, and you'll damn your people to the hells below.*

Baldur chuckled through his explanation of my threat, but it only deepened the burn of hate in her eyes. Enough chatter.

In three strides, I crossed the floor between us, only pausing when she drew in a sharp breath of air. Her stun caused her to press the blade deeper into her flesh, adding another drop of blood to the smooth center of her throat.

My gaze followed the descent, unblinking, until it cascaded between the cleft of her breasts.

To her favor, she didn't flush or look scandalized when our eyes met. "That will be the only look you shall ever receive, Sentry Ashwood."

She studied me, no doubt cataloging every scar, every twitch of my face. I, in turn, committed the small dust of freckles over her slender nose, tells of fear carved into her brow, her mouth, almost like each one was a forgotten memory.

Deep in the dregs of my soul grew an unnerving desire to keep her close.

"Take me," she said, voice low and rough, "and leave the rest. I am not asking."

A grumble of annoyance rolled out from my chest. I pressed a hooked finger against the side of my head and twisted, like tightening a bolt in a hinge.

"He says you are foolish," Baldur told her.

Her lips parted to spit back a reply, but I moved like a spark catching flame.

My fingers curled around her wrist, yanking the knife away from her throat. Seasons of training to drift in the shadows taught me to move as one, unseen until it was too late.

I peeled the knife from her grip, blade clattering on the floorboards, then pinned her body to my chest. One arm wrapped around her, keeping her arms tucked at her sides. With my free hand, I signaled to the Stav to move once more.

To the woman, I leaned in as though I could whisper. I did in my way, gently writing out my words against her cheek, taking a bit of twisted delight in the way she held her breath under my touch.

Say your goodbyes.

9

LYRA

BOOTS SCUFFLED OVER THE LONGHOUSE FLOOR. SOBS OF MY people split through my chest in an ache that felt like it would never heal—sharp as a shard of steel.

Night mists thickened the nearer we drew to the docks. I stumbled, but Ashwood refused to let me fall, keeping me upright, no matter how much my toes snagged across the pebbled shoreline.

Sconces marked the posts at the docks. The grim light played games with shadows, sprawling haunting shapes across the sails and hulls of the Stonegate longships.

One bitter tear dripped down my cheek when I took in the smooth, ashy stones of the Skalfirth beaches. I looked to the inky night sky bright with crystalline stars, to the crooked points of rooftops, then to Thorian's battered fishing nets. Hillsides and trees loomed around me like haunts in the darkness, watching as the village was torn apart.

"Lyra! Kael!" Selena sobbed on the path leading to the docks. The Stav Guard shoved her back into the crowds.

"Sel." My voice was a broken croak, too soft for her to hear.

Doubtless Selena took note of the wretched way my features contorted in fear, in pain, for she pressed a hand to her heart and did the same. She fell to her knees, pleading to the gods, who ignored us.

"You heartless bastard," I seethed at Roark.

The Sentry spun me around, pinning me to his chest. We were close enough, I had to tilt my head back to meet his stare. One of his palms cupped the back of my neck, squeezing until I stiffened beneath the grip.

For a drawn-out pause he held us there, nose to nose, then slowly pressed a finger to his lips. A command to keep silent and there was no mistaking the threat in it. His patience was spent.

Two longships bobbed in the tides. Clinker-built hulls bulged in the middle and were painted in the seal of Stonegate—a white wolf's head in front of a round shield and sword.

Most ships in the Skalfirth fjord came for trade, fishing, or passengers, and were fitted for only fifteen to twenty oars. These ships were built for battle and had places for sixty oarsmen.

My toe caught on the lip of the rail, but Roark caught hold of my hand.

I despised how warm his palm was against mine. There was an unwelcome gentility in the way he helped me over the rail of one longship, and I hated him all the more for it. Bruise me, batter me, be the creature I believed him to be. Kindness had no place in his actions.

When my feet were firmly planted inside the ship, I glared at Ashwood on the dock.

This was done under his command. Baldur shouted the orders, but the Sentry was to blame.

Another shoulder struck mine. Hilda, trembling and tearful, was shoved next to me. On the shore, Gisli, her husband, fell to his knees, a palm to his heart, like it might be breaking free of his chest.

This was wrong. Hilda had done nothing but carry bone craft in her blood.

Because of me, families were being ripped apart.

We did not know each other well. Hilda came from farmers, a loving home. Most of our interactions were had in the market and when the jarl offered the great hall for her wedding. Still, almost on instinct, she curled an arm around my shoulders, tucking me close against her side, no thought for the difference in our height, me standing half a head taller.

"Steady now, Lyra." Her voice cracked.

"Hilda, I'm so—"

"Hush," she said. "Not now. We need to keep our heads."

Edvin took up a place beside us. He took his sister's hand, but turned the pain in his eyes to the shore. The wife he adored, the three children he cherished, all huddled on the water's edge, broken and downtrod.

They would be forced to go on without a husband and father.

The Stonegate bone crafter materialized through the crowd of returning guards. She led the two men who carried Kael on a fur mat between them.

"In the center," she said, nodding as the two men placed Kael beside me and Hilda.

My hands fell to his chest, seeking the slow thrum of his heartbeat. Blood still stained his tunic, his shoulders were bruised and pulpy from the attack, but he was alive.

I curled my fingers around Kael's tunic, hardly noticing the shouts to take to the wind, the commands for oarsmen to take their places.

Through the blur of tears, the last sight I took from my home was of the fierce, unfeeling eyes of Roark Ashwood as he stepped onto the same deck—pain and suffering in his wake.

KAEL BURNED IN A FEVER THE DEEPER WE WENT OUT INTO THE short sea between Skalfirth and the hills of the royal keep. Black night cloaked all sides of the longships and only the steady dip of oars into the surface and lap of tides against the hulls were heard. The air was chilled, but Kael shivered like an early frost coated the sea.

With the help of Hilda, we draped him in any Stav cloaks that had been shed. I kept my arms wrapped around his shoulders, holding him close. When his fingers curled around my wrist, I grinned and pressed a kiss to the top of his sweaty head.

He was alive. He knew we were there.

Deep in the night, his groans grew louder, and the bone crafter from the great hall maneuvered to our sides.

"Get back." I tightened my hold on Kael's shoulders.

The woman shook her head like I was some sort of insufferable child. In her palms was a clay bowl filled with herb paste. The concoction smelled of damp bark and a bit of clove.

With two fingers she painted the pulse points of Kael's skin.

While she worked, she hummed a tune, a comforting song of old lore: *Kveða við min mórðir. Skip búask ok á morgun. Ek sigla til min folǫg.*

My throat tightened. From within the haze of a memory, the same gentle song lulled me off to sleep while slender fingers stroked my hair. Gammal sang it in the young house. Selena sang it while she baked.

To hear it from a Draven, an enemy I was raised to mistrust and despise, added a connection I did not want, a connection I resented, as though she'd stolen yet another thing.

"What is it you use on him?" I asked once her hands reached Kael's throat.

"Ortläk." Her eyes were like a sapphire sky, brilliant and fierce all at once. She couldn't have been much older than me, but there was a hardness in her features, like she'd already lived three lifetimes.

"I don't know of it."

"Most don't." She hummed for a few more breaths, caking the herbs over Kael's brow. "It is an old tonic made by my grandmother."

"Draven made."

She ignored the bite in my tone and nodded. "Craft does not have all the power. Sometimes our greatest gifts are found all around us in the water, the soil, the trees. This uses a moss that grows on the underside of logs. It seals wounds, reduces the chills of fever, and even extracts toxins from the blood."

I arched a brow, intrigued but furious enough to feign indifference.

The woman barreled on with her explanation as though her own concoction fascinated her. "Much like firevine and rosewood burn toxic in crafter veins, this moss is amplified. I found it heals a great many ailments for our folk."

"*Our* folk." I snorted and looked to the empty sea. "You are Draven and nearly killed him. You're not ours."

"Not the first I've heard those words." Her palms stilled. "I am born of both worlds and rejected for it. Because of this, I had to find my place and learn my craft. You will need to do the same.

By using your craft to save him, the strength of it will grow. It is like it has awakened, and will flow in your blood. Should your craft go dormant again, it will fester."

"Why should I believe you?"

She rolled her eyes. "Don't believe me. Believe the burn you felt when you touched that soul bone. Speak true: you felt a power unlike anything before."

I looked away, refusing to admit the truth.

The woman sighed. "I learned my craft well, Melder. Stonegate can help in that way. Be grateful it was me in the great hall. Darkwin would not have gone to Salur under my hand." With that, she stood and handed me the pouch. "If his fever remains, add more once the first layer has gone dry."

With each step she took toward the stempost, she sang the somber lines of the song—*at gafa skugga maðr . . .*

I blinked against the sting in my eyes, from the sea spray or something else, I didn't know. Softly, I murmured the final line in time with the Draven bone crafter, as though we were more alike than different for a moment, *Min sála, min sála.* My soul.

It was harrowing and true. Soon Stonegate would own not only my life, but my very soul.

"CRAFTERS, PAY ATTENTION." AT THE DAWN, THE BONE CRAFTER stood a few paces from the stempost. Her braids looked silver in the early threads of morning.

The second ship was spotted in the mists, distant from ours, but remained the only other sight. No land. No villages. Only Stonegate lay ahead.

Roark leaned against the coiled neck of the sea serpent stempost, arms folded over his chest, and faced the inner ship.

With my focus on Kael most of the night, I'd hardly taken note of the Sentry. Now he was a wash of somber, wretched beauty. Something cruel and hard, save the few moments of interaction he had with the Draven woman.

When she spoke to the Sentry, his features softened. The longer she whispered to him, the less tension seemed to stack on his taut body.

She mattered to him.

A lover, perhaps? I shuddered to think any sort could love a man like Roark Ashwood. Hate her as I did for the pain she'd caused Kael, the bone crafter had healed his fever. Without her rancid herbs, Kael might've faded from the infection and wounds.

"We will reach the shores of Stonegate by the morrow's nightfall," she announced, turning her back on Ashwood . . . as he turned to me.

The weight of his gaze spread an unnerving heat up my arms. A dozen stinging thorns on my skin. I kept my focus trained on the distant sea mists.

"The fortress is in the hills and will be reached by foot," she said. "Until then, you are under the watch and protection of Sentry Ashwood."

"We view protection as vastly different things, then." A low rasp jolted my heart.

My arms had long gone numb, locked in place around Kael's shoulders, but I shifted to peer at his face. He cracked one eye, and a weak smirk played in the corner of his mouth.

"Gods." The word slid over my tongue in a kind of plea. I hugged his back to my chest and practically throttled him from behind. "I think I hate you, Kael Darkwin. Don't you dare come so close to dying again."

"As you say." He let out a soft chuckle and gingerly rubbed my forearm around his chest.

A cinch of guilt tugged in my belly. "Kael, if I knew they planned to hurt you, I would never have argued with the Fox. Baldur knew what I was, and I . . . I tried to keep the lie too long."

"Don't." Kael squeezed my arm. "It isn't on you. I promised to keep your lies, and death isn't a sturdy enough threat to change that."

I rested my cheek on his brow, listening as the bone crafter went on with her instructions.

"You may know me as Emi Nightlark," the Stav Guard said.

Draven clans took odd surnames. Ashwood. Nightlark. Thorian explained to me that every Draven young one took a piece of the earth in their names—from the wood, the plants, the sea, the creatures—as a way to keep their souls connected to the wildlands where they lived.

Emi cleared her throat and went on, "I have lived in Stonegate since my fourteenth summer, and I understand what it is like to sit where you are." She hesitated. "So take my words and know it is not so dreary. This is not the end of your life, but there are expectations to remain safe within the gates."

"Nightlark isn't horrid, Ly," Kael said, hoarse and strained. "I met her, sparred with her. She did this under a direct command."

"She should have refused the command."

"Lyra." Kael sighed. "If not Emi, it would've been a blade from Captain Baldur. She even whispered to me before she used her craft that she would not let me die."

My anger at Ashwood, at Stonegate, at my own magic made it impossible to have a glimmer of appreciation for the woman. Kael and his endless optimism softened the disdain, but still I did not understand how another crafter could stand watch as families were torn apart.

There were means of surviving, then there were acts so vicious it would be better to die before committing them.

Emi described the trek to the gates. It would take long enough we would make camp in the wood before reaching the keep. From there we would be brought before the king.

A simple life, a purposeful life, that was how Emi described our new futures. Like all this was fated to be.

"For our journey," Emi went on, "you will be expected to learn a few hand signals Sentry Ashwood will use often."

Roark narrowed his eyes, but didn't move, merely took us in like he could not decide if we'd be better off in chains or drowned at the bottom of the sea.

Emi held up her palms, slowly moving through a few commands Roark might use on our journey and expected us to recognize.

To ask us if we were in need of aid, he would cup his palms and draw them toward us like a supplicant seeking food or coin. To signal an approaching fight or for us to take up blades, we'd watch for crossed wrists.

To claim something as his—a strike, a kill, a horn of ale— Ashwood tapped whatever he wanted three times.

Should a threat arise or danger grow close, Ashwood would pound one fist over the top of the other, then signal a count of how many threats we faced by tapping two fingers until we calculated the full amount.

"One tap signals there could be up to two assailants." Emi demonstrated on her own wrist. "Three taps means three or more. Understood? Naturally, if there are threats such as beasts or falling stone, I hope you all have enough wits to run without being told."

Herb bread and a few strips of dried herring and berries were passed about for a simple meal. Emi took the morning to guide us through more of Ashwood's commands, all while he kept his back to us, his focus on the sea.

I mimicked each gesture by my side; I watched every simple movement Roark made.

The man was not born of this land, yet he'd earned the trust of a king and the prince. Without the bark of captains or warriors, Ashwood could still bring a hush to a room, he could command the attention and respect of his men.

He was powerful and would not be a simple foe to defeat.

"You have not blinked once, Ly." Kael pulled himself up to sitting, back against the mast. "Do Ashwood's hands fascinate you for reasons I don't yet know?"

I rolled my eyes. "Emi taught us basic commands, but nothing to know his true words. I want to know what he says when he thinks we cannot understand."

"Why?"

I hesitated. "I don't know. I simply need to understand him."

The more I knew of the fiercest warrior of Stonegate, the more I had to believe I could find weaknesses in the walls. The more I had to believe I could get us free.

"When he speaks, I ask the woman Stav what it means."

"Making nice with Stav Nightlark?"

I snorted with a touch of derision. "Never, but she knows the Sentry enough to speak with him often, and she seems interested in earning my forgiveness for what she did to you."

Kael rolled his eyes. "Always scheming, aren't you, Súlka Bien?"

I ignored the jab and showed him a few subtle gestures with my fingers. "I've already learned more than the basic commands."

"You're picking up hand speak swiftly."

"Must be my craft. When I melded the shard into you, I could practically see the bones." The truth of the eerie phantom in the shadows died on my tongue. How would I explain such a thing without sounding like my magic had brought about an unnerving delusion? "Perhaps that is how I'm learning his words. I'm memorizing the movement of his bones, like I can see them."

I moved my hands in a new gesture Ashwood signaled to a nearby Stav Guard. In the next breath, the guard went through the unit, delivering orders for disembarking and making camp. The signal must've meant something about organizing the guard.

I blamed my craft, but there was something more, a pull toward Roark Ashwood that burned the words of his language into my mind. Like my own magic *needed* me to unravel anything about the man, and I could not help but want to learn the secrets he kept beneath his mask of cruelty.

"What if he's merely flicking at a pest near his ear?" Kael closed his eyes and tilted his face toward the misty sun. "You might be memorizing nothing."

I snorted a laugh. "Then I will learn it soon enough."

"You really think a man like Roark Ashwood will be so careless with his words?"

"I think a man like him underestimates those of us who have been forced to hide to survive."

"Lyra," Kael began, voice low. "Don't be foolish. Melder Fadey was constantly threatened by symbols and missives sent by commanders of the Dark Watch. The Draven army is known for spreading pieces of their victims across the Red Ravines. I don't want them to even breathe your name. Perhaps you should not fight this so fiercely. You might come to need his protection."

I picked at a few slivers in the damp laths. "How can you not see this as a betrayal? You've admired the Stav Guard—admired

Ashwood—for seasons, now look what they've done to you." When he didn't answer, I pulled my knees against my chest and propped my elbows on the tops to press my fists into my brow. "How can you stand it?"

A muscle ticked in Kael's jaw. "Because I am loyal to Jorvandal, but . . . I am also loyal to you."

We were silent for a long moment before I whispered a question for which I was not certain I wanted an answer. "Why would Vella want me dead?"

"I don't know, Ly. I never knew what Fadey's role was at Stonegate to bring such hatred for melding craft." With a wince, he pressed his hand to his side, and glanced over his shoulder before speaking. "For what she did, I do not mourn her death."

Damn this man. I kissed his brow.

Kael coughed through a groan and pressed a palm against his bandaged ribs, then looked to the stars again. "I believe Vella was manipulated to fear you by the Dravens. They despise Prince Thane's union with the princess of Myrda. And they despise that craft is strongest in Stonegate. King Damir has the power of melders and the support of the Myrdan king, and the Dravens want to take it all."

I rubbed the ache above my brow. "If Stonegate and King Damir are honorable, then why does no one truly know what goes on with a melder? Why are we forced to serve the king?"

"I don't know." Kael rubbed a hand on the back of his neck. "What I do know is when we reach Stonegate we must choose who we trust with care. This betrothal brings whispers of war, Ly. And the king will want our craft to be at the center of it."

LYRA

Y OU CANNOT REMAIN HERE, AND MUST WALK THE DECK."
Emi had rid her waist of her knives and the pouch with her herbs. Dressed down in a black tunic and simple hosen, the bone crafter seemed wholly unthreatening.

"Woman," Kael grumbled when she nudged his leg with her toe. "You've already tried to kill me once—"

"I did not try to kill you," she said in a huff. "For the last time, it was merely to spur *her* craft. I had it under control."

"Forgive me, Stav Nightlark, but I find your methods rather cruel. Now let me be."

Emi, at least two heads shorter than Kael, bent down and pressed a hand to his arm. For a moment, she didn't move.

Then Kael cursed and wrenched his arm away. "Damn you. Going to snap my arm now?"

"I will bend all your bones if you keep resisting my command." Emi grinned with a touch of smugness. "You need to walk. It helps the blood flow instead of pooling and hastens the healing in your wound."

"That you caused."

Emi pointed her face at the sky. "Get. Up."

Kael's protests and complaints faded once he was on his feet. His spine curved from the pain, but he was sturdier and had color in his cheeks again.

Dreary as our future seemed, Kael still managed to taunt and jest and brighten the journey. I did not wish this upon any of us, but was selfishly delighted I was here with him instead of facing it alone.

Hilda slept against Edvin's shoulder while he kept watch on the distant seas. There was little I could say to ease his heartache. So I said nothing, and merely squeezed his shoulder before rounding the mast to find my place.

Golden ribbons of sunlight drifted beyond the horizon, and opposite were shades of gray and black—the hills of Stonegate. As Emi promised, by nightfall we would make land.

On the other side of the mast, one elbow propped on the rail, was Ashwood.

Unlike Emi, Roark kept his seax on his hip and a bearded ax tied to a sheath on the small of his back. He curled two fingers, signaling for me to join him, and when I hesitated it only drew out a wretchedly intriguing half grin on his mouth.

I folded my arms over my chest, let out a breath of annoyance, and went to the rail. "What can I do for you, *Sentry Ashwood*? Come to thieve more plums?"

Gods, I was a damn fool. To provoke a man like Ashwood surely would end with my neck slit and my bones draped from the mast.

But Roark's wild eyes brightened, as though he took delight in my petulance.

"It amuses you, doesn't it?" I stepped closer, a mere pace away. "I know you marked my cart. You knew who I was from the beginning."

Ashwood took a slow, sweeping inspection of me with his eyes, drinking me in from brow, to throat, down my chest to . . .

I folded my arms over my body.

Roark plucked a scrap of parchment from a pouch on his belt. With his opposite hand he made a gesture of writing, then tilted his head, brows arched like a query.

After a pause, he waved his palms.

"You want to know if I understand you or you need to write?" He smirked. I hated when he smirked.

"I'm picking up your words rather quickly. Try me."

Again, the Sentry paused. Not from any sort of satisfaction, more like he was displeased he hadn't frightened me into submission.

With one hand, he spoke slowly, giving me time to catch the words. *Have you ever had a decent meal?*

Bastard. "I ate plenty before you tore innocent lives apart."

For a breath, Roark seemed stunned I understood. There wasn't time or desire to explain how his gestures resonated within me, as though the words were felt, not studied on his fingers.

I wanted to feel *nothing* for a man such as him, and certainly didn't want him to know I was failing.

He went on. *I was not the one who hid a melder.*

"No," I said, voice rough. "But you gave the orders to tear us from home. You ordered her to hurt Kael."

If Ashwood held any remorse, he didn't show it, merely nodded with a simple gesture. *True.*

Anger, fear, all of it was freeing my tongue. "Why did you not take me in the Fernwood? You find satisfaction in toying with the fears of others, is that it? How did you know it was me when we have never met?"

He didn't respond with his hands. Instead, Ashwood took up the parchment again and a narrow charcoal stick from the pouch. He hurriedly wrote out a few words and slid the parchment along the rail, waiting for me to take hold before removing his hand.

Our fingers brushed. I recoiled at once. His touch should've been cold, unfeeling, not . . . warm.

Roark frowned and flexed his fingers before curling them back into a fist, nodding with irritation for me to read.

My methods are my own.

When I merely scowled and looked away from his response, Roark added to the parchment.

You may ask questions, but do not expect answers from me.

"I would never expect anything from a Stav who is trained to strike down the defenseless."

Roark shifted abruptly, drawing closer, and I took a step back like a creature who spotted a trap. He paused, taking in the sudden stiffness of my stance. The Sentry dragged a hand through his loose hair and frowned, as though his patience for me was taxing.

With one hand he made small gestures, most motions Emi had taught me. *Remain beside me.*

He let the two fists he'd slid side by side fall when he finished. I narrowed my gaze. "Where else am I to go?"

Roark patted his chest with more force, adding firmness to his words. Next, crossed wrists—danger—but I could not follow the rest.

"Wait." I held out a hand. "Slow down."

A low sort of growl rumbled in his throat. Flicking one hand in the air, Roark snatched back the parchment. Jaw tight, he penned his thoughts.

You are under my charge until you are securely within Stonegate and afforded the king's protection. You already know there are many who despise melders and would see your head piked on a wall.

I read over his shoulder, interjecting like he was speaking the words out loud. "How would anyone even know we've arrived?"

The charcoal stick stilled in his hand for a breath. *Word travels fast when tensions are high. Folk are always looking for a way to King Damir. With our prince's betrothal, it is made worse. Stay close to me.*

Once I finished reading, I leaned my elbows onto the rail. "Stonegate has now imprisoned the only person I consider my family. You think I trust that Kael will not be killed? I assure you, I might welcome Salur rather than take what the king calls protection."

Roark frowned, flipped the parchment over, and added more to his missive.

If you think Darkwin's fate is the worst that can happen, then you have never met the blades of the Draven Dark Watch or their assassin's ravagers.

Sweat dampened my palms. "You say this, but you are Draven."

Roark stiffened, but hurriedly added another line. *All the more reason to trust what I say.*

"I will never trust what you say." The words came out soft, unintended, but there all the same. A poison between us.

With the charcoal still staining his fingers, Roark spoke with his hands, slow and direct, so I would catch each silent word. *Then you will likely die.*

I shrugged one shoulder and leaned onto my elbows on the rail. "The threat is meaningless, Sentry Ashwood. I'm certain, no matter what I do, it won't be long until I die anyway."

LYRA

THE SHIPS DOCKED ON A CURVED, PEBBLED SHORE.
A high moon muted the light of the stars overhead, and
all around were towering evergreens growing from rocky soil.
After endless strolls around the deck of the ship, Kael stood upright, holding only one side with his palm. Hilda and Edvin clung
to each other, but their faces, normally so lively, were like stone.
Cold. Hard.

We formed a crooked line amid the Stav.

Here in the lands of the king, the air was sharp with spice
from sap and spruce. Sea winds were still chilled, but didn't cut
to the bone. More subtle and briny.

Stav Guard shoved past me, took hold of the others, and pulled
them away.

"Wait." I reached for Kael, but was barred away from him by
four guards who gathered in a line. "Wait, where are you taking
them?"

One of the guards stepped in front of me. "Better not to travel with so many crafters in one camp. They'll travel with Captain Baldur's unit down the shore. You and Stav Nightlark will be the crafters in our camp."

"I won't be able to know if they're safe."

"They'll be safe and fed." The young Stav adjusted a leather strap over his shoulder that was lined in bronze throwing knives. "Until we reach the fortress, of course. After that, I think the Norns will have to decide their fate."

My stomach twisted. The risk of entering the gates of the royal keep was Kael might lose his life. I had one night to decide if it was a risk we took, or if we ran. With him gone down the shore, I did not know how I'd reach him.

Before he disappeared around a bend in the shoreline, Kael flashed his wide grin, no mistake, attempting to ease my troubles.

Roark's men maneuvered satchels, fur bedding rolls, and crates of water skins and dried meats in a tangle of lines for the journey.

"Melder." Emi approached with a touch of caution. "You'd be wise to keep close, the wood is dangerous. These trees house bears and fara wolves."

"Draven wolves?" The Draven folk were known to hunt their enemies not only with steel, but with beasts they bonded with from birth.

"Aye." Emi looked to the trees. "But more than all that, blood casts have been set in the groves to disorient and confuse wanderers away from reaching the fortress."

Gods. I knew Queen Ingir was born of Myrda and chosen to wed King Damir for her blood craft, but I studied so little of the three magical crafts, due to fear of my own, I did not realize she could cast such spells.

Perhaps there were many blood crafters in Stonegate.

Roark took a brisk step forward, shrouding his head in the dark hood, as though telling me he was to keep watch, but did not need to look at me.

The Sentry's contempt for melding craft was clear, and I hated the subtle bite of curiosity to learn why. Had he been harmed by a melder? Was it to do with the raids so long ago?

As a Draven in the royal court of Jorvandal, doubtless Roark Ashwood had learned to keep secrets the way I'd kept them all this time.

I could not see his eyes beneath his cowl, but glared at the strong line of his mouth until we stood chest to chest again. Roark removed his ax from the sheath on his back and handed it to me.

One brow curved. "What—"

I was unaccustomed to being interrupted by a man who did not speak, but Roark used his hands to command an interaction as fiercely as Baldur used shouts to overpower.

He spoke one word, a gesture Emi had taught us on the ship—*knowledge.*

"Do I know how to use it? I'm not as skilled as a Stav, but I can throw one. Might even know how to slit a throat if you'd like to test it."

Roark made a breathy sound.

Strange how his reputation painted him as a man of violence, yet he swallowed my sharp words with a hint of amusement. He never lifted a hand to strike any of us; he did not shove and prod like many of the Stav under his watch.

None of this eased the distrust. In a way, it left me wondering if Roark's demeanor was like the lure of a hunter's call. A ruse to get us to find a bit of composure around him, before he struck when we least expected.

Roark swept an arm, ushering me to take a step before him. My grip tightened around the ax, and I complied.

Through a narrow barrier of trees, a clearing gave way to a meager campsite. White wolf emblems marked the canvas sides of tents and bowers.

"There are several Stav camps in these woods," Emi said, her shoulder knocking mine as she strode past. "These are also the finest, with a few moss mattresses. You'll sleep better than on the longship."

One brow arched. "Should I be glad for it?"

"You might try." Emi flashed a tight grin and strode ahead of me.

I kept my pace aligned with Roark's. Murmurs and a few simple gestures from the Stav and Sentry gave up we would camp until the first mists of dawn.

"Keep your eyes peeled for Dark Watchers," a burly Stav passed down the line. "Those Draven sods know the wilds, they know how to blend, and are damn hard to see at night."

"They could attack the camp." The words slipped out in a whisper, and when Ashwood paused to glance at me, I wished I could snatch them back. I shook my head. "Never mind."

The Sentry faced me, tossed back his hood, and made slow, even gestures at an angle that caught the cold moonlight. *The blood crafter's betrayal has already alerted Dravenmoor to believe the child melder is alive.*

"But the missives were intercepted and—"

Roark interjected with a wave of his hand. *Her Draven correspondence did not receive a response. They are no fools and will suspect their plans have been foiled.*

The Sentry repeated his gestures three times before I nodded my understanding.

"I could've lived a quiet life." My teeth ground together for a breath before I went on. "I wouldn't have harmed anyone if you'd just left me alone. Now kingdoms are threatening kingdoms and you've torn innocent families apart. For what? What does the king want from me? Why is fusing bone to bone so damn coveted?"

Roark didn't move his hands for a long pause. *I did not want this either. If it were left to me, you would never have made it out of the raids. Now keep up.*

The callousness of his silent words settled like sour venom on my tongue. He despised me, cared nothing for Edvin, Hilda, or Kael, and I was expected to trust this man with my life.

The Stav had a torch lead at the front of the line, but no other lanterns or flames were permitted, an attempt to keep out of sight from beasts and any enemy arrows in the trees. The trouble was it made it damn impossible to see.

Soon enough, the Sentry had to take hold of my wrist. Roark Ashwood moved like he was made of the wood, at least the darkness of it. He kept a swift pace, never removing his grip on my arm.

His ax was made of fine materials—bronze on the head and a black handle carved in runes. Not manipulated bone like most Stav blades. Odd for such a man to trust me with a weapon.

Then again, I wasn't certain Sentry Ashwood knew how to truly fear. He was deadly enough he was always the predator.

Night mists thickened, the cold deepened, and the slope increased. My fingers around the handle of the ax had long grown numb from the chill. If anyone lunged, I would hardly be able to strike.

Whispers from nearby guards found me. Some wondered what happened to the rest of House Bien during the raids.

Dead. Most of the replies insisted my mother and father were slaughtered.

I ground my teeth, a new sort of anger boiled in my chest. So many seemed to know my story, but I did not.

All I had were screams and the haunting crackle of flames. Tense arms and muffled voices, running through mists.

A shudder rolled down my spine. There was a truth I could almost make out—someone pulled me away from the terror of the raids. Someone took me to that young house with gentle Gammal.

But I did not know how I would ever learn the truth.

My lungs ached by the time Roark paused in front of a small ring of huts tucked within a copse of aspen trees.

In the center was a fire pit with iron hooks for cooking, and casks of ale were still stacked against the mudded walls of every structure.

The Sentry pointed toward a shanty near the back edge of the camp. He pressed a palm to his chest, a signal that was his to use, and now it would be shared with . . . me.

LYRA

ASHWOOD PULLED BACK THE STAINED CANVAS FLAP THAT made a makeshift door over the hut entrance. His jaw flexed as he positioned his spine against the frame of the door, offering space for me to slip past without drawing too near.

I rolled back my shoulders and strode over the threshold.

The floors were made of dusty boards and cold clay. Crooked tallow candles lined a narrow table against one wall, and the bed was nothing more than a moss-filled mattress and an old burlap quilt haphazardly tossed over the top.

Ashwood shoved inside, took the ax from my hands, and stripped his cloak at once, tossing the garment over the table. He kept his back toward me.

The stance was a muted insult. I was no threat to him.

Roark tossed the ax onto the table and began removing knives and shivs from hidden pockets in his jerkin.

Disquiet twisted low in my belly. If he continued much longer, the Sentry would begin to undress.

Damn the gods, was that expected? Was my body his to use until we reached the gates of the fortress?

Kael spoke of Ashwood's honor, but many Stav Guard would view me as a conquest, a traitor who was no more a woman than the pebbles beneath their feet.

There was no honor that went with breaking an enemy.

I studied each position of the blades. Lined with precision across the tabletop, I counted five in all, but the Sentry kept his sword sheathed on his waist.

Should he lunge for me, it was possible I could slip around him and take hold of one of the small blades. Then what? I could throw a knife with accuracy, but if I managed to land a strike, Roark wore his leather jerkin, vambraces, and thick woolen trousers.

Not to mention, the man was broad and nearly two heads taller. He would have me pinned beneath him in moments.

The sound of fingers snapping drew my gaze back to his.

Ashwood dropped his hand, a befuddled look on his features, as though he didn't know what to make of me. After a breath, the Sentry opened his palm toward the mattress.

I swallowed the fear and shook my head.

He arched a brow, but turned to the table. Parchment tore and a few scratches of a charcoal pen returned a note.

Sleep here.

Blood pounded in my skull. "I won't let you touch me."

With a throaty scoff, he shook his head and added to his missive.

I've no plans to touch you. You will sleep here. We move at first light, so rest while you can.

A ruse. A bit of a false reprieve.

The hair lifted on the back of my neck; I skirted to one side when Ashwood gathered his weapons and placed them in a rabbit-fur pouch, then took up a folded linen from a basket and tossed it over his shoulder.

For a heartbeat or two, the Sentry peered at me with a touch of aggravation, then drifted toward the doorway. He held up a palm, motioning I was to remain.

"You're not . . . staying here?"

He shook his head and pointed at the canvas door. I took it to mean he would remain outdoors.

Strange, but the notion of being left unattended with other Stav Guard drew out a deeper knot of fear. Brutal as he was, Roark had power in this camp. His word would be honored, and for now it seemed he wanted to be nowhere near me.

"And will you allow your men to enter?" Gods, I despised how the words trembled over my lips. The boldness I'd felt when I leveled a blade to my own throat cracked with every step away from Skalfirth.

A shadow crossed Roark's features. I drew in a sharp breath when he crowded me near the bed until my knees struck the edge, forcing me to fall back on the mattress.

The Sentry placed his palm against my cheek. I stiffened, eyes closed. But all he did was tap my face three times.

Roark turned away in the next heartbeat and abandoned the hut.

Pulse racing, I touched where Ashwood held his hand. Three taps—his gesture for claiming something as his.

It meant *mine*.

A word meaning a dozen things—his to command, his to use, his to protect.

It didn't matter, there was truth to it. Since the moment he stepped foot on the pebbled shores of Skalfirth until he turned me over to the king, I belonged to Roark Ashwood.

THE HOLE IN THE CORNER OF THE HUT WAS HARDLY NOTICEABLE. Small rodents likely dug through the dirt and clay to seek refuge in the Sentry's shelter during the frosted months. Once it was clear Ashwood would not be returning, I took to clawing at the soil.

A reckless, stupid plan. Risks of Dravens, of creatures, and of the spell casts Emi mentioned all rattled through my mind, but the moment I began, I could not stop.

I dug and dug until I slipped into a bit of frenzy.

From rain and chill to heat and damp, the soil was hardened and rough. Sharp pieces of rock and twigs scraped at my callused fingertips. I kept digging. Sweat dripped over my lashes. When I blinked, the salt slid down to my lips.

Chipped stone ripped my fingernails, drawing blood. I winced and dug faster, careful to move as the night shadows—silent phantoms.

The longer I thought on the royal keep, the more I knew Kael faced too great a risk. We had to leave. Tonight. Even if I found Kael, I wasn't certain we would have the time or ability to free Edvin and Hilda.

I used my fists to dig deeper. They deserved freedom—they were here because I had been found out—but . . . I would always choose Kael first.

If we broke free, if we stayed hidden just long enough, perhaps we could find a way across the Myrdan border and slip back into obscurity, never use our crafts, and hide the silver curse in my eyes as we'd always done. I cursed when a jagged pebble sliced under my fingernail, and reared back.

I sucked away the blood on my thumb, somewhere inside knowing this plan was foolhardy.

Dangers hid in the wood, but there was also freedom.

By the time my spine was heavy with fatigue, the burrow was large enough to fit my bony shoulders.

With a glance at the canvas door, I slipped my head into the soil. Soon enough the frosted blue moonlight washed over my cheeks. I reached for it, the brine and chill in the air burning my lungs with each ragged breath.

The position of Ashwood's hut had added a barrier of trees with gnarled branches. I crouched in the tangle of leaves, watching.

Ten paces ahead, the Stav Guard first watch patrolled the edge of the wood. Pairs sauntered shoulder to shoulder, never glancing back when their route curved around the camp to the opposite side.

Baldur's unit camped just beyond the line of trees. Flames from their torches were hazy drops of gold in the distance. If I could keep out of sight long enough, I could come up on the camp, find Kael, and perhaps find a way to distract the Stav until we faded into the darkness.

Night mists coiled around the thick trunks of evergreens and oak trees. The wood felt haunted and formidable.

I maneuvered behind a wild fern, muscles clenched, when the patrols of Stav strode past again. One guard's mouth cracked in a sturdy yawn and he stumbled when his companion nudged his ribs, urging him to keep alert.

On my belly like a burrowing creature, I waited for the pairs of Stav to take a step in opposing directions, briefly leaving a gaping hole that would lead to the trees.

I tore from the burrow, sprinting free of the hut, never looking back.

The moment shadows swallowed me, I slammed my back against a crooked oak. Feverish heat scorched across my face, and my frenzied pulse made each draw of breath tight and ragged.

Gods.

All gods.

I'd done it.

I peered around the trunk of the tree slow like a rusted hinge, and studied the camp. No alarms were sounded, no blades, no Sentry.

How long my good fortune would last was not a game I would risk losing. I ducked my head beneath the night mists and hurried in the direction of the sea.

Baldur's camp couldn't be too far, not if we were to enter Stonegate together.

The trouble was from this new angle, no golden beams of torches broke the mists. Truth be told, the darkness thickened. Deep black devoured any gleam of the cold moon, coating the forest in shadows I could taste.

Dammit.

The blood casts. I cursed under my breath. Part of me considered Stav Nightlark lied about the spells, but the deeper I went, the less direction I had.

Lanterns from the second camp were lost to the darkness, and Kael was lost to me.

I jolted at every flutter of wings, every snap of twigs in the distance. Twisted vines coated the soil in a cloak of serpentine knots, climbing my ankles like tethers looking to chain me down.

Turn around. I needed to turn around and return to my camp, but I could not make out from which direction I'd come.

Haunts possessed these trees. Tricks of the mind kept folk lost and helpless lest they knew the wood to their soul.

It was no wonder why Roark was the lead party—Dravens were feral people. Some of Jakobson's servants told tales of how the people of Dravenmoor could speak to the souls buried in the soil to help guide their way.

A gust of wind battered my shoulders. I curled against it, but on my next step slipped down a dark slope, landing hard in a pile of brambles and dry leaves. I groaned, lifting my head. More pitch, more endless night mists.

Something damp and warm coated my arm. The sleeve of my dress was torn and the flesh split, blood dripping down my elbow.

Damn my reckless mind.

Damn my foolish plans.

Now, more than ever, I was lost in the trees, open prey for gnashing teeth and Draven arrows.

I did not know how long I traipsed through vines and hedges, but finally a glimmer of light burned through the haze of mists.

A torch.

Between two twisted, spindly aspen trees, the wood opened to a clearing.

The light was there, but it did not come from a torch or fire pit.

Light, like the faintest glimmer of dawn, skimmed across the soil. Tattered posts with ragged bits of canvas were arranged around a stone pit with scorched wood and an iron stoker still in place.

Another camp. One abandoned and left to rot.

No sign of Stav Guard, no ensnared bone crafters, nothing but bulbs of light buried in the brambles. I rubbed the chill from my arms and knelt beside one of the golden mounds.

Buried in a shallow pit was something pale, curved, and knobbed like it had not been moved for some time. Long. Human.

An arm, or what was left of one.

Flesh had long since been pecked away by creeping pests and birds, and all that remained was bone.

Nausea rolled from my stomach into my throat, hot and rank. I scrambled backward and took in the clearing of light. Bones. The same as the shard had spun in golden threads when I melded it to Kael, now dozens of heaping piles of bone gleamed through the soil.

I was surrounded by a massacre.

Branches snapped. Dead, brittle leaves rustled. A low, menacing growl broke the silence.

From between two leaning aspens came the flash of wet teeth. Red eyes like glowing embers locked on mine. Each hooked claw was elongated from the beast's paws. A fara wolf.

Teeth as long as my thumbs, hunched shoulders like a bear, but with the speed of a common forest wolf.

The wolf snapped its jaws.

I stumbled backward, my heel catching on one of the burial mounds. With a snapping bark the wolf plodded over the shattered camp on heavy paws. I screamed, scrambling to find a weapon, a stone, anything to fend off the claws and teeth.

My grip returned with a broken twig.

Shit.

I dropped to my knees, curled my shoulders, and waited for the pain of teeth sinking into my skin, but it didn't come.

A snarl was soon followed by a low whimper. I cracked one eye. Ten paces away, the wolf bared its teeth and flicked its tail at a man standing in front of its snout.

Gods. The Sentry.

Roark's golden eyes burned like a stormy sunrise; he looked nowhere but at the wolf. The Sentry stepped to the left, clicking his tongue and slashing a curved knife. The creature growled, but kept its ears pinned back, its head down.

Roark waved his hand. It took me a breath to realize he was signaling to me, telling me to run.

I rushed to my feet. The wolf snapped its bloody gaze, flinching like it might bolt after me, but Ashwood took a long step, becoming another barrier between me and a brutal end.

I kept my head down and raced for the tree line. At my back, the hiss of steel slicing through the air was met with snarls and the rustle of leaves.

I raced behind a thick oak and pressed my back to the trunk, drawing in deep gulps of air. A wash of guilt stirred in the pit of my belly. Roark Ashwood was the Death Bringer, a brute and heartless fiend for what he'd done in Skalfirth. Still, part of me did not want to see the man torn apart by a wolf.

When I looked back into the clearing, my pulse stilled.

Ashwood had one open palm on the top of the wolf's head. The beast was on its side, ribs rising in steady breaths, and its eyes were . . . closed.

As though the Sentry's touch had lulled it into a deep sleep.

Unaware of my scrutiny, Roark leaned forward, his hands making an arrow point shape on top of the wolf's head. The Sentry pressed a kiss to his hands over the crown of the wolf, then rose to his feet, sheathing the curved blade on his outer thigh.

By the endless gods . . .

Roark strode through the darkness, furious gaze on my tree, as though he were part of the mists. His hair was damp and his bare chest was coated in dirt and a splatter of blood from claw marks across his upper shoulder.

Once he reached me, anger flashed in his eyes like hot coals. Roark gave me a rough shake before releasing my arms. He twisted his knuckle to the side of his head—*foolish*—but he did not cease his silent rage. His hands spoke in rough gestures, some I had memorized, most I could not follow.

Strange, but I yearned to curl away beneath the shouts of

his silent language more than if he screamed the words in my face.

After a breath, the Sentry tossed his hands over his head, frustrated, and dragged his fingers through his hair.

In slower, steadier movements Roark made simple gestures for my benefit. The message clear—I could have died here.

"I wanted to see Kael," I said, voice soft and broken. "I . . . I didn't mean to go so far."

Ashwood closed his eyes for a breath, then lowered to a crouch, one knee bent. He tore out parchment from the pouch on his belt and penned a response. With the glow from the piles of bones, it was not so hard to read.

You were nearly killed to soothe your own worries. Darkwin and the crafters are unharmed. If you die on the journey, the king's wrath will be theirs to shoulder.

Tears of anger burned behind my eyes. "They do not deserve it. Let them go. They are innocent here."

Roark snatched the parchment from my hands and wrote against one of his palms.

Cease your childish naivety, follow my damn commands, and you all might live longer.

Before I had time to move away, Ashwood took hold of my arm and tugged me against the hard planes of his chest. Breath slid out in a gasp when he gripped my chin, forcing me to meet his gaze.

He shifted my face side to side, as though inspecting for wounds, his fingers almost gentle against my cheek as he asked, *Did it hurt you?*

The words were formed slowly, but it was another moment where I needed little help in understanding, like a deeper part of me *felt* his words.

I shook my head, uncertain what more to say.

After a moment, he jerked his head toward the shadows of the wood, an unspoken command that we would return to camp together.

"How did you calm it?" I looked at the slumbering wolf.

The Sentry's jaw tightened as he wrote in the corner of the parchment.

Fara wolves are loyal to souls who respect them. I spoke to its soul, let it trust me. Dravens are taught how to speak to fara before their fourth summer.

The soul. Draven folk used soul craft. No one ever mentioned if Ashwood had a talent with the magic, but it seemed even if he did not, Dravens knew how to communicate deeper than ears could hear.

"Are you . . . hurt badly?" Without a thought, I reached for the gash on his shoulder.

Roark pulled back, shaking his head.

I curled my hand into a fist and took a step back. "What is this place? There are bones everywhere." He paused, a muscle flexed over the hinge of his jaw. He tore a new scrap of parchment and wrote—this time using my shoulder as a tabletop.

What becomes of Stav and reckless women who wander the trees and face an ambush of ravagers.

I ignored his veiled insult and took in the massacred camp once more. "Skul Drek and his followers did this?"

This was how viciously the rogues of the untouchable Draven assassin left their victims?

Roark's mouth tightened, but he gave a rough nod.

I bit down on my bottom lip, taking a final look at the mounds of golden bones. "Do you see the glow?"

The Sentry arched a brow, but followed my gaze. Once more, he removed the parchment and wrote: *A melder's eye sees the souls that once were in the bones. Fadey could not summon the sight at will.*

I rubbed the inked runes on my neck. The insinuation came out like the Sentry thought me stronger than the former melder.

With the way Ashwood held me in a constant glare, I did not think it was a compliment.

The Sentry didn't bind my wrists, he did not level threats of maiming for my disobedience, he merely kept hold of my arm until we emerged from the harrowing shadows of the wood, returned to the ring of huts.

With a note that we would break camp at dawn and I would get my coveted glimpse of Kael, Roark settled in a rickety wooden chair in the corner of his shanty.

I slipped onto the makeshift bed, hugging my knees into my chest. Across the hut, Roark folded his arms over his chest, still covered in gore, and closed his eyes.

"Thank you," I whispered, tugging a thin fur under my nose to hide the quiver of my chin.

Roark cracked one eye, narrowed and angry, but after a pause he dipped his chin in a soft nod, and slumped deeper into the chair.

It was only in the moments before I fell into a fitful sleep that I realized Roark Ashwood found me without a torch. He was able to slash at the wolf, calm its soul, and find me in the shadows with only a sliver of moonlight to guide him. He'd written in the darkness without trouble.

Roark never truly responded to my query about the bones, merely spoke of a melder's sight, but he'd moved about the clearing as though he could see the strange, frightening glow of bones the same as me.

LYRA

THE STAV ROSE WITH THE DAWN. I WOKE TO ROARK'S BOOTS stomping out of the shanty at the first song of the morning birds.

He was replaced in the next moment with Stav Nightlark.

Her eyes sparked with something like annoyance, but Emi said nothing about my poorly executed escape, nor the blood that painted the chest of the Sentry as he strode past.

Emi supplied me with fresh hosen and an oversize tunic the color of forest moss. A strong scent of leather and harsh soap was wrapped in the threads, but to peel away from the brine-crusted hem on my woolen dress sent a shudder of pleasure down my spine.

She held up a cloak against the corner of the shanty, giving me a moment to scrub away dirt and sweat from the journey. "You'll be given time to wash fully before greeting the king once you reach Stonegate."

I nodded a wordless thanks. No one was required to give me

even a bed to sleep in, but Ashwood had done it, even after I fled, even after he'd tamed a damn wolf to save my neck. Nightlark did not need to take a pause to bring clothes or cool water to wet my skin, but she did.

It was disquieting how their actions did not fit into the simple vision of what I imagined. Cruelty, indifference, perhaps chains around the wrists and neck.

"Darkwin is outside." Emi folded the linen, her gaze turned away.

I whirled around, still lacing the front of the tunic closed. "Kael's here?"

"The Fox arrived with his men not long ago. The other crafters are alive and horridly somber."

My jaw tightened. "Couldn't be because a father was torn from his young ones, and a new bride was taken from a husband who adores her, could it?"

Emi shook her head. "Do not pretend any of us had a choice in this, Melder. Do not pretend you didn't nearly make their lives more unbearable."

I swallowed. The brisk, jagged edges to her tone gave up the first hint at how Emi Nightlark managed to stand as a respected Stav, Draven blood and all.

She stomped across the hut, kicking up dust and a few pebbles as she went. When her chest butted mine, she looked upon me with a narrow gaze. "What I *can* do for them—if you will allow it—is offer advice as a bone crafter torn from everything she knew. You are not the only ones who've lost family."

The desire to look away was potent. I held steady, giving her the decency of my attention, but a sheepish heat prickled up the back of my neck.

What did I know about the two Dravens in the Stav Guard?

They were in a foreign land, serving the enemies of the clan of their births. How did they come to be under King Damir's rule? Perhaps that was why Roark softened around Emi—they might've been all the other had from home.

I looked down, fingers fiddling with a loose thread on the hem of the tunic. "I merely want them safe. I do not know how to keep them alive when I do not know what we're facing by the day's end."

Emi let out a sigh. "Then I urge you to listen to us. Sentry Ashwood is honorable. He said he would get you to Stonegate, and I now believe he will."

"Did you not believe he would before?"

She smirked. "I didn't think he would risk his own neck against a fara wolf which did not share a bond to him, no. But like the Sentry, I said I didn't want Darkwin or any of you dead, and I meant it. I can offer the bone crafters guidance to their new lives in Stonegate. I could do the same for you if you would stop being a damn fool and stop risking your own neck in the wood."

With one finger, Emi signaled for me to join her near a narrow gap in the wall. "Look upon those trees in daylight."

I hesitated for a few breaths, then went to her side and peeked through the cracks in the daub between the laths.

Mists glided through the edge of the clearing. The trees were black and silent, gray clouds darkened behind the rich emerald leaves. Bursts of fiery orange clashed against the dreary bark and stumps with sea moss or blooming shrubs. But dripping shadows slithered across limbs and branches like dark serpents. Beneath the morning light remained a heady foreboding about the wood.

Darkness reigned here. Step too deeply beyond, and it would swallow you whole.

"It takes no time for wanderers to lose themselves, fall into the jagged ravines, meet the teeth of hungry fara wolves, or freeze until their skin is blackened and blue. There is a reason elders call these trees *draugaskógur*," Emi said, a hidden smile in the corner of her full lips. "The Phantom Forest. War and battles have brought too much death in these trees not to leave them a bit haunted."

The disorienting lure of the trees, the honeycomb of earthen paths, the tangle of branches and briars, all of it had drawn me in like a doe caught in a hunter's snare.

"The Sentry managed to find me swiftly." I turned back into the small room, gathering in my arms the dirty dress I'd worn on the ship.

"Because no one knows these woods like Roark." Emi stopped in front of the canvas doorway. "It is one reason why he holds his rank. Despicable as you find us Draven folk, we are taught from our first steps how to use signals in the trees to find our way, how to speak to the very soul of the forest. The ravines that divide the kingdoms are heavy with woodlands. It is where we learn to survive, or die.

Emi handed me a leather satchel to hold my old clothes on the rest of the journey. As I secured my dress inside, I lifted my attention back to her. "Do you miss it? Dravenmoor, I mean."

She lifted one shoulder in a shrug. "I miss the wildness of it, the trust my clan has for the land and the gods. But there was no longer a life for me there."

"Why not?"

"You trust me so little, yet expect me to give up my whole past?"

Heat flushed my cheeks, and I turned away. "You're right. Your business is your own."

I slung the strap of the satchel over my head, securing it on one shoulder. Before I could move for the door, Emi placed a hand on my arm.

"I was born with the wrong craft. Bone craft is not meant to be found in Draven blood. My father believed my mother must've been unfaithful, even managed to get her tried as a traitor, calling her a whore. She was banished, and not a full season later one of our hunters found her body half-devoured."

"All gods." I gripped the strap of the satchel, fighting the urge to take her hand for reassurance, almost like a brief urge to befriend the woman.

From beneath the thin mattress Emi gathered a knife I'd not realized was there and secured it inside her boot. "When a few more winters passed, I realized I no longer had a place in Dravenmoor. Roark was already established in Stonegate, and saw to it I was brought behind the walls. Is that enough of an explanation? We best be off soon."

Emi slipped around me, clearly finished with her tale.

"I don't remember the raids. I don't remember my mother and father." The admission spilled over my lips before I could think better of it. "Only in my deepest nightmares do I hear the screams and smell the blood. Someone took me away—I can almost hear his voice—but I don't know who it was."

One corner of Emi's full mouth curved when she looked over her shoulder. "Seems we all have broken paths that have led us here. What if this is exactly where the Norns intended for you to be, Melder?"

I frowned. If the Norns kept me alive all so my fate would place me in captivity within Stonegate, I rather hated them.

"So," I pressed once we stepped into the morning light, "what brought the Sentry to Stonegate?"

"That is his tale to tell. You're quite nosy when you start speaking."

I tugged my bottom lip between my teeth to muffle a soft chuckle. "I've seen little of the world; naturally, questions will arise. What was the reason you finally left Dravenmoor?"

When Emi faced me, her lips curled in a sort of snarl. "I had to flee."

"Had to? Didn't you say you were young when you arrived at Stonegate?"

"Only fourteen."

"They drove you out?"

"I ran before they could."

"What happened?"

Emi's eyes flashed with a touch of malice. "I tried to cut off my father's head."

With a wink, more condescending than kind, Emi slipped past me and entered the camp.

The bustle of Stav Guard was alive with curses and bawdy talk. Water splashed over the sound of palms slapping at bare skin as the guard tidied themselves for the king's court. Boots stomped, and spitting grease hissed and crackled over the snap of flames.

"Nightlark!" A guard, bare-chested and staggering near the fire, waved at Emi. "I signed up to watch your back near the creek should you wish to bathe. I'd even watch your front if you'd like."

Some of his nearby Stav brothers chuckled.

Emi didn't flinch. She turned to the guard, a smirk on her lips. "Ah, Henrik, I'm not interested in helping you practice."

The Stav grunted, palming himself over his trousers. "Trust me, I've no need for practice with this sword."

I fought the urge to groan. He reminded me of the aggravating stable hands at House Jakobson, always so impressed with what they had between their legs.

Emi pressed a hand to her chest in mock relief. "I'm so relieved to hear you've improved. Last I heard from the madam at the Golden Wing, her girl Asha felt rather guilty taking your florin. Said you were quivering like a pup, so worried you might put it in the wrong spot. The way I hear it, all you got for your coin was a kiss on your sweet little brow."

Henrik's fellow Stav howled and shoved his shoulders. His face flushed and his smile faded. "That's not true." He pushed the chest of one of the laughing men at his side. "Had her screaming for more, I did."

"Of course." Emi flashed a condescending grin. "Of course. Still, if you'd like, I can draw you a guide on the proper holes for next time."

With that, Stav Nightlark took my arm and urged me in the opposite direction of the laughter and taunts about why the guard's dalliance with the woman named Asha had ended so abruptly.

"I am one of few women in the Stav, Melder. The others are old and serve as advisors." Emi locked me with her sharp gaze. "In Stonegate, learn swiftly how to hold your blade and keep your wits. You are a melder, a survivor. Do not let these sods make you forget your power. Learn to use your voice, understand?"

I paused, a little stunned, but nodded slowly. If a woman from Dravenmoor could earn the respect of men like Baldur and Ashwood, I would do the same. Melders were valued by the king. A curl tugged at my lip. If I was of value, it meant I had leverage.

My service for Kael's life. I would demand it.

Lines were forming for the departures. Supplies were draped over shoulders in fur and leather satchels.

My gaze landed on Kael's messy golden curls. Without a

thought, I rushed for him. He was upright, the sun-dusted bronze of his skin returned, and a grin split over his mouth when he saw me.

Kael's wrists were bound in heavy irons, but the chain between them was long enough he could open his arms to embrace me.

"You pest," he whispered against my hair. "Everyone's talking about how the Sentry had to go drag the melder from the trees and he returned soaked in blood. Use your head, Ly."

I pulled back, eyes narrowed. "I needed to save you, fool."

Kael rolled his eyes and flicked my shoulder as he always did when he was annoyed with me. "What did I say? This is not a game, Lyra. We belong to Stonegate. Now we must focus on how you survive in there."

"Not just me, Kael." My voice dropped low enough, I wasn't certain he even heard. "You are to face the king, exposed as the one who kept melding craft from his hands."

Kael folded his arms over his chest, the chains clinking with the motion. "I'm not as worthless as you think." He held up a finger, ticking off each word as he spoke. "I have bone craft. I am a skilled fighter. I am of legitimate noble blood. And Jakobson apparently offered a payment to keep me from slaughter."

"What? The jarl . . . offered payment?"

Kael sniffed and looked away. "Disown me in name, but it seems the sod has some sort of affection for me. Nightlark told me before Baldur left, the jarl paid a fine with the request for the king's mercy. So, stop risking your bony neck." He glared at me. "As desperately as you want me to keep breathing, remember I feel the same about you. No more idiotic plans, no more pissing on the Sentry's limited generosity. At least not without telling me."

For a moment, I said nothing. Slowly, a grin crept over my features. I nudged Kael's ribs with my elbow. "Accomplices?"

He looked down at me like he did not want to indulge me, but it took a mere five breaths before Kael chuckled. "Accomplices always."

"By the way, I'm quite proud of you."

"Why is that?"

"You finally called Jakobson a sod."

Our levity lasted a moment longer before a shadow crossed over us. His presence was a force, a silky darkness that lifted the hair on my neck and turned my insides. But the maddening piece of it was I wasn't certain if they overturned out of disgust or intrigue.

Kael straightened out of respect in the same moment I looked over my shoulder. "Sentry Ashwood."

Roark had washed the dirt and blood from his face and wore a clean, black tunic. In his hands were a set of chains much like Kael's.

Emi stepped around the Sentry. "It's time to be on our way. You're to be bound, for your own safety, Melder."

I snorted, but bit down on the tip of my tongue. Arms outstretched, I didn't look away as Roark bound the iron around my wrists. His molten eyes poured into me when he gripped the chain and tugged me against him.

His hand was near my cheek when he spoke, slow and sharp. *By me.*

I grimaced. "As you say, *my lord* Sentry."

14

LYRA

L OATH AS I WAS TO ADMIT IT, TRAVELING BESIDE ROARK was not horrid. The man knew how to avoid the rockiest paths. He moved like a wraith, drifting from shadow to shadow, and kept us out of the heat of the day better than others.

On the winding earthen paths that carved through the damp and mists of the wood, it was in those moments when I learned the Sentry's face could seem . . . gentle.

Roark said little and was never unaware. Still, when the trees tangled in leafy canopies overhead and chirps of forest birds sang out in the distance, Ashwood seemed at ease, like he could breathe easier.

It must've been the Draven in him.

We descended a few rocky pathways that carved across the hillside like jagged claw marks.

Until we faced a flat pebbled ledge. Roark paused and, without looking at me, held out a water skin for me to take.

Gods, the man was a conundrum. One moment his eyes were

bright and heated, like he had a soul of passion buried beneath his scowls. Next, he was cold as a frost storm in the jagged peaks.

I snatched the skin with my tethered wrists and tilted the spout to my lips. With the back of one hand, I wiped away the dribble and followed Ashwood's stare.

Fifty paces down the hill was an arch made of thick slabs of stone and oak beams. The gates towered higher than ten men standing one on top of the other. The front entrance was block-aded by an iron portcullis, and watchtowers guarded every curve. Beyond the gates were dark speckles of homes, shops, and the gabled palace in the center.

"Stonegate," I whispered.

Roark let out a soft breath and stepped onto the wider path that would lead down to the gates.

Hillside cottages and hunting cabins tucked in tall grass and trees materialized as we walked farther.

A few folk loitered about, noticing the commotion as we marched past their huts. The Stav were greeted with murmured respect and a few fists to the chest. I stepped closer to the center of the path, and stumbled over a stone. The Sentry caught me under the arm, steadying me against his own body.

All the gods. Chest to chest, I could feel the thud of Roark's heartbeat against my own, I could make out the sharp edges of the scar that dug across his throat, and I could breathe in the leather and oakmoss on his skin.

It took a few moments to readjust, but the instant we were parted, the frigidness of the Sentry returned. He took hold of the chain between the irons on my wrists and urged us forward.

When we were on level ground, Stonegate appeared even more formidable than from above.

The journey from the sea was rocky and jagged, but trade

roads webbed across treeless knolls on the back borders of the keep. There, carts and caravans could wrap around the dirt paths to the entrance and join the market square.

Parapets and arched walkways connected stone walls to more stone walls. Stonegate was an endless maze of gates and towers.

All at once, the reality of what this meant crashed over me like a slab from the walls surrounding the city.

Roark slid one palm to the small of my back, as though he sensed the scrape of fear suffocating my every thought.

Gentle nudges kept me moving forward.

Shouts from Stav Guards in the towers echoed down the outer walls. Ram horns bellowed, announcing the arrival of the guard.

Heavy clanks from chains and rope released the portcullis, bidding us welcome into the jaws of Stonegate.

The inner township was organized with straight lanes and roads leading to shops for grains, meats, satin ribbons, and leatherworks. A smith's hut burned brightest from the roaring kiln, and hickory smoke from his hut coated the underlying hint of sweat and old ale.

The center path was paved in stone and did not bend on its way to the palace. My lungs ached and my legs protested when we made our way up a steep incline toward the royal house. It was the largest dwelling I'd ever seen.

It was made of three levels, with thatched rooftops that drew to a sharp point over nearly every window, and each doorway was built with sturdy black oak and topped with war shields bearing the white wolf head in the center. All around the courtyard and lower longhouses, ferns and evergreen shrubs grew in thick rows, as though the palace had burst from the bedrock in the center of a forest.

The late hour ensured there were few people in the streets,

and most cottages were shrouded in black like the sky. Anyone lingering nearby curled back when the huddle of Stav approached.

With both hands, Roark pressed against the doors at the entrance of the palace. A gust of wind blew against my cheek when he shoved the heavy wood open, revealing a gaping entry hall with arched rafters and iron chandeliers. Servants were there to greet us and moved almost at once to gather satchels and packs off the shoulders of the guard.

Roark tossed back his hood. More than one servant dipped their chins and shuffled to the other side of the hall, avoiding his attention. Now, more than before, I suspected his cruelty was shown in shadows. These folk were too frightened to admit what the Sentry did after he dropped his austere mask.

I stepped back and ignored the deliberate glance Ashwood shot my way. His brow furrowed, almost as though he were frustrated with my dismissal of him. I tossed the notion aside; it was utterly foolish. No mistake, Roark Ashwood was glad to be rid of me.

A hand curled around my arm. Emi offered a slight smile. "I'm to show you to your chamber."

"I want to see my people."

Emi gestured across the hall. A servant who was dressed in a dark tunic handed Kael, Hilda, and Edvin clay cups of a steaming drink. They were still guarded by five Stav, but unharmed.

Kael's bright eyes found me over his cup. He winked and mouthed, *Tea, stop worrying.*

Convinced they were not being poisoned, I let my shoulders slump. "Why can't I stay with them?"

"You are the melder, that means you have chambers of your own."

"Is King Damir going to execute Kael?"

Emi sighed. "The king will be more inclined to keep you breathing than kill him, and you've proven well enough you'll spill your own blood to protect him. Darkwin knowingly concealed a melder—it is against the ways of the Stav. He'll face consequences for it; you know that, right?"

I gave Emi a terse nod and followed her toward a wide archway that opened into narrow corridors.

Drawn by the sear of his gaze, I looked once more over my shoulder.

Roark's eyes burned like molten steel, his jaw taut like it was made from the stone at the gates. The way he looked at me, I could not tell if the Sentry feared for my life, or if he could not wait to take it himself.

Tall ceilings were made with rafters crossing this way and that, and more wrought iron chandeliers held dripping tallow candles. Bone blades, arrows, and whalebone bows decorated the walls, all symbols of King Damir's bold bloodline that won the land of Jorvandal through the centuries.

Emi stopped in front of a door painted in thin vines with violet blossoms on the corners. "Rest tonight."

"I doubt I will."

"Try. In the morning wait for the escort to arrive, then you'll meet the king and queen."

"You won't take me?" I was ashamed at the tremble in my voice, ashamed there was a strange, twisted piece of me that took a bit of comfort in the familiarity of Emi Nightlark.

"I am to see to your brother and the others." She hesitated. "Would you like me to return?"

"No. I hope you are sincere and keep those I love safe."

"You've no reason to trust me, or any of us, but I hope you give us the chance to try."

Without another word, Emi strode back down the corridor, unbuckling her vambraces and a few tight braids in her hair as she went, leaving me with the dreaded weight of loneliness.

15

ROARK

Emi sat with her back to me, her pale hair free and loose down her back. She was a woman who appeared harmless, dainty even. I knew better and stiffened when she caught sight of me in her mirror.

"Roark. Always lurking in the doorway." She spun around on the stool, the sharp blue of her eyes narrowed into icy slits. "Afraid to come closer?"

I waved my hand. *Always. Did you see the melder to her chamber?*

"I did, along with the other crafters to theirs."

Good. I hesitated. *I apologize for Skalfirth.*

A shadow crossed Emi's face. "You mean when you commanded me to break a man I knew? Even though you know why I vowed never to do such things with my craft again?"

Gods, I was a piece of shit. What was there to say? Emi was the only piece of my home clan I cared to keep. We had trust, yes, but in a way I'd broken a piece of it.

I will never ask it again. We needed the craft to take hold.

"I know, Roark. But next time find a way to leave me out of it."

Did it hurt you?

"Physically?" She stretched her neck and rolled her shoulders. "A little. My heart? Yes, it shattered. I actually like Darkwin. He was one of the few decent recruits who did not think I was only meant for his bed."

I offered a small nod of understanding. *Will you think I am an absolute ass if I ask another favor of you?*

"Oh, likely, but I do love having debts between us." She strode across the room, pausing a step away.

I held up the twine-wrapped sheets of parchment Prince Thane and I had been writing on since the first winter I was found at the gates.

Emi flipped through some. "What am I to do with these?"

For the melder.

"Oh, really." A bit of pink stained her cheeks.

Don't. You're doing it again.

"I didn't say anything."

She ought to know what I am saying. It means nothing more.

Emi clicked her tongue and propped her chin onto the heel of her hand. "Strange, but you cared little if Melder Fadey understood you."

I frowned. *Fadey was an ass.*

"I don't disagree." Emi's face grew somber. "Are you ever going to tell me what happened with the fara wolf?"

Doubtful.

"Roark, be careful how you go. With Lyra now in Stonegate, it's only a matter of time before the clan finds out. Lust for vengeance never dwindled, I told you this."

I know. My shoulders stiffened.

Emi tugged on the end of a lock of her hair. "Then be wary of getting close to the melder when—"

One wave of my hand cut her off. I jabbed a finger at her and spoke with my other hand. *Enough. I know my duty, and I will see it through.* I stepped back into the corridor. *Now, will you deliver the ledger? I need to meet with the king.*

"Gods, I said I would and I will." Emi hugged the sheets of parchment to her chest, still offering up the aggravating grin she'd mastered so well. "But I'm just saying you've never wanted to have anyone speak to you and—"

I'd already started down the hallway.

"There is no shame in it, Roark Ashwood! I support it, in fact," she shouted, unbothered if anyone in nearby chambers heard. "You could do with a strong woman to give you something to smile about!"

I offered a rude gesture over my shoulder before I rounded the corner, ignoring the snicker of laughter that followed.

KING DAMIR FACED THE ARCHING WINDOW, WATCHING THE bloody shadows of fading sunlight paint his empire in red and gold. Prince Thane was already in the study, seated next to a roaring fire, polishing a snake-hilt dagger.

Baldur was there, murmuring salacious words at the maiden delivering the king's mead.

I paused in the doorway and stomped one foot gently, signaling my arrival.

Baldur stilled his rakish hands, Thane stopped polishing the steel, but the king hardly turned his head away from the bubbled glass.

"Ah, Sentry Ashwood. Enter."

Thane stood and leaned against the wall between me and his father, like a shield. Most folk defended the king, but in the case of Thane, I was certain he was trying to protect me.

"Captain Baldur informed me that your uncanny senses for finding craft have come through for us. I do enjoy that side of a Draven. Always able to sense craft in the soul."

King Damir squared his shoulders to me. It was a simple statement, but there was a veiled threat beneath it all. Like the king believed I was keeping a skill hidden. I was no great hunter of crafters. There was a distinct pull to the magic of craft. It spoke to the soul; one merely needed to be willing to listen.

But the pull had been fiercer than before when I drew close to Lyra. I knew her from the first plum she'd tossed at my head.

Damir was suspicious and trusting of me all at once. I was a dark blade in his palace, a true warrior, but I was Draven. And that, to the Jorvan king, was always a risk.

The king had a youthful face beneath his long beard, but age had grayed some of his golden hair above the ears. "You've uncovered the lost melder?"

I dipped my chin in a simple response.

The king hummed in the back of his throat. "Finally. I assume the Stav Guard will be pleased to know they will once again move up in their rank with new bones to meld."

"Word is already spreading, sire," Baldur said. "They are thrilled."

Thane shot me a look of warning. My face must've twisted in a glimmer of disgust.

King Damir spun on me. "Tell me about her. How did she slip away during the raids?"

She does not recall. I flexed my fingers once, twice, then slowly, stoically responded. *She was raised in a youth house, then went to work in the jarl's household. The woman can read, but she knows nothing about her craft. I believe she fears it.*

Thane translated my gestures. Unlike the prince, who'd practically invented my hand speak, Damir could not be bothered to learn it.

"And what of this Darkwin? He had plans to join the Stav, but lied about a melder. My son seems to think you and Baldur told the girl he would live if she came willingly."

I doubted Lyra would see her arrival at Stonegate as willing.

Baldur cleared his throat. "My king, the woman had a knife to her throat to keep the man breathing. We had to say something. I, for one, care little if he lives. Stav do not keep secrets from their king."

I made a grunting sound and turned my back to Baldur and his snobbery. He would kiss the king's ass for any sort of advancement. No mistake, he'd suck Damir's cock if asked.

Darkwin has been raised as her brother, I explained, Thane murmuring my responses as I went. *In their eyes they are family. With her history, her craft left him fearing for her life.*

"So you would have me forgive treachery because he means something to the girl?"

"Father," Thane said, "I believe this man is loyal to you. He has been told lies like many regarding what happens to melders within these walls."

Damir's face fell. "Brutes. Ravagers. They robbed us of Fadey and now wish to rob us of our gods-given defenses." The king spun back to the window, face flushed.

More importantly, I said even if the king was not looking at me, *the woman will not be loyal if Darkwin does not live.*

The king peered over his shoulder once Thane concluded the translation. "Manipulative little thing, is she?"

The sneer on the king's face burned through my blood. I had no care for the life of Lyra Bien other than fulfilling my purpose here, so the jolt of heat wasn't from anything protective. The cinch in my chest wasn't for anything other than annoyance that I'd been brought into the middle of all this.

I had a duty, and I wanted to get back to it.

Still, only when Thane jabbed his knuckle against my ribs did I realize my fists had clenched at my sides.

I shook out my hands. *She is frightened. Nothing more.*

"Hmm. As she should be. Someone slaughtered her predecessor within my gates, and someone wants her kind dead." Damir stroked the braids of his beard. "I want you to guard her, Ashwood."

My fingers flicked, an instinct to state my refusal coming swiftly. It would be a horrid mistake to place me in charge of the melder.

I waited for a breath, then, *My king, certainly I am needed elsewhere.*

Thane glared at me when he recited my response. If I kept arguing, soon enough the prince would begin lying through his translations and insist I agreed with his father's every word.

Damir's eyes darkened. "Elsewhere? Is there anywhere else more important than protecting my strongest crafter?"

This would be a mistake. I did not need to know or see Lyra as anything other than a tool used by the forces of Stonegate. Melders worked in soul bones. To disrupt the resting place of the dead to collect their bones always left a mark of corruption.

It wouldn't be long before her own magic turned her into a greedy, wicked creature. The same as Fadey.

"I'll do it, sire," Baldur said. "I'm as skilled as Ashwood with the blade, and there will be no confusion with the woman understanding what I say."

His words were the slice of a blade. No, that wouldn't do at all. Baldur would torment her and try to bed her. The melder was my find; if anyone were to ruin her, the right belonged to me.

The captain has units of Stav to oversee. I will guard the melder.

King Damir grinned. "As I thought. I'm told you already did. Had an encounter with a wolf, did you? Not that I'm surprised. Dravens like to send their little pets after us anytime a soul bone is used."

The king was not wrong. When he used Lyra to fasten more bones to grow his twisted empire, more attacks would come.

Baldur slurped the last drops of ale from his drinking horn, then sloppily wiped his mouth with the back of his arm. "How'd it feel, Ashwood, killing one of your folk's pups?"

I did not kill the wolf.

"Ah, did you flee like a little, frightened girl?"

"Watch yourself, Captain," Thane snapped. "You speak recklessly toward my Sentry. Continue and I will enjoy taking out your tongue."

It was not often the prince showed the darker edges of his soul, but when he did it captivated the whole of a room.

Baldur's sun-roughened cheeks flushed. "Apologies, my prince. It is the drink and the long journey talking."

He dipped his chin and stepped nearer to the inglenook, recoiling beneath Thane's scrutiny.

Damir shook his head as though bored and looked back to me. "If the melder is harmed, remember, Sentry Ashwood, I will hold you responsible. I never want to see another death—not of craft or Stav—inside my walls again. Now go. Wash, rest. You look pitiful."

Out in the corridor, Baldur knocked my shoulder as he stormed away.

Thane leaned against the wall and blew out a long breath. "What was all that?"

I furrowed my brow and shrugged.

"Don't play the fool. You hated Fadey, though I don't know why, and you returned from Skalfirth so twisted in your snarl I thought I might never unravel it. Not to mention, every time Baldur opened his damn mouth about her you looked ready to gut him."

I waved him away and started my trek to my chambers.

"I mean it," Thane said, quickening his step to catch up. "Who is this woman and what has she done to you?"

She is no one.

Thane chuckled, not believing a single word, but left me to storm away.

16

LYRA

THE BEDCHAMBER WAS CAVERNOUS COMPARED TO MY ROOM in Jakobson's longhouse. Walls stretched with great corner beams etched in runes and symbols of the gods. Ravens and knives and runes.

The inglenook was empty, the fire long dead, and it gave way for cold—crisp and biting—to claw into the room.

I rubbed heat into my arms and went to the window. Below my chamber was a long stable and stacks of straw and feed. The room, for all its grandeur, was simple and dull. Smoky furs and heavy quilts made a bed. Two round, blue shields decorated the wall, and a simple russet woven rug covered the floorboards. There was a sitting chair made of pine boughs and a heavy yarn quilt tossed over the back.

Beyond the bedchamber was a washroom with a clay basin deep enough I could sit inside and stretch my legs. Tepid water filled it nearly to the brim, like I'd been expected.

A thrill quickened my pulse and I dragged my fingers over the smooth edges of the tub. We used wooden pails in the garden back home to wash our skin. Only Jarl Jakobson had basins in his chamber.

Dried petals of lavender and honey blossoms were kept in a jar. Pink and black salts from the seas took others. I popped a cork from a jar filled with powders to cleanse the hair. Selena made something similar but it had a savory scent that made my hair smell like rosemary and cloves. This was like rain on the sea, clean and cool.

A groan broke between my teeth when I sank into the water and took liberties with the different petals and scrubs. The powder lathered into a soapy layer over my long hair. I held my breath and dunked beneath the surface, escaping reality for a moment. Only the sounds of the pulse in my skull, the swirl of water, filled my thoughts.

For a moment I could pretend to be swimming in the Green Fjord with Kael; I could imagine the lap of water was the beat of the sea against Thorian's boat when he let us go fishing with him.

When I surfaced, I took my time washing off the journey until a chill chased away the warmth and my skin was wrinkled like rotting pomes.

I slipped into a thin night shift folded in the tall wardrobe, then returned to the truth—I was locked in a fine cell.

Shelves along one wall were stacked with parchment scrolls, vellum, and a few tomes bound in smooth leather. Near the bed was a new plate of boiled pears atop two books I'd not noticed before and a folded note on rosewood parchment. I popped one pear into my mouth, toes curling from the sweet juices.

My gaze scanned the books beneath the plate. One was a copy of *Tales of the Wanderer.*

The other brought a reluctant thrill to my pulse—a stack of

rice paper with notes about gestures, signals, and commands. With hurried fingers, I unfolded the note.

Didn't want to disturb you in the washroom. Thought you might want to read up on craft. The second ledger is a gift from the Sentry. Ashwood told me he caught your unbreakable fascination with his hands, so he thought it would save you time and less staring to simply read through some of them . . .

I huffed. "Bastard."

Even in writing, I could see his arrogant smirk, and had few doubts he'd said the exact words to Emi.

I think it is wise since you will likely see a great deal of him in coming days. Who knows, perhaps some understanding might alter your opinions of him.

Stav Nightlark

A slow grin cut over my mouth when I finished reading. Thoughtful of Emi, but I doubted it would do much to change my thoughts on the Sentry.

I plucked another slice of fruit and opened *Tales of the Wanderer*. The binding smelled of old leather and ink and dust.

Memories of Gammal's smoke-haggard voice telling the tale filtered through my head with each page. "Why did the Wanderer divide the magic of the gods?"

"Why should I care about your myths and legends, girl?"

It was her response every time, but always said with a glint of mischief in her eyes. I'd beg no more than three times before the old Unfettered woman would recite the history of my lands, all to make a young girl beam with intrigue.

"This Wanderer chose his fate through tricks and betrayal." Gammal would lower her voice to lift the hair on my arms. "The Wanderer's wife realized her husband—already powerful—craved more. He wanted immortality like the gods.

"The god-queen feared the power-lust in her husband's eyes. So, while the Wanderer slept, she stole three drops of his blood, then marked the brows of their three children, blessing them with the craft of their father, and taking it from her king.

"The first son was given craft of bone—to heal, manipulate, or rot. The second son, the craft of souls—to protect, control, or destroy. The third, to the Wanderer's only daughter, the craft of blood—to heal, disease, or summon."

One day, when I was bold enough, I asked the question I'd kept buried since I arrived at the young house. "Where does the silver curse fit, Gammal?"

The woman had paused for half a breath before kneading her seed bread with more fervor. "What I have read is the Wanderer was furious at his queen's betrayal. It is said one night, he stole into the chambers of his children and poisoned his own heirs. When his bride discovered her young ones thrashing and near death, the Wanderer vowed the antidote if she would tell him how to become a master of all the crafts, just like a god."

"Did she tell him?"

"In desperation, the god-queen told the Wanderer how to mark bones of those who'd gone to the gods' hall and summon a lingering piece of the soul left behind. Then the bone of the dead would be fastened to the Wanderer's living body, feeding new strength from the dead into his own soul. Since the fallen soul had already touched the magic of the gods' hall, the sagas say the Wanderer could then take slivers of wisdom from the soul he'd absorbed; he could borrow from the dead's former strength. With the additional soul, old scars healed, youth filled the Wanderer's bones, and like many of the gods, his skill with the blade grew tenfold. But it was a curse. With its strengths, the Wanderer also took on the cruelty and the vices of the dead bones. Each time made the Wanderer dangerously greedy for battle, blood, power.

"Disgusted by his corruption, the gods took back their daughter and her young ones, and marked the Wanderer with the scar of silver, leaving him to suffer alone until he met Salur. That is the legend of the silver scars. Who knows if it is true, but we both know when a melder uses their craft recklessly, they do not stay the same, don't we, girl? Be wary of those scars, child. Never use the curse in your blood."

As a child, I vowed to Gammal I would never be reckless. To save Kael was the first I'd used my craft.

Still, I could not deny the sense of power that hummed in my blood as I drew him back from death.

Was it truly possible to fall prey to the desire for more? Is that what King Damir wanted? A melder with insatiable desire to feed their own craft?

But how would such a thing grow the king's influence?

I thumbed through a few pages of the old poems and tales, stopping on the warning from the god of wisdom when he gifted the Wanderer his magic.

To harm the living, craft mirrors the pain.
To split the soul, craft sacrifices the blood.
To curse the body, craft devours the mind.
To bind dead and living, craft corrupts the heart.

Kael had used his craft only to shape blades, never to cause pain. The same could be said for Hilda and Edvin. Did Emi Nightlark feel pain when she harmed the living bone?

Soul craft, as little as I knew of it, was the magic that wallowed in blood somehow.

Blood craft was tangled in curses and spell casts. Used too wretchedly, it spun a mind with madness.

The last was the warning ignored by Stonegate. It was the risk of melding.

If the tales of the Wanderer were to be believed, to use meld craft in excess, the magic of it would feast upon a melder's heart until they were a husk of what they once had been.

Like a disease feeding from the inside out.

King Damir coveted melders. He would use my craft in excess, and if the tales were true, I would wither to nothing soon enough.

I slapped the pages closed and hugged my knees to my chest. On the morrow, I would be inspected by the king. No doubt, he would require me to prove my craft and I would be tossed back into that strange, mirrored world of mists and shadows.

My palms trembled when I lifted them in front of my face.

Gods, I wished Melder Fadey still lived. The questions I would ask. What was that place? Why did the connection to bone thrust it upon me?

Who or *what* lived in such a world?

I shook the thought away and took up the parchment of symbols and gestures. Craft and kings could wait for now. I held to the brittle trust in Emi's words that Kael, Hilda, and Edvin were safe. I held to the notion that Damir coveted craft and he would not want to execute three crafters.

They had to be alive, they had to be safe.

I kept reciting the words as I studied gesture after gesture of the finger speak until my eyes fluttered closed, and I drifted into murky black.

THE CROW OF AN AGGRAVATING COCK BLARED HIS MORNING welcome well before the mists of dawn had faded.

Today was my meeting with the king. I'd been given a refuge for the night—more than I expected—but what became of me after I left this chamber?

I made certain to summon some warm pots of water for the basin and soaked in dried petals and fresh salts until my toes wrinkled.

The wardrobes were stocked in simple clothes, a few shifts and frocks, some tunics and trousers and hose. I took a simple blue dress, a size too large, thin ankle boots, and braided my damp hair down my neck, tying it off with a pale ribbon hung on a hook in the wardrobe.

I'd only fastened the knot when a knock came at the door. I was met with a man's backside. Two Stav were pressed against the wall, and when my escort turned, my heart shot to my throat.

"Highness." I dipped my chin, avoiding the sharp, glazed-honey eyes of Prince Thane.

"Is my face so well-known?" he said with a bit of delight. "I'd no idea. I'm rarely afforded the chance to leave Stonegate save for the Wild Hunt each harvest. I might break my precious neck, after all."

I blinked. "My . . . Ser Darkwin described you, and I saw you at a recruitment once, several winters ago."

"Darkwin. Got himself into a bit of trouble with all this, didn't he?"

"Forgive me, Highness, but he was only trying to protect me."

The prince held up one hand. "No need to convince me, my

lady. He did what a loyal man would do for his family. I'm certain that will be taken into account when his actions are judged."

Prince Thane had the same pale eyes as the boy skipping stones on the shore. His hair had darkened to a dirty gold, and was shaved on the sides, revealing inked runes and symbols on his scalp. The prince kept a trimmed beard, customary for leaders of the land, and had two bones speared through the lobes of his ears.

Undeniably handsome, but Thane's smile did not reach his eyes.

"I wanted to meet you myself," he said. "A new melder. I'm certain you're filled with utter rage at being here."

"You mock me, Highness?"

"No." A bit of light left Thane's eyes. "Forgive me, Lyra. I've been told more than once my jests are spoken at the most inappropriate times." The prince held out one arm. "Still, if you can stomach me, I would be honored to escort you to the great hall. I've a great many questions."

When Emi said she would not return for me, I did not expect the prince himself would be my guide.

Anger had made me snap at the Sentry, but with the prince, I bit down any glimmer of resistance. In truth, if I wanted to survive Stonegate long enough to find a way to escape it, I'd be wise to bite down even my snarls at Ashwood.

We glided down the corridor. The Stav remained five paces behind, and occasionally Prince Thane would mention a tapestry or two, describing its origins from one of the many provinces until we made our way down another hallway with more arched beams.

"I am glad for a moment alone," Thane murmured from the corner of his mouth. His voice soft enough, I nearly missed it. "I wanted to meet you after what you did on the journey here."

"What I did?" Gods, would he punish me for my attempt to flee the camp?

"To the Sentry, of course."

I wasn't certain what he meant, but replied with a soft, "I did not intend to put your Sentry at risk in the wood—"

"I don't think we're speaking of the same thing," the prince interrupted, his grin widening. "I'm talking about how you've utterly discomposed the tightly stitched Roark Ashwood. If you keep at it, I think you might be absolutely perfect."

"Perfect for what, Highness?"

Thane paused our conversation to nod and greet a few courtiers passing by in the hall, then he drew us to a halt and leaned closer, voice low. "I think you will be perfect for a bit of entertainment in this dull fortress. In all our acquaintance, I've never seen my dear friend so undeniably frustrated. It's completely made my morning, Lyra. I thank you for that."

"I don't understand."

Thane placed both hands on my shoulders and spun me toward a wide set of doors. Emi was there, free of her Stav uniform, and clad now in a green dress edged in silver, her long hair free over her shoulders.

The prince leaned close to whisper into my ear. "You've done something to dig under his skin, and I must know what it was, for he is the most infallible, unruffled ass I've ever met."

Breath stuttered in my chest when Emi's companion turned around and I met the sharp golden glass of Roark's eyes. Soft for a moment, then his stare hardened at the sight of me.

Thane's deep chuckle pulsed against my back. The prince whispered as he readjusted to stand at my side again, "See what I mean? Perfect."

The Sentry was dressed in a new tunic, all black from the coat over his shoulders to the boots on his feet. Where had he gone after arriving? Did he have another room? Perhaps one shared with Emi? If they were lovers, and Thane believed me to aggravate the Sentry simply for existing, it would not be long until her calming demeanor wore thin.

The lack of contrast in Roark's attire only emphasized how lithe and tall he was, how beautifully vicious he might be.

His gaze roved over me, unashamed, as though he were soaking up every surface of my body. To be viewed in such a way was strangely intimate, and even more strange, I didn't despise it.

A thought I would never admit out loud.

Men in Skalfirth spared a look or two until Kael threatened them at the game halls. He thought I didn't know, but it was a small village. Folk whispered a great deal in the markets.

Now, to tremble under the watch of the man who'd upended my existence was shamefully laughable.

The prince bowed at the waist. "By the gods, Emi, once more your beauty lights the room."

Emi dipped her chin, but a smile teased the corners of her lips. "Always the charmer, my prince."

"And you." Thane's features hardened when he faced Roark. "I am told you tortured our guest the whole of the journey. It won't go unpunished, Roark. I swear to you."

My eyes widened. I reeled on the prince. What was he doing? I'd not spoken a word about Ashwood.

Roark's nose wrinkled, like he might snarl. In a frenzy he spoke with his hands to the prince, who observed each gesture as readily as if the Sentry were spitting his retorts vocally. Too fast for me to keep up.

"That is not the story she told," Thane said. Ashwood responded briskly, eyes like fire. Thane sighed. "Well, forgive me, but why would she lie?"

"Highness," I interjected. The last thing I wanted today was to earn more of Ashwood's blades and ire.

Then, Emi laughed. She clapped a hand over her mouth to muffle the sound and shoved—truly shoved—Roark's arm like he was nothing but a boon companion. "You fool. How long has it been since you've fallen for his games? What's gotten into you?"

Thane pressed his lips into a tight line, the sort of look when one was desperate to keep from grinning.

Roark's gaze bounced from the prince, to me, then back to the prince. He made a jerky signal with one hand.

Thane drew in a feigned gasp of scandal. "You cannot call me such names, I'll take your head. Ah, I will, don't press me. I never should've made that one up."

By the gods, this was . . . unsettling.

The prince gripped Roark's shoulder, a friendly sort of greeting, then returned to me. "Apologies again, Lyra. I had to poke him. He never smiles, you see."

"I've noticed." I turned my indifference toward the Sentry.

His jaw set and fists tightened in return.

"This is where I leave you. I am told I must also escort my mother. Seems no one can stroll the halls on their own these days." Thane bowed slightly and pressed a kiss to the top of my hand. His next words were heady with sincerity. "All will be well, I promise."

The prince asked for Emi to accompany him and give a recount of the journey. The two Stav Guards remained at my back, the only other presence crowding the silence between me and Roark.

Behind those doors the king would claim me as his new pet. Kind as the prince tried to be, this moment felt a great deal like facing the darkness of my end.

The air grew hot, like falling sparks bit into my skin. Walls were too near, too tight, too confined. All at once the corridor became my haven. The moment I went through those doors, I would be in chains. Perhaps not literally, but King Damir would have me in his sights. I would be a prize of a century-old treaty. Nothing more.

Sweat beaded over my brow. The space around my lungs tightened and I drew in sharp, jagged pulls of air.

Roark paused, eyes taking me in, a groove of concern—no, likely annoyance—on his brow.

Fog clouded my thoughts until all I knew was I could not breathe. I needed air, needed to be free of this suffocating hallway.

A hand took hold of my arm, pulling me from the doors. I met the sharp gaze of the Sentry. He braced my back to the wall, caging me—or shielding me—away from the open corridor.

With one finger he tapped on my cheek until I lifted my eyes. He didn't use his hand speak, didn't mouth a word, but kept his palm on the side of my throat, his thumb stroking the side of my neck.

Gentle strokes, almost soothing.

After a moment, I realized his other hand had taken mine and he did the same, only down the center of my palm, across my wrist. He added a bit of pressure and the weight of his touch drew my focus.

It pulled me from the thrashing fear, the tangle of thoughts. I drew in a long breath through my nose.

Roark stopped stroking the side of my neck and lifted his hand so I could follow his command. *Breathe.*

Where the Sentry could've mocked me, he calmed me instead.

I didn't understand it. How could he sit back with such indifference, watching families torn apart, but in this moment be a haven in a storm?

The door to the side of the hall opened. Baldur, dressed in his full Stav uniform, emerged. "The king is waiting, Ashwood." He noticed our position. "What's the matter with her?"

Roark waved the captain away.

"Tell her whimpering does nothing but prove her weakness. Dry your tears, woman, and meet your king." Baldur folded his arms.

The Sentry spun on him. I knew more of his words than I expected—like they had been burned in my mind after his banter with Thane—and from the flush in Baldur's face, the insults he leveled at the captain were not taken in jest as they'd been for the prince.

"Just get her inside," Baldur spat, then returned the way he came.

I buried my face in my palms. Wretched as Baldur could be, the captain wasn't entirely wrong. For now, I had little choice but to face the king. To remain here, spinning in fears, would do nothing.

Another tap to my cheek and I opened my eyes.

Roark held up a strip of parchment I never saw him take out.
When you are ready.

It was a kindness I didn't expect. True to his word, the Sentry leaned against the wall, like he might be settling in to wait the whole of the day.

I swallowed, cracked one knuckle, then another. Once my pulse had slowed to a tolerable pace, I cleared my throat. "No sense in waiting."

Roark took his place at my side once more.

"Don't let me fall in there," I whispered before I could think better of it. I wasn't certain I even meant the words for Roark, but he came closer all the same, until our chests nearly touched.

For a tense, drawn-out pause Ashwood studied me, then slowly took hold of my hand, guiding me through the doors.

LYRA

TWO GUARDS OPENED THE DOORS TO THE SAVORY SCENTS
and riotous company. My stomach churned when Roark
took us inside.

I anticipated endless rows of courtiers. There were few in the
room. A select few Stav Guard, a lady or two in pale gowns.

Roark led us down a woven runner, hardly glancing at the
others.

Despite the small numbers, the great table was topped with
hocks of meat and roasted roots and nuts, and seated at the head
was King Damir. Chairs down the sides were reserved for his
consorts, jarls, and Stav officers. Baldur was already fiddling with
a curled lock of hair on a young courtier at his side.

My steps were stiff, but I dared lift my gaze to the king.

King Damir shared the same storm gray eyes as his son, al-
though his hair was paler and speckled in silver strands. His
beard reached his chest, braided in two, and three bone shards
pierced his ears on each side.

Rugged and handsome like his heir, but there was an emptiness in his gaze, like he'd long ago lost the light his son still kept in his own.

The king rose, a tall drinking horn in his grip, and watched our approach.

Roark dipped his chin in a bow of respect. He did not gesture to the king, did not sign a word, merely nudged the small of my back until I stepped forward. Damir's gaze was cold, but the warmth of his smile fought to find a balance.

I mimicked the Sentry and dipped my chin. "Highness."

"Tell me your name."

"Lyra."

"What is your house sigil? Full name, girl. Or shall I look to the runes you have marked on your neck?"

My palm covered the altered symbols behind my ear. Air grew hot; walls were too near, too confined.

Roark came to my side, the storm in his eyes flashed like a summer squall.

Against the slope of my spine, his fingers moved. Slowly. It took half a breath to realize he was speaking. Small movements I'd studied on the ship, in the stack of parchment he'd sent, in the memory of his bones in my mind.

Don't fall, was all he said, again and again, ensuring I got his message.

My insides cinched. *Don't let me fall.*

Kael had always admired him, and it only made Roark's actions in Skalfirth more of a betrayal. Then in moments like this, I considered there was more to the Sentry than I knew.

"When the king speaks, it is customary to honor him with a response." Baldur's rough grumble drew me back.

My heart rate slowed, and my breaths grew even again. I met

Roark's stare. The look he gave me wasn't one of irritation that I'd gotten lost in a bit of fear. He gave me a subtle nod as if to tell me I could speak, I could *do* this moment.

"My sigil was changed, sire," I said, voice soft. There was no purpose to hide the truth, not anymore. "But it once said House Bien."

Damir clucked his disapproval. "Strange how the Norns of fate play their games. The same house name of the lost melder. How convinced I was you had died all those seasons ago. Who took you from your house, girl? Where were you hidden?"

I swallowed. "I don't recall, sire. Those early seasons are difficult to remember."

"Try."

I shifted on my feet, then took a small step closer to the dais. "I mostly remember living in a young house, then being given to House Jakobson on my twelfth summer. But . . . sometimes, I can remember someone . . . running with me."

My eyes fluttered closed. A voice, a rough shadow of a young man's beard. The race of a heartbeat beneath a leather jerkin.

See that she's forgotten.

I shook my head and blinked my eyes open. "I don't recall much more than that, sire."

King Damir's grin was like a wolf about to strike. "To have you here now, what a gift it is from the gods."

A side door opened and Prince Thane materialized, a woman with ink black hair toppled in curls on her head clung to his arm. Queen Ingir had pale skin like morning cream and wide, deep-set eyes that seemed to swallow everyone in the room in one sweeping glance. The queen was haunting, but lovely, and moved like her feet never truly touched the ground.

Attendants floated at her back. The prince's mouth was set,

but when his eyes found me—or perhaps it was Ashwood—he gave a subtle eye roll, like he wanted us to know the entrance was all rather ridiculous.

"You've begun without me, husband," Queen Ingir said in a voice that did not match her delicate features. Sharp as shaved glass, and directly aimed at the king.

Damir did not face her when he spoke. "There is nothing that requires your direct approval, wife, so I cannot possibly think of why I would wait."

Ingir flushed, the color hardly shading her cheeks, but allowed her son to offer up the tall chair to the right of the king. She greeted the king's consorts with a generous smile. Truth be told, I thought they might be the folk the queen adored the most for taking her husband's attention.

Thane sat next to his mother and slumped in the seat.

Damir, mouth tight, returned his gaze to me. "You've concealed your craft, Lyra Bien. A crime against the laws of our fealty treaties."

What was I supposed to say? Bone crafters were free to join the Stav, serve the king in Stonegate, live within their villages as crafters for jarls, or enjoy their own solitary lives. Not melders. Submission to Stonegate was their destiny. As little as I knew about the past, I understood what would become of me if ever the scars in my eyes were found.

Damir stroked the braids of his beard for a pause. The king was a formidable man. Tall and broad as any warrior, with a posture that seemed impossible to bend in the slightest. "Would you believe me if I told you I wish you were not here either? You make the death of Melder Fadey so real."

There was a touch of sincere grief in the king's eyes. Like he might've truly cared for the fallen melder.

Damir cleared his throat and paced in front of me. "But what does it matter? You are here, and I wish to witness your craft."

Roark's hand remained on the curve of my back. Where disgust should've been for the Sentry's touch, I took a bit of strength. "What if I do not wish my craft to be used in Stonegate?"

A few gasps rippled down the table. Queen Ingir locked me with a narrowed gaze. Even Roark shifted.

"I would respond with a query of my own," Damir said, voice calm as an untouched lake. "What rumors have you heard that would bring such fear in your eyes at the very thought? What life do you think you will lead here?"

I swallowed through a thick knot, snagging the gaze of Prince Thane. He gave me a nod of encouragement, but I read more into the constant bounce of his knee beneath the table. Now was not the time for brazen truths.

"I've . . . I've been rather sheltered. All I knew was to fear my craft. Forgive me, my king, my few interactions with the Stav of Stonegate have only ended in death."

I drew in a sharp breath, but kept still when the king took one of my hands between his. "Understandable and unfortunate. I ensure our people are well guarded here and the consequence of safety brings with it rumors and lies of what goes on inside these tight walls."

Logical, perhaps even true. Emi was not starved or battered. Even Kael spoke highly of his days within the fortress.

But fear of my craft was potent. If it was not so important—or formidable—melders would not be bound into servitude.

"Craft was meant to bring peace and light to our lives," King Damir went on. "That peace has been achieved with most craft, and you are part of that."

I blinked to Prince Thane, the lone face I even dared consider trusting. The prince gave me another smile, another nod.

"There is not much known on melder craft," I admitted. "Some say it harms the crafter. I've heard lore that it is a curse of greed."

"Yes, and lore can often turn to fable with mere glimmers of truth left behind. Craft did not harm Fadey unless he did not use it often," Damir said. "When craft awakens, it must be used, Lyra. Yours has done so. You'll have no choice but to use it or it will become a beast scratching to get free. I am quite protective of your craft. You'll note there are few here to witness our meet.

"The strength and power of melders is where those twisted tales of folklore emerge. There is more purpose to your gift than you realize. Greed to have the power I will teach you has become part of the frightening myths. They are believed enough that I have chosen to keep melders less known for their safety from our enemies. It was only beyond these gates that Fadey was lost to us."

My thoughts spun and I bit back tears. I'd never heard all this, but there was something about the way the king spoke that left me wanting to believe it. I'd noticed a constant hum of warmth beneath my skin since suturing the bone to Kael's spine. A new, unseen presence in my blood.

"Now." The king tightened his hold on my hand, patting the top, almost fatherly. "You successfully fastened a soul bone to the living, true?"

I drew in a sharp breath. The dark figure in the mists back in Skalfirth had hissed something about souls. I shuddered, tearing my thoughts away from the shrieking glow of the haunt that consumed me. "What is a soul bone?"

"Bone taken from the dead," the king said, "marked in runes that welcome the strength of that soul gone to Salur to unite with the ones left in this realm. That is the true power of the gods, the final gift in the legends of the Wanderer."

Just like Gammal's tales. It was the corruption that destroyed him.

King Damir did not seem to take the disastrous end of the Wanderer with any trepidation and barreled on. "A melder is a bridge to the magics. A connection that was meant to unify two beautiful affinities—the dead and the living. That is the bone you placed in Skalfirth."

The bone in Kael was from a corpse.

"The shard was powerful. It drew me in," I whispered.

The king hummed in the back of his throat. "A melder gives a mortal form a piece of an immortal soul. It strengthens them, brings vitality, more resistance to disease and death."

What was the cost? How was I to explain the darkness, the shadows that swallowed me? It had been a world similar to my own, only more like a dark mirror. If it was such a gift, why was there a foreboding when the shadows overtook me?

"Of course, soul bones are rare, and it is not the only duty of a melder. Have you heard of a binding, Lyra?"

"No, sire."

"It is a ritual of fealty. A true connection forged between me and my Stav as their king and commander. A sliver of their bone is melded to me. This creates a bond that is nigh unbreakable lest they wish to die from the power of it tearing them apart."

My heartbeat quickened. "All Stav do this?"

"It is the mark of a Stav's loyalty during their tenure. When they retire from the ranks, it is removed." Damir clasped his hands behind his back. "However there is one Stav who will keep the bond until death. You're to bind the Stav to me, and in return

I will begin to prove to you Stonegate does not mean the end of your life, Lyra Bien. It is the beginning."

The king looked over my shoulder when the same doors I'd entered opened with a groan.

My heart dropped.

"Kael."

18

LYRA

KAEL WAS TUCKED BETWEEN EMI AND ANOTHER STAV Guard. He flashed his wicked grin my way like there was nothing amiss, but his wrists were bound in thick rope.

"Bring him to me," King Damir said, stepping away from me to square against Kael.

I cast a look to Ashwood. His face was unreadable save for the twitch of a muscle on the hinge of his jaw. He hadn't expected this either.

When Kael reached the king, he lowered to one knee, chin dipped in submission. His golden curls slid off his neck, baring the flesh, and I hated the sight of it, like my friend—*my brother*—was offering up his neck to Damir's blade.

"Ser Darkwin, you completed training with the Stav Guard crafters, and you showed gratitude by concealing the very melder three kingdoms have sought for seasons." King Damir clicked his tongue in derision. "I'd be wise to flay you on the walls for treason, but it seems your fellow Stav and even the Sentry think I ought to give you an opportunity to explain yourself."

Roark spoke for Kael? I blew out a soft breath to keep from glancing at the Sentry. Doubtless he would not care for the scrutiny, and his odd show of gentility might again return to violence.

Kael lifted his head, but remained on his knees.

"I do not deny it. Lyra is my family." Kael glanced over his shoulder, giving me a weak smile. "My actions came from a misplaced fear that the only person I loved was in grave danger and should be kept from all the kingdom's sights."

King Damir had the decency to give Kael his time to speak uninterrupted. My heart beat against my ribs like a mallet. I didn't move, didn't dare breathe.

"And what do you think now?" Damir asked.

Kael hesitated. "I will always be loyal to my family, my king. I will not do you the dishonor of lying. But I am loyal to Jorvandal in equal measure."

Once more, King Damir clasped his wrists behind his back and took to pacing. The brush of his steps rattled in my head the longer he took to respond.

All at once, he stopped. "You are a naïve man, Ser Darkwin, but I am a merciful king who takes the word of my most trusted into account. I will not be so forgiving a second time. Still, if you wish to live, I'll give you the chance, but you will be bound to the Stav Guard. Your life will be to serve Jorvandal and its people. Any future aspirations belong to these walls, any family home you wish to build will be in these peaks. Do you understand?"

Kael nodded. "I do."

The king's bright eyes lifted to me. "We have need of a melder,

Súlka Bien. Stav Darkwin will be bound to the royal line of Stone-gate until he meets Salur."

Every limb, every muscle tightened like a rope growing taut. If I refused to fasten Kael's life to this fortress, he would die. But it was taking away his choice, his own will.

"Ly," Kael whispered. "This is what I want."

Liar. Kael wanted to serve the Stav to see the kingdoms, to traipse over the knolls and valleys of Jorvandal, then he'd always dreamed how he'd settle down with the most beautiful wife and take up the life of a fisherman like Thorian.

Until his death, Kael would be locked into the life of a war-rior, of bloodshed, and battle if it arose. There were tales of Stav who lived such lives. They were never the same—built strangely, like battle fashioned their bodies in new ways.

They seemed empty.

Still, how could I refuse when it meant the world would be without Kael Darkwin and his good heart, his rakish way with women, his gentle soul?

"If it is what you want," I responded, a thickness to my voice.

"Stav Nightlark," Damir said, flicking his fingers to signal Emi. "Retrieve the bone."

Emi approached Kael. She gave him a soft smile. "Again, I must manipulate your bones. I assure you it won't be like the last time."

Kael snorted. "I think you take pleasure in my pain."

Emi shook her head and turned Kael's palm upright, so it faced the ceiling. With a small paring knife, she cut a slit in the top of one of his fingertips. After she dabbed away some of the blood, Emi took the tip of his finger between her own, like she was pinch-ing the nailbed.

Kael grimaced and blew out a few ragged breaths through his

nose, but no screams, no horrid agony was written on his face. More discomfort and irritation.

When Emi slid her fingers off his, a shaving of something pale and blood-soaked followed. Kael clutched his hand to his chest until the second Stav Guard handed over a linen cloth to stop the blood.

Pinched between Emi's fingers was a piece of bone so thin it was nearly diaphanous.

With care, Emi handed the sliver to King Damir. Prince Thane approached his father, saying nothing, but made a small gash behind the lobe of the king's ear with his own knife.

The king didn't flinch, simply chuckled at my widened eyes. "You can understand why I only trust my own flesh and blood to draw a knife so close to my throat." Damir held out Kael's bone in his palm. "What you did in the jarl's house, do again. It will not be so overwhelming, for this is no soul bone."

"You will sense Kael through his bone?"

"At times."

"Is it not maddening? To feel so many others, I mean?"

"It takes a great deal of focus to sense another soul through the binding, but it is not impossible."

"Even though you are not a crafter?"

Damir smirked. "Yes. Something about the melding power connects me to these slight pieces of my Stav, creating a sort of bridge between us. I can choose to access it if necessary, or burn it should they betray me."

Skalfirth was small, secluded, but I thought we understood more than all this. Never had I heard of such a thing being done before. Jorvandal's Stav Guard was the envy of the kingdoms. Strong, formidable, and some of the most fiercely loyal warriors across the lands.

Because they'd given pieces of themselves.

I laced my fingers together to hide the tremble. "How do I bind the bone, sire?"

The king slid half the shard into the gash in his neck. "Touch it, and your craft should lead you from there."

The weight of every eye fell over my shoulders. My fingers were unsteady, but with care I reached out to the sliver of bone.

A bite of something sharp, almost like a thorn, pricked my skin. The roar of a furious tide filled my ears and soft light wrapped around the shard.

The same as with the soul bone I melded to Kael, filaments like gold threads webbed around the bone and into the open wound on Damir's neck, a sort of pattern I could use to stitch the new bone into the king.

I touched one strand, dragging the tips of my fingers downward. The gilded threads fastened along the edge of the shard and I made quick work of nestling the piece half inside the gash on the king's neck.

It was bloody work, a little sickening to mold and maneuver flesh aside to make way for additional bone fragments.

My jaw tightened against a swell of sick in my belly the deeper I shoved the piece. Each new tug against the glow of craft threads squished and slipped into blood and tissues. I was no healer and the whole of it reminded me of gutting days-old fish.

Soon enough my lips parted, allowing short puffs of breath to flow, all to keep from breathing in the hint of copper and sweat on the king's skin.

More stitches, more threads, more gold and heat stitched Kael's finger bone beneath the surface of the king's neck, shifting it like a bulge of creeping maggots to the hinge of Damir's jaw.

Melding was curious, subtly powerful, and I could not look away.

It felt as though a dormant edge of my heart awakened with a new thrum and pulse. Kael told me when he used his bone craft to manipulate a fishing hook or blade or to heal a cracked shin of a child, his body heated and his blood swelled in his veins with a new sort of strength.

Before the horrors of Jarl Jakobson's great hall, I'd never felt the burn of being anything but ordinary. Too bony, too freckled, too dull. In this moment, my craft drew out a side of me I did not know.

Someone braver, bolder, even stronger.

Absorbed in the motion of threading the sliver into Damir's neck, I never took note how the walls darkened, like a shade pulled over the lancet windows, blotting out the sun. Flames in the inglenook died, filling the hall with the gust of a winter wind.

The eerie glow from bodies of the consorts, the prince, and the queen lined the tattered and chipped table.

My hands stilled and I pulled back. The king's features burned like a noon sun, his flesh more like a flame than anything. I could not make out his fine tunic or the beads in his beard. All around, much the same as in Skalfirth, bones burned through bodies of those in the palace hall as though their very souls were aflame.

Black dripped off the walls, from the corners and edges of the tables, like moldy refuse.

A mirrored reflection of the world I knew, but rotted and dreary.

Smoke and salt expanded in my lungs with every breath.

I shuddered in the chill, too unnerved to look over my shoulder at the shuffle of steps across damp stones. I clenched my eyes for one breath, two, then shook out my hands and tried to continue stitching the golden thread into Damir.

The small shard gleamed like a polished gold coin, half inside Damir's aura, but a different shade. In truth, I could make out endless shades of gold on the king. All different shapes and sizes.

"Come to take more souls, Melder?"

Ten paces away, the harsh glow of the phantom's eyes held mine. His cloak billowed like mists of the night around broad shoulders. This time he was not towering over me; he'd perched atop a blackened stone that dripped in rotted moss and vines.

The golden rope keeping the creature tethered around his waist seemed weaker, more frayed, almost ready to split.

Tricks of the mind, that's all this was.

"I'm not here to disturb anything." I turned back to the king's bones. The threads had faded and what was left was a molten glow around the edges of the sliver, melted down into Damir.

The phantom drifted to my side, the brilliant rope shifted with him, going slack when he stopped at my shoulder.

"What is it that has brought you here?" He tilted his cowled head.

"The command of the king."

The phantom merely hummed, gaze sliding across my throat, almost as though he were hungry to cut it out. My eyes clenched when he leaned close enough the cool mist of his darkness brushed along my cheeks.

"Why are you seen here?" He spoke like he was asking the question to himself more than to me.

"This is simply in my mind."

A heavy, strained sort of laugh grumbled from the spectral. "You don't really believe that. Learn this now, Melder—not everything is as it seems. Those who seem trustworthy might be enemies. Those who seem enemies, well, they might be the fiercest allies."

"What are you?"

Another hum. The phantom billowed, almost iridescent, like he was fading. "Take a soul, Melder, and I will take one in its place."

The memory of the screaming figure when I melded Kael's body would not leave me. A soul for a soul.

The world spun and the same suffocating fog began to fill my head, until I was flung back.

Warmth from an open hearth stung my skin, and my cheek was pressed against something hard, something sturdy.

Gods. My knees must've buckled, and I fell against Roark's damn chest. His strong arms held me around the waist, my face buried into the embroidered wolf head over his heart. For a moment, I didn't mind.

For a moment, he was my strength.

King Damir chuckled. With care, and a bit of a tug from Ashwood, I found my footing again. The king dabbed a hand over the thin, sealed scar across his neck. Where blood and opened flesh had been moments ago, now it looked like nothing more than a healing scrape.

The king's eyes flashed in a new kind of life. "I feel it. The addition of it, the strength of it. It took so swiftly. Not even Fadey could settle a binding so painlessly." He laughed and clapped his hands, delighted. "How glad I am to have you here, Lyra Bien."

A few courtiers and mistresses offered a gentle applause, with murmured praises.

Damir placed his hands on my shoulders, nudging Roark to step back. The air was colder without the Sentry so close.

"You will be honored in these walls," Damir told me. "A crucial member of the royal house and Stav Guard. I still see the fear in your eyes. Tell me what I can do to ease your worries."

There was sincerity in the king's words, his eyes. What was it about melding that brought such peace, such hope, and fear? How was I to find a way to be free of these walls if I did not understand the craft that brought me here?

"I do not know much about melding craft. I think it would be wise to understand it."

"I agree." Damir glanced over my head. "Sentry Ashwood, you'll see to it."

Roark dipped his chin and nodded. I schooled my features into what I hoped was something unreadable, something flat. Why Roark? The thought was both a fear and a delight, and I could not explain it.

"You and I will speak in my chambers, Lyra. Then you will be given time to adjust to your life here. You will be shown about the borders of Stonegate and train with the Stav. Melding is a rare craft, and should you find yourself unprotected, you must be able to do so yourself." The king cupped my chin with his large palms. "Your comfort is my greatest concern. The Sentry is under my command to keep you safe, but I'm certain you'll hardly know he is there."

19

LYRA

OUTSIDE THE KING'S CHAMBER, ROARK TOOK HIS PLACE against the wall. I didn't need to look to know his gaze followed me until the door closed at my back.

King Damir had one hand on the edge of the hearth as he slowly sipped from a drinking horn, watching the flames. The king kept his hair loose over his shoulders, and a pale tunic hung undone from his trousers.

"Lyra." He grinned. "Come in."

I kept my hands clasped in front of my body, stopping in the center of the chamber. The space was wide and arched, filled with benches and high-backed chairs covered in soft furs. A chandelier made of antlers was overhead and held at least three dozen tall candles.

"I heard you know how to handle a blade. Apparently, you pulled one on my Sentry in Skalfirth."

"I did not pull it on the Sentry, Your Grace. I pulled it on myself."

Damir made a low grunt in his throat. "There won't be any of that now, am I clear?"

I swallowed with a nod, but said nothing, made no promise.

"I want to speak with you about your duty as a melder without so many prying eyes. But you must understand, to meld brings risks, Lyra. It is the lot the silver scar delivers to those born with the curse. Ravagers of the assassin Skul Drek are often sent by the Draven court whenever a melder works."

"How do they know, sire?"

"I suspect spies and traitors have something to do with it," said Damir. "But when you meld at my request, I will see to it precautions are taken."

"I melded today." I stared down at my palms as though I might see the gold threads on my fingertips. "Will they retaliate?"

"Perhaps. They seem keener to prevent us from melding soul bones than binding bones. Souls bound to another bring more power, you see."

Damir returned the horn to a table near the hearth and sat in one of the chairs. The king crossed one ankle over his knee, his gaze never leaving me. "Soul bones are offered to Stav Guard advancing in rank. That is your main purpose as my melder. So you can see why the Draven folk despise you, for you, Lyra Bien, are what makes my army stronger."

Dread weighed heavy in my chest from the unshakable fear of my own craft, of being tossed into the mirrored land where the shadow and his glowing eyes would at last catch hold of me.

Damir took a slow drink. "Rank melding is a practice restored from the myths of the Wanderer by my father's father."

Heat prickled beneath the neckline of my gown. "The craft that destroyed the Wanderer's kingdom?"

"Ah, you've been reading from the lore." Damir's lip twitched.

"Many tales are meant to teach lessons. That version of the tale warns of greed, does it not, Lyra?"

I didn't disagree, but I did not agree either. Tales were there for us to learn where caution ought to be taken in our lives.

"My grandfather studied myths and sagas to near obsession," said the king. "He won our place in these lands during old wars, but he also found a new use of melder craft. With the aid of a bone crafter, my grandfather marked the breastbone of his own father in a summons to the realm of the gods—a soul bone."

"Like the lore of the Wanderer demanding the power of the god-queen."

Damir lifted a brow but grinned. "Yes. My grandfather believed the god-queen marked the bones used by her husband to summon the power of the fallen. It worked, Lyra. It wasn't only myth."

I cracked a knuckle. "So your grandfather melded his father's bone to him?"

Damir gave a wolfish smile. "He did. The soul bone provided wisdom, like our father-god. Strength, like the god of war. Compassion, from the goddess of the heart. Insight, health, cunning. Power flowed once again as it did when the Wanderer held the gifts of craft."

Those gifts came from corruption and deceit in the folklore, and I was not so certain much had changed.

"Once my grandfather realized melding soul bones to living bone brought such gifts to his own abilities, he added more and more. He began using a melder to armor his warriors with the bones of those who had fallen in battle. Bones from the strongest among them. Not only did the king gain strengths, but his army became a true threat against our enemies."

King Damir had large, rounded shoulders and thighs. His

knuckles were thick and looked nearly jagged. Was it his natural figure or could it be that bones of the dead were melded onto his own?

"Melded bone becomes a conduit for the strengths of the fallen soul to flow into the living body. It becomes an armor that never leaves," Damir explained. "For some it is so fierce not even the strike of blades would cause harm."

All gods. He was talking of an indestructible force.

"You understand what I am saying, Lyra? My grandfather discovered how to create a true, undefeatable, Berserkir army. We have continued the tradition in Jorvandal. It keeps Myrda desperate to be our allies through marriage treaties, and it keeps Dravenmoor seething with their hatred that we have power and they do not."

I took a step for one of the chairs, placing my hands on the fur draped over the back. "But there is a reason this angers Dravenmoor. It takes from the dead, from souls. They use soul craft, yes?"

Leave the souls. It was the plea—not a threat—of the phantom in the dark mirror land.

Was this what he meant?

"Dravens do not despise us because we absorb the strength of fallen souls. They have done worse with their twisted craft." Damir's mouth tightened. "They are angered because they cannot overpower us. They want to slaughter melders to level the battlefield, Lyra. For without melders, soul bones would never be. You see why you must not step outside the gates without protection? More than me, they will strike at you. That is saying a great deal, for Queen Elisabet of Dravenmoor would sooner slit my throat than talk peacefully."

I knew little of the Draven royal line—only rumors passed on by Skald tales or hungry traders in Skalfirth that the queen was a fearsome woman who could rend the soul of her own people with the flick of her hand.

"Craft was meant to be unified." Damir's voice drew me away from my thoughts. "Dravens do not agree. They use their soul craft to manipulate and punish their folk. It is cruel. Look at our Sentry. His people tortured him, left him scarred and brutalized as a mere boy."

I blinked, a little horrified.

"What we do here is for the protection and benefit of our folk," Damir said.

By creating his manipulated Berserkir army. I rubbed the chill off my arms. "If I may ask, sire, why give such power to the Stav? Forgive me, but why not meld soul bones only to you?"

"If I found soul bones powerful enough to leave me invincible, perhaps I might." Damir chuckled. "Stav deserve the honor of the gods as much as their king. This brings us back to rank melding. Within the fortnight, four Stav Guard will be named captains. Their honor is a soul bone, which you will place within them. The same as you did for Stav Darkwin."

Damir uncrossed his ankle and leaned his elbows onto his knees. "There is more you must do, Lyra. What I am about to ask, I urge you to speak truthfully. When you meld the bones, tell me, is there anything you feel, anything you see in your mind's eye?"

My throat went dry. Stun must have been painted across my face. Damir grinned like he'd won some grand victory.

"These lands are filled with the fallen of the first kings. Warriors who had craft from the Wanderer. Fadey explained there is a feeling, a sort of glow, that led him in the direction of unmarked burial mounds from across the centuries."

"He did not go into the shadows?"

Damir cocked his head. "Shadows?"

Gods, what was the shadow and phantom I saw? "Nothing. I have felt something, but did not know what it meant."

Damir's face softened. "That is your craft reaching out to bridge the living souls to the fallen. You will follow it and tell us where to forage."

"You use these bones for rank melding?"

"And for bone crafters to fashion stronger blades. But most are marked as soul bones. They save the lives of our armies, Lyra, like it did for Darkwin. It gave him strength from the fallen once it was melded."

"What is it about the bones of the dead that add so much more power than the shard Kael gave to you?"

Damir sighed. "Some believe a soul yearns to keep living. To do so, it shares its strengths with its new soul. I will show you areas we've already harvested, and you will continue the search Fadey left behind."

What about the phantom? His rage at my presence?

Before I could press the king again, Damir rose and took a step for the door, clearly finished with our conversation.

"As promised, I will give you time to get accustomed to living within Stonegate. Before the rank melding, I will have tomes sent for you to study and learn." Damir led me toward the door, pausing before he dismissed me. "This is what the gods have prepared you to do, Lyra. Trust in that, and you will serve your people with honor."

20

LYRA

"U p." HEAVY CURTAINS SKIDDED ACROSS THE ROD OVER the window.

The boil of sunlight seared against my eyes. I groaned and shoved my face into the pillow, blocking the light. Craft was tiring. Even melding Kael's bone shard had left me desperate for bed last night.

"Get up." Emi's impatience was felt with every heavy step to the side of my bed. "You're to learn the borders of the fortress today and you're going to be late."

"Be gone."

"Fine. I'll get the Sentry. He can toss you into a now-frigid bath. Naked."

I tossed one of the down pillows off the bed. "I've been here mere days and already I detest you the most."

Emi wore her crimson Stav tunic. Her pale hair was braided in a tight plait down her back. She grinned and threw back the furs guarding me from the morning chill. "Detest me if you must, but we are due to meet Ser Bjorn Stonehands so you can see the grounds by the morning bell. He's less patient than I, and holds no care if you are the melder. And you're in luck. With the pleasantries of the upcoming royal vow, the prince has insisted Stonehands deliver his guests to the Boarshead Tavern for a revel."

I arched a brow. "I've never been to a revel."

Emi paused. "You lived in a jarl's household."

"As a servant."

"Well, tonight you shall go as a guest. Wear something nice, but a gown that breathes, if you want my advice. Gets all sticky with so many drunken souls in one room."

"The king wishes to expose his melder? Just last night he said enemies would want me dead more than him."

Emi chuckled and plucked a small glass vial from her leg pouch. "The king desires his melder to feel at ease here, as promised. You're not leaving the walls, and you'll have protection." She gestured at herself. "Besides, he's recently learned a thing or two about thorn blossom dye."

My lips parted.

Emi removed the cork on the vial and handed the dye over to me. Her expression sobered. "You are not the servant girl any longer. The prince especially encouraged his father to let you live freely, as best you can within a fortress."

"I don't understand why," I admitted.

"You'll find Prince Thane knows what it is like to have a duty forced upon him. He tends to try to make the best of it."

"But . . . the king fears for my safety—"

"Lyra, it is a revel in the royal tavern. Take moments you can to live beyond duty. You'll be surrounded by Stav Guard and your shadow. No harm will befall your pretty little neck."

Unbidden, a groan slipped through my teeth. Ashwood. My

assigned watchdog. The worst part wasn't that I detested the thought of the man following me, it was more that I didn't.

I'd done little else since I was given the guide from Emi but study the language of the Sentry. Each gesture was inked across my thoughts, unforgettable, and it had become a strange sort of obsession to know more.

I recalled Gammal teaching me to read Jorvan and even symbols from her lands across the Night Ledges as a girl. Neither came to me as simply as Roark's words.

I didn't understand it, but his hand speak came clearer with every passing day.

Truth be told, it was a little frightening. Almost like a spell cast had captured my mind, I was pulled into his mystery, his violence, and the way he looked at me like he might wish to slit my throat or step a little closer whenever our paths crossed.

Naturally, the hidden pull needed to die a quick death before anyone in Stonegate caught wind. Kael would be one. Gods, he could smell it if I looked twice at a man. But Emi was another. She had a strange relationship with the Sentry, one I still didn't know.

"Was I not clear enough?" Emi's voice cut through my wandering thoughts. She placed her hands on her hips, her pale features flushed. "We're to leave shortly. Get washed. I'm certain it is as frosted over as the Black Fjords in the North."

I fought the urge to roll my eyes. The Black Fjords hugged uninhabitable lands that snowed even in the warm months. A place where rapists and thieves and unwanted crooks went to labor until their penance was paid on jagged mountain walls between a distant Dravenmoor border and the cold edges of Jorvandal.

I closed the washroom door, stripped, and bit down on the tip of my tongue to keep from freeing a gasp from the shock of cold. No sense in giving Emi Nightlark more to gloat about.

With haste, I scrubbed my skin, ignoring the clack of my teeth and the gooseflesh dotting my limbs. By the time I emerged, the tips of my fingers were a shade of purple and numb enough I could not fasten my own bodice. A servant who said little braided my hair while Emi ducked into the tall armoire and tossed out boots and satin slippers, hunting for a pair of shoes.

"Don't you have other duties besides interrupting my mornings?" I glanced at her in the mirror.

"I"—Emi grunted the deeper she dug—"think you are not sincere in your disdain for me."

"I think that is your hope."

Emi returned with black ankle boots, polished like the gloss of a raven's wing. "Darkwin holds no ill will. You could learn something from him."

"Kael was always the more forgiving one of us."

Emi scoffed and placed the boots in my lap, shooing away the servant so she could finish my hair. In the mirror, she lifted her bright eyes to meet my gaze. "The Sentry trusts me to be alone with you much more than his men, so me you shall get."

I picked at a thread of my skirt, annoyed at myself for even wondering if Roark would join the tour today. "You are close with the Sentry?"

"Very." She spoke the word in a way that left little room for more questions. They weren't affectionate, but not all lovers were.

From somewhere inside the fortress the bellow of a bell rattled the glass windows.

"Dammit." Emi looked me up and down once in the mirror. "You'll do. Hurry. Stonegate is no small place, and Bjorn waits for no one."

BJORN STONEHANDS WAS A MAN WHO'D EARNED HIS NAME from the thickness of his fingers and the heavy strike of his fists.

While she tugged me through the corridors toward the great hall, Emi offered a few hurried tales of his youth as a Stav Guard. Rumors insisted Bjorn had killed no fewer than five opponents in sparring matches with his bare hands.

He was a towering man with a silver beard that struck his chest and nothing but inked runes over his scalp. A crowd of folk visiting the fortress had gathered in the square beyond the great hall to await Bjorn's tour. Travelers passing through the vales of Jorvandal on their way to the Myrdan border. People from Myrda visiting their families who took up houses in Damir's realm. Some were elders with silver-wrapped hair and age carved in the lines of their eyes and cheeks. Others were young, gawking at the towering walls with a look of awe.

Being buried between the rocky cliffs brought rogue gusts of wind, but the square within the palace walls always breathed of fresh basil and lavender.

Emi nudged me aside when a trio of Stav Guard stomped over the cobbled paths. I thought it more for show. They plodded their boots with unnatural force to jangle the buckles on their ankles, and more than one Stav puffed out his chest when a cluster of young ladies traveling for a wedding in the township to the north whispered and snickered and sighed when they passed.

We arrived at the square outside the great hall after the final bell, and the way Stonehands pinned me with his gaze, I feared I might fall to my knees merely to escape his attention.

"Let's be off, then." With a grunt Stonehands adjusted a pigskin satchel on his shoulder and stomped toward the first portcullis leading away from the palace.

"I think he likes you," Emi muttered.

I turned to frown at her, but caught movement beneath a shadowed arcade.

Roark, dressed in a black Stav tunic with a gray wolf fur cloak over his shoulders, stepped onto the road. The Sentry kept a distance of more than fifteen paces, but moved as though weightless.

He maneuvered around the inner guards and courtiers, barely snatching the attention of others, yet my gaze found him in the crowds as if he were dressed all in red, waving his arms to steal my notice.

Annoyed as I wanted to be at the king for demanding the Sentry stand as my personal guard, I could not deny an unsettling sort of relief knowing Roark Ashwood kept watch on my back.

Melder Fadey was slaughtered just beyond these walls. Roark was swift and dangerous with a blade, a sight I'd witnessed firsthand, and he had what appeared to be unwavering loyalty to the royal house. Perhaps the Sentry despised me, but I was of value to the house of Oleg.

I'd few doubts that Roark would take countless heads in order to keep me safe.

When his sharp eyes found mine from his place in the shadows, breath caught in my throat. In haste, I turned away and blended into the back edges of the touring crowd.

"Keep close," Stonehands called out. "Makin' our way to the inner market, roads get a touch narrow."

I felt a great deal like a hog being squeezed into the slaughterhouse the way folk pushed through the arched gates into the lower township.

Stonegate palace sat on the top of a rocky hillside and below were homes and the market square that bustled with hawkers trading their hogs and goats and hens. Fish and smoked meats passed hands as swiftly as florin coin, and beneath it all was the scent of damp grass, soil, and salt.

"Wars were fought over these knolls for centuries." Stonehands led us up a sloped cobbled pathway, pointing out stones and foundations that belonged to ruins of an original palace. "It is believed the Wanderer once ruled here, making it the most coveted land across the realms of Stìgandr."

"The Wanderer lived on Jorvan lands?" a woman asked. She was joined with two young boys and a bearded man whose belly sank low over his belt.

Stonehands gave a stiff nod. "So the sagas say. Here, his warriors bled, his children played. There is power in these lands, and lust for more of it breeds hate. It was much of the cause of the Divisive Wars that split the kingdoms in the modern three of Myrda, Dravenmoor, and Jorvandal. Now, follow me. I will show you the painted windows."

My fingers trailed over the moss-soaked stones of the old fortress. "Stav Nightlark."

Emi wove backward between a few other visitors. "What?"

"Is it true?" I tilted my head back, squinting through the sunlight toward the upper towers. "Did the Wanderer live here?"

The Wanderer King was no mere king. He was the father of our lands, the legendary genesis of craft across the kingdoms.

"It's a common belief back home."

"So, Dravenmoor accepts it."

"Some do." Emi placed her open palm on one of the walls. "Others believe the old Jorvan king who won his treaties was simply lucky in battle and selected the richest lands, then called them gods-blessed to become more important than was true."

She followed the flow of the crowd. I held back a moment, looking around the towers, the roads, and onto the distant hills beyond the inner walls. Could these be the knolls where myths were born?

"Who can tell me what this signifies?" Stonehands paused beside a stone juncture where three paths convened into one.

Over the archway that covered the single lane was a bind rune made of gold, bronze, and crimson iron. Silver filigree made the edges, like the rune was nestled in a night bloom.

When no one spoke, Stonehands let out an irritated growl and pointed to each shade of the rune. "Crimson in the rune of a warrior signifies the blood of those lost in the Divisive Wars. Bronze in the rune of loyalty stands for the treaties of craft between Jorvandal and Myrda. Gold in the rune of protection, a vow from these walls to always protect those who remain loyal and steadfast against our enemies."

Stonehands barreled on about the grandness of King Damir's distant grandfather in battles that divided the folk and kingdoms. Divisive Wars made Dravenmoor the enemy and signed treaties that demanded Myrda deliver the craft of melding to the service of Stonegate if ever it was found in their borders.

While he rambled with pride over the feats of Jorvandal and the depravity of Dravens, I rolled the end of my braid around one finger, casting a glance at Emi. She was focused ahead, her face unreadable.

I looked back at Ashwood.

He kept a steady distance, back to the wall, his attention wholly placed on a knife he spun in his hands.

Could he hear Stonehands and the mutters of hatred toward his people? Did Roark even consider Dravens his people anymore?

My fists curled at my sides. My pulse quickened; unbidden

words to remind Bjorn Stonehands to watch his words in front of two prominent Draven Stav danced over my tongue.

"Moving on." Stonehands frowned at the lot of us and ushered the crowd forward.

I blew out a breath as the moment to be bold faded, the way it always did.

We were led to the upper bridges that looked down over the lower roads of the township at the base of the hillside. Vendors and tradesmen crowded the bridges and upper roads. It gave Stonehands a bit of respite to set his gaggle of visitors free to spend florin coin on a few pearl combs, exotic pastes for skin spots, or sugared strips of vibrant fruits from mountain orchards.

A woman in front of me clung to a man's arm. She handled a new satin coin purse with delight while the man gave up two large silver florin.

I stepped across her path to be free of the crowd, but she waved me over. "Here alone?"

"In a sense."

"Bold of you." She looked at the man by her side. "We were recently wed, and took to traveling for a fortnight."

Her new husband kissed the corner of her mouth, eyes alight with sickening affection. "How dull it must be to travel by oneself."

"I've grown rather fond of it." I offered a narrow look at Roark and Emi, both standing at the end of the bridge.

The woman lowered her voice, as though sharing a bawdy secret. "Ligstaad, the township in the easternmost hills, is the territory of Jarl Hendrikson and has a great many young men. You might go there next and find a husband of your own to join you."

"Then I would be forced to share all the food." I plucked a small sample of seasoned fish a vendor passed around.

"Jarl Hendrikson is my father," she went on with a touch of

pompous propriety. "Travel back with us. It's dangerous for a lady to be on her own."

"How wonderous it sounds, but alas I'm doomed to die in these walls. See that man?"

Roark's face shadowed when I pointed his way.

The jarl's daughter blanched. "The Sentry?"

"Yes. He is my captor. Or guardian, if you ask him. I prefer captor. I am told I must attend the prince's revel with him at my side. His sour disposition frightens away all the suitable . . . well, suitors."

"Gods." The woman pressed a hand to her heart. "Poor girl. Whatever did you do to be taken?"

"I fear I had the gall to exist."

From the corner of my gaze, I watched Emi draw her bottom lip between her teeth, the way someone might if they were fighting back a laugh. By her side, her fingers ticked off to a count of three. In the next moment, heavy steps approached and Roark curled his hand around my arm, tearing me away from the crowd.

"Pardon me," I said over my shoulder to the stunned woman. "My captor has need of me, it seems."

What are you doing? Roark's gestures were harried and angry.

"Making new acquaintances. Is that not what I should do since this place is doomed to be my fate?"

You want her to report you to her father? A tale of a captured woman?

My skin heated. Perhaps my moment of what I thought was cleverness was not so cunning after all.

He took a moment to write on the parchment.

It seemed Roark did not wish for me to miss a single word.

The Sentry leaned in, our noses nearly touching, and the grin he wore was colder than mine.

He did not pull back, not even when I read the scrap of parchment.

Let me tell you of Jarl Hendrikson. He would send a summons to King Damir. If you were not the melder, and the king gave you leave, Hendrikson would take you as a wife. When he tired of you, he would give you to his horrid sons to bed as they pleased.

I swallowed through a new thickness. "You are making assumptions, Sentry Ashwood. And they are wrong. I was not trying to leave."

His cold grin grew colder as he spoke with one hand. *I doubt that.*

This close, I could make out the bits of black in the gold of his eyes. I hated him—*tried* to hate him—but was undeniably pulled into the fury and violence of the Sentry.

"You also assume I would allow such a man to touch me," I said, voice low and rough. "I learned long ago to sleep with a blade beneath my head."

The corner of Roark's mouth curved. *That I believe, though I doubt you know how to use it.*

"Pray you never find out."

Roark's eyes darkened. *You are understanding hand speak well.*

I took a step back. "Another of my talents. I have a knack for studying the movements of bones."

The lie would serve me well, for the last thing I ever wanted was Roark Ashwood discovering how tirelessly I'd studied the written guide of his words. That would bring the man too much satisfaction.

He gestured to Emi, who informed Bjorn Stonehands I would meet the rest at the Boarshead when the revel began.

I did not miss the parted lips of the woman as Roark dragged me deeper into the market.

21

ROARK

THE BOARSHEAD TAVERN SAT ATOP A KNOLL WITHIN THE palace boundaries. A crooked pipe puffed smoke from the large inglenook, and the sod atop the roof grew wildflowers in the wet months. Tonight, lanterns hung from iron hooks and set the whole tavern aglow against the purple dusk.

A revel was the last thing I wanted tonight. Tension rippled across my shoulders and had for the better part of two days. The sort that felt more like an instinct than annoyance.

There was something coming, and I could feel it brewing. The walls had been too quiet since Lyra entered the fortress. She'd already melded a soul bone, ignited the power in her blood, then bound a jarl's disowned son to the king.

Something was coming.

Enemies of the king never allowed Damir to bask in his small victories for long. They always knew when Fadey melded, and it was long past time for them to realize the lost melder had been found.

The wolf in the wood was only the beginning.

"You're hurting my arm." Lyra tugged against my grip once we reached an arched bower outside the tavern. "The king said I was to be kept comfortable, not dragged around like your personal pet."

I looked once over my shoulder, and seeing no one, pressed her back to the mossy stones of the wall.

Her lips parted with a gasp and her eyes, darkened with dyes, widened when I crowded her. I flattened one palm beside her head and with my other hand, I gripped her jaw, holding her gaze for a breath.

Her chest rose in harsh gasps, brushing her breasts against me, but she didn't look away.

Slowly, I pulled back one palm to speak. *If the king knew what a fool his new melder was, he would bind you in iron and keep you tethered to his side. Test me again and I'll see it done.*

Her full lips curved up, annoyingly captivating. "And if the king knew his son's Sentry was such a brute, he might station you outside the wall with the wolves."

The last word came out in a hiss. A furrow built between my brows. I expected her to catch the anger in my face, not my actual words.

I leaned closer, pressing her body firmly to the wall. *How is it you understand me so well so soon?*

"That's what bothers you?" Lyra snorted a laugh. "That I understood your words enough to catch your insult?"

Gods, she was aggravating.

How? My fingers brushed along her cheek.

I'd used hand speak against Emi's palm, or Thane's at times, but I didn't touch others. Truth be told, the thought of it often repulsed me beyond sparring and battle and the occasional tryst.

There was no reason to draw near to anyone in Stonegate.

But brushing a word against Lyra's skin caused a bit of pleasure to burn in my veins when her breath caught. As though I unsettled her as fiercely as this gods-awful woman was peeling back my ribs, peering inside to see my every secret.

How? I pressed again, slower, gentler.

Lyra frowned. "I've studied them. Is that not what you intended when you sent the guides?"

No one has picked it up so quickly.

Lyra's eyes tracked my hands. When I lowered my palm, she swallowed, her voice went softer. "As I said, must . . . must be my craft."

It wasn't craft. This draw, this dangerous pull, was something more.

I hated her for what she represented. Pain, blood, anger. I hated her for the risks she brought merely by having melder craft.

But another part of me wanted to hate her at a nearer distance. And each damn day the desire to stay away cracked and shed more of its strength.

My fingers curled around her jaw again, tilting her head. Every breath I took was filled with frostrose petals from the oils left in her chamber and sugared honey scrubs in her hair.

Gods, unwanted desire was there, and I'd be wise to remember the risks of getting too close to a melder. She was a tool to be used and destroyed by royals. Nothing more. The fara wolf in the wood was proof Lyra Bien was fated to fall like Fadey. A truth I couldn't forget.

I took a step back. *Since you understand me so well, there is no reason my commands should not be obeyed.*

"You are not my king."

No. I rested one hand on the curve of the crescent pommel of my sword and spoke with the other. *But I am the one your king tasked with keeping you alive.*

Lyra's jaw worked for a moment. "You're so angry I spoke to that woman, but do you know what I think, Sentry Ashwood? I think there is nothing so terrible beyond the gates. A few ravagers perhaps, but caravans and travelers are everywhere in the fortress. How can it be so deadly on the trade roads? I think you and the royal house want to keep me afraid, so I never fight back."

Gods, this woman.

I stepped nearer, head tilted until my nose nearly touched hers. My fingers spoke against her face. *You do not want to test that theory, Melder.*

Before she could say another word, I took hold of her arm and pulled her toward the doors of the tavern.

Already, rawhide drums thudded a steady beat in the corner alongside the songbird tune of a panpipe and the plucking strings of a tagelharpa. Too many bodies shoved inside. Folk from across the kingdoms traveled to and from Stonegate for trade, and to catch a glimpse of the capital of Jorvandal.

Mothers with their daughters laughed and daintily sipped from drinking horns near tables. No mistake, until Thane took his vows with Princess Yrsa, the daughters of Jorvandal would be tossed in front of the prince's feet.

As though Thane had any say in the matter of his bride.

I led Lyra to a back table. A line of young Stav Guard tasked with watching the doors stiffened on our approach, all arching their faces to avoid my scrutiny.

Lyra huffed when I placed her into a chair at the table and snatched a horn from one of the trays being passed around. Ale sloshed over the rim after I pounded the horn on the table too hard.

She glared at me. "I never expected my first revel would be spent hidden in the corner, drinking alone. Might as well take me back to my tower and lock me away, Sentry Ashwood."

I would love nothing more.

She snorted with derision and took a long gulp, wincing through the bite of the drink, muttering something like *ass* under her breath.

This would be a damn long night.

"Ly!" The boom of Darkwin's voice lifted over the heads of the patrons.

Emi stood at Kael's side, and behind them were the two bone crafters taken from Skalfirth. Truth be told, I hadn't seen them since arriving at Stonegate. Damir would let them stew in their misery until the next full moon, for the sake of his melder, no doubt, but soon enough they'd be taken up into society to strengthen the king's influence.

The man—I could not recall his name—looked practically murderous behind his sister.

"Kael." Lyra waved, a look of relief replacing her disdain for me.

Darkwin paused at the table, dipping his chin with a hurried, "Sentry Ashwood," then sat beside Lyra. Kael adjusted his new Stav blade with the wolf head pommel and made room for Emi and the other crafters to find a place.

"Hilda." Lyra took the woman's hand and squeezed. "How are you?"

The bone crafter woman had dark eyes that collided with the paleness of her hair. They hardened when she lifted her gaze and met mine. "I was torn from my husband after being wed a month." Hilda pasted a false smile on her lips and peeled her attention to Lyra. "How would you be?"

I did not feel guilt over what was done. That would be reckless and hint that I cared about crafters.

I didn't.

In truth, I would rather live in a world without any craft at all. Too many wars had been fought for a drop of the gods' magic. Too many families much like Hilda's had been upended.

Darkwin did not allow the somberness of the table to last long. Perhaps the side of him that was raised as a jarl's son was still there. He had a knack for drawing folk to laughter and drink and entertainment, like most jarls saw fit in their oversize long-houses.

Soon enough Hilda was laughing and mocking Darkwin for his overwrought tale of his skill during the day's training. Her brother's mouth twitched like he might grin before he hid it through a long draw of ale from his horn.

Emi cut Darkwin at the knees by regaling them with a story of how he wore his leather training gambeson backward for the whole of the first week during his training in the warm months.

Lyra's head fell back when she laughed, and I did not realize I'd gotten lost in the sound of it until cheers and applause drew my attention to the center of the tavern.

Thane stepped into the hall.

The prince had braided his hair in a ridge down his head and donned his favorite sea blue tunic and was, no mistake, reveling in the endless genuflection of the inner fortress travelers.

Thane was gracious enough to greet most, but the way the prince shouldered through the crowds, he was aiming for the familiar.

His gaze caught mine across the hall, and he smirked before clambering atop one of the tavern tables.

"My ladies, good sers, so rarely do we have such a gathering for a revel in the fortress. You honor us." The prince allowed a bit of applause before going on. "Now, eat, drink, and be entertained. You are honored guests tonight."

The moment the prince hopped from the table, drums thundered to life again.

"Ah, here are my friends." Thane clapped one hand on Emi's shoulder, the other on Kael's. "Darkwin, I hear Captain Dahl was quite pleased with you today."

"I told you," Kael murmured to Lyra. He grinned back up at Thane. "I'm honored to hear it, my prince."

Thane took Lyra's hand and pressed a kiss to the top. "Súlka Bien. Forgive me for not using your proper title." Thane leaned closer, voice low. "Might bring danger your way, and I'd be left to deal with the grousing of that somber sod at your back."

Lyra lifted her chin, watching me in the corner of her eye. "I fear it is just what he does, my prince. No matter what joyous thing might've happened in the day."

Thane barked a laugh.

I frowned.

"Oh, don't look at me like that." The prince stole a horn from the table and stepped beside me. "It isn't as though you weren't aware of your constant state of annoyance. It is a revel, within the gates, Stav at every door. It would not kill you to enjoy a horn or two."

It might and that might kill you. I gestured low enough that only he would see. *There is tension.*

Thane shook his head. "There is always tension. We have enemies who are never appeased and will be less so the moment they discover our lovely Lyra is behind these gates."

I started to gesture that the feeling went deeper, but Thane was pulled away by Emi to dance. Darkwin was spotted by a bold young woman who whispered in his ear, and in the next moment he followed her to the center of the tavern with other couples.

Lyra sat away from the two bone crafters, sipping on her horn. She looked back at me for a long breath, then replaced Thane's spot at my side.

"You've not taken a drink of your prince's ale, Sentry Ashwood. Not thirsty?"

All at once a thought—perhaps a memory—snapped through my head like a lash across my mind.

Shadows were thick, only the flicker of golden light from a few lanterns danced across the mossy stones of a feed barn.

Keep low. Keep down.

He'd flog me with his belt if I stepped out of line of his command. He was already in a piss-poor mood since I snuck away to join his march.

"You look thirsty. Have you been lost in the wood?"

My stomach backflipped. I whirled around, yanking a small whittling knife from my belt. I was met with dust-covered cheeks, messy soil-brown braids, and dark eyes with the faintest slash of silver carving through the centers.

"Sentry Ashwood?"

I blew out a rough breath when the memory faded and met Lyra's befuddled gaze.

She arched a brow. "Are you all right? You looked to be in pain."

I swallowed thickly and snatched the horn from her hand, taking a brisk drink, and gestured a rough, *Fine.*

Lyra pinched her lips. "Hmm. Pity."

In the center of the tavern, a Skald was calling for the attention of the crowd. The woman's arms were draped in vibrant linens, her head topped with a flat cap, and a spike of bone pierced through the center of her nose.

"Gather round, ye kin of the king. Hear this, a tale of a wicked queen."

My chest tightened, but I'd learned long ago not to show disquiet. Not to anyone.

"I always loved listening to the Skalds at House Jakobson." Lyra's mouth raised in a smile, but when she seemed to realize it was me she'd addressed, she cleared her throat and took a step away. "They always have good tales."

I didn't respond and listened to the Skald go on about the saga of a vicious queen who lost it all after she tried to take from a good and honorable king.

"A cruel woman she was," the Skald sang out. "Sent the heir of her throne to take the first king's spoils, a place a young princely boy ought to avoid, he should've known."

Stay down. Go. I closed my eyes, barring out the phantoms of a night I hardly recalled.

"What is this tale?" Lyra's whisper drew my attention. "I feel like I've heard it before."

The Skald barreled on when the crowds chanted and cheered with her. "And oh, what screams rose when the young princely boy lost his pretty head. Raiding he went when he ought to have been in bed. Bloody waters marked the shore, and the queen was sent to the pits of the ravines forevermore. Lost her heir without a care. But everyone from vale to sea knows there is no heart in those who master souls."

The tavern bellowed with cheers and harsh words leveled at the enemies across the ravines when the Skald ended her tale with a flourish of her hands.

Lyra cast an uncertain look my way. "They should not speak so foolishly in front of you."

I faced her. *Foolishly? Where was the lie in the tale?*

"I-I don't know," she stammered. "Is that true? Did the prince of Dravenmoor die in the raid looking for me?"

Many souls died that night.

Lyra's face paled. "I hate that so much death came because of the curse of my blood. I want to go back to not knowing all the truths."

She blamed herself? Then again, I had done the same thing for seasons.

As Emi often told me, I might've been a bit of an ass.

With a rap of my knuckles on the table, I drew her attention. *Lust for power spilled blood that night. Not a girl.*

"Well, it hasn't stopped you from hating me for it."

For a long, drawn-out pause words died between us, as though her tongue had gone as silent as mine.

She cleared her throat and looked back at the crowds. "All the same, I don't think it's fair to Emi or . . . or you to have folk speak so harshly of your people."

By the frosted hell, she was befuddling.

I dropped my chin, drawing my face a bit closer to hers. *I have no people. Only duty.*

"Must be lonely." Without another word, Lyra scooted down two seats.

I folded my arms over my chest, ignoring the aggravating desire to take the chair at her side for the rest of the revel.

On the last beat of the drum, a heavy thud pounded on the door to the tavern. The crowd hushed when it came again, like someone tossing themselves over and over against the wood.

The tavern matron bustled across the room and flung open the door, mouth opened to berate the one who'd disturbed the tune, but she screamed when a young Stav Guard staggered inside, blood dripping down his lips.

His eyes were wild, unfocused, but his words were clear. "Ravagers . . . attacking at the gates."

The Stav fell facedown on the floorboards, and let out a final, gurgling breath.

LYRA

TWO HANDS TOOK HOLD OF MY SHOULDERS BEFORE MY mind could even fathom what had happened.

Roark ripped me from the seat, knocking the table filled with horns, and shoved me toward the back door of the tavern. His gestures were collected, calm. But I did not need his voice to know he was barking commands at the Stav Guard.

I did not need to hear him to feel the way he demanded I be taken out of sight at once.

The Sentry drew his sword. He did not look at me before careening into the frantic mess of the crowd trying to flee from the fallen guard.

A ram's horn bellowed and the tavern went hauntingly still.

My shoulders rose and fell in heavy breaths.

"To the gates!" Baldur the Fox stepped across the threshold, not sparing a single glance at the dead Stav beneath his boots.

At once, the Stav Guard maneuvered into organized lines—axes, blades, bows—ready to defend the walls of Stonegate.

"Melder Bien, this way. Hurry now." The Stav left to look out for me urged me into the back rooms of the tavern.

There, we were met with another battle.

"I will defend these walls as well as you." Prince Thane was surrounded by a trio of guards, but his ire was pinned on the cowled face of his Sentry.

Roark gestured wildly at the prince and shoved—*shoved his palms*—against the prince's chest when Thane tried to follow.

"Roark," Thane shouted, but the three guards stepped in front of the prince in the same moment Roark disappeared into the main room of the tavern. Thane's eyes flashed with heady rage at the guards. "Your orders come from the royal house, not the Sentry."

"Apologies, my prince. Not when the royal has a desire to get his throat slit."

The prince cursed and spun around. His features were contorted in unmanaged anger until he caught sight of me. "Lyra."

Without a thought, I reached for the arm of the prince. "What's happening?"

"Damn ravagers. They've been getting bolder in recent seasons." The prince's jaw worked. "But I fear rumors might've reached them, and they are beginning their retaliations."

For me. Because Stonegate took me, just like the night I lost my past, blood would spill.

I swallowed through a scratch in my throat and tightened my grip on the prince's arm. "Then I hate to tell you, my prince, but I agree with the Sentry and you must get into the palace."

Thane returned a narrow look. "I'll never forgive you for saying that."

"I've been banished too."

"Well, that makes it a little better." The prince looked about, then took hold of my hand. "Come with me. The melder will be guarded in my chambers. Now get us to the palace," he commanded the Stav.

I tucked in close to the prince's side the whole of the journey back. Shouts and the stretch of leather from rushing guards surrounded the outer walls. Doors slammed and locked, the heavy iron around the portcullis clanked into place the instant we passed under the arch.

"Lyra! No, please!" Hilda gripped the bars of the heavy gate, tears glistened on her cheeks, and the watchmen shoved her back with the ends of wooden spears.

"Wait, let her in." I spun back, trying to shove past the three guards escorting us forward.

"Gates are closed, Melder Bien, we—"

"You can't just leave her out there." I looked for Thane to help. The prince wouldn't leave Hilda, but he was no longer at my side.

Thane shoved a Stav Guard against the bars of the gate. "You'd leave a woman alone in the streets? She is under the protection of this fortress, and you will let her in."

With a jumble of apologies, the Stav Guard signaled for the men on the walls to lift the jagged gate just enough for Hilda to slip underneath.

She fell against me, trembling. "Edvin left. He just left with the Stav. I can't lose my brother, Lyra. I can't . . . lose someone else."

"Hush." I stroked a palm down her braids. "It'll be all right. Edvin is skilled with the blade, you know that."

"Come, my ladies," Thane said. "We must get out of the open."

Hilda sniffled, but followed closely, keeping her hand in mine.

Inside the palace was quiet—oddly quiet—like we'd stepped from the chaos of reality into the peace of a dreamless sleep.

"My mother and father will be barred in their personal

wings," Thane explained when we reached his door. The prince moved like a man who'd done this too many times. "Their guards will be standing watch behind their doors, not in passages. When the horn blares, servants know to remain in their quarters."

The three Stav positioned themselves outside Thane's door. Wooden sofas with fur pillows were neatly arranged inside the prince's sitting room. A heady scent of pine and leather filled the room. There was an empty inglenook coated with dark ash, and the prince's windows were arched and painted like a wild forest with ivy and aspens in the glass.

I wrung my fingers together. "Kael would've gone with them."

Thane paused near the back wall. "Darkwin is a Stav and a man of honor. I have few doubts he was one of the first to run out."

Hilda hiccupped and hugged her middle.

The prince plucked a hunting bow from a peg on his wall and slung it over his head so it fell across his chest. From behind the inglenook he took out another one. "Any experience with bow hunting?"

Hilda shook her head.

I lifted my chin. "I'm not a fair shot, but I've done a little to keep the hares from Jakobson's gardens."

The prince handed over the second bow. "Good enough. If the thought of remaining barred and clueless behind the walls drives you as mad as it drives me, then follow me, ladies. I've something to show you."

I WAS IN A DAMN TREE HOUSE.

While our unsuspecting Stav Guards remained outside Thane's chamber doors, the prince led me and Hilda through a passage-way in the wall. He explained it was built half a century ago, a better way for kings and advisors to move about the palace un-seen before the stone walls were securely in place.

The corridor opened to one of the numerous back gardens with towering oaks and maple trees. Tucked behind walls of thick leaves and branches was a small fort. Childish in many ways, but useful in the fact we were now high enough we could see over the wall and still keep concealed.

"Built this with Roark when we were stupid boys who wanted to be watchguards."

Strange to think of Roark Ashwood as a boy, maybe smiling with the prince as they built their war tower.

Thane removed the bow from his shoulders and unearthed a quiver of bone arrows beneath a dusty tapestry. With a nod, he urged me to take one as he set his own arrow and aimed out a small oblong window. "Godsdammit."

"What is it?"

Breath caught in my chest.

Beyond the walls, just where the wood began and Stonegate ended, pikes with bloody heads were aligned in front of a torchlit evergreen shrub. Arrows with blue and gold fletching had pierced through each skull.

They were the Stav Guard who patrolled the wood.

From this position, the clang of steel on steel sent a shudder down my spine. The guards from the revel flung blades at men in dark cloaks. The gleam of the white wolf on the Stav Guard flashed here and there.

"What a cunning queen Elisabet has become." Thane tight-ened the bowstring again, his eye ticking as he tracked move-ment. "This is an act of war, but she will deny involvement since they fight ravagers down there. They're considered rogues, not under her command."

"You think the Draven queen commands them?" My voice was hardly steady, nothing more than a rough whisper.

"I do. Along with that bastard assassin of hers."

Skul Drek. Hair lifted on my arms. Was the unkillable assassin out there?

"Once we fire," Thane said, a touch of warning in his tone, "Dravens in those trees will fire back. They always have a few archers hidden in the dark. Watch your heads."

I kept low beside the prince. Hilda knelt on his other side, frantically tugging at the end of one braid.

Thane cursed when a Stav Guard ran past the wall, a ravager with a long, bearded ax three paces behind. The prince let an arrow fly; the point split through the side of the ravager's neck.

"By the gods." I stumbled back when he loaded another arrow.

Thane winked. "I'm more than just pretty, Lyra Bien."

Hilda let out a scream when—as promised—the thud of a stone arrowhead pierced the side of the hut in the trees.

Thane fired below, unable to see an archer in the trees, but reeled back inside the protection of the hut in the moments before two arrows returned, missing the window by two fingers.

"Let us pray they do not light the tips," the prince said, quickly loading another bone arrow.

I blew out two sharp breaths, then spun toward the window and steadied my borrowed bow. The trees were haunting and dark, and this range was wickedly far, nothing like I'd done on Skalfirth.

With the string taut beside my cheek, I scanned the branches. A hum of warmth brushed against my face, and for a moment I could've sworn a glimmer of gold burst in the trees and along the arrow shaft. Like the threads of my craft.

I aimed for a tree near the wall and let the arrow loose. The point struck the soil ten paces from the trunk. A poor shot, but it drew a nearby ravager's attention long enough a Stav Guard was able to strike his knee and bring him to the ground.

"Don't overthink the shot," Thane said when he fired another. "Be quick, be steady, and trust your eyes to get that arrow where it must go."

Warmth bled from the second arrow I nocked. Now there was a distinct glimmer of threaded gold coiled around the bony tip.

A wicked sort of grin teased my lips. A bone arrow could meld to other bone.

In position to fire again, I scanned the tree line.

I blew out a breath, embracing the heat off the arrow until it glimmered like the fealty bone shard. My pulse slowed, and for a heartbeat, it seemed as though the entire world grew darker, colder. The mirror land.

Golden filaments erupted from the towering limbs and branches across the wall. By the gods, I could make out the Draven archers' every movement, their every bone was a brilliant burst of gilded light, there to guide my arrows in the dark.

Threads of craft floated eerily around the sharp tip. With one finger, I touched a thread and pointed at the nearest pine where a ravager sat poised to fire another shot into the madness.

The thread shot forward, a tether of light from the point of my bone arrow to the skull of the distant attacker.

I let the bowstring go.

"Lyra, by the gods." Thane's voice shattered the dripping shadows of the mirror land and snapped me forward into the moment. The prince looked at me when an archer fell from his perch in the trees. "Woman, now *that* is the proper way to shoot an arrow."

I blinked, stared at my palms for a breath, then grinned as I nocked the next arrow. More than rank melding, more than fealty bones, I could meld damn arrows to the bones of our enemies.

"There's Edvin." Hilda's fingers curled into fists. I wasn't certain she even breathed.

True enough, her brother stood among the Stav, one of the only men who wore nothing but a loose tunic and a leathersmith jerkin. Edvin swung a stone mallet, cracking jaws and spines and knees.

Never had I seen the quiet-spoken bone crafter with such hatred in his movements.

My muscles clenched with every arrow the prince shot over the wall from his childhood hut. I took longer to fire since I guided the strands of my craft to my targets, but the shots were clean. Deadly.

It was a mark to Thane's character and devotion to his folk that he was here, fighting unseen for them. The more the fighting raged, the more violence coursed through me. Not so long ago, I would keep to the back of the great hall, head down.

Now I wanted to stand beside the prince and charge into battle to defend this keep.

"Last arrow," I said when Thane's hand brushed mine on the quiver.

The prince handed it to me. "Your accuracy is impeccable."

I pushed it back toward him. "But these are your men. You do the honor."

The prince studied me for a breath, then winked and nocked his weapon, firing into the battle.

In the frenzy of searching for Kael, I found Roark instead.

Gods, the Sentry was mesmerizing in the way he moved. Like a secret on the wind, he fought with a finesse and agility the ravagers could not meet. In one hand, Roark had his battle-ax, in the other a short blade.

He spun and ducked and jabbed. The Sentry dug fissures through skulls in one breath, then turned and opened chests in the next.

The Death Bringer.

It was no wonder so many looked upon him with a sort of reverent fear.

Ravagers fled toward the trees. The Stav pushed them back, cheering and calling out their threats.

I looked nowhere but at Ashwood.

The Sentry stalked a ravager, a man who was scrambling backward on his hands and heels. He was shouting something I could not hear, but it was enough to bring Roark to pause for a breath, two. Then, with a mighty heave, the Sentry swung his ax, catching the curved blade between the ravager's eyes.

With a jolt, the ravager's body went slack.

The siege was over.

Thane let his shoulders slump and his bow fall to the floor-boards. "Not how I planned for this night to go. Damn Dravens always pissing on us when the ale is flowing."

Hilda let out a nervous chuckle and Thane grinned, rather pleased with himself for managing to have his wits in such a dire situation. He helped Hilda to her feet, going on about how they'd be wise to safeguard the woods before his future bride arrived for the wedding festivities in coming weeks, then something more about bone blades for the princess to use. I wasn't listening anymore.

I could not peel my gaze away from the weary units of Stav returning to the gates. Behind them all was the Sentry. At this

distance, I could not make out his features, I could hear only muffled shouts and the rumble of voices in the lines.

No one would see us even if they glanced our way. The same
moment the thought crossed my mind, my blood heated.

Roark paused a pace from the arched gate, one pace from
stepping out of sight, and turned. His gaze was aimed at the tree
house, as though he knew we were here.

His gaze was aimed at me.

LYRA

"IT IS A FEELING UNLIKE ANY OTHER, LY," KAEL SAID THE morning after the attack. We tied dried lilac and sage to the stacked logs that would be the funeral pyres for the fallen Stav. "After so long of not belonging anywhere, I belong here."

He fought alongside the Stav and helped pike one of the ravager heads. More than one courtier had already taken note and, no doubt, more women would be carving his name like a shrine on their mantels much the same as poor, naïve Märta back home.

I turned away to hide the pain in my gaze. Kael wanted to belong so badly he would ignore the truth—he was forced to be here. This was not a choice.

"I hear the Sentry thought you fought well," I said, desperate to speak of anything but eternities at Stonegate.

Kael's grin widened. "Truly? It is quite a compliment coming from Ashwood. He battles like he is a spectral, untouchable. All those Draven bastards recognized him as one of their countrymen and fled from sight."

I gingerly placed another bundle of dried herbs on the pyre. "I heard a ravager spoke with him."

Thane had not let on the king's melder had flung arrows into the trees and risked her neck.

I wanted to keep it that way. Even with Kael. More than anyone he would chastise me for the stupidity and likely request a second Stav join Ashwood in my constant supervision.

Kael added bits of silver florin for the Stav to take with them to Salur. "I did hear a ravager spoke to the Sentry. Mad fool kept shouting about duty, like Ashwood was here to serve *them*." He chuckled. "The bastard died with a look of shock when the Sentry cut through his skull."

To me, Dravenmoor had done nothing to deserve Roark Ashwood's service after trying to slaughter him in childhood.

"I think I saw Skul Drek, Ly." Kael's voice lowered.

"What?"

He nodded. "I think I saw him in the trees. There was this darkness, so thick I couldn't make out where the soil began and the trees touched the sky. But for a fleeting moment, right when the final ravager fell, I could've sworn I saw his eyes. Like the molten hell—red and wretched." After a breath, Kael laughed and shook his head. "Sounds mad. Perhaps it was a trick of the mind. Hard to know with all the blood and chaos."

I laughed and followed behind him, but I could not shake the discomfiting feeling there was more to what Kael saw than any of us knew.

THERE WAS A SHIFT SINCE THE SLAUGHTERED GUARDS WERE found beyond the walls. Desire to break free was now edged in sharp fear.

I despised the helplessness, the dependence on men who held blades that had torn my life apart. Edvin's skill with the mallet had earned him undeniable respect from the Stav captain who led the smiths of the guard, men and women who pounded anvils and aided bone crafters in forming Stav armor and blades.

The light had not returned to Edvin's eyes, anger and a dark rage still festered under the surface, but his fury was now homed in on breaking iron and steel and sweating out his pent disdain.

Hilda said he still spoke little, but she anticipated it was how her brother would be until Salur. The emptiness from bidding his wife and young ones farewell was a stain on his soul.

What was most unsettling was Roark Ashwood. Where I had kept the secret of our battle in the old tree house, the prince ardently boasted about my aim to his Sentry.

For a moment, Ashwood looked at me with fleeting concern before briskly chastising the prince until Thane shoved his shoulder and ended the conversation.

After the battle at the gates, I looked at the Sentry differently. Impossible not to when I'd seen the way he killed, the ferocity in his devotion to keeping me, the prince, and all of Stonegate protected.

He was a man made of brutality and secrets, but there was loyalty beneath the surface.

I did not resent his presence as much; some mornings I almost anticipated the sight of my dark shadow.

Twelve days inside the gates, and I stood in the round entryway of the palace, hair braided, boots tied, and a dagger sheathed to each thigh.

I was to train with the Stav Guard. With Kael.

Emi was in the corridor when I emerged from my chambers.

"You wake before the sun now, yet all other days you are a petulant child when I try to rouse you."

I didn't even fight the grin. "Kael and I used to spar as children. This almost feels normal. I've missed it."

The sparring fields were dotted with Stav. Most had removed their tunics and battled one another with dull blades, bearded axes, or practiced footwork with captains.

Near a rack of daggers and knives, Kael wrapped his wrists.

"Ly." He waved, grinning. "Ready to fall on your ass?"

I plucked a stiletto knife off the rack, spinning it in my hand. "Darkwin, prepare yourself. You are about to become the mockery of the Stav Wing tonight."

I tightened my grip on the hilt of the sparring blade. Kael had a kind heart, but he was a warrior. As a jarl's son, even disowned as a bastard, he'd been taught with wooden blades at his earliest steps.

We backed away from the racks onto the field.

Kael struck hard and with purpose. Swift, deliberate, and unseen.

The edge of his practice blade came down on mine. My shoulders throbbed from the attack, but I spun out. Kael struck again; I parried. He jabbed; I sliced. When he ducked, I attempted to knock him off-balance. With his elbow he slammed me between the shoulders, but I kicked at his ankle, causing him to stumble.

I hooked an arm around Kael's neck and managed to get him to his knees. My weight was not enough to drag him down completely, and he was actively pushing me away.

From the edge of the field more than one Stav had stopped to watch. Emi shouted her horror and disgust on my form, then would switch to her annoyance with Kael.

"Darkwin, are you Stav or not? Why are you still on the ground?" She shook her head.

I grunted and tugged, trying to get Kael to fall. He managed to hook his arm under my knees and flipped me onto my back. I wheezed when the breath fled from my chest. When I opened my eyes, cool steel was leveled against my neck.

I froze.

Roark stood over me, chest bare from the waist up. Planes of hard muscle from his shoulders to the sharp carve of his hips that disappeared beneath his low-slung trousers added a touch of heat to my pulse.

Kael laughed and backed away. "If you meet ravagers or Skul Drek, Ly, they'll come at you from all sides."

You closed your eyes. Roark crouched, his hand over my face. *Never close your eyes in a fight.*

Roark leaned closer, his fingers moved deftly against my cheek, a sign the Sentry was whispering. *Fight me.*

His silent words burned through me like liquid fire. I swallowed and rolled onto my side, hurrying to my feet.

A dark gleam filled Roark's eyes. He spun a short blade in his grip.

I kept low, circling the Sentry. Kael stood beside Emi. More Stav took positions to watch. Even a few courtiers and servants preparing the courtyards for the arrival of the Myrdan royals stopped to observe.

You have enemies you do not see. Prove you can defend yourself. Roark gestured with sharpness, like a command. Like he would not accept anything less.

Then he lunged.

Like Kael, Roark moved with the glide of a shadow. His strikes came before I caught up to the previous move. I fought to gain the offensive, but kept backstepping, blocking every strike in a frenzy.

I managed to spin out and get behind him, but Roark took a long stride and found a position behind me before I had time to turn around. He was a force and I could not follow him. He swung at me, and I stumbled, falling backward to the ground.

Roark gave me no time to breathe before he made a cage with his arms and legs over the top of me, my own damn dagger in his control at my throat.

Dark hair pinned to his brow from a thin layer of sweat. His body was carved in divots of muscle and pressed too close to mine. The bastard only made it worse when he leaned his mouth over my lips, one hand in my sights. Heat from his bare skin burned against my chest.

You are dead.

His fingers brushed below my jaw, and I had to fight the horrid urge to lean into his touch. "Does it please you?"

A snide kind of smirk split over his mouth. *Depends on the time of day.*

"It is a shared feeling."

He leaned in ever closer. One slight lift of my head and my lips would brush his. Roark shifted. His chest ran over my breasts, forcing my teeth to clench to bite back a moan.

Your grip on that blade is the worst I've ever seen.

I huffed in annoyance. "Get off me, Sentry. I tire of looking at you."

Doubtful.

"Bastard."

Roark held out a hand to help me up. I took it, almost on instinct. The instant I was steady on my footing, Roark's smile faded and we pulled apart.

Emi will guard you tonight. Roark turned to go.

"Why? Where are you going? I thought you were to be my shadow."

I have duties with the Stav Guard. I am glad my absence is distress-ing and you will miss me.

"I will not miss you," I fired back.

"How do they talk so fast?" Kael's irritated grumble came from my back. "Lyra hardly pauses to read the hand speak."

"Sometimes souls just understand each other, Darkwin," Emi returned.

I pretended as though I did not hear her because she was wrong. There was nothing about my soul that wanted to know the deeper edges of Roark Ashwood.

It wasn't until I was alone in my chambers, reading the last page of hand speak, that I admitted such thoughts might be more of a lie than truth.

LYRA

HERE ARE SOME MORE." EMI DROPPED A STACK OF BOOKS onto the narrow table.

"Thank you."

With a nod, Emi left the room, pausing long enough to give Roark a greeting where he stood in the corner of the library, a dark phantom.

Hilda rose from her seat, inspecting the pile. This morning she'd received her first response from Gisli since being parted. I'd missed Hilda's smile.

She took the top book, brushing her fingers over the gold-embossed symbols. "Oh, blood spells from the common craft."

Common craft was a phrase for those who did not have magical blood but made their own magic from runes, blood, and verbal spells. Like Selena and her tonics and protection totems.

I didn't lift my head away from the page of gestures Roark might use if he were expressing care or concern. All day, I'd read the page like a compulsion, imagining Ashwood offering condolences or giving tender words like *beautiful* or *love*.

When I ought to be studying more about the approaching rank ceremony, I'd obsessed over studying more of Roark's words.

We spoke little to each other, but when he thought I was not looking, I observed his interactions. Usually terse and simple unless the prince or Emi was nearby.

He spoke more freely with them.

Roark insulted the prince often, but the expressions on their faces were usually light, as though they could not help but taunt each other. To Emi, Roark spoke of her emotions, always asking if she'd heard from her home or if she was well. Part of me still wondered if they were lovers. When I'd slyly asked Kael, he seemed taken aback with the notion anyone would dare be a lover to the Sentry, and certainly not Stav Nightlark.

As days passed, I could understand why someone might find favor with a different side of the Sentry. Days when he gave up a touch of gentleness or playful taunts added a sweet kind of humanity to Roark Ashwood. In truth, I'd rather he remain heartless and cold. Indifference made him simpler to ignore.

"Soul craft often requires blood," Hilda read, then turned the page, a frown on her face. "Draven craft is eerie. I know some see the use of bones as disgusting, but to manipulate the soul? Sounds wretched."

If Roark heard Hilda, he made no show of it.

"Ly." Hilda nudged my arm and turned her opened book under my nose. "I'm going to find Edvin, see if he heard from home, too, but I think I found something on the ceremony. You might want to read up on it."

I tugged the pages closer. Drawings of rune-marked bones were fitted into the corners.

"See you at supper?" Hilda paused near the door.

"I hope."

When the door closed behind Hilda, I was all at once aware the room was filled with only me and Roark's silky presence, which kept clawing under my skin.

I propped my chin on one fist, scanning the guidance for the ceremony of rank melding.

. . . *A ceremonial meld, meant to enforce the strength of a warrior. Taken from the lore of Berserkirs in the gods' armies, rank melds are a gift from those fallen in battle to those still living.*

I used one finger to track each word, afraid to misunderstand. As Damir explained, bone was taken and marked in runes through the manipulation of a bone crafter to create a soul bone.

Soul bones were harvested from jarls, kings, queens, and warriors, believed to be the strongest and most potent for a meld of bone armor or healing mortal wounds.

"The wounds heal quickly, but how?" I could not find any reason such bones would strengthen the body, other than adding thickness to limbs or chests. A true, manipulated armor beneath the skin.

A hand clapped against the wall. Roark waited for me to look, then said, *The fallen soul.*

"The king said something similar, but I don't understand how?"

With a sigh, he approached the table and wrote on a piece of parchment.

Once a melder bridges the dead to the living, remnants of the soul absorb into a new body and add strength, even against dire wounds.

"But if it is so powerful, I don't understand why healers,

common folk, and the Stav are not given such powerful bones constantly."

Short supply.

"Of bone?"

For a moment, Roark seemed to consider returning to his corner, but he tugged Hilda's abandoned chair free from the table and sat in it backward, his arms propped over the high back, legs straddled on the seat.

He briskly scribbled another thought on the parchment.

There are only so many soul bones that come to us naturally.

"Naturally? What is that supposed to mean?"

Roark's face was unreadable as he wrote. *What is the opposite of natural death?*

I frowned. "You know, you could simply answer my questions."

The Sentry smirked, flashing the white of his teeth, almost like he was amused, not agitated.

I could.

"Ass." I rolled my eyes. One hopeful thing about being Damir's new melder, my importance rivaled that of the Sentry. I could call him what I pleased without fear of repercussions. "An unnatural death, do you mean murder?"

Roark flourished his hand as if to announce I'd drawn the correct conclusion. It made a bit of sense, why there was a limited supply.

The king wouldn't murder his own people simply to harvest their bones to place into other warriors. He wanted a grand army, and as many of his manipulated bodies as he could get.

Peace lived between Myrda and Jorvandal, and only a few Dravens ever made it through border patrols. The consequence would be sparce burial mounds of warriors and fierce souls lost to battles. Doubtless the mounds and pyres of Stonegate were left for the sick and elderly who fell to Salur.

Roark wrote another line. *Rank melding is not a beloved practice to those outside the kingdom borders.*

He did not need to say it out loud for me to understand the warning in his words. "This is why Fadey was killed?"

Roark hesitated, then with his hand said, *Likely.*

Heat rippled down the back of my neck. "Berserkir warriors are known in the jarldoms, but we always assumed they were highly trained Stav Guard."

Roark let out a little huff that sounded like a dry rasp. He chose to write again instead of hand speak.

They are manipulated men who often suffer from what we call ber-serksgangur. It is an insatiable violence that can occur when many soul bones collide. Each unique soul feeds the living, and too many can bring darker consequences.

"Like the violence?"

Ashwood nodded, a harshness to his eyes that wasn't there before. *Along with madness, brutality, and bloodlust.*

Damn the gods. The risks were vicious and I was required to hunt these bones whenever I used my craft. How could I when each meld drew out the haunting spectral in the dreary mirror realm? The phantom never left me, and seemed to despise the use of soul bones. Doubtless he would not allow me to hunt them.

To my soul, I felt the phantom's hatred of me. Like it had cut down to an unseen piece of me, deep within. A scar I could not heal.

For a moment, I considered admitting what I'd seen to Roark, then shook the thought away.

I slumped in my chair. "I see why Dravens despise the Berserkirs. With enough manipulated bone as armor, they can't be defeated."

Roark shrugged. *Tensions have always been there between the kingdoms. This makes it worse.*

"Being a melder is nothing but a slow death sentence." I despised the tremble in my voice, the fear in my veins.

Roark's molten eyes dug into me. He didn't blink for a long pause, then slowly wrote his response.

Your craft is rare, so it is misunderstood and hated, especially by Dravenmoor. But it is my duty to keep you breathing, so I will not let you slip into Salur yet.

Roark did not mince words, he did not hide the troubles of the world, and still this was, perhaps, the gentlest the man had ever spoken to me.

"What do you think, Roark Ashwood?" I folded the paper over once, then twice. "About the use of soul bones, I mean? Have you been melded?"

He reached out for the parchment.

"Wait. Speak as you normally would. I'm proving to be a quick study, remember?" I tried to keep my voice light to hide the tremble of embarrassment.

It was pointless. Roark's arrogant grin returned. He moved his fingers in smooth, graceful words, slower than was normal, for my benefit, no doubt. *It is satisfying to know you've been reading the guides so dutifully.*

I folded my arms over my chest. "Don't preen. I'd rather know what you're saying in case you decide to slit my throat after I agitate you."

A smile, cautious and shadowed, found his mouth. *Wise. It is bound to happen.*

"I thought so. You never answered; have you been melded? Is that why you're so skilled with the blade?"

He gave me a narrow look before slowly responding. *I have only given a bone shard of fealty, nothing more.*

"Like Kael gave to the king?"

Yes. But mine went to the prince.

"I'd think the king would want a Draven warrior bonded to him." I bit the inside of my cheek after hearing my own words. "I didn't mean just because you're Draven that you—"

Roark held up one hand, silencing me.

Damir holds no love for my blood, but that wasn't what brought him to reject my bone. It is this. With the tips of his fingers, Roark traced the long scar across his throat. *The king did not think I would amount to much, so I was given as the prince's servant.*

My knee bounced under the table, and a sly grin cut across my lips when I took in the twitch to Roark's mouth. "Well, I'd say you proved him wrong."

Roark drummed the edge of the table, then, *I tried hard to do so. Now the king would like me to give up the shard from Thane and meld it to him.*

"You won't do it?"

Roark hesitated. *Thane is the reason I am alive. I owe him a great deal.*

Silence cloaked the room as the truth settled against me. I wanted to ask everything—Why was he abandoned? Dravens did this, but why? Was the scar what stole his voice? I didn't ask any of it.

I'd never admit it to the man, but his resistance to giving up his fealty to Prince Thane was rather . . . admirable.

I leaned forward. "Do you approve of these soul bones, Sentry Ashwood? Of melders?"

I wasn't certain if I did.

Before Roark could answer, a servant entered. We jolted back as though caught in some sort of scandal. Roark was on his feet in another breath, paces away from me.

The servant cleared his throat and lifted his chin. "Forgive me, but it is time for the feast."

25

LYRA

OURTYARD GARDENS SURROUNDING STONEGATE WERE
alight in golden torches. An open fire pit burned with sage
and hickory wood, and long oak tables were arranged with opu-
lent tiered platters of iced cakes, saffron braids, and crisp wafers
that were sweetened with honeysuckle.

I smoothed my hands over the blue satin of the gown I'd
found laid out on the bed. Not as warm as my woolen tunics and
skirts back home, but the breeze around Stonegate did not cut as
sharp as the shores of the Green Fjord.

On a dais, tall wooden chairs were draped in black satin.
Queen Ingir sat between King Damir and Prince Thane. Each
royal bore a circlet made of black iron and in the center was a likeness of the white wolf head.

The queen chattered with her son, ignoring Damir, and the
king drank from a golden horn, his eyes locked on one of the
nearby courtiers spinning and dancing with partners.

"Ly." Kael pushed through the sea of fine gowns and tunics. A wide grin painted his face, like he was alive at long last.

My heart squeezed and I could not help but wrap my arms around him and hold him close.

Kael grunted, patting my back. "Not that I don't enjoy feeling wanted, but what's all this for?"

"I've missed you."

He chuckled. "We ate the nightly meal together last night."

"I know." I forced a grin to conceal the swell of disquiet growing tighter in my belly.

Kael used his thumb to tilt my chin. "You're unsettled about the ceremony?"

"I wish I'd learned so much more about craft. I feel like I have no choice but to fall into that . . . place."

"What place?"

I sighed. "Nothing. Melding is simply consuming at times."

"I felt that way when I was first learning how to use my own craft. Remember what happened after I helped old Fen go to Salur?"

I nodded. One Jul season, Thorian had gifted Kael and me an old wolfhound. For two summers Fen was our constant companion, until one day the hound stumbled down one of the rocky hillsides near the fjord.

The beast was in such pain, Kael couldn't stand it.

For the first time, he used his bone craft to decay the bones until Fen gently faded to Salur. Kael grew ill with chills and nightmares for three days.

"It becomes more natural." Kael nudged my arm. "We might have different craft, but if you give in to it, if you let it flow when it roars within you, I've found it becomes as natural as a draw of air. Craft is yours to command, Ly," he said, voice soft. "No one else commands your power, even if it feels that way being here. Stand firm, do not fear it. I believe the magic in our blood can sense it and will not trust us in return."

I considered the idea for a pause. Fear was potent and sour the few times I'd used my magic. I'd been terrified when Kael was dying, terrified to prove my worth to the king. What if fear made the shadow? A projection of my terror.

With a forced smile, I squeezed Kael's arm. "You seem at ease, at least."

"I miss home, don't mistake me, but I was made to be a Stav, Ly." Kael looked at the crowd almost wistfully. "No one cares I'm the unwanted son of a jarl. No one cares that I come from nothing. They see me as one of theirs, a part of a great warrior clan."

Selfish of me, but there was a stab of envy at the awe in Kael's voice. We'd grown together, and I never cared that Jarl Jakobson disowned him, I'd always seen him as mine.

We kept close to each other, me the silent one at his side, Kael the boisterous Stav who'd earned respect for his skill in the battle of the wall.

When some of the young Stav Guard surrounded us, I wanted to sink into his side, but he'd been pulled away by his fellow guards, leaving me alone, cut off from the crowd.

A young officer, not much older than me, eyed me over a wooden goblet. "Súlka Bien."

He approached, his broader body like a shield against the revel. All at once, I felt cornered, intentionally trapped.

I dipped my head in response, one arm across my middle, and looked away, praying he wouldn't want to converse much.

The guard stepped closer, scents of leather and wine on his skin. "May I ask a question?" He didn't give me a chance to respond before his finger tapped the center of my chest. "What does the king make you do to earn his trust? Melders do not give their bones of fealty, some say they can't. Doesn't meld properly, I hear. Fadey got on his knees for the king's delight, I wonder if you do the same."

I stepped back, eyes narrowed. "Wonder all you like."

"Hmm. I can't help but think of the things this mouth might do. It's been so long since the melder was a woman." He gripped my jaw, hard enough my teeth cut into my cheeks.

The way we were positioned, no one could see. I tried to slip his hold, tried to bend and reach the knife I'd stashed in my boot, but he squeezed until tears slipped over my cheeks.

Until, all at once, the guard's hand was torn off my face. He stumbled backward.

Roark had one palm gripping the side of the Stav's neck, his other hand cutting the drunken man with words—silent and fierce.

"Sentry," the guard spluttered. "My apologies."

By now, Kael returned to my side and nudged me behind him.

I looked nowhere but Ashwood. His eyes were like bright fire, consuming the pale fear on the guard's face.

Touch her again, and I will stand by as she melds your jaw shut and you take your food through your nose.

"Is there trouble, Sentry Ashwood?" King Damir stood on the dais.

Roark tilted his head, fury locked on the Stav. *Is there?*

The guard shook his head. "No. No trouble."

Then beg forgiveness.

"No—" I tried to interject, but Roark had already shoved the guard in front of me, forcing him to kneel. Like I was some sort of goddess.

The Sentry gripped the guard's hair and wrenched his head back. The man swallowed thickly. "Apologies, Melder Bien. Forgive me."

"Fine." I waved a hand, wishing the damn soil would swallow me up. "Forgiven."

At long last, Roark released the guard, watching him scramble away. When he looked back to me, there was a sort of smugness to his grin, that faded the moment he took in my glare.

"Was that necessary to do right here?" I gritted out through my teeth.

"Ly," Kael snapped. "You're not to be disrespected."

I ignored him. "I wish you wouldn't have done that."

Roark's eyes shadowed. He crowded me with his broad body, unbothered that Kael stood so close. *Is this your gratitude? It needs work.*

His hand was in front of my face. I pushed it aside, lowering my voice. "I am grateful, but I do not like attention drawn to me. When you spend your life hiding, to have endless eyes watching can be too much at times."

Too many people, too many gazes pointed my way, felt like the air, walls, wherever I might be, were crushing in on me. My chest tightened, blood heated, fog gathered in my head, until I wanted to flee.

Where I thought Roark might mock me, maybe gesture one of his snide comments, instead he simply dipped his chin in a nod.

"If there are no more delays, Sentry Ashwood"—King Damir's sharp tone sliced through the tension between us—"then I would like to get on with the ceremony."

We were taken from the courtyard. Only Roark and a few highly ranked Stav followed.

"With attacks on the rise and Dravens always seeming to know when my melder works," the king said once we were behind a black velvet curtain in a chamber filled with ferns and potted plants, "I will have our ranks advanced in private."

Four Stav Guards stood in front of a platform with thin twisted trees in stone pots. Fine black tunics, crimson threads around the wolf head on their chests. Beside each guard was another officer, holding a silver raven pin and a slender knife.

Damir opened one arm, summoning a skittish-looking servant with a wooden tray in hand. When the linen cloth was pulled back, four pale shards of bone were displayed in a straight line. Some looked like they might've been taken from a thigh, or shoulder, and one appeared to be a piece of a finger.

A wizened bone crafter woman entered the chamber from a side door. Her hair was the color of frost and the crimson robes drowned her knobby body. Under the watchful eye of the king, the crafter etched runes into the shards—protection, wisdom, strength, joy. Where her fingers traced across the surface of the bone, a thread of gold followed.

I looked about, but no one seemed stunned by the light, no one made a whisper of awe at the beauty. No one could see it, the remnant of a soul still living within the bones left behind.

Gentle applause from the small crowd followed when the servant showed the finished shards, marked in their manipulation as soul bones.

"Lyra." King Damir gestured for me to step forward. "Once the officers have been cut in their chosen locations, meld the bones so they might reach their new ranks and power."

There was a somber kind of hush that fell over the chamber. Anticipation, maybe a bit of trepidation, lived in each suffocating gaze. They'd witnessed Fadey do this, no doubt, and it was obvious many had missed the spectacle.

Some of the Stav awaiting their bone looked practically ravenous.

I looked over my shoulder. The only eyes I found reeled me in like a line in the sea. Roark's features were steady and unmoved. He did not look away.

Strange as it was, I took a bit of strength from the scrutiny of the Sentry. He was a shadow I did not always want, he was the cause of my being here in many ways, but Roark was also becoming the constant on which I could rely.

A firm bit of ground that was dependable and sure.

My fingers trembled when the first bone was placed in my palms. The Stav who'd receive the shard was tall and lean; his hair, the color of red sand, hung long down his back.

He said nothing and removed his tunic. A protrusion on one side of his ribs seemed misplaced, along with a bulge over one hip. Other soul bones? He was advancing to a captain of three units—more than fifty Stav would be his to command—and each bulge might be the addition of impenetrable bones under his flesh.

The officer with the knife cut a deep wound into the side of his ribs without the bulge. Blood fountained down his waist, but he didn't wince in the slightest.

My fingers trembled. Sick burned the back of my throat when I needed to dig at the torn skin to nudge one edge of the bone inside, like a bloody pouch.

"Remember your purpose, Lyra," King Damir said.

I held the king's stare until the bursts of golden threads flashing over the new bone pulled my attention. Lovely guides and whispers to the magic in my blood on what it could do, what it should do. Stitch in the bone, meld it, move on.

I would fall to the darkness, face the shadow, if only to prove I could stand before my fear. With my back to the king, I touched the bone and a veil of cold mists coated the world.

LYRA

ARKNESS BLED INTO ITSELF, DRAWING ME DEEPER THAN before, consuming me whole. The chamber transformed into inky shadows that slithered from corners like spreading rot. Gentle flakes of wispy snow kissed my cheeks now, and the only light came from the golden bones in every direction.

Beneath my hands the soul bone burned like it was wrapped in flames. Slender threads tugged it deeper against the Stav's rib cage. My fingers moved without thought, like Kael promised. The more I accepted the power in my blood, the more instinctual it became.

Each movement became a trance.

With one bone placed, I gathered the next, the pale heat of cold alight in my palms, then drifted to the form of the next Stav Guard.

Those present for the melding drifted like they did outside the mirrored land. Bones shifted when folk leaned in to whisper, to gossip. Some people lifted horns and goblets to parted jaws for more wine, and others returned to seats near the front.

Again and again, I stitched the bone to the Stav, forgetting the unease of this place, of the magic here.

Until the cold came—sharp and jagged. I quickened my fingers, securing the bone against the third Stav's upper thigh.

I'd only pulled my hand away when the darkness coiled around my shoulders. I closed my eyes. There was the urge to flee, to fall out of my own power, but I was here to find more. King Damir required it of me.

The king carried a demeanor of gentility, but there was a cruelness behind his eyes. A man not above threats and brutality to get what he desired.

I could face the haunt of the shadows. This was fashioned through my power, and I did not need to fear it.

I released the breath in my lungs and spun around.

Sunken copper eyes filled the dark cowl over the shadow's head. Ribbons of darkness radiated from the places where shoulders and arms ought to be. In the dim light, the rope keeping the phantom tethered had frayed, like something started to unravel his chains.

Fear. He was nothing but a nightmare built from the uses of my craft. There were always consequences from craft, after all.

"To harm the living," I whispered, stepping back from the phantom and focusing on the glow of the Stav Guard in front of me. I had to meld. I had to break free of this place. "Craft mirrors the pain."

A low rumble, some sort of dark laughter, came from the haunt at my back. No doubt, he mocked me for my fear.

Still, I repeated the ramifications of each craft, as though it might prove to my fearful mind the creature standing watch at my back was not real. Until I reached the consequences of melding. "To bind dead and living . . ." I lifted my hands off the fourth guard in line, a man who'd chosen to be melded between the blades of his shoulders. "Craft corrupts the heart."

"Am I your heart, Melder?"

I peered over my shoulder, summoning whatever thread of courage still burned in my veins. "Leave me be."

Refuse to fear, and he would leave.

I heard the glide of steel. A dark misty blade lifted, ready to strike at me again. Another clack of teeth, another growl, and the blade lowered to strike.

This time I didn't bend. I didn't try to run. I held up a hand and shouted, "Stop!"

A rush of air rippled from my palm. The shadow blade halted against the gust. Some of the mist peeled back to reveal a true steel.

I kept my hand out, for protection or to feel powerful when I feared I was helpless.

"Stop," I said again. "I do not fear you."

For a moment the burning eyes tilted, as though the billows of darkness truly had a head. As though it was lost in a touch of stun itself.

Then the low, cruel laughter followed. "Liar."

Its voice was low and raspy, like it was a strain to speak. It was a voice I felt thread through my veins, stitching deep inside me, as though it were part of me.

"What do you want?" I took a step closer. More satin-black skeins of mist pulled away from the phantom, shaping a defined figure with a hood and thick, sturdy boots over true feet. "Tell me and be gone, so I might finish this."

"I warned you, Melder. Take the souls, and I take the same to replace them."

"Yes, you keep saying it, but I've yet to understand what you mean." I squared my shoulders. This specter had to be a manifestation of my own hesitations toward soul bones.

Speckled throughout the darkness were faint, flickering gleams of gold. Bones of the fallen were there in the distant hills, and the strength of the power they once had beckoned to me, a moth to the flame.

A ghostly shape of the palace surrounded me, but it was as though I could see it from all sides, nearly omniscient. With the slightest lean to one side, all at once, lawns, courtyards, and palace towers flowed into view.

Near the queen's wing was a mist of shadows, darker than the rest.

"I do not want to do this, but I must. It keeps those I love alive and safe. It protects our people."

The phantom let out a rough laugh like broken glass. "The lies you tell your heart. Melders craft monsters."

I frowned. "I am no monster. I never wanted to be here, but if it keeps my family alive, I will meld every damn bone the king places at my feet."

"Hmm." The shadowed spectral took a step closer. More like a man now. Legs wrapped in darkness, arms, the cowl over his face. "Your soul smells familiar." With a long draw of breath through a nose I could not see beneath the cowl, the phantom breathed me in. His hellish eyes snapped open. "Why do the gods let you come here to me?"

I followed his steps, twisting the more he prowled. "I don't know. I've been ordered to find more soul bones. Perhaps they are allowing me to search. You can't argue with the gods, can you?"

The phantom barked a rough, throaty laugh. "The gods left this land to tear itself apart long ago. Look how selfish thrones have corrupted the power of those gods they pretend to worship." He stopped his prowl. "But never has a melder faced me here. Until you. Why is that, I wonder?"

I faced away from the palace chamber. Instead of ferns and trees in clay pots, thick darkness flowed over crumbling walls of the outer gates, and opened to the eerie shapes of the distant knolls tucked behind the line of trees on the edge of Stonegate.

This place held no barriers. If I desired to look elsewhere, the mirror would adjust, it would shift; the cold would pull back shadows until I found where I wanted to be.

Bones were in the knolls facing Myrda. As Damir said, there was a sense of where old burial mounds might be unearthed.

"My craft pulls me toward bones of the fallen. We must forage them."

The phantom said nothing, merely followed me with his gaze.

Beneath the shadow of the hood I could make out a sharp jaw-line, skin like gray stone. Lips, colorless and pale, were drawn tight. A man of sorts, a demon, perhaps. He stepped in front of me again. Cold rose from him, adding a puff of white in front of my lips with every breath.

"Who are you?" The question came out in a whisper, rough and edged in fear.

"I am he," his rasp of a voice frosted against my cheek. "And we are we."

"Yes, you said that before. It explains nothing." I stepped around him. He allowed it, studying my movements with a harrowing curiosity. Like he might still be considering using his blade to cut me down, but was a bit more intrigued than blood-thirsty.

I flexed and curled my fingers once, twice, and kept my spine rod straight. If he was an illusion of my fears, of my own mind, why was he not fading?

If anything, he'd damn well gotten more solid.

The shadow's silky presence followed me. Sometimes a cold

strand of mist would curl over my wrists and shoulders, as though he were tasting me with his darkness.

"Screams." The phantom's eyes closed into blackness for a breath, then sparked open, almost with a strange touch of humanity when he pulled back. "I remember your screams." With a quick motion, he drew me against him. I struck a cold, broad chest, and a shriek split from my throat. "How are you doing this?"

"Doing what?" I pushed back. "Leave me be."

With a rough snarl the shadow recoiled, fastening us together. Left in the space between us was a thin thread of sunlight gold. I screamed and tried to step back. The thread only stretched, and the phantom groaned as if unsettled.

His hellish eyes locked on me. "What *are* you? What have you done?"

"Nothing! You touched me, now . . . break this away." Gods, what if I was trapped here, chained to this creature. I stepped back. The thread between us only stretched longer. "I-I-I don't know what this is."

He pulled me closer, his shadowed nose cold and dry along my cheek. "What cruel games the Norns play." His nearness sent a tremble dancing up my arms, and the whisper of his rasp bit like a frosted wind. "You will not claim me with whatever dark casts you've spun."

"What?" My eyes darted between his. "I don't want to claim you. Craft is pulling me toward you. Let me go and it will break."

"Yes. This thread is doomed to be severed. It must be or it was all for naught."

He made little sense, but there was an odd touch of melancholy in his hissing tone.

"Continue taking the bones, Melder, and the Thief King will

corrupt everything," he snapped. "There will be no voice but his, and you will force my hand to end you."

I struggled against him. "Soul bones add strength to an army, they don't corrupt everything."

A sort of low rumble rose from his chest. "With you, the Thief King will find the one he wants. Let the ancient one rest."

"Ancient one?"

In the distance something snapped, like the crack of a heavy tree bough. The shadow tilted his head and sniffed. He took an abrupt step back. "Let him rest. Tell the Thief King to do the same. I will see you again, Melder. It would seem fate demands it."

He flicked the weak thread sewn between us.

"Let who rest?" Another crack echoed in the distance. The shadow drew his blade, those thin lips curling into a snarl. I held out an arm. "Wait. What or *who* are you?"

The phantom paused. When he turned to look back at me over his shoulder, shadows billowed like silk in the wind around his shoulders.

"When your enemies ravage, what name do you whisper?" A low, throaty chuckle followed. "You have seen the signs of me in the darkness of the wood." Again, the phantom sniffed the air, then flashed sharp, jagged teeth when he grinned. "Remember, a soul for a soul."

Signs in the wood? An enemy who ravages with a whispered name?

All at once, my blood went cold. Gods, no. It . . . it wasn't possible.

I trembled and lifted my gaze back to his vicious eyes. "Skul Drek."

He gnashed his teeth.

No, Skul Drek couldn't be here. He was a creature, an assassin, not a shadow of a being. I was so lost in the horror, the confusion, I did not notice he rolled the sword in his grip.

"Four were stolen this night, Melder. So, four I will take." Skul Drek paused, his mouth tightening. "Ready your blades."

"Whatever you plan to do, please don't. We have little choice and—"

My words choked off when Skul Drek drifted deeper into the smoky, thin mists. "Ah, but this is what we are made to do, Melder. Battle until we destroy each other." His fingers twisted around the thread of craft drawing me into him. "But this is cruel, and this time it will hurt to kill a melder."

Darkness devoured his horrid eyes, and in the next moment, I was flung backward into the salt of the mists.

My head was lost in a haze and it took a moment to realize I was moving, but not walking on my own. I was pressed against something hard, warm, something that breathed of smoke and oakmoss. I tilted my chin.

The dark stubble on Roark's jaw scraped against my brow. The Sentry had me in his damn arms.

My cheek was pressed to the steady cadence of his heart. I bit down against the urge to nuzzle against his throat. It was wholly unfair for a man so stoic and harsh to smell like a spring morning after rain.

If Roark knew I was awake he made no show of it and shouldered into my bedchamber.

His long strides took us across the sitting room, a gentle crackle from the inglenook the only sign of life in the room, then into the bedchamber. With care, the Sentry placed me on the edge of the bed.

I pressed the heel of my hand to my head, vaguely aware Roark was pulling back the furs and quilts over my bed. "What happened?"

He paused and raised a hand. *Parchment or hand speak?*

I gestured at his palms. "I told you, I'm a quick study." With his words, at least.

The Sentry stepped back, giving me room to settle against the goose down pillow before he spoke again. *You fell from the melder's trance, and didn't wake until now. Four soul bones was too many.*

The way he formed his words was sharp, almost like he was spitting them through his hands. A true show of repulsion for the soul bones—perhaps for me—but written in the groove between his brows was something akin to concern.

Roark hovered over me. *How do you feel?*

I forced a grin, a weak attempt to mask the pain of exertion, the way my fingertips were frigid in numbness, the bone-deep ache from using such a force of power. The fear of the phantom's name I could not stop repeating in my head.

"I feel as though I have raced the length of every corridor no less than a dozen times, but I am well enough."

His vibrant eyes were narrow, but he did not back away as he gestured slowly, *Liar.*

I ought to send him back to the ceremony, keep our distance and disregard, but a sob broke free when I shifted too swiftly on the mattress.

Ashwood stepped closer, lowering to one knee. Overcome with the pain of the meld, the fear of the mirror, I hid my face against his chest, tears soaking his tunic.

When his hand cupped the back of my head, letting me break, I'd never felt safer.

ROARK

KEEP DOWN.

I kicked a pebble from the forest path, frowning. I didn't need to keep down, but that's all anyone ever told me to do.

I was old enough to fight with the damn clan, and tonight I'd prove it.

From a small leather scabbard on my waist, I removed my father's old whittling knife, etched with runes and a double-headed raven on the blade, and slashed at the low-hanging branches.

My foot caught on a gnarled root, and I toppled—head over foot—down a lumpy slope, landing in a heap with a cough and groan.

"What's a boy doin' out in the trees? Don't you know the drums sounded? They're barring the gates to town."

A hand touched my shoulder and I scrambled backward, sloppily holding the knife out in front of me. This was not my fate. No damn enemy clan would slit my throat without me drawing a bit of blood first.

"What's the matter with you?" she snickered.

A... girl? Oh, by the gods, no. I was not—in any of two hells—dying because of some *girl*.

"You look thirsty." A hand touched my shoulder. "Have you been lost in the wood?"

I spun back toward the hill, knife outstretched, and met her eyes. Dark and bright all at once. There was a shock of silver through the centers. The color we needed. The color that meant an end to war.

But it was more. The first look at her stole my breath, the same that happened when stupid Gunter rammed his fist in my belly last week in the sparring circle.

This time it didn't hurt. This was warmer, like waking after the dawn to the full sun. The knife in my hand lowered.

Until the screams began . . .

I SNAPPED AWAKE, SWEAT ON MY BROW, PULSE RAPID IN MY skull. I blinked against the gray light of my chamber, screams and smoke and blood in my ears and on my tongue.

With a silent curse, I kicked off the furs and sat on the edge of my bed, threading my fingers through my sweaty hair.

A damn nightmare was what brought down the Stonegate Sentry. Pathetic.

Silver scars. I dreamed of Lyra, but . . . as a girl. Through the mind of a boy.

I dropped my palms and let my head fall back, face pointed at the thick rafters overhead.

The rank ceremony had to be the cause. Soul bones left me in disquiet for days, waiting for blood to follow.

I slumped forward, leaning onto my elbows over my knees, and caught sight of something pale beneath the crack of my door. A missive.

The wax seal was Thane's symbols—stag antlers behind the white wolf. I scanned the prince's steady writing, my blood heating with each word.

Damn you, Thane. The coward of a prince must've delivered this several bell tolls ago. He'd slipped out of the gates, bound for a ride in the wood with half a dozen Stav Guard. Bastard had the audacity to tell me not to feel a drop of frustration or anger at his recklessness of leaving the fortress.

There was nothing else to feel.

I crumpled the parchment and threw it at the wall.

Thane oftentimes forgot I was duty-bound to keep his precious royal head atop his shoulders. But to leave the walls without warning, this was a deliberate attempt to give me no choice but to wander, fret, and curse his name until he returned.

He thought it was a kindness, a way to give me some respite, but waking to the missive left a darkness in my chest, a dread that prickled over my scalp. Wretched things happened after a melder used craft. Thane knew my beliefs on this, but did not feel the same.

I felt out of control and I could not rid myself of the tension of *why* and what might come of it.

Sleep evaded me and my temper heated the longer I paced my chamber.

Soon enough, I bit into a strap of leather, securing it around one wrist, and trudged toward the training field off the east wing of the palace.

Long lines of racks with silver-bearded axes, longswords, seax blades, bows, arrows, and throwing knives were there for the taking. Wooden round shields all bore the white wolf of Stonegate and the clank of dull steel over the boards echoed across the morning mists.

Morning, the moments when dawn was pale and weary, seemed to be the only time I could train.

After last night's feast, I'd not been able to sleep long. Unrest at the sight of Lyra locked in the strange craft-induced trance kept sleep from ever settling fully. The way she'd sobbed against me, more broken than before, cut through me to the marrow of my damn bones.

Fadey never stayed under the control of his craft so long. For a moment, I was not convinced Lyra would wake. More unsettling than her stupor was the jolt of concern for her if she did not pull away.

I finished wrapping my wrists and selected a practice seax from one of the racks, then rolled the blade, testing the give and weight.

Frustration over my misplaced interest in the melder was like a slow bleed, yet I couldn't find the wound.

In the weeks since she arrived, I'd followed her every step under the king's order. Whether it be from a corner during the queen's many luncheons, or in silence while she studied books on craft, I kept aloof, agitated.

But my resolve was failing.

Lyra was skilled at masking, I'd give her that. The woman was well practiced in smiling and nodding, while slowly dimming the light in her eyes. She knew how to become faceless in a crowd, never drawing the eyes of too many.

She kept drawing mine.

I thought I might hate her for it. Never had I been so unraveled. Now I was having damn nightmares with her face.

Since building my life in Stonegate, I kept my focus on my
duties, my strength, and keeping our people safe. Mere weeks after bringing a stubborn woman into these halls, I slept less,
thought of the way her lips twitched as she read, and I'd grown a
bit of smug pride with how she took to heart learning the language of my hands.

I thought too damn much about the way her skin, when it
touched me, no matter how briefly, lingered like venom I wanted
to drink again and again.

A festering energy to beat a sword against anything had me
storming the practice fields before my new charge woke for the day.

"Lord Ashwood." Darkwin cut through the mists, shield and
blade in hand, eyes alight after I'd battled in solitude for a full
bell toll. "Care for a partner?"

I arched a brow. *You're early to rise.*

Kael studied my hands. Stav learned most of my crucial
gestures—the ones I used for commands—within the first weeks
of training. Most never tried to learn more. Only Thane and Emi
knew every word I spoke—well, Lyra was catching up quickly.

Kael was a curious sort, and he'd learned enough to hold a decent conversation.

"After last night, I couldn't sleep." Darkwin paused. "Thank
you, by the way, for helping Lyra."

A muscle flinched in my jaw. *Is she awake?*

"No." He hesitated. "I'm sure it was exhausting. That was the
longest she's pushed her craft."

I didn't want to speak on Lyra Bien any longer. *Have you settled
here?*

"I have. My unit is honorable and I'm pleased to see Edvin and Hilda have started smiling again."

A bite of something like guilt gnawed at my chest. Worthless to feel guilt over something beyond my control. We were ordered to take the crafters, so we did.

"They're a bit like Ly, reading up on craft a great deal," Kael went on. "Edvin enjoys sparring ever since the ravagers attacked the wall. But I think Hilda might find more joy with the herb healers. She was often at the bedsides of the sick back home."

The brother and sister did not leave anywhere without each other. Darkwin might've been trying to find the good of their new existence, but I was inclined to see the darker pieces of folk— they were in pain.

True love of family was lost on me. Thane was the closest I had to a brother, and I tried to imagine being torn from him like the man had been torn from his family and the woman from her husband. Difficult, to be sure.

Nothing I could do. I was not king here.

Kael's smile widened and he tossed his blade to the other hand. "So? What do you say? Up for a round?"

Already sweat beaded my brow from slicing straw-stuffed canvas sacks, but I rolled my sword in my hand and bent at the knees.

When the sun was high overhead, the sparring fields were filled with Stav not assigned to watchposts, and Darkwin was about to be defeated for the fifth time.

Kael let out a curse through a grunt when I slammed his back to the grass, breaths heavy, blade at his throat. Teeth bared, he tried to break free, but the shield strapped to my arm kept him locked in defeat.

I grinned, sweat and dirt spilling into my eyes.

Another curse and Kael let his arms fall to the side in surrender. "Gods, I concede."

One palm clasped with his, and I tugged him to his feet. We'd long since stripped off our tunics. Smudges of dirt and streaks from the green grass painted our skin across shoulders, spines, and chests.

A small half circle had formed to watch. More than one hand clapped a few florin coins into palms. Seemed some guards had placed bets against me. Fools.

Buckets of water for drinking or washing were dotted across the fields. I splashed my face once, then tilted water into my mouth, soothing the burn in my throat. Kael slumped back on the grass, catching his breath.

"Have you been rank melded, Lord Ashwood? Is that why you're so damn impossible to defeat?"

I stiffened for a breath, then shook my head.

Kael lifted his brows. "Truly? Not even as the Sentry? I spoke to some of the men in my unit last night about it. Those who Lyra advanced, they say, will be brutes with the blade."

If they were bonded to a cruel soul, soon they would not know how to leave the brute on the field.

"I know rank melding is not required," Kael went on, "but what are your thoughts on it?"

What were my thoughts on the practice of melding dead Stav bone to living Stav? Despicable.

I took another drink, then waved one hand in reply. *Merit of a warrior ought to be earned through skill.*

Kael considered it for a moment. "But if it gives a Stav an advantage over an enemy in battle, is it not worth it?"

Darkwin was a good man, but naïve. He would see the strength and ferocity of the Berserkir Stav, not the downfall. It was a form of glory in Stonegate, but like so many others, he'd never see—or choose not to see—the lust for destruction and battle that followed if a cruel bone was chosen.

It was the risk of soul bones. If the fallen was horrid in life, they poisoned the bonded soon enough.

Find those answers on your own, Darkwin. I rammed the point of the practice sword into the grass and continued. *Don't take from the opinions of others. It is your life, not theirs.*

Kael studied a few pairings as they sparred across the field. "Captain Baldur insists more ravagers have been moving closer to Stonegate with the upcoming arrival of Princess Yrsa. Sometimes I think it might be nice to have more than a wooden shield to protect against their blades."

I faced him. *Ravagers are not warriors. If they overpower you, perhaps you are not a good Stav.*

With an unfamiliar grin, I slashed at him with my sword.

Kael rolled out of range. "Bastard."

He hurried to his feet, clashing his own blade against mine. Where he jabbed, I parried. When I aimed at his spine, he blocked, kicking at my legs. My muscles throbbed with the frenzy of a fight, my chest ached with each breath, but if I could belt a laugh the way Darkwin did, I likely would.

Somehow we'd managed to lose our blades, and there was no skill in our steps, simply sheer desire to best the other. With a shout, Kael rammed his shoulder into my side, encircling my waist in his arms and dragging us to the ground.

My elbow caught his lip, his knee my ribs.

We both rolled onto our backs, faces to the sun. Gasps followed, a few breathless chuckles. I could not recall the last time I'd fought for the sheer enjoyment of it.

"Ly," Kael shouted through a ragged pant. "I defeated the Sentry."

I snapped up. Lyra stood on the edge of the sparring field, alone. The gown she'd chosen was red as blood, and drew out the dark shade of her eyes and pink of her lips.

Gods, what was the matter with me? Her lips?

I spat my frustration and shoved Kael back to the ground when he tried to stand.

Where you belong, I gestured quickly.

He let his head fall back, smiling through deep draws of breath.

I'd never admit how much I enjoyed the spar. Most Stav were fearful around me and would never rise to the challenge. I gave them reason to be wary. I was brisk, brutal, and Draven.

Most of all Draven.

Lyra wrapped her arms around the curves of her waist. When I came closer, she lifted her chin the way she did when she planned to be defiant.

"Sentry Ashwood." She tried to sound annoyed by the sight of me, but there was a tremble in her tone.

I unsettled her as much as she unsettled me.

I didn't miss the way her eyes ticked to my bare chest for a moment too long. With one knuckle, I tilted her chin to look at me, then brought one hand up for her to read.

You are not to leave your chamber unaccompanied.

She scoffed. "My escort was nowhere to be found."

Then you wait.

"I should not be held prisoner because you wish to puff out your chest on the sparring field."

One half of my mouth quirked. *You were looking at my chest?*

"Gods." Lyra's cheeks reddened. "You're insufferable. More so than most men. My tower is right there"—she flung an arm behind her—"I hardly think I was at risk of being assassinated on the short walk here."

Lyra's breath stuttered when I shifted and pinched her chin between my thumb and finger, and gestured my retort near her cheek. *That is for me to decide. Not you.*

"Is this my fate, then, Sentry Ashwood?" Her words were warm against my bare skin. "Never being free to go where I like, or do what I like, without you?"

I understood her meaning, but despised the cinch it brought to my own chest at the thought of days not filled with the sight of Lyra Bien. I was a wretch, a fool, and an embarrassment to my position.

This draw to the woman was a hindrance.

But I wasn't so certain I was alone in it. Lyra spoke like I was a nuisance, but she had not pulled away either.

A ram's horn sounded from the tower and my stomach bottomed out. *No.*

"What is it?" Lyra looked about when Stav shot into action.

One possessive hand held on to Lyra's waist. Fear lanced through me like a molten blade. The prince had not returned from his feckless trip outside Stonegate, and a warning was rising from the gates.

I whistled, drawing the attention of a few Stav, and ordered pairs to form a line at the gates.

"Roark." Lyra looked at me with wide eyes.

I waited to speak until she was carefully focused on both my hands. *This is that moment when you go straight to your tower. Lock the door. Do not leave unless you hear three knocks, a pause, then two short knocks.*

"What is it?" She dug her fingers into my forearm when I turned to go.

She would find out soon enough. *Dravens. Go.*

LYRA

ANY DESIRE TO STAND AGAINST ROARK'S ORDERS FADED when Stonegate erupted into a wild frenzy. Stav Guard seemed to appear from the walls, from every corner, sealing in Queen Ingir and King Damir.

Thoughts about Kael lifting another blade for more than practice filled my head with worry. I half expected Prince Thane to round the corner and demand I join him in the tree hut to slaughter with our arrows.

The prince never came.

I hurried up the wide staircase to my chamber. More than one drifting thought of the Sentry stole its way into my head.

"Lyra!" Hilda, skirt clutched in her grip, raced up the stairs at my back.

"Thank the gods." I wrapped my arms around her shoulders. "Has Edvin gone with the Stav?"

"Only to the inner gates." Her eyes were blown wide. "Do you know what's happening?"

"Roar—the Sentry said it means Dravens were spotted."

Hilda kissed her fingertips and pressed them to her head in a swift prayer. "Stav were headed into the wood. No doubt, they'll keep them as far from the walls as possible, like they did last time. Gods, I thought Stonegate was meant to be the safest refuge in the kingdom."

I bit down on the inside of my cheek. Perhaps it was before the damn melder was dragged inside.

Emi materialized around a corner at the top of the stairs. She was clad in her dark Stav Guard tunic, but her hair was let down her back in soft, pale waves, not braided in her typical slick plait. "Roark told me to see that you listened. Good thing he sent me, for I see you have not."

Damn that man. "I was going until Hilda found me."

Emi's sly grin ticked at her mouth. "Seemed rather unnerved at the thought of you being unprotected."

"I don't know why you're saying it in such a way." The tips of my fingers tingled. "He doesn't want to be reprimanded by the king, I'm sure."

"You're probably right." Emi took a step toward the wooden staircase leading to my chambers. "Shall we?"

When we got to my bedchamber, the room all at once felt too small. No matter how much idle talk the three of us offered up, thick silence always followed. I leaned one shoulder against the wall near my window, peering down at the commotion below. Stav Guard were aligned and orderly, even around the stable doors below.

Where was Kael? Edvin? Where was Roark? Doubtless the Sentry would be drawn to the heart of all skirmishes. He was Roark Ashwood, skilled enough to be named the Death Bringer of the kingdoms.

I peeled away from the cold glass. Why was I even fretting over the man at all? He wore a constant scowl and looked at me like he couldn't decide if I ought to go headfirst out the window or down a winding staircase.

But there was a draw to him. An undeniable truth that there was more to Roark Ashwood than I knew, and the part of me that wanted to learn more of him kept expanding with every sunrise.

"How far out do the patrols go?" Hilda asked Emi.

"Nearly to the shore, then to the open lands between Myrda in the north and the ravines of Dravenmoor in the west."

Perhaps I'd feel more at ease if Emi were not twisting a lock of her hair around her fingertips until they turned purple.

"They'll return soon," I said, more for myself than anyone.

We poured wine we never drank, tried to play a game with smooth wooden rune chips that was inspired by battles between the different realms of the gods, and paced and paced and paced. Sunlight deepened in the sky the more the sun faded toward Dravenmoor.

Hilda replaced me at the window, and Emi kept clicking two game chips against each other, watching them collide and snap apart.

The door burst open, wood clattering on the wall.

Kael, sweat-soaked, hair on end, and blood over his lip, gasped in the doorway.

"Kael!" I nearly tripped over my hem with my hurried steps.

"Ly . . ." He tried to gather his breath. "Hurry. We . . . we need you. Hilda, Nightlark, you too."

"What happened?" Something had gone horribly wrong.

Kael raked dirty fingers through his hair. "Skul Drek."

Dammit. A vow, a threat, a promise to attack had felt half like a dream. It was a nightmare. The phantom of the mirror land also lived in reality—not a myth, but a true killer.

A killer who knew exactly who I was.

Out in the corridor, Kael tried to keep a cool demeanor as we hurried down the staircase, hallway, then another winding set of stairs, leading toward the Stav Guard wings.

Kael paused outside a door. Behind it, muffled voices gave up at least two other people in the room. "You must keep quiet. We don't want a panic. He was . . . he wasn't supposed to be there."

I spared a glance at Hilda and Emi, but nodded and followed Kael into the room.

My pulse froze.

Blood-soaked linens covered a bed. Edvin moved about gathering supplies, cursing and pleading to the gods all in the same breath. Roark was hunched over the man on the bed, holding wounds closed with his bare hands. Sprawled on his back, tunic shredded over his bloodied chest, Prince Thane was unmoving, too still, too pale.

"*Thane.*" Emi rushed to the bedside of the prince.

Her cry drew Roark's attention. In his eyes was a look of pure fear. In three steps the Sentry was in front of me, bloody fingers waving in a panicked plea I couldn't follow.

I clasped Roark's fingers; blood—the prince's—was slick on my palms.

"Roark," I whispered gently. "Slow down. What do you need me to do?"

He blinked through his haze, swallowing with effort, then lifted a trembling hand. *Soul bone.*

It was then I took note of a basket—taken from the king's stores, no doubt, and filled to the brim with pale bones.

"For Prince Thane?" To heal him, the way it had healed Kael.

Roark's mouth tightened. He gave me a stiff nod.

"Yes," I said, squeezing his hand still locked in mine. "Of course."

The Sentry did not approve of soul bones—to ask it meant he truly believed the prince would not survive without one.

"Edvin." I knelt beside the prince's bed, taking up a shard. "Will you mark it?"

He didn't hesitate. His ability to bend and manipulate bone grooved new rune etchings into the flat piece of bone, symbols to summon the essence of the soul who'd left their bones behind. When the edges burned in the familiar gold, I pressed the bone into one of the many wounds over Thane's chest.

I let out a rough gasp when golden threads burst from the edges of the shard like iridescent yarn. Hands on the prince, I began to stitch it in place, sinking the piece deeper toward his breastbone under the blood, the sinews, and torn muscle.

I stitched the strands until darkness pulled me away.

Fear did not come when black water dripped down the rotted walls of the space.

Soon, Edvin's form glowed with his frantic steps, and Kael's gilded body didn't move, a silent observer, but his arms were folded in a way that had me convinced he was gnawing on the nail of his thumb. On the opposite side of the bed, a glowing Hilda and Emi had taken up the positions of Kael and Edvin, likely manipulating any broken bones on the prince while I melded.

Silky shadows draped over my shoulders. Cold and smoke filled my lungs.

He was there. I didn't need to turn around to know it. I ignored the ominous presence of whatever piece of Skul Drek stood at my back.

Was he like me? Able to slip into this plane when soul bones were used? Was he a true demon, a spectral sent by cruel gods?

"I don't know how you cross realms. I don't know if you're a melder—"

The shadow hissed in disgust.

"It doesn't matter," I went on, voice rough. "But you attacked a good man. A kind man."

My fingers worked quickly, securing the soul bone against Thane's chest. When all the stitches were placed, I cupped both palms over the top, embracing the heat under my skin. The bones brightened as the edges grew molten, fusing into Prince Thane's natural bone.

I sat back on my knees once the heat faded, glaring over my shoulder.

Red eyes were buried under the misty cowl, but bits of his gray skin were visible, not so shielded. His golden rope, which disappeared into the distance, was tattered and weak.

But the new strand that fashioned between us during the rank melding was thicker and stronger.

I looked away from the unwanted golden rope tying me to a monster, more vengeful than afraid. "Why him? He does not have craft and he isn't selfish or cruel. The prince is no threat to you."

Billows of darkness rolled over Skul Drek's shoulders in greater swells, and I was beginning to think the heaviness of his shadows was his only tell of emotion, a source of feeling. Cruel or gentle, I couldn't know. He'd left me in peace to work, but still studied me like he craved the sight of my blood.

"Four souls were stolen, four souls must take their place. It is not a matter of choice, but purpose." There was tension in the rasp of Skul Drek's voice, like he spoke through his teeth.

I followed his burning gaze to the bone under my hands. Perhaps it was the exhaustion from a day of worry, perhaps it was anger that the prince—who'd been kind and safe—had been harmed, but I faced Skul Drek, fists tight at my sides. "Then change your damn purpose. He deserves to live, you bastard. Give one soul away, even this once."

Skul Drek took a moment to speak. "Perhaps."

Was he complying or mocking me?

"What do you want? You attack without care, slaughter men with lives, homes, with people who love them. You're a *monster*."

"Like you will be."

I looked down at the threads of golden light fastening my heart to his. With a cry of frustration, I pulled and yanked, desperately trying to be free of him.

"You're keeping me here with you." I bared my teeth. "Is that what happens when I meld? Is this how my heart is corrupted? You destroy me."

For a long pause, Skul Drek said nothing. "You brighten the dark. It calls to me, it reminds me . . ."

The shadows of his form shifted, as though he turned his back on me.

Bursts of warmth cut through the cold. I was falling back. I made a move to turn away, but let out a scream when all at once, Skul Drek's phantom was a mere pace away. The cruel shade of his eyes pierced through me, like he'd never seen me before.

"Melder." The word hissed against my skin, a scent of brine and sea, as though a storm made the shadows. "Not all is as it seems."

My chin trembled. "The prince did not deserve your wrath."

"Then the Thief King must stop the search."

"Tell me what he wants me to find, then."

Another hesitation, another pause. The rope keeping Skul Drek chained to the darkness flickered, almost growing dimmer.

He faced me again. "Hear me—let him rest. More blood spills if he does not rest."

"I don't know what you mean." I tilted my head, watching as the great Draven assassin—or the ghost of him—looked about, almost like he expected an attack from behind. I followed his gaze into the unknown darkness. "Are you . . . are you protecting something? Does that strand of craft that holds you lead to something hidden?"

"Something hidden." Skul Drek's words were jagged as broken glass. "Not all is as it seems, Melder."

There was something of power here. Something King Damir wanted. Something Skul Drek did not seem entirely free to mention.

"What is here? What is the king looking for?"

Skul Drek faded more into his darkness while the heat of the bedchamber called me back.

But his final words cut against my heart like the crack of a lash. "The Wanderer."

ROARK

E MI SLEPT, CURLED ON A PAD OF FUR ON THE FLOOR NEAR
the foot of the bed. She did not want to leave Thane.

I didn't blame her.

Seeping gashes were slashed over the prince's body. Bruises
were swollen and black over his skin. But his chest rose and fell
in steady breaths. Clean linen bandages encircled his bare chest
where Lyra had placed the soul bone.

Thane wouldn't be pleased. He didn't protest soul bones like I
did; his resistance to them was more aesthetic. The way they
bulged in bodies like a nodule or growth went against his vanity.
Lyra's work was hardly noticeable.

I cared more for the nature of the soul inside him.

In my frenzy to save him, I struggled to pause long enough to
sense the power of each bone. Corrupt and cruel bones could be
felt if given the time to listen to their craft.

Thane was a man of honor. I had to hope his soul was strong
enough to blot out any corruption of the fallen.

I leaned over my knees, forcing a smile as I gestured to the silence of the room. *Wake up and I will point out the small lump often, you bastard.*

"He'll wake."

I spun in the chair. Lyra held a tray with a tin cup and a plate of sliced pomes. Dark rims of fatigue shadowed her eyes, and for the first time she looked almost frail. Her dark hair was free around her shoulders, and the simple shift she wore was two sizes too big.

She placed the tray on a table beside the bed, studying Thane's sleeping face. "He'll wake, Roark."

I slouched in the chair. Each arm felt as though it were made of stone. I didn't respond.

Lyra pulled another wooden chair from against the wall and placed it beside me. "You should eat something, maybe go rest. I'll watch over him."

I shook my head.

"There is nothing more you can do."

Against my leg, I used one hand to reply. *He did not leave me.*

Lyra blinked, her gaze scanning the scar across my throat. "How old were you?"

Twelve. Thane was fourteen.

"He didn't know you, but stayed as you healed?"

I nodded. Three days and three nights, Thane stood by like a silent defender, seeing to it his father kept his word that healers could tend to the dying Draven boy they dragged in from the gates.

"You know, scars are considered attractive to Jorvan girls."

A weak grin tried to spread over my mouth at the memory of the first words he spoke when I opened my eyes after I'd been found at the gates.

Lyra handed me the tin cup, refusing to pull it back, even when I refused twice. With an eye roll, I took the mug, steam from the herbal tea soothing a bit of the noxious fear. I wouldn't let on lest she return one of those arrogant smiles.

The smile still came when I took my first drink.

Lyra fiddled with a snag in her shift when silence thickened. "May I ask how you were injured?"

I tapped the side of the mug for a long pause. *My people.*

"You said that, but how?" Lyra's face wasn't one of pity, more of anger. "How could they do such a thing to a child?"

Nightmares, strange memories, more and more of the night my standing in my own clan shifted was returning. I did not recall much, and wasn't certain I wanted to know every dark truth of the raids, but I remembered enough to know Dravenmoor paid for those raids in blood.

I replied slowly. *I made a fatal mistake.*

Her eyes narrowed.

I shouldn't speak on it. There was no need to give up bits of a past so few knew. I kept going anyway. *Cursed marks are carved when a clansman dies by another Draven's hand, or a betrayal is committed. I was accused of both.*

"You were a boy, surely nothing was intentional."

It was not seen that way.

She wanted to ask, I could see it in her eyes, but Lyra dragged her bottom lip between her teeth, as if biting the question off before it could form.

I brushed a hand over her shoulder, drawing her attention.

I do not recall everything, the mark—I gestured at my scar—*is a curse in a way and must have shadowed memories. But as time goes on, I recall more. One of my choices caused the death of the Draven prince. Where blood is taken, blood is given.*

"The prince?" Lyra fiddled with the end of her hair. "Thane said you were found at Stonegate after—wait . . . you were found after the raids."

I looked away. It was foolish to be speaking of this when so much was at risk, when I was half-convinced my nightmares of a silver-eyed girl in the darkness might be more than a dream.

Lyra drew in a sharp breath. "Roark, you were in the craft raids as a *boy*? Weren't you?"

I told you, I remember little but—I hesitated, my hand stilling in the air—*I remember smoke, blood, and screams.*

Her chin dropped. "So do I. When I was taken from Skalfirth, small moments from the raid started returning. Mostly in dreams."

My stomach tightened. A muscle pulsed in my jaw. Why were we both all at once recalling moments of that bloody night?

"I'm not sure they're even real," she said. "But I remember my father. He . . . he had dark eyes and a deep laugh." The corner of her mouth curved into a small smile, but it faded swiftly. "I remember the heat of fire on my face, and I think someone pulled me from the longhouse. I don't know, but since using my craft, slowly my mind seems to recall horrors it wanted to forget."

Perhaps it is better to forget, I responded. *I would rather not remember any more.*

"You did not deserve what was done to you," Lyra insisted. "Forgive me, but customs or not, that is terrible. What I am assuming was an accident, gods, to punish a child in such a way . . ." Her voice trailed away like the words were too bitter to form.

How do you know it was an accident?

"I suppose I don't." She pointed at Thane. "But your eyes when you mentioned the dead prince looked a great deal like they do now—with this prince. Fear is in them, the kind that comes when someone does not want to live through heartache again. I had the same fear when Kael was dying on the jarl's floor."

I studied my palms for a breath. *Emi would not have let him die.*

"But I didn't know that." Lyra cleared her throat. "I understand you were under orders to force out the melding craft; Kael holds no bitterness . . . nor do I any longer. I know there is no returning for the two of us, but"—Lyra shifted in her chair, hesitating—"but Edvin and Hilda, they left behind children, a wife, and a new husband."

I knew what she was asking. *I am not the king here. Nor is Thane.*

Her face fell. "Thought it was worth the ask."

I leaned closer. *In time, you could have enough of Damir's respect to barter for their return.*

"In time." She closed her eyes for a moment. "How long might that be? When Edvin's eldest boy is a man himself?"

I didn't know how to respond. Once Damir had a crafter in his walls, the king became a bit of a collector of magic, believing it only added to his power. I doubted the two crafters would ever be welcome to live on the shores of Skalfirth again.

"I don't mean to offend, but Dravenmoor sounds harsher than even Stonegate." Lyra forced a small smile and picked at some of the fruit she brought for me. "Emi told me why she fled the clans."

I nodded. *The Draven clan holds little patience for bone crafters. Even when they are born of their own blood.*

"How did Emi escape when she was only a girl?"

I sighed and sat back in my chair. *She managed to send a raven to me with a plea for help. I had been here two summers already, and with Thane's aid, we saw her safely behind the walls.*

Lyra watched Emi sleep for a pause, then grinned. "I thought I'd hate her, but she's rather likable. Started liking her on the longship when she forced Kael to walk."

She is stubborn and aggravating. A little like another woman in Stonegate.

Lyra chuckled, but started picking at one fingernail. "I'm certain it's . . . well, I'm sure it's good to have someone from your own lands."

I suppose.

A flush of pink washed over her cheeks. "You seem rather close. I, well, I hope you treat her well, Sentry Ashwood."

One brow shot up and a grin followed, the first since Thane was harmed. Lyra avoided my gaze, and I took a bit of pleasure from it. With my center knuckle, I tilted her chin to me. *Are you insinuating she is my lover? That curious about me?*

She pulled her chin away, frowning. "I knew you'd be pompous about it. Gods. No, I'm not curious, it's called conversation. Since I like Emi a great deal more, yet I'm stuck with you, I figured I'd better get to know you. Perhaps find out what she could possibly see in the Sentry."

She spoke a great deal when nerves took over. My grin widened.

I took hold of her hand, spreading her palm so I could respond against her skin. *She sees a cousin.*

Lyra made a sort of choking sound when she drew in a sharp breath. "You're blood?"

Why do you suppose she sent word to me when she needed help?

"Your reputation was my first guess." This time, she didn't pull away. "Folk in the kingdom call you Death Bringer."

My lip curled. *Because I will. Should anyone harm someone under my charge, I will kill them.*

"I am under your charge."

I didn't respond but for a flick of my brow, a tilt of my head, and a final glimpse at the burn in her cheeks before I forced myself to pull back.

"He does not even speak out loud, yet I cannot find rest around him."

I shot to my feet when Thane groaned and went to rub a hand against the bandages over his face.

Lyra caught his wrist. "Prince, don't."

He groaned again. "It itches. I'm going to go mad. One scratch and I'll stop."

She laughed softly. "We can find pastes to relieve it a bit."

Blood pounded in my skull when Thane cracked his eyes and found me in the dim light. "What? Do I look as awful as you?"

Too close. I had to speak it twice, my hands were so unsteady. Guilt at nearly losing my oldest friend, guilt that it had happened at all, the whole of it burrowed in my chest, making it hard to draw a deep enough breath.

Thane sobered. "Looks like it is what you and I are fated to do, brother. Nearly die, then survive."

"Well, you both might be fond of that," Lyra said, tucking a fur tighter around Thane's waist. "But I could do without it."

"I will do as you say, Lyra Bien." Fatigue was heady in Thane's voice. "You frighten me more than the Sentry."

THE GREAT HALL WAS LADEN IN TENSION AND QUEEN INGIR still dabbed at her swollen, damp eyes. She had not stopped since word of Thane's injury spilled through the corridors of Stonegate.

"A dozen Stav in Salur, five in the healer's wing, one with a missing eye, and a prince nearly sent to the gods." Damir's features were ruddy with anger and aimed at his son, who seemed content to remain lost in his cups. "I want to know why you went beyond the gates."

Only two days since I found Thane bleeding out in the wood and one of his eyes and top lip remained swollen and blackened with bruises; the wounds over his chest were still wrapped in pungent herb presses.

In every other way he was Thane—irritated he'd been forced into the great hall and content to drink his way through it.

"I should think it quite obvious, Father." The prince filled his horn with more foamy ale.

Damir's eyes flashed. Somewhere within the Jorvan king, I believed him to hold true affection for his son as more than an heir. But siring only one child left the king more concerned about continuing the Oleg line than Thane's thoughts, hopes, and attributes.

"You should not have been there for any reason."

"My lord," Baldur began, "the prince explained he left with a small unit of Stav to set traps and markers along the roads out of concern for the Myrdan caravan when it brings his bride."

"Thank you, Baldur," Thane said through a long gulp of his ale. "I could not have explained my own thoughts and actions better if I spoke them myself."

The king cursed. "Stupid fool. We will provide Stav aplenty for King Hundur." Damir paced, his every step drew another whimper from the queen. "You were struck by ravagers?"

Thane shifted in his chair. One of his fingers traced the rim of the drinking horn. "They fought more like warriors, but they were led by Skul Drek. In fact, my numerous wounds are a shrine to the assassin. He could've done worse."

My jaw pulsed in a touch of fear, knowing how truly near to Salur Thane had been.

"Worse?" Ingir wailed. "Look at you."

"Well, if you must know, Mother"—Thane waved his drinking horn about—"the bastard might have more fear for our rule than we thought. Seemed the moment he saw the royal seal on my cloak, he thought twice about killing me."

"Dravenmoor would know we'd storm their gates if the prince of the new empire were killed." A deep grumble broke from Damir's throat.

No one knew for certain where the assassin hailed from. Attacks against bone crafters and Stav Guard who willingly used soul bones merely left assumptions and suspicions pointed toward the enemy.

Thane sat back. "I've already received a lashing from the Sentry for sneaking away, I do not need more. I needed to see the roads cleared personally or I could not allow Yrsa to travel them."

Thane was an honorable idiot. I would tell him as much the moment we were free of this damn hall.

He was right to fret over the princess. It mattered little to those standing against their union which of the pair died to prevent the vows. Thane merely drew the ire of the enemy first.

Damir spun on me. "I am told you took swift action to secure a soul bone in my son to save him."

Yes. Gestures with Damir were direct and straightforward. Simple enough for Baldur to translate.

"The sort of thinking we need around this damn palace." Damir butted his chest with mine. "You should be the king's inner guard, Roark."

It was the same request I'd heard since my eighteenth summer when I showed greater aptitude than most with the blade. *I am honored, but will remain at the service of the prince.*

"Why?" Damir had never pressed more. "Your station and rank would improve, along with your power to command."

"I'm more tolerable, perhaps?" Thane's voice dripped in irony.

Damir shot his son a narrow look, and before he fell back into shouts and rants, I offered a response I'd practiced more than once.

To serve the prince is to serve the future of the Oleg line.

Damir returned a tight glare when Baldur repeated my words, missing a few here and there.

"True enough. I will let it go, for now." The king turned to face some of the courtiers who surrounded the despondent queen. "We will honor the Sentry and the melder for their quick actions to save the prince. King Hundur and the princess will be arriving within the fortnight, then we will feast, and praise our gods that the line of Oleg lives on."

A thrilled sort of applause filtered through the hall.

Lyra deserved the honor. I deserved nothing. Thane never should've been beyond the gates.

His near death was mine to shoulder. Not praise.

LYRA

I DID NOT KNOW HOW TO SPEAK OF SKUL DREK. TRUTH BE told, I was half-convinced Thane's injuries, the deaths that followed, were wholly my guilt to bear. But the warnings of the phantom would not leave me. *Let him rest.*

The Wanderer.

The damn Wanderer King was meant to be a myth based on dozens of sturdy kings. A saga to explain the origins of craft. He was not meant to be a man who once lived in these knolls, with bones buried in this land. Bones coveted and sought for the power of the Wanderer's soul.

Once Thane was no longer at risk for the gods' table, the king pressed me on whether I had sensed any bones in the ground. The way Damir spoke, I wasn't certain Melder Fadey stepped into the mirror land. It seemed more like the former melder had inclinations or instincts where new bones might be found.

I wanted to know why Skul Drek could step into the mirror like me, then kill beyond the gates as well as a Stav. I wanted to know why he spoke to me, why a thread of craft seemed to tether me to him whenever I melded.

Several days after the prince recovered, mists crept over the lawns of the fortress like spreading poison.

I tightened a fur mantle around my shoulders, watching as a line of cloaked Stav Guard rode into the gates, saddles laden with pouches and bags.

They'd recovered the bones I'd seen glowing in the rotted knolls after the rank melding.

Across the courtyard, I caught the king's gaze. It wasn't kind; his eyes burned with something sharp and greedy. Damir dipped his chin toward me, a grin spreading.

He was pleased.

He would ask for more; he would search for more.

Let him rest.

I did not know how to end it. If I did not comply, perhaps Kael would be used against me.

If I did as the king asked, a deadly creature built in the darkness would level his blade at my throat soon enough.

"I DON'T EVEN KNOW WHERE TO GO FOR A FITTING." I FINISHED tying off the end of my braid and faced Emi, who looked less like a Stav Guard and more like one of Queen Ingir's courtiers in the pale dress. "In Skalfirth, ladies did not get fitted for gowns. They had us—their servants—make them."

"Your days of pricking your fingers and untangling yarn are over."

I tossed my braid over my shoulder, inspecting my face in the mirror. Since using my craft for the king, the scars of silver in my eyes had brightened.

In truth, I rather enjoyed the times when Lady Jakobson would demand her daughters' or her own dresses be sewn. Selena and I would sit and snicker with other women, catch up on gossip, who might be courting whom, while Kael got to go gut rancid fish and eel in the deep seas with Thorian.

I slid my palms over my hips. Fuller than they'd been back home. The hearty meals sat on my bones better than seed breads and root stews.

Emi offered me a bemused look and nudged my side with her elbow. "You'll enjoy yourself, I swear it. The market is diverting and you could use it. These last weeks, you've been jolting at everything."

"Could it be because ravagers have attacked? The prince nearly died? Feels like I brought a curse to this place."

Emi tilted her head back and forth. "You certainly brought changes, in more soul than one. Come on, you'll enjoy the market."

A bit of heated panic rose like a wave from my belly to my throat. "I've spent most of my life avoiding strangers and folk I don't know."

With a gentle smile, Emi placed a hand on my arm. "I'll be with you today. No market beginner should haggle with Margun alone, it'd be rather cruel."

"Margun is the silk merchant?"

"I suspect she's a troll in a woman's body." Emi waved a hand, erasing the thought. "She's tricky and loves a good scheme. Cunning as she is, the woman knows how to supply this fortress with the finest of silks, yarns, and wool."

All the ladies of the palace were to be fitted. The watchtowers blew their horns before the sun rose this morning, a signal the royal Myrdan caravan was spotted beyond the knolls and would be here by nightfall. On the morrow, Damir ordered, a celebratory feast to honor the Sentry and me would occur at the first star of dusk.

I plucked a cloak from a hook near the door and draped it over my shoulders, glancing at Emi. "Why are you in such a pleasant mood?"

Emi blew out her lips. "I am never in a foul mood."

"Stav Nightlark," I taunted, "only this morning you rampaged over the consistency of your pottage. I think you even insisted the cook was trying to poison you."

Tucking a stiletto knife in her boot, Emi lifted her gaze. "Don't let her fool you. She has it in for me. Loves Darkwin, though. His plate arrived with two additional spiced rolls."

I snickered and stepped into the sitting chamber of my room. Truth be told, I was a tangle of thoughts. One moment, I was knotted in my stomach with excitement at the thought of leaving the inner walls of Stonegate again. Then, in the next, I did not want the crowds, the questions, the glances.

Weeks here, and . . . some of it I did not despise. Emi. Prince Thane. Where I thought I would hate them, I dared consider them friends. Stonegate was a force, and I feared it was drawing me in, deeper and deeper with its mystery and glamor.

EMI SPOKE TRUE ABOUT SÚLKA MARGUN. ONE BELL TOLL IN THE market found me perched on a stool as the woman circled me, a wolf with its prey. She tapped one hooked finger against her lip.

The silk merchant was slender, with sunken cheeks, but she moved like a queen in her own shop. Margun brazenly inspected the length of my hair, my hands, my arms, my shoulders, the natural bend of my knees, all while her knuckle kept tapping her lip.

Where I wanted earthy brown, Margun insisted on evergreen. When I said silver trim suited the shade well, she smacked my hand away from the threads and held up an iridescent spool of thread that reminded me of starlight.

I argued over the plunge of the neckline; she battled me on the cut of the sleeves, hem, and bodice.

By the end of our encounter, Emi was red-faced from holding in laughter, and I had a roll of different silks draped over my arm to choose from before Margun finished the gown.

When all the selections were made, I scurried from the silk shop—a satchel of lace and ribbons Margun insisted ought to be braided into my hair tossed over one shoulder—and into the streets of the market, desperate to finally breathe again.

Emi paused to inspect a cart with bone and jade bands, and woven necklaces.

"I didn't take you for a woman who wore stones?"

The curves of her ears heated in a soft pink. "I was thinking it might be a fine welcome gift for the princess Yrsa. She's remaining at Stonegate from now on, after all, and I thought it might suit her."

Generous. Yrsa was a mystery to me. Rumors insisted King Hundur was a protective father, and some said he never allowed his girl beyond her own private gardens lest she was visiting her betrothed in Stonegate.

Still, Emi seemed to hold the woman in high regard, and Thane did not loathe his match.

I looked forward to meeting her.

I leaned against a stone wall near a short tunnel that cut across one side of the market and opened in the other. Young laughter drew my attention.

I peered around the wall and a flush of heat prickled across my cheeks.

Roark, clad in his Sentry tunic with his crescent moon sword on his waist, was turned away from me. A trio of Stav were with him, grinning as the Death Bringer held his hands up over the heads of a gaggle of young ones.

Tucked between each of the Sentry's fingers were parchment-wrapped sweets—smooth creams made from honey and milk and sticks with sugary glaze.

Roark would taunt the littles by tempting them with the sweets, then tuck them behind his back, slip them into a pouch tethered to his waist they could not see, and return empty-handed.

I muffled a laugh when the groans echoed along the tunnel.

Until the Sentry held up one finger, telling them to be patient.

In a few theatrical motions, Roark reappeared eight sweets, one tucked between every finger. Cheers, giggles, and muttered thanks followed as Roark and the Stav gave up the sweets, watching the young ones scatter gleefully through the market, their prizes in hand.

I leaned against the curve of the tunnel. "I've been your charge for some time, Sentry Ashwood, and I've yet to receive anything sweet from you."

The three Stav at his back dipped their chins at the sight of me. Roark spun around, eyes like a fading sun drawing me into its brilliance.

Gods, I was a fool. Yes, he was handsome, and competent, and loyal. Perhaps he was not the worst of company to keep, and now I knew he respected the most innocent, but he was still Roark Ashwood, a man who saw me as a duty to his position.

I had no business wishing he might come a bit closer.

Why are you out here alone? He wore a shadowed expression.

"Emi is only there." I gestured toward the pearl cart with one hand, adjusting the weight of the satchel on my arm. "I'm not a fool, and I didn't mean to interrupt your time away from your nursemaid duties to the melder."

Roark tilted his head, then replied with his fingers against my cheek. A secret delight of mine. *A duty I enjoy.*

He pulled his hand away as though he'd replied without thinking. The Sentry rubbed the back of his neck for a breath, then took note of the leather pouch filled with ribbons.

With a signal to the Stav Guard, he instructed them to take my things to my chamber.

Do you wish to return? he asked once the three guards had gone.

"No." I allowed my eyes to flutter closed. Scents of baked breads and rosy skin oil, leather and a bit of woodsmoke. "I was going to beg Emi to stay a bit longer. I'd like to see the whole of the lower township."

Roark glanced over my shoulder. *You have been abandoned.*

I followed the point of his finger. True enough, Emi's tight, icy braids were nearing the bridge to cross over onto palace grounds. She held her own purchases, but waved wildly as she bid farewell. With the distance between us I couldn't see her sly grin, but I could damn well feel it.

My insides twirled when I faced Roark again. "I should follow her, I suppose."

He shifted on his feet for a breath. *I can stay with you.*

What was this new . . . pressure that always seemed to gather in wretched places near Roark Ashwood? Chest, head, and somewhere low, low in my belly. "Well, then, lead the way, my lord Sentry."

He feigned irritation at the mock propriety in my tone and stepped into the flow of the market, keeping close to my side.

Strange, but folk in the market seemed to revere the Sentry more personally than the Stav Guard.

Old women slipped him more than one fresh herb roll or strip of seasoned venison. Carpenters and street sweeps waved and bid him a good day. Roark responded with respect and something gentle, but there was a touch of shyness in each dip of the head, each twitch of his mouth. Seemed the Sentry cared for the attention of others as much as me.

The sun hung low in the sky when we paused over a wooden bridge to eat a parcel of sugared nuts one of the merchants had practically shoved into Roark's belt.

I popped a nut onto my tongue and spun around, so my back was against the rail of the bridge. "I never knew you were so beloved, Sentry Ashwood. It is you who slows our pace from all the greetings and well-wishes."

He stared at the nuts, a bit of heat in his face. *I'll try to be crueler so I do not delay your market days in the future.*

"See that you do." I grinned and stole another nut from his palm. "Is Dravenmoor like this? Markets, trade, old women trying to pinch your ass when you pass by?"

Roark smiled, and a sort of grumble rose in the back of his throat—his laughter—a sound I could pick out of a boisterous hall by now. *I was young when I was exiled, but I recall each Jul going into town, lining up with other children, and receiving a sweet stick if I had been well-behaved.*

There was an ease to his features as he spoke of childhood, even with the proof of agony and pain carved into his flesh.

"Selena, a cook in Jarl Jakobson's house, would take me out to the star plum trees when they bloomed. We'd spend half a day braiding flower crowns and eating berries, then she'd tell me I was the queen of the whole orchard." I smiled with a touch of sadness, and looked down at the river below. "I think she did it to brighten my heart whenever noble folk spoke cruelly."

Roark's shoulder brushed mine when he leaned onto his elbows over the rail. *Then you've known good people.*

"Yes. Some of the servants took to looking after me and Kael more than others. Selena is always convinced water nyks or huldufólk are invading, but she is so gentle. Thorian is a groundskeeper and fisherman. He knew Kael would be forced to see his father disregard him over and over, but never spoke of Jarl Jakobson. Instead, he taught Kael to fish in rough seas, told him he was powerful and a good man."

I paused, sparing a glance at Roark. His eyes were focused nowhere but on me. I tucked a lock of hair behind my ear. "I'm sure it seems rather simple, but when I could not show the truth of myself, it felt nice to be accepted for any piece of me, I suppose."

Roark's brows tugged together. He faced the river. His reply was slow, gentle. Whenever the Sentry responded—frantic, stiff and stern, or slow and calm—I imagined it like his voice might be. Brisk or soft. In this moment, I imagined it low and kind.

All pieces of you are not so bad.

"I think you nearly gave me a compliment, Sentry."

You read my words poorly.

I laughed. "I read them perfectly."

Roark stared over the rail of the bridge. Together, we reveled in silence for a time until he brushed a hand across my arm, drawing my attention. *You are more than the scars in your eyes.*

On instinct, Roark rubbed the line of puckered flesh on his throat.

Blood heated. I drifted nearer to his side, so our bodies touched from shoulder, hip, to legs. This close, I was surrounded by his strong oaky scent.

"You are more than the scars on your skin." I shuddered when his eyes dropped to my mouth, unashamed.

Roark tilted his head. Heat and desire pulsed across my body. His mouth, full and parted, drew closer. A need to lean in, to taste him, throbbed low in my belly. I tilted my chin up, and our noses brushed, a whisper of a touch.

The gods-awful ram horn bellowed from the towers of Stonegate.

Roark blinked, his heavy breath heated my lips, then wretchedly slow, he pulled away. *The Myrdan caravan has arrived.*

LYRA

THE CARAVAN HAD GATHERED NOBLES FROM ACROSS JOR-
vandal, all here to celebrate the vows. Gowns the color of
bone or blue dewberries glittered in the fading sun as folk crossed
the bridge from the lower marketplace to the palace gates.

Furs from high-mountain bears or meadow foxes were added
to the shoulders of men. Newly shorn beards braided in bone
beads. Gold chains around wrists and necks of ladies.

Territory jarls strode in with pomp and arrogance. They offered greetings to their fellow noblemen and rulers, but underneath their felicitations was subtle measuring—as though each
jarl wanted to be counted greater than the others.

I dipped my chin at the sight of Jarl Jakobson; his wife, Mikkal; and Astra, who looked around with awestruck delight.

Jakobson scanned the crowds, and I hoped he was searching
for Kael. I hoped he knew his son would not greet him.

Kael had enough regard among the Stav and Sentry. I did not

think he would crave the slightest attention from his blood father.

From Stav reports, the seashore was clotted with longships. All here to pay tribute to the prince and his betrothal. Then there were those who were surely here to gawk at the new melder and the Sentry who'd been brought together in violence only to work side by side to save the prince.

I could not soothe the heated waves in my stomach.

"Oh, there's the Myrdan royal coach." Hilda patted my arm, pointing over the heads of people.

Canopies over carts, flags of black and crimson, marked the arrival of royals.

Courtiers, jesters, and Skalds clad in finery, they all made merry on their way. Some regaling the folk of Stonegate in grand sagas of the gods' chosen formation of the kingdoms.

The traveler's lullaby Emi sang on the longship rose among several different factions of the caravan.

Kveða við min mórðir. Skip búask ok á morgun. Ek sigla til min folǫg . . .

Drums beat a tune by which they marched, ominous and powerful. More than a beat, it was a threat not to underestimate King Hundur and his forces.

The king and his queen, who kept her face hidden from the burn of the sunset, rode in a cabriolet with satin cushions. Seated across from Hundur was the princess. Yrsa was lovely. She waved shyly to people as they pulled nearer to the palace doors. She had dark hair, fine as spider's silk, woven into a crown of braids around her head. Her skin was a deep brown, her eyes were warm and kind. Thane hinted once Princess Yrsa had a slight talent with blood craft, but was not as skilled as his mother.

Perhaps the touch of craft in the princess's blood made this betrothal all the more advantageous for Damir and his proclivity to catch magic.

Small as the kingdom was, Myrdan warriors were formidable. Strong grips on craft-made bone blades, piercings through the center of their noses, and runes tattooed across their throats. Selena told me once that Myrdan ink was a mark for every Draven warrior they'd slaughtered.

King Hundur was a broad man with a lighter complexion than his daughter. Suspicion rimmed his gaze that cut through the crowd like jagged glass. At his side, the queen was petite and wore a look of unease. She held a linen cloth to her nose, as though the smell of so many bodies had long grown rancid.

Beneath the arch of the front entry to the palace, King Damir bore the weight of his dark crown, a fine sword with jagged bones shaped like serpents on the hilt lined his waist. The thick cloak he'd draped across his shoulders made him broader than was true.

I thought it might be intentional.

"Hundur, my friend." Damir clapped his palms against the Myrdan king's shoulders once the man was free of his coach. "Welcome. I trust your travels were uneventful."

Hundur sniffed. "Cold and rocky."

Damir chuckled and draped an arm around the shoulders of his fellow king. They staggered into the palace, chuckling through chatter with each other like the oldest of friends.

"Lyra." Hilda dug her fingernails into my arm. "Lyra, gods, tell me . . . tell me I am not imagining it."

I winced and gently eased my arm free of her grip, following her look of stun down the long line of travelers.

My heart stuttered when he caught sight of us in the same instant.

"Hil!" Gisli's voice cracked and he barreled through the crowds, desperate to reach his wife. He wasn't alone. Three young ones shrieked and giggled, following him close behind.

Edvin's children.

A sob broke from Hilda's chest. She raced for her husband.

I didn't understand. Only noble families, their inner courts, and their guards would be invited into the palace for the feast.

Movement across from me revealed Edvin running forward. Only when he wrapped a woman cloaked in a tattered woolen cape in his arms did I realize Freydis, his wife, was here, bound furs and satchels strewn about her feet. She sobbed against her husband's chest.

Their three children darted for their father.

Hilda had arms and legs entangled around Gisli. She kissed his brow, his cheek, his throat, over and over, as though she had forgotten the very taste of him.

"They've been granted land here." I startled when Kael materialized at my side. He grinned, watching our fellow crafters love their missed families.

"What do you mean granted land?"

"They're here to stay. Hilda and Edvin can have their families again."

I pressed a hand to my heart, tears rising in my throat. "What made King Damir allow it?"

"Ask your guardian." Kael winked and jutted his chin across the bridge. Standing beside Prince Thane at the doors, Roark observed the crowds with the same silky darkness as the night we met. Now I wondered if it was more that he became unsettled by those who strode past the Draven Sentry, whispering and wondering.

"Ashwood is right terrifying." Hilda emerged from the bustle, tears on her long lashes, Gisli's hand curled in hers. "But I'm not so convinced he's all stone and cruelty now."

I squeezed her arm and beamed at bashful, kind Gisli, who could not peel his eyes away from his wife, as though he could not quite believe she was beside him again. "How did he do this?"

Gisli lifted his head. "The Sentry? Oh, as we understand it, not long after Skalfirth, he petitioned the king for our families to be relocated to Stonegate. We heard after your service to the prince, the king finally agreed."

"He petitioned the king right after we arrived here?" Why hadn't Roark mentioned it?

Hilda's melancholy faded. Joined with Edvin and his family, she babbled on about the jagged points of the palace and how the style was not to her liking, yet still rather majestic.

I only heard bits and pieces, my mind and focus skirted over the heads of the caravan until I found him.

The same sharp pull, a hook on a rope, fastened in my chest. Soon enough, Roark's gaze sifted through the chaos and found mine.

I returned a watery smile and moved my fingers in his gesture, *Thank you.*

The Sentry took me in a moment longer, then bowed his head for a drawn beat before he looked away once again.

LYRA

COTTAGES WOULDN'T BE READY FOR EDVIN AND HILDA until the dawn. I gave up my bed to Edvin's three young ones while Edvin and Freydis took furs on the floor beside them. Gisli and Hilda laughed in my sitting chamber with me and Kael over mead and sliced plums.

Gisli told us about the despair in Skalfirth after the raid. Jarl Jakobson had not left his longhouse until now, and it seemed old Thorian thought the man deserved his anguish for not intervening for his son.

Kael said little about House Jakobson or the fine his estranged father had offered to entice the king to spare his life.

When the bells rang a midnight toll, Gisli and Hilda left with Kael, and I tried to find sleep beneath a soft quilt near the inglenook of my sitting room.

My fingertips touched the edges of my lips, as if I could feel the warmth of his breath, the nearness of his features. Good gods, I'd nearly kissed the Sentry.

I flattened my palm over the steady thud of my heart, the corners of my mouth curling. Roark Ashwood was beautiful mayhem. Austere and impassive, then aimable and gracious. He was a storm rolling off the tides, but I could not find the strength to run.

Instead, it seemed, I stood at the water's edge, willing the gale to devour me.

From the glimmer of the next dawn to the twinkling twilight, debauchery filled the gardens, corridors, and halls of Stonegate. King Damir promised a celebration and he delivered mightily.

With Hilda and Freydis at my flanks, we strode through the courtyards with courtiers and ladies. Queen Ingir took the head along with Breetha, the Myrdan queen.

Hilda would not stop beaming, and it lessened the dullness of the evening.

She could hardly contain her joy knowing she would share a house with Gisli again. He was a talented woodworker, and I had few doubts he'd find work aplenty in the fortress.

When the queens settled beneath a bower lined in fresh blooms, other ladies found spots to soak up the last rays of sunlight. I wanted nothing more than to return to my chamber to be free of crowds.

"Lyra." Freydis took hold of my hand. "We're to see one of the cottages the king has given us before the feast. Care to join? Or must you remain here?"

My shoulders slumped. "I'm not permitted beyond the gates without an escort. One who happens to be missing."

I'd not seen Roark the whole of the day. The man did not speak out loud, but his absence had become thundering and aggravating. Whatever affection I festered for the Sentry, I'd be wise to crush it before the king, or Kael, or worse—Roark—found out the truth.

"Pity you can't join." Freydis placed a hand on my arm. She was a gentle woman, from her features to her temperament, so it was unnerving when her lips curved in a sly sort of grin. "But I don't think it will be so terrible to stay behind. You've caught someone's attention."

A man, from the colors cascading over his tunic I guessed a Myrdan, shifted on his feet, occasionally looking my way.

My palms started to sweat.

"Surely he'll escort you back to the palace." Hilda winked.

Before Stonegate, we'd been nothing beyond friendly, chatting at market stalls or in the great hall. Through all this, we'd fashioned a new bond. One where I was not the servant of the jarl, but we were simply two women who looked out for each other.

But I cursed her now.

The woman I thought I could trust took Freydis's hand, grinned when the young Myrdan took a step my way, and turned to abandon me.

"See you soon, Lyra," Hilda said through a muffled snicker, then disappeared with her sister-in-law down a set of stone stairs leading to the lower township.

"Súlka Bien," the man said, voice smooth and light.

My heart stalled. With a soft breath through my teeth, I faced him.

I said nothing, merely held his stare, feeling a fool. Never one to know how to act in front of strangers, I was more accustomed to growing silent, invisible. Nothing but a bit of the foliage in the background.

He swiped his tongue over his lips, and grinned brightly. "My name is Tomas Grisen. Son of King Hundur's fallen seneschal."

"My sympathies."

Tomas lowered his chin. "The raids took many lives."

Dammit. Another house with blood spilled at my feet. Still, he didn't look at me with anger, more demure interest.

"I don't mean to disturb you," he said, "but I have been look-ing forward to meeting the new melder."

"Oh?" A prickle of defensiveness rolled up my arms.

Tomas held out a hand, perhaps a little taken aback by my abrasive tone. "Yes. I, well, one of my ancestors was a melder in old wars before the kingdoms were so divided. I'm not a bone crafter myself, but I find all magics fascinating. Did you know, it has been centuries since a female melder was born?"

"I didn't, only that it has been some time," I said, intrigued despite myself.

Tomas nodded vigorously. "Many sagas believe the female melders have stronger craft. Tends to connect deeper with their gentler souls, I suppose."

If only he knew an assassin's shadow drew me in whenever I slipped into the mirrored lands of the fallen.

"I wouldn't know." I clasped my palms in front of me. "I've only recently been introduced to my craft."

Tomas flushed in a bit of embarrassment. "Of course. Forgive me for rambling. I'm merely awed by melders."

I took a step back. "Well, I must dress for the feast. It was good to—"

"Allow me to walk with you."

I wanted to be alone. There were few whom I enjoyed walk-ing with to my chambers. Kael, Thane when he was mocking folk under his breath, Emi, and Hilda. And Roark.

My insides tightened. Gods. Roark was fast becoming a con-stant, comforting presence.

Before I could summon up a word of refusal, Tomas had threaded my hand through his arm, and strode with me toward the palace doors. He spoke fondly of craft and Myrda, lauding his accomplishments, even going so far as to say if Jorvandal did not have a prince, he would've been a candidate for Yrsa's hand.

Pleasant, but pompous.

We crossed into the front hall, me speaking a handful of words, and Tomas having said much more.

"I would love to escort you through the Myrdan glades, Súlka Bien." Tomas flashed a white smile. "The Grisen lands are surrounded by endless knolls, quite lovely countryside."

"I do not think I would be permitted to leave Stonegate, Ser Grisen."

"With our position in the court," Tomas said, disregarding my words, "anyone who dared disrespect you would be punished. I would personally see to it. I would see to it you had the finest gowns."

"How thoughtful."

Tomas beamed like he'd won some great victory, utterly missing the bite to my tone.

"Any lady would see it as an honor to be a guest of the second-most-powerful house in Myrda." There was a bitterness to his tone. After a breath, Tomas softened his features and smiled. "I suppose that will all change with this betrothal. You serve the royal house at Stonegate, but Myrda is soon to be tied to that house. I am certain your craft will be shared across borders."

Unease slithered low in my belly. I did not care for being seen as some sort of possession merely because of the blood in my veins.

King Damir saw me as such. Now, it would seem, so did Myrda.

"Thank you for walking me," I said, unthreading my arm. "I can manage from here."

"It is no trouble. I can walk you the rest of the way."

I didn't want Tomas of Myrda to know my chamber door. "Thank you, but—"

"Lyra!"

Gods, a swell of relief bloomed like a second heart in my chest. Prince Thane strode down the corridor, already dressed in his fine clothes and polished boots. Bruises still marked his features from the attack, but he was a great deal more like himself.

Tomas bowed at the waist. "Highness."

Thane greeted the man with a flick of his brows, then turned to me. "I hope you'll forgive me, Melder Bien, but your presence is needed elsewhere before the feast."

"Oh. Of course." I took a step closer to the prince.

"Súlka Bien." Tomas held out a hand between us. "I hope you might do me the honor of sitting with me."

"Afraid she'll be considered an honored guest, ser." Thane took hold of my arm, tugging me against his side. "She'll be at the high table."

"A dance, then," Tomas said, the slightest snap of irritation in his tone.

"Perhaps," I said in a rough breath as the prince bid a prompt farewell and spun us away.

When we were around the corner, I snorted a horrid-sounding laugh, stumbling against Thane's side.

"Gods, Lyra." Thane nudged my shoulder. "How do you manage to attract such odious company? Tomas Grisen is one of the haughtiest men in all of Myrda, according to Yrsa."

"Aggravating men simply find me." I nudged him back. "Some rescue me."

"I shall take that as a compliment." Prince Thane used his chin to direct me toward a winding staircase that would take us to his wing of the palace. "You have truly been summoned. Before the tedious chatter suffocates us at the feast, come have a bit of enjoyment."

"What are you talking about?"

Thane winked and flung open the door to his chamber. I breathed a sigh of relief. Emi stood near the tall, arched window with the princess.

Here, I was simply Lyra. I did not need to be the melder.

"Lyra." Emi waved. She kept the black fur cloak of a Stav Guard on her shoulders, but underneath was the fine blush-dyed dress she'd purchased at the silk merchant. Her lips had a touch of color on them, and she'd added gold bars through holes in each of her earlobes. "Come meet Yrsa before your time is stolen. Thane thinks you both will get on."

"Of course they will." The prince sauntered to a table with ewers and polished wooden drinking horns.

Yrsa's brown skin had been painted in gold shimmers and her dress reminded me of the star plum skin—silver over sea blue with a cloak made of furs dyed to appear as honey over her narrow frame.

"Princess." I bowed my head.

"Yrsa has shirked her ladies by lies and deceit all to debauch with us," Thane said with a laugh.

Yrsa clasped her hands in front of her stomach and looked away shyly. "You know how *fitful* I find travel. My insides are not well at all. I suspect I have a bit more time before someone tries to enter the washroom to check on me."

"And until then, we drink and laugh and avoid the masks we wear." Prince Thane handed Yrsa a horn of pearly wine. "For you, my bride. Nightlark, what will you take? Lyra?"

I waved a hand. "None for me. Not sure I could stomach it tonight."

"Unsettled by people again?" Emi touched my arm. There wasn't judgment in her tone, more a call to arms to those in the rooms to keep me in their sights.

"She ran into Tomas Grisen."

Emi's nose wrinkled. "Arrogant ass."

When Thane offered a sort of salute with the second drinking flute, as if to say he understood, a wash of affection bloomed in my chest. They ought to be my enemies, but I found a sort of belonging here, in this room, with these people.

Yrsa tilted her head, smiling my way. "So, you are the melder."

"I am."

"You saved his life." Yrsa gave the prince a tender smile. "You don't know me, but I thank you for it."

It was heartening to see a genuine fondness between an arranged match. They hadn't shown affection through touch, but the smiles, the comfort with each other being near, it was clear Yrsa and Thane held each other in high regard.

"I was not alone," I admitted. "Without Sentry Ashwood I wouldn't have known the prince was injured at all."

Thane chuckled and looked over his shoulder. "Did you hear that? Something else to get all haughty about. I wish you hadn't said it, Lyra."

Heat and a strange pinch to my chest fought to double me over when Roark emerged from the prince's bedchamber, securing his seax on his belt.

Gods, he was captivating. Like a warm memory.

Tonight, his eyes were brighter than a sunrise after a rainstorm. His hair was freshly braided on the sides, and the oakmoss scent on his skin was a beautiful tether, drawing me nearer.

Roark's mouth was set into a smug sort of grin, like he knew exactly what he was doing to me.

With one hand, he lifted my knuckles to his lips, then with the other gently spoke against my cheek. *Red suits you.*

"Oh. Thank you." I patted at the simple woolen gown, dyed a rich crimson. My heart bruised my ribs, as though I no longer knew how to be around the Sentry. "I don't know what to say," finally slipped out in a low breath.

He tilted his head. *About what?*

"What you did for Edvin and Hilda, for bringing their families here."

Roark seemed to gnaw on the words. *You were right when you said they ought not be punished for the actions of others. Craft should not deny you the people you love.*

My throat tightened with emotion. I refused to grow weepy, and Thane seemed to agree.

"All right. Enough, the both of you." The prince heaved himself onto one of the fur-lined lounges and crossed his ankles. "Yes, Roark is magnificent, but we're not here to watch him grow insufferably conceited. He already does it enough."

Roark knocked Thane's feet off the edge of his seat.

The prince was undeterred and raised a horn. "We are here to celebrate our own rebelliousness and distaste for being flaunted as the tools of two kingdoms."

Princess Yrsa laughed at something Emi said. Roark stood at my shoulder, and I found I wouldn't mind if he came closer.

The levity ended too soon, when a servant announced we were to dress. The first star had brightened the sky and the feast would soon begin.

Emi invited me to dress with her and Yrsa. I took advantage of the offer, continuing to laugh after we entered the princess's bedchamber.

"Oh, Lyra." Yrsa covered her mouth once I stepped around the dressing shield. "You are stunning."

The fabric of my first commissioned gown was the color of a green sea. The sleeves were split, revealing most of my shoulders, and on one side, a slit opened to my upper thigh. Carved bone beads were stitched along the bodice in the shape of the gods' tree. Yrsa was skilled in braids and had maneuvered half my hair into tight rows along the sides of my scalp, leaving the rest flowing down my back in long waves.

"As are you." It was true. Both Emi and Yrsa looked made for royalty.

The princess wore a gown of delicate gold lace, her lips painted to match, and more shimmery powder lined her dark eyes.

Emi kept her hair long over her shoulders. She chose Margun's black satin, but it was a trick of the eye. Every step past a sconce with a flame, and the ebony skirt shimmered in midnight blue.

Emi stood guard by the princess with me behind them until we reached the corridor near the great hall. Roark waited for us outside the double doors. The princess entered the hall, chin lifted, Emi at her back, and I was left to enter with the Sentry alone.

Roark's verdant gaze took in my dress, then blinked as through a fog back to my face.

I tightened my grip on his hand for a breath, then two, until he offered an arm for me to hold instead.

"Don't let me fall in there," I whispered.

Unlike the first time we stood beyond this doorway when Roark said nothing, he took my hand and lifted the back to his lips. I did not blink, watching until his mouth met my knuckles.

When he pulled back, he traced one word against my palm. *Never.*

ROARK

THE HALL WAS PACKED WITH TALL HEADDRESSES AND DOU-blets the color of hummingbird wings. Lyra's fingers dug into my arm, the only hint she was unsettled. Her face was a mask of unbothered indifference.

Darkwin caught her in his sights and winked. He was seated at one of the tables with the Stav Guard and more than one noble daughter.

We took our places on the dais beside the king and queen, a position of honor.

I handed Lyra into one of the high-backed chairs. Hundur and his harsh eyes watched her every move, and he wasn't alone. Beady gazes devoured her, a sea of serpents waiting to strike. Melder craft always brought with it fascination and awe, but also fear and suspicion.

A dangerous combination.

One I disregarded in the seasons I knew Fadey. He was a boor, snobbish and cruel.

Lyra was both timid and bold, mild and fierce. I took in the gawkers while she settled into her chair. Something cold, almost dark, drove through me like a lash. A possessive sort of need to tear her away from their scrutiny.

"Roark. Are you all right?" Her eyes, dyed dark as black cherries, grew wider.

I'd not realized how stiff I was, how much pinched disdain tightened my face. I took my place beside her, tossing back a long gulp of sour mead.

The feast opened with a winded speech from Damir about the rescue of his son. Lyra's name was spoken like a reverent secret. Mine was chanted by the Stav. I kept my gaze trained on the stone floor, wishing to be anywhere but there. Then Damir began to boast about his army and Thane's utter devotion to the safety of his future wife as though the king hadn't chastised his son viciously for his stupidity days before.

Part of me wondered if Damir would have us speak. The king always took a bit of twisted amusement watching me finger speak and needing another to translate. More than my hope I would not be urged to stand, I hoped Damir would stay his amusement for humiliation for Lyra's sake.

Blood had long ago drained from her cheeks. The woman could hardly sit still as the king droned on. Beneath the table her knee bounced, and she'd wrenched the linen cloth in her hand so fiercely it looked like she was twisting the head off a pigeon.

The desire to touch her had not left since the moment we'd stepped close on the bridge, since I'd pressed her skin to my lips in Thane's chambers. No good came from a Draven and a melder. Certainly not a match.

But when King Damir drew gazes our way once again, Lyra's

breath stuttered, and I placed a grounding palm on her thigh beneath the table. She stiffened at once.

I was a fool, thinking she'd want my touch. After a moment, I began to pull my palm away until Lyra's grip took hold of my fingers.

She squeezed once, then lifted her chin. "Stay," she whispered. "Please."

I swallowed, then slowly maneuvered my hand so her fingers laced through mine, and kept hold of her until Damir ceased his speech and demanded the feast truly begin.

Rawhide drums boomed and tagelharpa strings plucked. Folk danced, drank sweet ale and dewberry wine. Partners kissed and rocked against walls and posts. The king and queen sat on the dais with Hundur and his frail wife, like scavengers in the treetops looking at the weak below.

Baldur had long since moved to seduce one of Hundur's servant girls. The daughter of the Skalfirth jarl tried to draw the same attention Baldur had given her in Skalfirth, but the captain shoved her away, forcing her hips to strike the table's edge.

From across the hall, Darkwin stood, a rage in his eyes. Edvin had to tug on Kael's arm, murmuring what I hoped was a call to stay his temper.

If he could not, I would need to pull him away.

Baldur was an ass, but he was Kael's superior.

I signaled to Emi to keep watch on the servant woman should the captain try to take her from the hall.

When plates were cleared and more wine and ale served, I was called to intervene more than once with drunken Stav, leaving Lyra to endure King Hundur. The Myrdan king was brisk and foul with his words when he took too much ale.

From my position across the great hall, I could make out the steady, practiced expressions she kept in place. Polite nods of her head, the occasional taunting smile, she kept the king engaged, while never needing to speak in return.

"She's always been unique." The bone crafter woman—Hilda, I thought—stepped to my side. She followed my gaze, grinning. "Lyra, I mean. I can't tell if you are about to attack her, or the Myrdan king for looking at her."

I frowned, but didn't attempt to reply. No doubt, the woman had not learned many of my gestures.

"But I think you know that," Hilda went on. "She was a quiet girl. A simple servant, but even as girls I told my mother it felt like Lyra was stronger than she let on, like she was bound for something more than the shores of Skalfirth. I always thought Lyra was a hidden princess, running from her enemies. I suppose, in a way, I was right."

I heaved a sigh, hoping the woman could hear my question of what she wanted to truly say rather than attempting to finger speak and storming away in frustration when she couldn't understand.

Hilda chuckled. "I think you've fallen into the pull of Lyra Bien."

I looked away with what I hoped was a fierce expression of annoyance. Hilda was undeterred.

"I can't blame you. But let me say this—I wouldn't care if you were the king," she said through a dainty sip of ale. "Should you choose to hurt her, I will manipulate that spine of yours until it snaps."

She was . . . *threatening* me?

I spun into her. Most might cower, maybe back against the wall, but not Hilda. She took another sip, pinning me in her gaze over the rim of her horn.

"I wouldn't be alone," she whispered. "Kael admires you and all the Stav, but Lyra is his sister in every way that matters. She is like a beloved niece to Edvin. We are watching you closely, Sentry Ashwood. Do not hurt her heart, or yours will stop beating."

For speaking in such a way, I could have the woman's flesh flayed from her bones, her naked body strung up in the square for townsfolk to mock and bruise with rotted pomes.

Hilda was no fool; she knew the risks and spoke her words anyway.

I should've penned a response—I always carried charcoal sticks and parchment for such an occasion—I ought to remind her of her place, of my interest in the melder being nothing more than obligation.

I did none of it, merely lowered my chin in a subtle nod.

Hilda grinned and patted my arm. "Good. Enjoy the revel. It is in your honor, after all. Threats aside, I have no words to convey my gratitude for your part in restoring our family."

My lips parted in a bit of stun when she sauntered away. A heartfelt thanks and soul-deep vow of death and gore in one conversation.

Hundur's barking laughter drew my attention back to the high table. The Myrdan king was chortling at one of the jesters tossing platters atop a long spinning rod, but Lyra was gone.

A touch of frenzy took hold as I scanned the hall until I caught sight of her intricate braids and the pale skin of her thigh showing through the dangerously high slit in her skirt.

I'd be certain to send Súlka Margun a basket of the finest silk threads for her contribution to Lyra's attire by week's end.

Lyra shifted, giving up that the sod, Tomas Grisen, had trapped her in conversation near the back doorway. The man was a bastard who thought himself equal to a prince in Myrda.

As though she could sense my glare, Lyra looked over her shoulder. Those warm eyes locked with mine.

Just a duty, a purpose.

That was all she would be.

The thought was potent enough, I tasted the lie on my tongue.

HAVE YOU SEEN LYRA? I PATTED KAEL'S SHOULDER WHEN THE crowd in the hall had thinned. Damn Baldur tried to drag me to a room with him and a Myrdan man and woman. His drunken request drew my frustration long enough that when I looked back to the hall, Lyra was gone.

Darkwin's eyes were rimmed in red from too much ale. A Myrdan courtier had her slender arm around his waist, keeping him steady.

"Say again?" He squinted at my hands.

I let out a rough sort of growl. *Lyra?*

Kael blew out a breath. "Ah. I think I saw her . . ."

His voice trailed off when the courtier nuzzled his neck. I smacked his shoulder, hands moving in sharp gestures. *Darkwin!*

"Apologies." Kael cleared his throat. "I, uh, saw her leaving with that Myrdan nobleman. The one with a nose like a beak."

Dammit. Tomas. Cold stacked heavy in my gut. A lone nobleman had no business tearing the melder out of sight from the court.

"Ashwood. She was tired, I'm certain she went to her chamber." Kael's rasp was slow and slurred when I shoved past him and his courtier.

A panic, unseen and vicious, took me from behind after I found the first corridor empty. The next was filled only with lovers sneaking away for the night, and the vise around my throat tightened.

One hand on the hilt of my seax, I quickened my step and rounded the corner.

"You refuse so swiftly, Súlka Bien. Why? You are revered as near royalty, as am I."

My blood chilled when her firm response followed. "I would not care if you were a king, ser. A match with you, after your behavior, would be the last thing I would ever do."

There was a harrowing pause, then . . .

"You little bitch." Boots scuffed over stone. "You hold no power unless a bone is in your hand."

"Care to test that?" Lyra's biting retort shot back.

"I could take you here, ruin your pretty little body, maybe fill you with my heir, so your king would have no choice. Call it dues owed from the raids that killed my father."

I moved at a near run until I skidded in front of a staircase. Panic dissolved to rage, the sort that blinded the mind, that brought the darkest edges of a soul to the surface.

Tomas, drunk and red with desire, curled his hand around Lyra's throat. The back of her head struck the stone of the wall. She shoved against him, but he pinned her with his hips.

I took the stairs two at a time, a haze darkening my sight. A rush of cruel violence heated my blood, crackled along the scar on my throat. I could snap his neck, open his chest; I could cut him in all the places that would force him to bleed out slowly, painfully.

Lost to bloodlust and gore, I did not notice the way Lyra bent one knee, the way she tugged something free of the top of her boot. Not until she sliced the small knife over Tomas's cheek.

He cried out, scrambling backward, and held the gash on his face.

Lyra did not let up. In his distraction, she shoved him backward, so he stumbled against the rail of the staircase. She pressed two fingers against the wound on his face.

I came to a halt, from surprise, but more to admire this moment properly.

There was a pulse of power, the same ripple that struck against my chest whenever she used her craft, like it called to a deeper piece of me. I felt the pulse to my soul, a slow roll from my head to my heart.

Tomas cried out, loud at first, but it soon muffled, like he was screaming into a thick quilt.

His teeth clamped. He mumbled and shouted through a taut jaw.

My mouth quirked. She was melding his mouth shut, the same threat I'd leveled at the disrespectful Stav Guard weeks earlier. I wanted her to crush his skull, but when I looked at her eyes, the silver scars widened, glazing over the brown of her eyes until they were milky white.

I hurried to her side, taking hold of her wrist, and pulling her away before she could not undo her actions. I trapped her face in my palms, stroking the bridges of her cheeks with my thumbs. Slowly, Lyra blinked into focus.

"Roark." Her voice was low, almost frightening.

I did not know what drew me to do it—the fear in her eyes— but I pressed a quick kiss to her brow, then faced Tomas.

The wretch had crumpled to the stairs, moaning and holding his melded face. He could hardly even separate his teeth.

I gripped his hair, holding him steady, and used my other hand to speak to Lyra. *He needs to know what happens when he touches you.*

With the same knife she used, I pressed the edge against one of Tomas's little fingers. The sick sound of steel cutting through flesh and bone was buried beneath his roars of pain. I palmed the severed fingertip and sneered at the sobbing man.

Without pause, I slammed my palm over his mutilated mouth, shoving the bloodied tip onto his tongue.

Lyra covered her mouth with her palm, eyes wide, when I looked back at her. In a swift gesture, I said, *Finish what you began*.

After I stepped aside, it took Lyra a few heartbeats to return to Tomas. The man kept choking and spitting, desperate to remove the bit of his own finger from his mouth. A stunningly vicious heat blazed in the silver of Lyra's eyes. She pressed her fingertips to the front of his mouth, ignoring Tomas's screams, until his teeth cracked and shifted, melded shut.

I brushed my knuckles down her arm, drawing her from the haze of the melder's trance. *I will end him. You need only ask*.

Shouts from guards echoed in the corridor, answering Tomas's first cries.

Lyra's breath came rough and heavy. She shook her head. "No. Gods, what did I do? No, leave him. You can't be here. Myrda only sees you as a Draven. They'll place all blame on you. He . . . he told me Hundur wants to find a reason to turn Damir against you."

I wanted to spill his blood at her feet, and she feared for me.

Footsteps approached. Lyra took hold of my arm, leaving Tomas moaning on the staircase, and ran until we came to the upper corridors. She wrenched open an arched door tucked in an alcove and dragged us inside. It was a small sitting room with only enough room for a single chair, a narrow lancet window, a shelf of parchment and old books, and a bench against the other wall.

Lyra slammed the door at our backs and slumped against it.

There was little room, but I paced, anger and bloodlust hot in my veins.

"Roark." Her breathless sob slowed my pace.

A tear fell onto her cheek. With hesitation, I reached out to wipe it away. She didn't pull back, didn't whimper under my touch.

Lyra took my palm and held it to her face, and whispered, "I don't . . . I don't know what came over me. I-I-I wanted to . . ." She studied her hands, still splotchy with Tomas's blood.

I spoke with one hand against the warmth of her face. *He deserves his crushed skull piked on the wall.*

Lyra covered one of my hands with hers, leaving the other free to speak. Her chin quivered. "I've heard melders become monsters."

I have seen my share of monsters, and you are not one.

Another tear, another swipe of my thumb.

"You wanted to kill him. You could lose everything for doing something like that. Don't you dare think to risk your life for my stupidity."

Your stupidity is endearing.

Lyra frowned.

I drifted closer. The swell of her breasts brushed against my chest. I tightened my body against hers, caging her to the wall, and moved my hands in sharp, angry gestures. *He should never have put a hand on you.*

"And you should not put yourself at risk." Heat flooded the bridges of her cheeks. "Do you go around ending everyone who looks at Emi improperly? Or anyone who speaks poorly of Thane?"

I slammed a palm against the wall. Lyra stopped speaking, but looked at me with a touch of defiance.

"Do you?"

I tipped my head, drawing my nose along her cheek. She drew

in a sharp breath. I mouthed the word *no* against her skin, shaking my head and watching the heat of the word lift gooseflesh over her neck and cheeks.

One of Lyra's hands skirted up my waist, her fingers curling into my side, holding me closer. "Then why do it for me?"

I lifted one hand, making certain she would see. *Thane and Emi have not infected my soul like you.*

Lyra's lips parted, as though she might respond, I did not give her the chance before I kissed her. Hard.

For a moment, she was stiff with surprise, but in the next breath Lyra dug her fingertips deeper into my waist, slamming my body to hers.

Those sweet lips parted and my tongue slipped through her teeth, meeting hers in a frenzy of need and lust.

There was no easing into the kiss, nothing gentle. I demanded her mouth and took it. She tasted like rain in the forest, fresh and wild. This, I shouldn't want it. Her taste, her body, her skin, I should not be such a weak thing and crave it, but a spark in the blood settled in my chest. Heat that drew me closer, keeping me ensnared by her touch.

It was a feeling like coming home, like I'd been here before.

A craving took hold deep inside, a bit of madness unraveled at the edges, and left me needing more of her softness, her kiss, her touch. More of her.

I wasn't alone.

Unease faded from her features into something darker, almost feral. One hand held my waist, keeping my hips aligned with hers, and the other dug into my hair, tugging at the roots. She arched against me and a soft moan glided from her throat.

One kiss slid to the next, rough, desperate. All teeth and desire. I tasted her jaw, her throat.

"Roark." My name spoken in such a cry of want snapped something inside, something greedy. Something dangerous.

One palm flattened next to her head, the other dragged along the length of her thigh, up the divots of her ribs, to the underside of her breast.

I paused and Lyra cracked one eye. She took hold of my wrist, a beautiful bloom of pink flushed her skin. The silver scars flashed with heat when she guided my hand over her breast.

A groan escaped my chest. I crashed my mouth back on her, working the shape of her, rubbing my thumb over the peak of her nipple under her bodice.

Lyra reached between us and palmed the bulge in my trousers. Blood abandoned my head. Couldn't be helped. With every touch, this woman had my body raging for more, like a boy who couldn't control his own damn cock.

She would be wise to turn from me, and I'd be wise to let her. But I was a selfish bastard and could hardly stomach the thought of anything but Lyra's body wrapped around mine, the slap of our skin, her eyes looking at me like I was more than the Death Bringer of the kingdom. Like I was more than a silent Stav who was only here because a boy prince had taken pity on the enemy at the gates.

I tugged at the neckline of her gown, desperate for a taste of her skin, but went still when voices rose from beyond our hidden sanctuary.

"Sentry Ashwood! Melder Bien."

Thane's voice followed. "Keep looking. Find them."

The prince's voice was next to the door. My chest tightened. Thane would lead the guards away, but he had to know exactly where I was. He'd never used the bone shard from my fingertip, but it gave the prince the ability to sense my whereabouts.

He knew I was tucked away like a coward.

If he knew that, he would suspect the fallen Myrdan noble had something to do with me.

Lyra's breaths were hot against my lips, but the poisonous fear filled her gaze again. I dragged my fingertips across the line of her lower lip, pressed a soft kiss there, then stepped back.

I will say this was my doing.

She clutched my tunic. "Don't you dare. You did not want his hands on me, I do not want their hands on you."

Wicked, beautiful woman. I pressed a kiss to her palm. *Thane will know.*

I stepped for the door, and Lyra tried to protest, but stopped when I unlocked the latch. As expected, Thane leaned against the wall, picking his fingernails with a small knife, a look of annoyance in his eyes.

"Normally this disheveled state of you might bring me joy." Thane used the knife to point at a moaning Tomas. "Alas, tonight feels a little different. Care to explain, my friend?"

LYRA

THANE'S MOUTH PARTED IN SURPRISE WHEN I EMERGED from the small chamber behind Roark. My skin was still flushed from the passion of his kiss, and doubtless my hair was unkempt and wild.

I knew enough about the prince to know he would've laughed any other night. Tonight, he shoved a palm against Roark's chest, eyes dark with frustration.

"How do you expect me to protect you when you pull shit moves like this? Tomas is an ass, but he's a noble ass, and you broke his damn jaw. You know Hundur despises Dravenmoor because of his brother-in-law."

"What happened to his brother-in-law?" I asked, voice soft. Gods, how could it get worse? If Roark was implicated here and the Myrdan king already had a vendetta . . .

Thane flicked his gaze to me, frowning. "The late Draven king was once challenged by the queen's brother for a rumor that his younger sister was kidnapped by a Draven nobleman. Let's just say there was one less Myrdan soon enough. Hundur has claimed it as murder for seasons."

I looked to Roark, who'd gone stoic and stern, all Sentry while the prince spoke.

Thane looked away again, glaring at his guard. "Hundur will see this as another aggressive act by a Draven. What if he takes Yrsa away? You know what her life is like in Myrda."

Roark glanced at Tomas, still moaning on the steps, hands over his face. From the sneer on the Sentry's face, I wasn't certain Roark felt much guilt for what happened here.

Still, I refused to watch him take the blame on my behalf.

"It wasn't him." The admission was soft, but steady.

Without a pause, Roark waved his hand, signaling the prince to look at him, not me. *He is fortunate my blade is not in his heart.*

Thane folded his arms over his chest. "What did you mean, Ly?"

"He's not broken." I intentionally turned away from Roark's glare. He wanted to take my actions as his, but one kiss and I could not stomach the thought of never having another one. "Ser Tomas is melded."

Thane's brows lifted. "You sealed his mouth?"

Again, Roark intervened, stepping between me and Thane. *He attacked her. Hurt her. Had her against the wall.*

Thane peered at me. "That true?"

What was the point of hiding the truth? I rested a hand on Roark's arm, a silent plea to keep steady, and straightened my shoulders to the prince. "Tomas seemed to believe I was his simply because of his station in the Myrdan court. He said if he assaulted me, put a child in me, the kings would see me as ruined and give me to him as a wife."

A wash of rage twisted Thane's face. Kind and personable, but harm someone he loved, and Thane could reveal the dark edges of his soul with ease. "Did he, now?"

"Roark had the opportunity to kill him," I went on, "but he didn't. He insisted on trying to take the fall for me"—I turned to the Sentry with a narrow look—"but I was the one who did this."

The prince said nothing for a dozen heartbeats. Then Thane descended the few steps to Tomas's side and nudged the bastard in the ribs with the toe of his boot, and crouched, elbows on his knees, waiting for Tomas to crack his eyes open.

"You won't be able to eat," he said, voice rough. "Nor drink. What a horrid way to die. I suppose you should have kept your hands off her."

Tomas moaned, eyes imploring the prince for aid.

"Yrsa told me about you, the things you say to her. It is unfortunate your family has such prestige and my father will crave diplomacy. But hear me." Thane gripped a tuft of Tomas's hair. "If you are healed, if you can speak again, you say nothing against the melder or the Sentry.

"Refuse and I will see to it a bone crafter snaps each bone in your body, then Lyra will be given the chance to repeat what she has done today. I will leave you on the Night Ledges, where the crows or Unfettered Folk will decide your fate."

Thane kicked his boot into Tomas's ribs, revealing a brutality in the prince I'd not seen. Then again, as Gammal told me, one never truly knows another until they see the darkness inside. Then we made the choice to love all their jagged, broken edges or not.

I spared a look at Roark. What darkness lived within the Sentry? It was there, I could feel it—dangerous and beautiful. I'd shown him a sharper piece of my desires tonight, admitted I wanted to slaughter Tomas Grisen.

Roark had not turned from me, even did the opposite by pulling me in and unlocking a new, greedy temptation with his wicked mouth and powerful hands.

Should he ever give up his darker edges, I hoped I would do the same.

"Roark, take Lyra to her chambers," Thane said. "I will see to this, but expect both kings to have words about it all."

Blood drained from my face. I jolted when Roark took hold of my hand, gently guiding me up the staircase.

Outside my chamber door, two Stav Guard were positioned for the night.

I bit down a laugh when Roark nearly snarled at the two men until their spines stiffened like rods of iron. If I had to guess, the Sentry was, all at once, regretting his choice to have more bodies near us tonight.

Roark slammed the door behind us. I stepped away, my back toward him, my arms around my middle. "Your men might tell the king if you . . . if you don't leave my chamber tonight."

Gods, did I want him to stay with me?

Yes. I wanted more, and feared what such a desire could bring. Damir would never condone it. Truth be told, if ever I wanted a lover, I had few doubts the king would take me for himself all to keep me close.

The way Damir coveted his melders, it was clear he did not want their attentions distracted by anyone else.

Roark's slow steps came up behind me. His chest brushed against my back until he gently turned me into him and lifted my palm to his lips, kissing me there.

Too soon, Roark stepped away. Perhaps I ought to have feared such a brazen shift in my thoughts about the man I wanted to despise, but I was drawn to him—a moth trapped in fire-golden eyes.

Without hesitation, I cupped the back of his neck and slammed his mouth down to mine.

I kissed him, deeper and deeper, until sweetness faded to frenzy. Roark's fingers dug into my hip bones, my back struck the wall. His tongue, his heat, his need pressed against me and I was lost to it.

I raked my fingers in his hair, tousling the dark strands. His teeth scraped along my bottom lip when he pulled back. For long, breathless moments Roark pressed his brow to mine, holding me close.

I lifted my chin when his fingers touched my cheek in his gentle words. *I will keep watch on the corridor.*

"You already have two men at my door."

They are not me.

My lips curved into a sly sort of smirk. "A little possessive, don't you think, Sentry?"

Roark's hand gripped around my chin, then lowered to my neck, his thumb running along the smooth slope of my throat. *More than a little.* He pulled one of his palms back enough to say, *I should go.*

I allowed my palms to slide down his firm chest. "Don't do anything foolish like turn yourself over to the Myrdan guard all to be some hero to honor my tarnished name."

I'm no hero.

"Probably best. I never favored the hero in sagas." I gnawed on my thumbnail while Roark straightened his tunic and smoothed his finger-raked hair. At the open door, I dipped my chin. "Good night, Sentry Ashwood."

Alone in my chamber, I fell into bed, only to drop into a fitful sleep. Screams, smoke, terror filled the night.

"Go, elskan! Run, keep your eyes down." The woman's voice carved through me like sharp glass. My mother. I could smell her—bread and honey and lavender soap—and she was screaming for me to run.

Dreams were timeless. Where the smoke and clang of steel swords had been, now there was only darkness, the chill of the night, and a sharp taste of brine from the sea.

My head rocked back and forth. Two sturdy ropes held me—no, arms. I was in arms.

"Stop fidgeting, godsdammit."

His voice was older, sharper, and lined in fear.

When he came to a pause, breathless and frantic, I let my head loll to the side. My heart shot to my throat. We weren't alone. There was someone else nearby, someone clad in black but for two brilliant eyes the color of a golden sun.

ROARK

S HE'S MINE." AN EMBARRASSING STING OF TEARS BURNED behind my eyes. "I felt it. They can't take her."

At long last, he lowered his sword—crafted from the black iron of the ravines, a royal blade—and knelt in front of me. "You know what you're asking?"

I nodded. "I'm dead if they catch me."

"And that can't happen." He blew out a long breath. "If you're certain, I'll help you."

My heart raced like I'd been running for days. "You will?"

"I don't take such bonds lightly, but this doesn't mean you can keep her." His eyes were deep blue, like the tides near the coves. That was why he was a prince; he looked like Dravenmoor. "They'll *never* let you keep her, but we can keep her breathing. That's what it means to claim another soul, you understand? Sometimes you must give them up if it's what's best."

But I wanted to keep the silver-eyed girl. She burned through me like wildfire at the first touch, the first laugh when I slurped back her spoon of water.

It was exactly how Father described Mother once.

"We do this my way or we don't do it," the prince said again, shaking my shoulder slightly.

My chin dropped. I was not going to let him see my lip quiver. Wouldn't be right, and he wouldn't trust me to stand as his blade ever again if I was some weepy sod.

"I swear it," I muttered.

"Good." The prince stood again. "Then let's take your little melder before we both lose our damn heads."

I STARED AT THE CEILING. THE DREAMS WOULDN'T STOP. THE closer I stepped into Lyra Bien, the more she haunted my nights.

I didn't even know if they were real, but something *felt* real about each dream.

It would be better for us both if I walked away, ignored her as before. I owed a debt that could not be paid, but like in the dream, one glance at her and the roar of something fierce, something dangerous awakened inside me.

Now I'd had a taste and unlocked a deeper need to have more. No doubt, if I gave in, Lyra Bien would consume me—heart and soul.

"Roark."

One hand shot to the pommel of my sword where it leaned against my bed, only easing back when Emi emerged from the shadowed corner of my doorway. She was in a nightdress, hair free over her shoulders, looking well-bedded and flushed.

Still able to stand? It's been some time, cousin.

She shot me a glare. "I heard what happened."

I looked away. *Tomas deserved everything he was dealt.*

"I've no doubt he did," Emi agreed. "Yrsa is speaking for Lyra. She's made a convincing argument about Tomas's character, but her words are the only thing keeping Hundur tame for now. The two kings have argued the whole of the evening, and I fear Damir may concede to some punishment to keep the peace."

I made a note to thank the princess the next time we met, then made another vow that if the Myrdan king claimed his punishment from Lyra, he would be found without a head come dawn.

"Hundur is furious and demanding Lyra be turned over to Myrda," Emi said.

Heat gathered under my collar. *He touches her and Myrda will be without a king.*

"I was worried you would say that." Emi's shoulders slouched. She sat on the corner of my bed. "Something has changed, Roark. Tell me."

My jaw tightened. I turned away and unsheathed my blade, working on the buckle of my belt. When I tossed the weapon aside, I faced my cousin. *Nothing has changed.*

Emi scoffed. "Really? Because I thought your duty regarding the melder looked vastly different than what it seems like right now. Not that I'm complaining."

My cousin was no fool, and I was a piss-poor liar when it came to Emi Nightlark. I looked down at my palms and gestured slowly. *I am recalling more.*

Her eyes widened. "Really? Do we know the truth?"

I shook my head. *Truths have been altered, but I don't think this is the first time I have met Lyra.*

Emi shot to her feet. "I knew it. The gods pointed you to her. Of course it would change your motivation, how could it not? If you've met before, then this has happened before, the draw to her. That's why he helped get her free of the bloodshed."

What are you talking about?

"Don't play the fool. I know you've felt something. I saw it in Skalfirth. Gods, *I felt it.*"

What?

"The connection. A sjeleven bond."

I waved her away, annoyed, but her words dug into the marrow of my bones. Tales of sjeleven—bonded souls—were spoken at marital vows. A sentimental notion that was nothing but dribble to add sweetness to a union.

Still, with the flashes of a past breaking through the shadows, perhaps there was more truth to the myth than I wanted to admit. From the first sight of Lyra, it was as though a dormant piece of my soul awakened and broke through the powers keeping it buried, only to live again near her.

"Roark, you were pulled to Lyra in House Jakobson. Nothing could break your attention away. You even took my longship to keep watch—"

I waved my hand to interrupt, but Emi silenced me with a look.

"You opened your words to her, something you rarely do. You leap into the battles at the gates like it is a personal attack on *your* home. So, I'll ask again. What are you doing, and how?"

I am doing my duty. I replied briskly. *As always.*

"But you're not." Emi squared her shoulders. "You seem . . . freer."

I hesitated, but nodded. *I suppose something has changed.*

"It won't go unnoticed, Roark. That is what has me concerned— you creating enemies on both sides of a wall. With your heritage, the line you must walk is narrow."

The same can be said of you.

"I hear a few insults about Dravenmoor." Emi popped one shoulder in a shrug. "Hardly anything worthy of distress. You hold more power, more responsibility, and have more to lose. What do you plan to do with Lyra?"

I closed my eyes for a long pause. Emi would keep my confidence. Never had she broken my trust, and she never would. I was not certain I could even summon a lie.

I would do anything to protect her and keep her from the soul bones.

Emi rested a hand on my shoulder. "Can you give her that loyalty?"

Every day is easier.

My cousin sighed, worry written in the furrow between her brows. "Then perhaps you should tell her, let her know the risks. The truth."

I need more time.

"If you feel as you do, be wary, cousin. Others will want the Sentry free of his distractions. I would not wait long."

With a final squeeze to my palm, Emi retreated into the darkness of the corridor, leaving me alone with my tormented thoughts.

Lyra already feared her craft. To tell her the fate awaiting her, without a means to free her from it, would be cruel. I wasn't certain that was the only truth Emi meant, but it was the one that mattered most.

The more Lyra used her magic for the greedy purposes of kings, the more they devoured the goodness of her own soul.

LYRA

THERE WAS A GREAT DEAL WRONG WITH ME. REMORSE AND heaps of guilt should've plagued my thoughts, but my mind could not keep focused on Tomas Grisen. Instead, whenever the panic rose, I drifted to warm hands on my skin, lips against mine, the hardness of his body.

One finger absently twirled a lock of my hair while I sipped a bit of rose tea. Across the morning meal, Edvin taunted Kael over his drunken, reckless desire last night to confront Baldur's disrespect of his half sister during the revel.

Astra was young and likely hoped to find a warrior lover during her visit to Stonegate.

I chuckled through the exaggerated tale and took another drink. Baldur the Fox likely didn't even understand how to kiss a woman. No mistake, he would not understand the delicate balance of softness and passion, how to torment a body with only his hands, no words spoken.

I was not convinced Astra would ever find such qualities in a man, for they were owned by Roark Ashwood.

The hint of a grin played over my lips. I slipped back into the clean scent of his skin, the scrape of the stubble on his chin.

Until the peace was shattered by a missive delivered by a palace steward when he took away our plates.

"What's that, Ly?" Kael tossed the belt holding his seax over one shoulder.

I read the missive under the table. It was a summons from the king to join him in his wing once all the other guests took their noon meals amid the games and entertainment in the courtyards.

My heart fell to my feet. I blew out a long breath and forced a smile. "Nothing. I merely need to perform for the Myrdans while you lot get to enjoy besting the Stav in ax throwing. Kael, if you do not win, I'll never speak to you again."

He scoffed. "I was practically born with an ax in hand."

Edvin chuckled and clapped a hand on Kael's shoulder, challenging him to a friendly competition before the actual games began. I feigned a grin, tickled one of Edvin's daughters beneath the chin, and slipped his middle girl an extra sweet bun beneath the table.

I was well practiced in burying my disquiet behind false grins and laughter.

If I did not, those I loved would see the cracks in the facade; they'd see the fear I carried that day after day, the deeper I was rooted here in Stonegate, the sooner the king would discover I was not his ally.

Now I feared what I stood to lose if Roark discovered the same.

A BULKY STAV GUARD ESCORTED ME TO THE KING'S WING OF the palace. From open windows, laughter and chatter filtered through the somber corridor.

The guard had a rounded chest and protrusions on his skull that appeared almost horn-like. Soul bones. He was a melded Berserkir, but there was an emptiness about him I hadn't seen in the younger guards I'd first melded.

The paleness of his eyes was cold and distant, and his mouth seemed permanently set in a stern frown.

He did not bid me farewell when the door to the first sitting room was opened, did not address me in the least. In truth, he seemed wholly aggravated with the air I breathed, and every time his gaze looked my way, his grip tightened around the hilt of his sword until his knuckles turned white.

Glad to be rid of him, I hurried into the open room.

There, the queen, King Damir, Prince Thane, Princess Yrsa, and her parents were all standing near the open hearth. Another man, dressed in a rich emerald tunic, with silver hair shorn close to his scalp, glared at me down the hook of his nose.

My stomach twisted at the sight of Tomas. Nursed by a few palace healers with numbing pastes and oils to soothe tooth-aches, he moaned more furiously than he had last night.

No doubt, he made the whole of his agony worse than it seemed.

Fingertips brushed across the curve of my back. I startled, then nearly crumpled in a fit of relief. Like a phantom, Roark stepped from the far edge of the room—a position I hadn't seen— and stood at my side.

I wanted to take his hand, squeeze the rough skin of his palm until his fingertips went numb.

"Melder Bien." Damir's words were as cold as a north wind. "King Hundur, along with myself, would delight in hearing your reasons for attacking not only a guest of Stonegate, but a nobleman of Myrda."

"Choose your words carefully, woman," Hundur grumbled. "They very well could seal your fate."

Roark stiffened. His hand went to my back, a touch of possessiveness and protection in one motion.

"Sire, I did not attack Ser Grisen. He spoke threateningly to me, insisting he would . . . force himself upon me, so you would give me to him as a wife."

King Damir's eyes flashed.

"A story, no doubt." Hundur grunted. "One carefully crafted when a man cannot even speak for himself."

Roark stepped nearer to the dais, hands speaking in direct, harsh swipes. He did not need to make a sound. I could sense his rage in every gesture.

"The Sentry was there, King Hundur," Prince Thane translated. "He saw your seneschal's son with his hands on the melder." The prince paused, watching Roark. "She made her refusals clear, and he ignored them. He planned to harm her."

King Hundur's glare fastened on Roark. "We cannot know if they both are lying. Your so-called Draven thrall—"

"I would watch how you speak, Hundur," Prince Thane cut back. "Of those whom I am loyal to in this room, Roark Ashwood nears the top. But your resistance to harken to your own daughter's words, a melder, and a respected warrior of Stonegate have me curious as to why. Embarrassment that it was Myrda who stirred trouble? Is this retribution for the loss of your seneschal during the raids? What is it?"

King Hundur's wide face deepened to a fierce shade of red, as though he held his breath far too long. "I seek the truth. Nothing more."

"It would seem you have it." King Damir drummed his fingers over the arm of his throne. "What would you have me do, Hundur? She is the only melder we have. Would you have me maim her, make her hideous so men do not wish to touch her?"

My heart dropped. Roark took a step back to me, steady as a predator. A fleeting thought left me curious if the Sentry might stand against his own king for this.

The notion of it stirred something inside, something darker. More and more, his actions in this room gave up that Roark would be willing to draw a blade for me.

More and more, I was convinced I might want to do the same.

"I propose a compromise, so we might get back to celebrating." Damir clapped his hands together. "My melder will heal Ser Grisen. Fadey could unravel his craft at times. I'm certain Lyra will manage much the same."

A harsh sound crackled from Roark's chest, but I was not certain King Damir heard. There was darkness in the way the Sentry tracked the king. Heat pooled low in my stomach, and I had to curl my hands into fists to keep from reaching out to touch him.

This was madness. One heated moment, and I was allowing this man to consume me.

"In return," the king went on, "I propose a gift for King Hundur, a show of good faith."

The Myrdan king huffed. "What sort of gift?"

"You've always desired your own melding, my friend." Damir's mouth quirked on one side. "Whatever you desire, the melder will put in place."

There was no choice given to me.

I did not want to meld. I did not care for the sly gleam in King

Damir's eyes. This was nothing more than another excuse to search for whatever power he desired in the mirrored world.

The king was cunning. With little hesitation, Hundur's mouth split into a wide grin. He flexed his fingers, once, twice, then dipped his chin. "Agreed."

A Stav took hold of my arm, only loosening his grip when he caught sight of Roark's murderous glare, and guided me toward Tomas.

He scrambled to get free of me. I bared my teeth and leaned close, my words meant for him alone. "I'm to do this by the king's command. I've never done it. For your sake, I hope it goes well."

The fear in Tomas's gaze brought a twisted bit of satisfaction. Perhaps I was a monster. I fell into his whimpers, his protests, and trapped his face between my palms.

A sick glide of molten bone shifted under my palms. Tomas cried his pain, still muffled behind his melded teeth.

Queen Ingir gasped when bone cracked. A new cleft formed, splitting Tomas's mouth. He drew in a sharp gasp of air. More teeth were cracked and jagged from breaking apart, but the opening was wide enough he could drink and slip small bits of food inside.

The room spun and I pulled away my palms. Golden threads only I could see frayed and split, freeing the melded parts of his jaw. I swallowed bile when Tomas spit out the mangled piece of his fingertip onto the floor. At my back, I caught sight of Thane leaning into Roark.

The prince's voice was low, as though he wanted only his Sentry to hear, but I caught the soft words. "I know the symbolism of the swallowed finger, Roark. That is a damn Draven punishment to those who harm a woman already claimed by another. Take heart no one else cares to study their rituals or you would be blamed entirely."

By the gods. Roark punished Tomas in a way folk of his clan harmed those who hurt their lovers? I shook my head and split more of Tomas's teeth.

It was not so taxing as I let on—forced breaths that heaved my chest, false dabs at my brow for sweat that was not there—when I faced the king. "My lord, I've done all I can do."

"No." Tomas's words were muffled, slurred. A bit of spittle slid from the corner of his mouth. "I can . . . cannot speak as I . . . did."

I raised trembling palms and swayed on my feet. "If King Hundur is to receive your reward, I cannot do more. I fear I might . . . stumble."

I leaned forward. Arms surrounded me. Roark lifted me, holding me against his chest, with the slightest gleam in his eye. He knew the truth and played along in a new role, morbid concern furrowed on his brow.

Gods, the man was convincing, even Ingir murmured to the guards to fetch herbs for a spinning head.

It was cruel, a little vicious, but I refused to undo every stitch of melded bone on Tomas. He was a wretch and he would survive with a jaw that did not extend fully.

"Your decision, my friend." Damir grinned at his fellow king, dark delight in his eyes, like this was all a game.

Hundur hesitated. "I suppose he looks fine enough, doesn't he?"

Tomas began to protest, but his king waved him away, instructing his servants to see to it the man was kept comfortable through the rest of the festivities.

"Now." Damir rose, one arm opened to a Stav holding a black box lined in velvet. "Select your pieces."

LYRA

SILKEN DARKNESS WHIPPED AROUND ME. THE PHANTOM OF Skul Drek was a silent observer as I melded jagged bones to the Myrdan king's knuckles.

The tether between us was stronger, but the first rope that led off somewhere deep in the shadows of the mirror land had shredded into something brittle and weak.

Skul Drek said nothing as I worked.

Hundur was vicious and he wanted it to be known. Seen as a threat. Instead of hidden soul bones, he insisted they be cracked into shards with points. A bone crafter was summoned, and he made quick work of shaping the soul bone piece into ten curved claws to be melded on his top knuckles.

I glanced at the assassin. There was no time to be demure. "Why does Damir want the Wanderer?"

Skul Drek shifted and his cold voice breathed against my ear. "Why tell you when you serve a Thief King?"

I had already inferred Damir was the Thief King. Truth be

told, I found the title fitting. "I only find the bones for the king to strengthen his army."

"Making him powerful."

"That isn't what I want." Ribbons of darkness caressed my cheeks like cold fingers. "You seek to kill us on the other side of the mirror whenever I meld bones. What if I helped you, so you could leave us be?"

"You take a soul from its rest, I take one to replace it." Skul Drek's thin lips curled.

"You could stop."

His sneer faded. "Not all is as it seems."

"I'm sure it isn't, but I do not want to be a pawn. Help me and no more souls will be taken from their rest."

"Tell me why, Melder."

I took a cautious step closer. "I think you might want to. I think . . . you don't want to kill me. Do you?"

Skul Drek said nothing, but turned away, looking off into the darkness where his battered, splitting rope faded.

"Our desires align," I said. "We could help each other. The king finding the Wanderer's bones frightens you. Why? What would happen?"

Hot, crimson eyes locked with mine. Teeth clicked. A low rumble of a growl rattled from somewhere in his cloak of shadows. "The power of all. A new Wanderer, a lord over the lands. All the gods' power would once more belong to one. A soul to corrupt, a soul to enslave, a soul to rule all."

"Because soul bones from the Wanderer would have every vein of craft. Is that why? He was the last to have all three. Only melding had to be shown to him, a craft used for greed."

Skul Drek hummed his agreement.

I faced another hooked claw, watching my fingers meld the

golden hook to the gleam of Hundur's form. "I don't want Damir to have all the power. I want to be free. Perhaps you do, too, from whatever curse keeps you killing for the sake of soul bones."

Half of Skul Drek's face was hidden in darkness, like a mask of night, but his eyes flashed like he might've grinned. "You brighten the night, Melder." A coil of shadows flicked the golden band between our hearts.

He spoke in riddles, but there was meaning underneath it all. I simply needed to discover it.

Another step closer. I could breathe in the salt and chill of his skin beneath the darkness. "I want to help. I don't want any more deaths. *I* don't want to die."

Copper red deepened in his eyes. A coil of darkness wrapped around my throat, not enough to choke off air, but enough I could not move. I wasn't certain I wanted to.

"Once you know, you cannot unknow. I speak the truth to you, then you cannot betray it." His shadowed mouth brushed across my ear. I held my breath. "Or I will find you; I will end you. I will not be able to stop."

"I want to know."

Without a word, Skul Drek stepped back and sat atop a heap of darkness that could've been a mirrored chair or windowsill.

"The first king lies in places unseen."

"Places?"

"Four." Skul Drek spoke clearer, firmer. As though I were speaking to a simple man and not some spectral of a killer. "Four pieces to make the bearer the gods' ruler of their craft. The arm, to swing the sword as the first king. The ribs, to wear his armor. The breast, to have his warrior's heart. And the skull, to claim his wisdom."

I pressed a hand to my stomach, ignoring the final two fingers of Hundur, and knelt in front of Skul Drek. "Are the *bones* of the Wanderer all here in Stonegate?"

Skul Drek clicked his tongue twice. "I do not know, but . . . some have felt close."

Close could mean the damn fjord beyond the wall, for all I knew. "This is why your ravagers hunt the Stav. To slaughter them before anyone can stumble onto the Wanderer's bones."

"And to leave fewer warriors for the Thief King."

"What if you're wrong?" I said. "What if the Jorvan king is hunting only for soul bones to build his army? He rarely keeps them for himself. You might be slaughtering people for nothing."

"So sure?"

I added another bone to the glow of Hundur's hands. "No, I'm not sure, and that is the reason I'm asking you."

"Should the Thief King find the power he seeks, those he has bound to new souls will bend the knee to their first king."

"I don't understand."

Skul Drek hissed like I'd angered him. "The Wanderer's soul commands all craft and it will bow to him. Soul bones are crafted, are they not? Manipulated and filled with a melder's touch." Skul Drek's eyes turned a poisonous sort of red. "No crafted soul will be free of their king and all will bend the knee to the new Wanderer."

Shit. King Damir was not simply crafting Berserkirs.

He was crafting an indestructible empire where no one could stand against him.

"I want to find the bones." I lifted my gaze to Skul Drek. "I want to find them, so he never does."

He cocked his head. "To hunt the bones you must take them. You will be hunted in turn."

"Then stop." My voice came sharp and edged in ice. "You are

the one hunting and attacking us. Stop doing so and give me time to help."

Mists billowed, hiding his eyes for a breath, then Skul Drek stood a pace away. "Not all is as it seems."

Gods, I didn't know how to do this. To find the bones, I needed to be connected to the dark mirror land. I needed to meld. Should I meld, Skul Drek seemed content to continue attacking as penance.

"Time grows short." The assassin took a step away. A skein of darkness flicked the strange tether between us again. "I may find ways to stay my sword. Will you keep your word?"

I didn't hesitate. "Yes."

His cold grin sliced through the shadows. "I suppose we shall see."

The final threads tugged the hooked claw onto Hundur's knuckles and, as though a rope fastened around my middle, I was pulled away.

I TOOK ANOTHER SIP OF THE PUNGENT TEA. IT TASTED A GREAT deal like sap and tree bark, but it softened the furrow of Roark's brow and he eased back on the bench. If not for the Sentry insisting I'd exhausted myself from the use of my craft, I was certain Damir would've forced me to parade around the luncheons and game yard.

Hundur needed to reveal his new horrid claws, after all.

I was becoming a reminder that the Jorvan king had a weapon.

A weapon the Death Bringer saw as weak enough he forced fetid herbs down her throat, like a tonic on a deathbed.

"I'm fine, Roark," I said, forcing a weak grin when he tapped the edge of the table again, a signal I needed to drink more.

You were entranced too long.

Entranced. It was a good way to put it. Emi always described my eyes as a glassy lake. Glazed over with a sheen they could not break through. Not until I was thrust out.

I winced through another sip. Part of me yearned to tell Roark the truth, of the conversation I'd had with a phantom of Skul Drek. Some sort of dark spell craft was at play.

It meant the phantom knew exactly where I was in both the mirror and the waking world.

But his threat of giving up what I knew would not leave me. Doubtless Skul Drek would make good on his threat to find me, to end me, should I betray him. Of course, he might betray me first because he was a killer at heart.

He might be using me to find the Wanderer for himself.

I returned the tin cup to the table, one half of my mouth twisted in a grin. Roark's eyes heated, watching me as I drifted around the table and took a place at his side on the bench.

A muscle jumped in his jaw when my palm dropped to his thigh.

"Worried for me, Sentry?" My whole body was alive with a rush of desire. I was not one to be bold or licentious. Life had trained me well to be demure and unseen. When I realized what I'd done, I slowly drew back my hand.

Roark caught my wrist. His fingers came to my chin and tilted my head so I could meet his dark, golden eyes. He was close enough I could feel the deeper draws of his breath against my hair.

The rough tip of his thumb brushed over my cheek. Roark did not gesture or write a response, merely nodded and hooked an arm around my waist, urging my body closer.

Close enough I leveraged my legs on either side of his hips, straddling him.

My brow pressed against his. Roark dug his fingertips into my hips, lips parted. A dark groan rumbled against my body, and in this moment, whatever he asked of me I would do. I wanted to scream at him to command me, to take the whole of me.

I was overwhelmed, confused. I did not know how to stop the spinning that rotated around a man who should've been revolting, should've been an enemy.

Now I could not get my fill of him.

Roark held my gaze. One palm roved up the side of my waist, his long fingers touching every divot of my ribs. The other hand glided down until he reached the ruffled hem of my skirt gathered around my bent legs.

I hooked my arm around his neck, my fingers playing with the ends of his hair, and I watched as his hands disappeared beneath the folds of my skirt.

Everything slowed. His palm on my bare thigh drifted slower, drifted higher. My blood was molten. I couldn't think.

For a man enrobed in darkness, he touched with a scorching gentility that drew out ragged breaths and embarrassing moans I could not stop if I tried.

Roark gripped my jaw in his palm, drawing my eyes back to him. He released me only long enough to say, *Tell me to stop.*

"We should."

He nodded, but his hand remained under my skirt, his thumb drawing small circles on the sensitive skin of my inner thigh. This would not be accepted. King Damir's prize with the prince's personal guard would be seen as a distraction the king would not allow.

"We should stop." My lips hovered over his. I adjusted my position on his lap, settling my core over his hardness. Roark hissed through his teeth, and his fingers dug into the flesh of my leg. I tilted my head, drawing my lips to his ear, and whispered, "But don't you dare."

A breathy sort of groan was all I was given before Roark kissed me. Where his touch had been gentle, his kiss was desperate. Fingers tangled in my hair, he pulled me closer. I clawed at his shoulders, gripped his tunic in fistfuls, circled his neck to allow me to lose myself in the feeling of his hard body.

His domineering mouth parted my lips and gave me the warmth of his tongue. He tasted like mint and heat. A fierce collision that tilted the ground beneath me.

A shudder of a gasp fell against his mouth when Roark's fingers teased the line of the thin undergarments over my core. His eyes spoke a thousand words, a dark declaration to stop him was there, but underneath was a hope, a plea that I wouldn't.

I clasped a hand around his wrist, guiding his palm to the slick heat of my center.

Roark breathed heavily against my skin, one finger touched me, teased me, then slipped inside me.

I bared my throat, wishing I could bite back the mortifying sounds. His hips bucked gently and the Sentry added a second finger.

I kissed him. The movement of his mouth spun my head in as much delirium as the curl of his wicked fingers. Roark's mouth claimed my jaw, my throat, his teeth scraped over my skin. With his other hand, he tugged the sleeve of my dress off my shoulder and kissed me there.

I held the back of his head against my skin, my body arching into his touch, his tongue, his kiss.

I wanted to unravel him the way he was destroying me.

With one hand, I reached between us, gathering the latches of his trousers, but Roark pulled my hand away and shook his head.

His eyes burned in a molten blaze when he opened his palm over my heart, patting the place three times.

A gentle declaration this moment belonged to me alone.

My neckline slipped low over my chest, barely shielding the peak of one nipple. Roark slid his fingers deeper inside, and his thumb rolled across the sensitive apex between my thighs, in the same moment his mouth found the swell of my breast.

His touch was too much, it stole my restraint, and I bucked my hips with every motion of his hand.

Roark grinned against my skin when I whimpered. Heat coiled taut in my lower belly. My thighs clenched. As though sensing the build, Roark lifted his head, holding the back of my neck, and crashed my mouth against his.

I broke.

Roark kissed me through the wave of my release. His name rolled over my tongue. He held me closer, pulsing his beautifully cruel fingers in and out of me, and in the same breath steadying me through the rush until my pulse slowed again.

One palm brushed over his flushed face. I traced the curve of his lips. He studied me, face unreadable.

What were we doing?

"I want to touch you," I whispered, embarrassment heating my cheeks.

Roark's eyes glistened with dark need. He seemed to consider the words, no doubt weighing the risks and worth of this, then gave me a slow nod.

The way I'd done to him, Roark guided my palm to the front of his trousers where his desire strained against the laces. I stroked him over his trousers for a moment, then reached for his belt. My palms settled on his thighs. "I have never done this, but will you . . . let me taste you?"

Roark's jaw flexed. He took hold of my wrist and flattened my palm so he could speak across my skin. *I do not expect it.*

"I know," I whispered. "I want to."

His eyes heated. A small smirk teased the corner of his mouth. Roark gripped my chin with one hand, drawing my mouth close, but with the other he made certain I understood his every command. *On your knees.*

All gods.

I leveraged off his lap and lowered to my knees between his legs.

My fingertips slipped under the waist of his trousers. Heat swirled in my belly when I brushed over the taut crown of his length. I lifted my chin, taking note of the way Roark's fist clenched when my fingers gently caressed back and forth.

One breath, another, and Roark readjusted on the sofa, helping me tug down his trousers. The ruddy length of his cock sprang free. I swiped my tongue over my lips, uncertain if I was bold enough.

I closed my eyes and sealed my lips around the tip.

A sort of rough cough broke from Roark's chest. His hips bucked on instinct. With another groan, he let his head fall back, his fingers tangled in my hair, holding me in place when I took him in deeper.

I dragged my tongue along the underside of his length until he looked down at me with hooded eyes. Roark's lips were parted; he was panting softly. What he did not speak with words, he said with touch. Every lick, every kiss, Roark would tighten his fingers in my hair, he would stroke his thumb across my cheek, my throat.

When he gently tapped my shoulder three times, then again, emotion knotted in my throat. *Mine.* He kept claiming me—Lyra— not the melder, but me.

And I wanted to claim him. Not the Sentry, not a brutal Draven, but Roark Ashwood.

The taste of his skin and musk pooled heat between my thighs. My tongue curled around the tip of his length. What I could not take in, I covered with my hand, stroking in tandem with my mouth.

One glance at the flush in his face, the way his body rocked with pleasure, and my core throbbed as I watched the desire written on his face. There was a wondrous power that came from knowing I brought those breaths from his lungs, that it was me he touched.

Roark thrust into my mouth deep enough I let out a strangled cough. He stilled, but I shook my head, gripping his thighs, a wordless command for him to never stop.

A moment longer and Roark frantically tapped my face, he tried to pull back.

I didn't stop, not when his breaths were sharp and jagged. Not when he groaned and pressed his fists against his eyes, I wanted all of him and did not stop until his hot release was spent on my tongue.

When it ended, I pulled back, smiling and wiping my lips. Roark let his palms slide down his face, a heat to his skin. He cupped the back of my neck and pulled me over his exposed lap, kissing me, hard and deep.

"I want to—" Words were cut off by voices, laughter, and footsteps outside the door.

We froze for half a breath, then made quick work of untangling from each other. I shot to my feet. Roark refastened his belt and trousers, adjusted his tunic, and helped me with the sleeve of my dress.

He'd taken four swift paces away from me by the time a heavy knock pounded on the door and, without invitation, Kael strode inside.

"Oh, good. You're back." Kael looked between me and Roark, a glimmer of suspicion on his features. "I was going to wait for you. Emi asked me to help keep watch on the princess in the market. She thought you might want to join. If the Sentry agrees, of course."

Roark was all warrior, all somber shadow once more.

"Princess Yrsa . . . wants me?"

Kael clasped his hands behind his back. "Seems most of the women are going to market today to commission gowns for the vow feast."

"We just commissioned gowns not long ago."

"Seems you get a gown for every occasion. I know little else except she thought you might want to join after dealing with that bastard Grisen. Apologies for my harsh words, Sentry Ashwood. But it's true."

"Oh." I swallowed, forcing a smile, praying he could not see the flush to my face. "I, well, if it's all right."

I glanced to Roark, not truly asking his permission, more hoping we might find a way to continue whatever was happening here.

Kael's smiled faded. "Well, it does come from the word of a princess, who you will likely be serving until we all have flesh sagging off our bones. Might be wise to befriend her early on."

I knew the tone in Kael Darkwin's voice. A tone he used often in the past whenever stable hands commented on my features, or if village boys tried to get me alone. Kael was always there with a warning in his eyes and threats at the ready should they be untoward in the slightest.

He was suspicious of us, protective of me, and now wary of a man he'd always respected.

Roark must've heard the same, since he moved for the door.

Myrdan guards and Emi will be with you, I shall give you ladies time to yourselves and go see to the prince.

I wanted to tell him not to go, but in the same breath, feared if he remained, the way I could not cease looking at him would make it quite clear to the entire palace what we'd done here.

With a slight nod at Kael, Roark quit the room.

I bit the inside of my cheek and smoothed my dress. "Let me . . . just get a cloak."

"Right." Kael folded his arms over his chest, watching me disappear into the bedchamber.

When I returned, he was already standing in the open doorway. I forced a smile and pinched the back of his arm for good measure. "Shall we?"

"After you," Kael said once we were in the corridor. "But you might want to let down your hair."

I flipped my braid over my shoulder. "Why?"

Kael lowered his voice. "The Sentry left his bite behind."

LYRA

MYRDAN GUARDS WERE TANGLED WITH STAV ON ALL sides of the inner court procession through the streets of Stonegate.

Much the same as when I'd stepped into town with Emi, hawkers shouted prices, hoping for a royal sale. Margun had orders of custom gowns with lace, silk, and satin ribbons to fund her shop until the next frost.

Kael kept a distance, allowing me to drift along with courtiers who followed Yrsa.

The princess and Emi kept the lead, but soon enough most of the crowd bled into shops of their own interest, and I was shoved back into the hordes. As the melder, I would be expected to commission a fine gown for Thane's vow ceremony, but I found little interest in the bustle today.

In truth, all I wanted to do was find my Draven guard.

Gods, I needed to tread with caution. Both Roark and I knew Damir would never sanction any sort of affection between us. If

Roark were to have a lover, I had few doubts the king would use it strategically. A high-ranking Stav with Draven blood would go to a noble Jorvan woman, a slight to Dravenmoor or a branch of peace.

I knew little of Roark's folk in his homeland, but perhaps he would be a bridge between kingdoms. My heart dropped. If Damir found the Wanderer's bones, none of us would have any choice or power to speak against him.

There was true, dangerous trouble facing the kingdoms, but I was a wretch. My thoughts would not stop wandering to the Sentry.

We'd kissed, we'd touched, but none of it meant Roark would want me for his match. No mistake, the king would never allow it anyway.

My fingers trailed over a wooden table laden in bands made from bone and glittering threads, necklaces of blue pearls and gold, and broaches of all kinds. I selected a curious ring of silver and bronze. Two serpents entangled, jaws spread, like they were readying to devour the other.

"Pretty thing, isn't it." The woman behind the stand grinned, polishing a cloak pin with a thick linen cloth. She nodded at the ring. "The symbol comes from the poem of the nymph and her night and day lovers."

I slid the ring on my center finger and glanced at the woman. "I don't know that tale."

"Ah. 'Tis a tale of a beautiful nymph from the gods' wood. First, she gave her heart to a man who was bold, kind, and good. But one night on her journey home, she came across another man. He was not like the first. He was strong, cunning, and wicked."

The woman winked and placed the polished pin on the table-top and leaned onto her palms. "The nymph's heart was drawn to both. Uncertain what to do, she prayed to the goddess of love. Touched by her plea, the goddess combined the two men as one. And that, they say, is what it means to love a heart—the lightest pieces, and the darkest."

True love. To accept another soul—the good and the bad—and love them through it all.

I slid the ring off my finger and returned it to the table. "I suppose it's what most of us want, right?"

"The legend says this symbol calls to those whose hearts are torn." The woman winked again. "I hope you find what your heart wants soon."

What my heart wanted? I thought it yearned to be free of these walls once. But now I yearned for more of Roark's wicked hands on my skin, more of his sly grin, more of his soft laughter.

My insides cinched. In another breath, I recalled the icy touch of a phantom in the mirror land. The way his nearness quickened my pulse. A cruel soul, yet I didn't pull away. A piece of me, deep within, almost anticipated the sight of him whenever the king used my craft.

Gods, I was a fool. I allowed a man to touch me, so intimately, yet I was betraying everyone by conversing and plotting with a killer.

Heat rushed to my head and turned my stomach. I needed to be free of these crowds.

While Kael was turned, speaking to another Stav standing watch, I slipped around the corner where tall tenements and arched bridges shadowed the streets from the burn of the sun.

I followed a set of narrow steps to one of the lower streets. Noise from the market faded. Only simple conversation and a few voices followed.

There were a few lingering Myrdan guards about, laughing

with one another as though they were waiting for someone. Strange.

I went back the other direction, but stopped at the sound of breathless sighs from inside a small cottage with boarded windows and a roof that leaned to one side. Moans and more feminine sighs followed. One glance over my shoulder to ensure I was alone, and I peeked through a crack in one of the boards over the window.

My breath caught in my chest.

Emi was inside. She wasn't alone. Her slender fingers were threading through the dark waves of Princess Yrsa's hair. She claimed Yrsa's mouth, kissing the princess like she did not know how to let go.

Yrsa dug into Emi's waist, holding her close, her back to the crooked wall.

I blinked, one hand to my chest. My heart snapped against my ribs, and I feared it might crack in two at any moment.

Prince Thane would be devastated. I did not know how much passion lived between the prince and princess, but I knew enough that Thane genuinely cared for her. He looked forward to their vows fondly.

Anger grew more so toward Emi. She was not only a Stav, but Thane's friend.

I peeled away from the wall, conflicted. Prince Thane was not a brutal man. I was confident he would not punish either of them should I speak of it, but in another breath I wasn't convinced it was my place to speak at all.

From one of the towers of the palace, a bell rattled through the market.

The evening gates would be locked soon, and more feasts

would be had. I gathered my skirt and hurried back to the main square, desperate to forget what I'd seen.

"Lyra." Kael shoved through a few men. "By the gods, where were you?" He dropped his voice. "Were you with him?"

I frowned. "No. And if I were, what do you think you would do about it, Kael Darkwin?"

His jaw worked. "Lyra, this is not a game."

"I know," I snapped. "Please, just . . . I know. He is not a game to me."

"And what is he? You think this will be allowed? You think when Ashwood settles with a wife it will be you? The king has already told Thane he will force Ashwood to take a noble Jorvan woman by the next frosts. Did you know that? I assure you there is no shortage of ambitious fathers who would want their daughter paired to the future king's most trusted warrior. Where does that leave you?"

Mortifying tears burned in my eyes. I didn't know why; nothing Kael said was anything I had not considered myself. The blame fell to what I witnessed with Yrsa and Emi, with the truth that I had allowed myself to feel something more than was wise for the Sentry.

Kael's features softened. He took hold of my hand, holding it between his palms. "Lyra, I'm sorry. That was harsh."

I shook my head. "No. It was true. I'm fine, Kael."

"He"—Kael cleared his throat—"Ashwood didn't force you to do anything, right?"

"No. Gods, no. We didn't even . . ." I hurriedly waved details away. "He knows as well as I we should not cross such lines."

Kael didn't look appeased, but he nodded. "Remember, I am loyal to Jorvandal, but I am more loyal to you. Accomplices?"

I smiled and hooked a hand through his arm. "Always."

IT WASN'T MY PLACE.

I kept repeating the words the entire time I dressed for the feast.

Despite the warnings from Kael, despite knowing within the full seasons I would likely lose Roark to an arranged match, I craved his steadiness now. He was stoic, but there was a sense of calm that soothed my nerves when the Sentry was near.

Likely, he was with the prince.

I remained with his cousin.

Emi had chattered on as she dressed. I offered distant, simple responses, bitterness at her deceit growing the longer we were near each other.

Why did it matter? Loyalty among royals was hardly common. King Damir and Queen Ingir could hardly spare a glance at each other. The king's lovers were openly paraded in the palace, and I had few doubts Ingir took her own.

Thane was different from his mother and father. He saved Roark, even saved Emi. Perhaps that was it. The prince had done so much to be different, to bring peace and safety to others, and this felt a great deal like she'd dug a knife in his spine.

"Are you going to tell me what has you so sour?" Emi heaved a rather theatrical sigh and perched one hip on the edge of the vanity where I finished dabbing a touch of kohl under my lashes.

"I'm not sour."

She puffed out her lips. "I'm not sure you know the meaning of the word, then."

"It's nothing."

"So there is something." She nudged my shoulder and I clenched a fist. "Did something happen in the market? Did someone bother you? Tell me, and—"

"No." I rose and turned my back on her.

"Lyra. What is it? If you've been disrespected again, I will make sure—"

"I saw you!" *Dammit.* I closed my eyes, wishing the words back onto my tongue. I let out a harsh breath. "I saw you, and . . . how could you?"

Emi's face paled. "You mean, you saw me and—"

"The princess. Yes." My blood heated. "He is your friend. He is her friend. How long? How long have you been at this?"

"Lyra." Emi drew closer. "You don't understand."

"I may have lived a sheltered life, but I know what lovers look like, Stav Nightlark."

Emi's shoulders slumped. "Let me explain."

She would not get the chance. A knock sounded on the door and without an invitation to enter, it swung open.

"I figured we are all such boon companions that you will not mind if I see you in whatever state of dress you are in." The prince—as if he knew we were quarreling over him—entered, his back facing us. "But all the same, I will give you time to dress if you prefer. Tell me when you're decent."

At his side Yrsa snickered. "They're dressed. Though both look rather somber."

Roark followed behind them. As anticipated, a silky calm coated the anger lashing through my chest. He met my gaze from across the room. One corner of his lips twitched into a smirk.

Until he saw the state of his cousin.

Thane turned to Emi. "What has you out of sorts, Emi?"

"Nothing," I insisted and took a step for the prince. This was not the sort of thing I wanted to face. Not now.

Prince Thane's smile faded. "What is it?"

I looked away, arms folded over my chest.

"If ever you question whether Lyra will stand on your side, Thane, you need not wonder. She will." Emi mimicked my stance and held my glare. "She feels I've betrayed you greatly."

"What are you doing?" The words hissed through my teeth.

Roark came to my side, one brow lifted in a silent query.

Emi opened her arms. "She saw me and Yrsa, and I'm convinced she's considering stabbing me—"

"I am not."

"I think she might. All to protect your feelings, my prince."

"Ah." The prince faced me in the same moment Roark turned away.

Was he *smiling*?

"I had no plans to say anything. It was not my place. Wait." I tilted my head. "Do you already know?"

"I do know." Thane nodded. "I've known how Yrsa and Emi have felt about each other for seasons."

I looked to Roark. The bastard *was* smiling.

"Lyra." Thane came to me and put both palms on my shoulders. "I told you, Yrsa and I have known we would be wed since infancy. We became friends, but that does not always mean the romantic heart will ever take hold. It did for her and Emi. Who am I to stand in the way of them?"

"Why wed, then?"

Prince Thane scoffed. "If I refused, do you think King Hundur would allow his daughter to be with Emi merely because he learned she prefers women? No. She would be placed with another nobleman of Myrda, forced to bear his children, and be banned from Stonegate."

By the gods, he was protecting her. Marrying her to let her be free.

A gentle touch came to the back of my arm. Roark leaned

close and spoke in soft gestures. *They protect each other. Understand why few can know?*

I nodded, feeling utterly foolish.

"I love Thane," Yrsa said. "But we knew we would never be *in love* with each other. Like he has let me follow my heart, I will always do the same for him."

They could fall in love with others, but never be allowed to truly claim the ones in their hearts. "I'm sorry."

"Don't be." Thane flashed his roguish grin. "We are happy, which is much more than I can say for many arranged marriages. You might have seen some in these very walls that look truly miserable."

Yrsa chuckled and nudged his ribs.

"What about heirs?" It was customary if a royal bride did not bear children within the first three full seasons, her husband would be given a new bride. "She will face the same trouble soon enough."

Thane cleared his throat. "We've spoken of it many times. We will do what we must do."

"Prince Thane is safety to me, Melder Bien," Yrsa said. "He is a friend I will always trust, even if it is with my body."

"I like to think I would make a decent father too."

"You will." Yrsa snickered, but sobered when she looked back at me. "I will be honored to be his wife. I will be honored to watch him fall in love with another as I have. I only hope she will be as understanding to our situation as Emi."

The prince kissed Yrsa's knuckles.

"Now that all this has been cleared, may we get on with the feast?" Emi's face softened.

I glanced to the floor. "Forgive me for assuming."

"Nothing to forgive. It is reassuring to know you care for the prince."

"It is." Prince Thane strode past, Yrsa still linked to his arm, but he patted Roark on the side of the face as he went. "How do you feel knowing I've won her over?"

I'd learned enough of Roark's vulgar gestures to know he leveled no less than three at the prince.

Thane simply laughed and escorted both Emi and Yrsa from the room.

I looked at the Sentry. "Next time your cousin is a princess's lover, tell me."

Roark took my hand and squeezed it twice. *I did not think you would be so nosy to deem it necessary.*

"I am not nosy. I happened to stumble upon them and have been torn over what to do all afternoon, I'll have you know."

A short gasp broke free when Roark had my back to the wall in the next breath. The others had rounded the corner, but alone in the corridor, the Sentry made a hard cage over me.

His fingers traced the line of my jaw before forming his words. *I could help with the distress.*

I'd be wise to heed Kael's warnings, be wise not to let up my heart so easily. I should've done all that before Roark's damn fingertips traced the neckline of my gown. An ache gathered in my chest and spread lower in my belly when Roark brushed his palm over the swell of one breast.

"How would you do that?"

Wickedness burned in the gold of his eyes. *On my knees with a kiss.* His palm slid over my hip.

I dug my hands into the wall, feigning indifference. "I've had your kiss. Not certain it would be enough."

Not here. Roark touched my lips with his. His other hand glided down my thigh, toward the inner leg. I jolted when he paused over the apex between my thighs. On instinct, I widened my stance, wanting him to touch me deeper. Roark's fingers brushed over my skirt, adding pressure to my core. My breath caught when I looked down to see him forming a single word.

Here.

Damn the gods. My breaths came too swift, too heavy. His silent words bled into my pores until they pulsed the ache to the lowest part of my belly.

Roark grinned, like he knew exactly how easily he'd found the loose thread, tugged, and unraveled me.

He stepped back, one hand in front of us. *Later, of course. We're needed at the feast.*

The feast. More crowds. More simple chatter. More folk wanting claws like Hundur.

More. More. More.

In this moment, all I wanted more of was the Sentry and his wicked, silent mouth.

ROARK

WHEN THE SUN FADED, MOONLIGHT BROUGHT OUT THE darker pieces of a soul. Chaos and blood always followed a meld. No matter how privately the king kept the melding of soul bones, he still added more Stav to the walls after the craft was used, as though anticipating trouble.

It was no different tonight.

Myrdan guards were the overwhelming presence of blades in the hall. More Stav were in the towers, on foot, and in town. But since Lyra had melded Tomas's jaw, cracked it open again, and added Hundur's claws, there was still no hint of ravagers, no Dark Watch.

Tomas, the bastard, hadn't shown his face, and I doubted we would see much of him until the day of Thane's wedding. Perhaps not even then if we were fortunate. The way he'd looked at Lyra with such disdain, such dark rage, I would not mind if he scurried his pitiful ass back to Myrda like a haunt in the night.

Silence added only more weight to the discomfiting sense that something was out of place in the great hall. Tension gathered in each muscle, from my shoulders to legs, but there were no horns from the watchtowers, no calls from the border walls.

And Lyra was unharmed.

Truth be told, it was one of the few nights I'd seen her laugh with her head tossed back, a few crystal tears in the corners of her eyes. Lyra had joined the great hall, silver scars mottled with dyes. A few whispers had already spread about unfortunate Tomas. Damir did not want any guests beyond the inner chambers of Myrda and his inner guards to recognize Lyra as the melder.

She sat on the right hand of Thane, but Darkwin and their folk from Skalfirth took her other side.

I could watch Lyra laugh all night.

One palm gripped the crescent moon pommel on my blade and I turned the opposite direction. Stonegate might be quiet, but the night wasn't over, and I couldn't soothe the sting of apprehension.

I prowled the walls, keeping sight of the high table with the kings and queens, and more than one look at Lyra. No one spoke to me, no one even seemed to realize I was there.

To be the Sentry meant becoming a man worthy of note in one moment, and an insignificant shadow in the next.

One corner had a huddle of men pounding different sizes of drums. Others plucked at strings or blew over panpipes and lurs.

There was a man standing atop the center table, with hair cropped to his scalp and a beard that was twisted in a tight knot with bone beads clicking as he spoke. The Skald had enraptured half the hall in a new tale of the Wanderer and how he defeated a Jotunn's bear before the creature could devour one of his children.

A tale of how the great Red Ravines were carved into the land from the giant paws of the beast clawing free of the Wanderer's bone snare.

I walked on, hand on my blade, head turned inward, searching, and searching, and searching for a threat, the slightest taste of retaliation for the soul bones.

No one shared my discontent.

Damir was enraptured by a man from Myrda and a woman from one of the lower jarldoms. I expected him to take them both to his chambers soon enough. Ingir was engaged in chatter with the Myrdan queen, and Hundur could not get enough of his new bones.

I made it to the other side of the hall where Baldur stood, nursing a tall drinking horn.

"Ashwood." He took a long drink. "Why so stiff? Double watch has been placed at the walls."

I ignored him and looked to the empty upper eaves.

Baldur snorted and took another drink; the last of his ale drizzled down his chin. "By the gods, man. Go find a damn hole for your cock. Does wonders for tension."

I dodged his hand when he tried to clap my shoulder, like we were true Stav brothers. We weren't. Baldur let out a wet chuckle and staggered off.

Loathe him as I did, I still knew Baldur wasn't entirely wrong. There was little to do in here when the trouble I kept seeking had yet to rear its head. I gave in to the pull.

One step at a time, I made my way over to the bench between Thane and Lyra. With my palm, I shoved at Thane, forcing him to scoot down to a new position as I took his place.

"By all means, Sentry Ashwood, please sit with us." Thane lifted his plate and placed it in front of his new seat.

I ignored him and turned toward Lyra. *Súlka Bien.*

A bit of pink dusted Lyra's cheeks. "Sentry Ashwood. Decided to join us after all your lurking?"

Noticed me, did you? You were the only one.

"I wouldn't be so certain. I saw many gazes of curious ladies following you around the room. What brought you here now?"

"Perhaps he wanted to sit beside you, Ly," Hilda murmured, low enough I didn't think anyone but us heard. Lyra tilted her head, eyes wide, as though silently communicating something hidden to the woman.

I tapped the table, drawing her attention back to my hand. *Perhaps I did.*

Thane leaned in, his mouth too close to my ear, exactly how I hated it. And he knew it. "You can do better than that, you ass. I'm embarrassed for you."

I shoved him back with an elbow to the chest. The prince coughed and laughed, rubbing the ache off his stitched doublet.

The corners of her lips curled. Lyra made quick work of gathering a silver plate and topping it with strips of roasted pheasant, boiled spiced roots, and a pudding made of star plums. When it was positioned in front of me, she handed me a horn and tipped the ewer. "Tell me when to stop, Sentry."

I would never.

Thane groaned. "Gods, I should not have helped you find your words, they're mortifying."

Lyra topped off the drinking horn, then slid close enough our legs brushed. "You say that often, Prince. What do you mean you helped him find words?"

"Has he not told you? I'm appalled. It is one of my grandest achievements."

I shook my head. This was the prince's favorite boast.

"Roark's injury robbed him of his voice, but we started communicating with a few gestures. It inspired pages and pages of signals and words we memorized together those first seasons. We'd add or adjust if we pleased."

"Thane," Yrsa said with a small grin. "You told me you had tomes from the healers on hand speak and you took it from there."

He likes to pretend he invented a new language, I added.

"Begging all of your wretched pardons"—Thane feigned disgust—"those previous writings were mere inspiration to my brilliance. It was meant to be made of secret signals for myself and Roark to cause a great deal of angst in these walls. For the most part, we've succeeded, but you, Lyra Bien, have picked up on it rather quickly. I'm curious how. Most Stav Guard take months and still aren't as fluent as you."

"I've taught myself since coming here, but after a few days, I realized each gesture is almost burned in my memory. I know it sounds impossible, but once I see them, the words are felt more than understood. I simply know them. Doesn't make sense, I know."

"Almost like something wants you to hear him. How fascinating." Emi raised one brow, staring at me over the rim of her horn.

I responded with a frown, and stifled the urge to kick her shin under the table.

"It is interesting," Thane said. "Maybe a unique trait of a melder. But I don't recall Fadey being the same."

Fadey hated me and would rather cut off my hands than listen to them, I insisted.

Thane tilted his drinking horn my way. "Well, you hated Fadey."

"Why did you hate the last melder so much?" Lyra's eyes glistened.

He was a pompous ass.

Talk shifted to other things, like predictions on who would become lovers after tonight, how many times Ingir would complain about Damir's presence at the wedding, and how Lyra wanted the prince to place Jarl Jakobson in the back of the hall so he could not see a thing.

Food grew heavy in bellies, and some folk abandoned the hall to sneak away to rooms. Damir had taken his two new interests to his chambers. Ingir, too, had done away with the debauchery. Hundur dozed in his throne, and it was the first time his wife seemed at ease as she picked at a few extra bites on her plate.

Thane and Emi dug their heels into an argument on who was the better knife fighter, and even dragged a breathy laugh from my chest.

"Ly." Darkwin nudged her shoulder. "I've had all the ale I can stomach for the night."

He winked when she rolled her eyes. Darkwin had a woman with dark curls wrapped around his arm.

Lyra bid a swift farewell, then returned to her place at my side, her thigh pressed firmly to mine.

"What interesting folk you claim, Melder Bien." A Myrdan woman with dark hair fashioned in a circlet of intricate braids, and each finger dressed in silver rings, leaned over the table. "Forgive me, I overheard the prince speak of the former melder as though you might be like him. I took a guess. I'm Lady Solveig, and have been interested in meeting the young melder."

Lyra shuddered at my side. She didn't respond.

Yrsa lifted her chin. "Lady Solveig, what need do you have for the melder?"

"So I was right." The lady returned a wolfish sort of grin toward Lyra. "No need, my lady. Mere curiosity."

"Regarding what?" Lyra cracked a finger under the table.

Where no one could see, I took hold of her palm and rubbed the same finger, as though soothing the knuckle from the pop.

Solveig grinned, as innocent as a viper in the grass. "I merely find it fascinating the Jorvan king keeps you in his hall."

"She is not one of my father's hounds, Lady," Thane grumbled.

"Of course." Solveig snickered. "I only mean, with the history of your disappearance, and the vengeance our enemies must feel, well, it places all our heads under the blade in a way."

Lyra blinked. "I would never intentionally bring harm to anyone."

"I'm not sure Tomas Grisen would agree."

"Lady Solvieg." Yrsa clapped her drinking horn on the table. "You are crossing a dangerous line."

The woman feigned stun. "Forgive me, Your Grace. I should not have said a word." Solveig dipped her chin, but lifted a glare at Lyra. "If you care for your prince and my princess, Melder, I do hope you will consider staying out of sight. The Dravens care more for your blood than the previous melder since their prince died trying to hide you, after all."

Violence was no stranger, and it throttled me now. I had never slaughtered a woman for insults, but tonight seemed a good time for a first.

Solveig took note and chuckled. "Then again, you already have your own Draven watchdog."

Yrsa shot to her feet. "Gerta Solveig, leave this hall. You will not step foot at the royal vows. I will personally cast blood wards to bar you out. Should you attempt it, I'll be certain my father returns you to Myrda in chains.

For the first time, Solveig's face paled. No lady of Myrda would want to be excluded from the royal wedding. The woman hesitated for a pause, then lowered her head and scurried away.

There was rage inside me, unwise and unexpected. Lyra's shoulders curled, and the light that was in her eyes not moments before dimmed.

"Think nothing of it, Lyra," Thane insisted.

"Truly." Yrsa lifted her horn. "Solveig has yearned for the eye of House Grisen since our gentry studies. She must've heard about what happened."

"It isn't like Hundur is being silent about it," Thane snapped.

Yrsa's mouth tightened but she nodded in agreement.

Lyra gave them both a tentative grin, but it was a mask. There was pain behind the mottled dyes in her eyes.

I moved my palm higher on her leg and took on a firmer, near-possessive grip. She sucked in a sharp breath and shifted closer. Lyra held my open palm over her leg, a silent encouragement to never let go.

I didn't. Not until more drunken fools tried to speak with her, some begging for their own claws like Hundur's.

Through the corridors, I kept a hand on the small of her back until we reached her chamber door.

"Is it true?" Lyra turned to me. "What Solveig said? Did the heir of Dravenmoor die trying to take me from the raid?"

I winced.

"That is my answer, then." Her tone grew cold.

I waited until she lifted her gaze back to mine. *I don't recall everything about that night. But I know the prince helped hide you.*

"Why?"

I didn't know what to say, how to explain what I wasn't entirely certain I understood myself.

Lyra studied her hands for a breath. "I keep having these . . . dreams. Someone is holding me and running through the wood. At our backs there's only smoke and screams." She rubbed her brow with her fingers. "He tells me to keep my eyes closed. What if it's not a dream? What if it's a memory?"

Dammit. Her dreams aligned with my own, and I couldn't explain any of it.

I don't know. I brushed a lock of her dark hair off her brow. *Queen Elisabet hates Damir's use of soul bones. But her son had mercy on a child.*

There was a new somberness in her smile. "Then I will always have a debt I cannot repay."

She did not know that I did too.

I touched my thumb to her bottom lip, tugging gently. *Ravagers have ways of knowing when bones are melded. Be on guard these next days. Royal vows make threats worse.*

"I don't go anywhere alone, thanks to you."

Sometimes it was not enough. It was not the ravagers I did not trust; they were predictable enough. It was the one who led them.

Lyra turned to me. "If it is true. If an enemy gave his life for mine, I cannot—will not—ever be the melder Damir desires, Roark. I don't want to meld for Stonegate, and I know you might find that treasonous and cowardly, but—"

I cut off her words with a kiss, hard and deep. Lyra moaned against my lips, her arms wrapping around my neck.

How long I took her mouth, I didn't know, but when I pulled back her lips were full and swollen, her visible silver scars pieces of moonlight.

I pressed a palm to her cheek, and with my other hand, I said, *You are no coward, Lyra. You are no monster. Your soul is too bright.*

Lyra laughed softly. "You're not the first to mention the brightness of my soul." I tilted my head, but she waved the thought away. "Never mind."

Shoulders to hips, I pulled her closer. *I regret taking you from a safer home, but I am not a good man. I have no regrets that you are here.*

She dragged her plump bottom lip between her teeth. Her fingertip traced the wolf head stitched over my gambeson. "You are unexpected, Roark Ashwood."

And you'd be wise to keep a distance. I didn't lie when I said I am not a good man.

She stepped closer, arching her neck so our noses nearly touched. "You never truly know a heart until you see the darkness inside. I might like to see yours."

I tilted her chin, our noses grazing. My fingers danced against her cheek. Lyra closed her eyes, listening, feeling the words. *That would be a mistake.*

Her cheeks lifted in a grin. "You don't frighten me, Sentry Ashwood."

She rose on her toes and kissed me sweetly. I craved more, a beast wanting to devour her. My fingers dug into her waist before I broke away, my brow pressed against hers. *I will be here on watch tonight.*

Lyra took a step back and opened the door to her chamber. "Then I will sleep well."

I flattened a palm against her door when it was closed and the lock clicked in place. A simple declaration—to sleep well knowing I was here—but it cut beneath my ribs, a molten blade to the heart.

After the life I had lived, Lyra Bien would be wise not to trust me. I'd be half-decent if I left her be, if I kept a watchful distance.

I settled in front of the door, hand on my blade, senses alert. Trouble was, I wasn't certain there was much decency left in me.

40

LYRA

I COULDN'T BREATHE. THERE WAS PRESSURE OVER MY mouth, my body.

Someone was on top of me.

My eyes snapped open and a muffled scream peeled from my chest. A gaze of copper and blood hovered above me. Darkness in the room shaded the cowl over his head, the mask covering his mouth, the pallid gray sheen of his skin, but I needed little light to know who pinned me to the furs on the ground.

Skul Drek raised a finger over his masked lips, mutely demanding I keep quiet.

A whimper sliced through his leather-wrapped fingers. His palm still covered my mouth, but I tried to nudge my face to the side.

The assassin merely added more pressure, holding me still.

He was oddly solid and heavy, a body of muscle and strength, but also cold shadows. He'd played me a fool, drawing me to a strange sort of ease near him, and now he found me in the night and would end me.

Outside light glowed like a bleary lantern through the open window. My head spun when the walls cracked and peeled with blackened rot. Cold washed over me in a roaring wave and all at once, the heat of my chamber faded into a dank, mirrored chamber.

Gods, all gods, Skul Drek could drag me away into the trance of his wretched mirror world without melding. What was he? A blood crafter? A demon from the hells?

I kicked and thrashed, desperate to scream, desperate for a hint of my voice to break through the trance. Roark was on watch; if he could but hear me, the Sentry would take the assassin's head.

My insides twisted in sick knots—or Skul Drek would take Roark from me.

"We had to slip away. You can't be heard." A scorching heat boiled in my skull, and the gritty, thick rasp of Skul Drek's voice.

I let out a scream all the same, muffled under his palm. Skul Drek hissed and stroked a finger down my cheek. "You needed to be warned."

I blinked through the coils of his inky cloak, my body going still. With my other hand, I patted his arm until he eased the unnerving pressure of his weight off my mouth.

I rubbed my jaw, glaring at him. "Warned of what? How did you do this? How did you bring me here?"

Skul Drek leaned forward, drawing close enough I felt the scratch of frigid wool over his face, half-solid, half-dark. "The gates have cracked. Keep out of sight."

He lifted slightly, letting me breathe.

"How am I here?"

"I called to you." Skul Drek pointed to the place over my heart where the golden rope burned bright and heavy between us.

"Release me! I am not yours to summon or chain or—"

I cried out when the phantom reared over me as he'd done before, his flashing, cruel eyes a hairsbreadth from mine. "Soul to soul, I called you. If you desire to die, then do so."

Soul to soul?

By the gods. My lips parted. "You are not a man?"

A cruel, thick, heavy laugh danced a shudder up my arms. "I am he, we are we." Skul Drek placed an open palm over my heart. I shuddered beneath the frost of his touch. "But you brighten the dark."

I swallowed, dropping my gaze to the hazy skeins of darkness billowing off his long fingers against my breast. "My soul . . . calls to you?"

"Yes."

All gods. "That's what happens? I speak to you, *see* you, in my soul?"

A low, haggard sort of hum was his only response. After a drawn-out pause, the assassin stepped back, dropping his hand. "I brought the warning. Stay away."

For the first time, through the fissures breaking away bits of my own terror, I saw a flash of something in his eyes, something like his own worry. One breath, two, three, then I nodded briskly.

His palm slid away painfully slow. Skul Drek braced on his elbow, merely studying me from beneath his cowl.

I swallowed. "Why are you here?" *How* was he here?

Skul Drek's head canted to one side, then back. He was studying me, absorbing me, as though trying to puzzle through a riddle. "You brighten the dark, and I do not want it to stop. No matter what you hear, do not chase it. Stay quiet. Stay back."

The assassin touched my jaw. My skin hummed with a strange heat. He had me vulnerable, could apparently draw me into the mirror without my control, and still his touch stirred something like unbidden desire in my blood.

Gods, what was the matter with me? He was a trickster, a killer who'd nearly sent Prince Thane to Salur, and had caught me in his snare.

This close I could see the rage buried in the crimson of his eyes, the haunting flecks of black and copper. Otherwordly eyes.

I did not know what he was—a demon, a man, a dream.

Whatever he was, there was a disconcerting draw tethering me to a killer, and I did not know how to break it.

"You've come to attack," I said, voice steady even when the realization struck. The only reason Skul Drek would be here was to draw blood, and he did not want me to be in the middle of it. "You don't need to do this. We . . . we were working together, I thought. We were going to find the scattered bones of the Wanderer."

"Not all is as it seems." There was a bite to his tone, the cruel assassin was bleeding through the somber, curious creature he'd been.

"People I love are in these walls," I bit back. "Good people. You take them from me, and I will never help you. I will not stop until Stonegate hunts you down."

Skul Drek leaned closer until we were brow to brow. His skin was cold, like bathing in a frosted lake, but his breath was warm like the scent on his clothes—cloves and pine and dying embers. "I will say for a final time—stay out of sight."

A rattle echoed in the room, like a pick worked against a lock. A fist pounded at the door.

Skul Drek reared back. At full height he was enormous, a looming shadow that drew in light until it blotted out.

The harrowing blare of a ram's horn sounded from the distant towers. Sound was muffled at first, but with each breath grew clearer and clearer. The shadows of the mirror faded across the room, but for the first time, Skul Drek did not go with them. He remained, dark and harrowing, more solid than before.

How was he here if the dark realm faded?

In a rush, he made it to the window at the same moment the door crashed open.

Roark stumbled into the room, breathless and with a dark hate in his eyes when he saw the assassin. He cast a look at me, ensuring I was breathing, then swifter than a spark of a flame, Roark ripped one of two twin daggers from the sheaths on his thigh.

"Roark, no!" Strange as it was to feel drawn to the brutality and villainy of Skul Drek, I could not stomach the thought of Roark being harmed.

The dagger flew, drawing a shout of pain, a clack of snapping teeth. The blade buried into Skul Drek's side to the hilt. In another breath, Roark rushed the assassin.

Skul Drek waved a hand and the dagger clattered to the floorboards when Roark met him with the second blade.

"No!" I snatched hold of the stoker near the inglenook.

My cry snapped Skul Drek from his haze. Like a haunt in the night, he slipped through the open window without a sound, fading into the darkness.

Roark stumbled toward the window, clutching his side, sweat on his brow. Gods, he'd been struck.

He remained there for only a moment, then spun back into the room. With a wince, he took five long strides and trapped my face in his palms. Hot, sticky blood coated one of his hands where he'd pressed it against his wound.

My hands trembled when I covered his palms. "You're wounded. Roark, let me see it."

He ignored me and scanned my features instead, searching for injury.

"Roark." I patted his bloodied hand on my face. "I'm fine. You are not."

He shook his head and waved one hand, a simple signal the wound was nothing.

More horns rose in the night. Shouts. They filtered through the window from outside. The call of an attack against the fortress.

Listen to me. Roark released me and the ferocity of his position took hold. *Go to the washroom. Lock the door. Barricade it. Do not leave it until I return for you.*

"No. You and Kael will be there, I'm not—"

Roark silenced me by gently covering my lips with his palm. He shook his head, a desperate plea in his eyes. Against my cheek he spoke, *Stay out of sight, Lyra.*

His plea mirrored the command of Skul Drek. Two deadly forces standing on either side of a battle, yet both shared the same demand of me.

Lyra. Roark touched my chin. *Go now.*

I hesitated. There was a sharp jab of painful fear knowing Roark would lead the units against Skul Drek and whatever ravagers had breached the walls. Roark would stand before them all. He would be the most at risk.

Roark lifted one of the slender daggers from the floor. The hilt was made of bone and carved into a flame. He placed it in my palm, curling my fingers around the hilt, then gave me a slow nod.

I squeezed his hand, memorizing the heat of his skin, the rough patches from blade calluses, and it was over too soon. He pulled away and rushed for the door, disappearing into the corridors. Only after he'd left did I take note of the trail of blood that followed behind his every step.

He was wounded and going against the Draven assassin.

I blinked back into focus, head spinning. I understood his desire to see me safe, but I shared the same desire. To leave was a risk. I was no Stav warrior, no Berserkir, but I could handle steel well enough. Perhaps Thane was tucked away with his arrows again and I could help. Truth be told, I felt compelled to do so, for I could not shake the feeling that this battle was caused by me. I never spoke of Skul Drek, yet now he'd found me within the walls of the fortress. Now he'd found those I loved.

The dagger Roark placed in my palm was stained with blood. Doubtless more would spill before the night's end. I tightened my grip on the hilt and slipped out of my room to the sound of battles rising in the night.

41

LYRA

UPPER CORRIDORS AND STAIRWELLS WERE PROTECTED by Stav Guard. Two kingdoms faced danger in Stonegate tonight, and they took no risks. It was a stroke of good fortune there were Stav Guard aplenty, so I could fade into the chaos without being seen.

Word of me in the halls would reach King Damir and he'd chain me to the walls.

Sweat gathered around my palm the tighter I held the dagger. I fought for Stonegate tonight, when once my heart yearned to watch it fall.

No. I fought for a man I was forbidden to love. I fought for a brother who was not my blood. I fought for Emi, a friend I never expected. I fought for a prince with a good heart who might one day change this wretched fortress into something worthy of protection.

I slipped out of the front gates. Walls were stacked in Stav Guard, their dark tunics like stalks of scorched wheat all in a row, all willing to join the gods in Salur. Another horn blared in the night. I pressed my back to the wall when a heavy gate cranked free. From inside the bowels of a dark tower, rows of new Stav Guard marched forward.

My mouth went dry. These warriors bore crests of crossed seax blades, not the head of a wolf. Their hair was braided alike, no matter the thickness or shade—a ridge down the center of the skull with the sides shorn close to the scalp.

Their shoulders were too thick, too bulky. Some had jaws so square it appeared they had an extra set of teeth.

Berserkirs. These men—no less than a hundred—had been melded over and over, crafting soul bones to their bodies like bulky armor beneath the skin.

Their eyes were soulless, blackened. Tassels of colorful leather pinned to their tunics were symbols of their brutality, of how many lives they'd sent to Salur. They were far enough away I could not make out the numbers in full, but many of the Berserkir Stav wore their kill marks like a cloak across their shoulders.

Their heavy steps trampled across the bridges and cobbled roads until they reached the gates. I sprinted to the end of one bridge, leaning over the edge.

Along the outer gates, lines and lines of warriors—Myrdan and Jorvan alike—crashed swords and daggers against the bronze edges of a sea of invaders.

Ravagers. The crimson paint across their faces looked like they'd bathed in blood. Fara wolves howled and snapped at the ankles of the Stav, their tapered ears flicking to the whistles and commands from their masters.

A gate near the southern wall hung crooked on the hinges. Wood beams were tossed aside. Four Stav Guard were sprawled across the grass near the opening, dead.

That was their entry point.

From this vantage, I could make out the vibrant tunics and cloaks of Myrdan fighters tangled with Stav Guard. My head felt like it spun in delirium. So many angles, so much blood that the air was hot with the tang of it. I wanted to be everywhere, yet I could not move my feet.

"Lyra, what in the gods' names are you doing here?" Kael's sharp tone broke my stupor.

His hair was pasted to his brow from sweat and mud, and all along the edge of his Stav blade were bits of cloth and thick blood. He wasn't alone. Mikkal Jakobson stood at his side, breathless and dirty much the same.

"Get back in the palace." Kael gripped my arm. "Did Ashwood let you out?"

I shook him off. "I made my own choice. I could not sit there and do nothing. I helped in the battle of the wall."

Kael looked ready to argue, then his gaze widened. "The hidden archers?"

"Thane will tell you."

"Gods." Kael looked over his shoulder at Mikkal. His younger half brother let his sword sink to his side for a moment. "We don't know how the ravagers breached the walls, but they despise you most of all. Skilled as you are, you bring more risk to us here than in the palace."

It was a blow to the chest, but not a lie. Should any of the ravagers catch sight of the silver scars, they would force the Stav to move and drift from positions to keep me safe.

"I can't sit and do nothing." I held Kael's stare. "Skul Drek faced me. He knows of me and Roark . . . he went after him."

Kael cupped the back of my head. "And do you think Ashwood can focus on surviving if he sees you rushing into blades with a single dagger, Lyra? Think. Do not risk your life or his tonight. The palace—"

"Is warded," Mikkal interrupted, using the pommel on his sword to gesture at the clank of the portcullises falling into place on every gate.

"Dammit." Kael looked about, puzzling through a next move, then spun on me. "Listen to me, Ly. The ravagers will be hunting you out there, but you can protect lives here in the township. Mikkal is wounded. Edvin's new house is near the satin shop. Go there. Most of the inner homes are guarded well enough, but with their children, I doubt Freydis and Edvin will refuse a few extra blades. They can tend to his wound before the fool gets infected or worse—wakes in Salur."

Kael glared at the brother he was not given a chance to know. Mikkal Jakobson had been schooled by Henrik to be the future jarl after Kael was disowned, but he was not a hateful soul. Part of me believed he still viewed Kael as his elder brother, a leader.

"Go." Kael shoved me into Mikkal's chest.

"Kael Darkwin." I fought the tremble to my chin. Kael paused long enough to look back at us. "Don't you dare die."

One corner of his weary face curved. "Same, Ly."

Roads were clear through the market. Doors were sealed. Lights were doused.

By the time we reached the new household of the Skalfirth crafters, Mikkal stumbled a bit, his breath more like a ragged wheeze.

"Sit there." I urged him to take a place on the stoop, his back to the cool clay-and-wood wall.

"Súlka Bien," Mikkal said, voice rough. "If I meet Salur—"

"Hush, Mikkal."

"If I meet Salur," he barreled on, "tell him . . . tell my brother, I never stopped caring. He did not deserve what was done."

I closed my eyes and rapped on a window with my knuckles. "He didn't." I pounded again and called out to Edvin in a hushed voice.

"Tell him, won't you?"

"No. You're not going to Salur, you fool. Edvin, open the damn door!"

Mikkal let his head fall back. A weak smile spread over his mouth. He looked a bit like Kael. The same eyes, the same strong jaw and full lips. Mikkal's hair was icy and straight while Kael's was golden and messy.

I hated Jarl Jakobson more for denying his sons a life together.

The door cracked. We were met with the gleam of an ax blade for a few heartbeats before Gisli pulled it back. "Lyra."

"Help me. Mikkal Jakobson is badly wounded."

Hilda's husband was a soft-spoken man, but strong as stone. Woodwork and hauling logs had built him into a warrior without the blade.

I hardly did anything to help drag Mikkal into the longhouse other than ease his ankles atop the table in the center room once Gisli had him sprawled on his back.

Hilda emerged from a rear room, Freydis at her back.

"Ly." Hilda gingerly touched Mikkal's shoulder. "Gods, what is happening out there?"

"Ravagers broke through the gates."

"They're growing stronger, then." Hilda's face paled. "The walls haven't been breached in decades."

I waved the truth away, unable to confess my belief the horrid tether chaining me to Skul Drek brought this attack. Mikkal would die if the wound wasn't dealt with soon. "Hilda, can you craft a bone tonic for Mikkal?"

Without soul bones, the touch of a crafter to crushed marrow could amplify strength and health against specific ailments. I prayed to the gods—who seemed to have turned their faces from us—a tonic would be enough to seal Mikkal's wound.

Hilda's brow furrowed. "Chicken bones will need to do."

She fled from the room, leaving a back door open.

Whimpers overhead drew my gaze to the loft. I forced a smile at the curious, tear-filled eyes of Edvin's children.

"All right, loves." I went to the ladder, one hand on a rung. "Try to sleep and perhaps your fylgja guide will visit your dreams and give you a peek at what good fortune awaits you."

Freydis gave me a gentle smile and set about peeling back Mikkal's tunic.

"Edvin left," she murmured, avoiding my gaze. "Went to help again."

"He survived the last, he'll do so again." I schooled my face into something flat. Edvin would see it as a dishonor if he did not protect his family, but he'd only just won them back. Now it was all at risk again.

Should anything happen to him I would meld a dozen bones until I faced Skul Drek. I'd find a way to do to the assassin what I did to Tomas.

Hilda returned with thin, bloody bones in her palms.

It took little time for her craft to crush the bones, manipulating them into small bits of powder and narrow pieces. A wince contorted her features from the ache of using bone craft, but Hilda didn't stop, shouting for a few herbs and oils to be gathered and added to the bone dust.

Gisli and Freydis did as she asked and held Mikkal down

when the burn of the bone tonic hissed and crackled along the gash carved deep into his ribs.

"Never said it was comfortable." Hilda wiped a drop of sweat off her brow, fingers battered and red from crafting too fiercely.

A tug on my hand drew me to a little face at my side. Edvin's youngest hugged a linen rag doll and peered at me with crystalline eyes from behind a mess of red hair. "Kris left."

"What?" I lowered to a crouch.

The girl pointed to the open back door. "Kris went to find Papa."

Gods. No. Krisjan, the eldest of the three, wanted nothing more than to be like his father.

I took hold of Roark's dagger, told the girl to stay put, and rushed outside to confused shouts from the others at my back.

"Krisjan!" I screamed his name, racing down the cobbled streets.

Cries of battle drew too near. My lungs burned, my body ached, and when I rounded a corner near the opened gates, I let out a sob of relief. There, crouched behind a wooden cask, a boy too small for the seax he carried was crouched, watching the destruction near the border walls.

I ducked behind his cask. "Krisjan. You cannot be here." Big, wet eyes lifted, filled with fright. I wrapped an arm around his small shoulders. "Come. We must go back."

The boy didn't protest. He hardly uttered a sound when I pried his little fingers off the hilt and took hold of the seax. I clung to his small hand, pausing to look over my shoulder to the gates, searching, fearing.

Kael was out there. Edvin. I did not find them, but an unseen hook, an undeniable draw, pulled me to Roark at once.

He was impossible to avoid, a predator.

Blood clung to Roark's cheeks, his lips, the blaze of his eyes spun with a bit of madness. One hand gripped a seax, the other his dark battle-ax. From hilt to point, both blades were soaked in blood.

Ravagers made their attempts to strike at the Sentry. He crouched, then landed the second blade in necks, hearts, bellies.

Roark moved with mesmerizing violence. A bloody dance where one partner was left standing and the other in pieces.

I swallowed down the need to run to him and turned to the boy. "Hurry now. We need to get inside."

Together, we rushed toward the longhouse, but when we rounded the bend, my heart stopped.

A bulky warrior blocked our path. His skull was misshapen, a look of rounded points like horns. The Stav Guard who'd been there the day I was brought before King Damir. What was he doing?

The guard's eyes were wild, like a flame caught up by the wind. He rolled a short blade in his hand, teeth bared. There was a hunger in the way he looked at Krisjan, like the boy was nothing more than a beating heart to slash open.

I'd never wondered how bloodlust might appear until now. It was feral and wretched, a wicked trance the Berserkir couldn't escape.

This was the untamed violence of the berserksgangur poison taking hold.

No mistake, the Berserkir's mind was overtaken by the ferocity of the many soul bones. Impenetrable, unbreakable. He craved battle, and would not let a moment of shedding blood go to waste.

Only now his desire for slaughter was placed on the head of a child.

The Berserkir roared a cry, one laden in a twisted glee, like death thrilled him to the bone.

I slid in front of Krisjan, my arms encircled around his trembling body, nothing more than a fleshy shield. I clenched my eyes, waiting for the killing blow.

It never came.

With my arms still cradling Krisjan's head, I glimpsed over my shoulder.

My heart stuttered.

From the shadows of the arcades and crevices, billows of darkness draped over broad shoulders. Skul Drek materialized at the Berserkir's side. Red, wild eyes met the dull emptiness of the warrior's.

With a guttural cry, the warrior crashed his blade toward Skul Drek.

The assassin drifted to one side, like stepping from one shadow to another. Ropes of inky darkness wrapped around the Berserkir's arms, ankles. Skeins rammed through the warrior's nose, blotting out the whites of his eyes.

The warrior slashed and jabbed, cutting through the murky shadows like slicing through cobwebs on the rafters.

Rage burned through the deadened stare of Damir's manipulated Stav. Whatever brutality burned through his soul from the bones of his armor now contorted his features into something frightening, like the sneer of evil.

Skul Drek rolled his shoulders, readying to strike. The way he fought wasn't natural. There wasn't a clash of steel against steel. When Skul Drek struck, it was more like he attacked something else, something beneath the flesh of the Berserkir.

The Berserkir snarled when the assassin slashed another ribbon of darkness across his body, forcing the warrior to a halt. A rabid bear in a trap.

Skul Drek whirled around and waved one hand. He didn't shout. There was no scrape of his raspy, heavy voice in my head.

I blinked and spun toward the boy. "Run, Krisjan." I could see the rooftop of his longhouse. "Go! Do not look back."

He obeyed. Head down, the boy darted down the street, never once looking at the phantom who'd become a defender.

I took the bone dagger from my chamber in hand and watched as shadows clashed with a Stav blade. The Berserkirs were unstoppable. Iron and steel from blades could wound them, but rarely kill. But the lashes from Skul Drek's mesmerizing darkness landed the warrior on his knees, yet I could not see a drop of blood.

Coils of dark tethers strangled the warrior's thick neck. Positioned behind the Berserkir, Skul Drek moved his fiery eyes to find me.

He didn't speak. He didn't tell me to run. Heat flushed through my blood, and my heart quickened.

"Are you speaking to me?"

His skin was cold slate, but when his lips curled his sharp teeth gleamed against the darkness surrounding his head.

All at once, my body careened forward. Frosted wind pummeled my cheeks the same as in my bedchamber. Salt and smoke filled my lungs with each breath. Longhouses, sod rooftops, and cobbled roads were mirrored in dripping darkness.

Once again, he'd pulled me—perhaps my soul—into the mirrored space.

"Leave." Skul Drek's strained voice shattered my stun.

His darkness remained, but was now wrapped around a collision of different shades of gold. Here, the Berserkir's glowing body was made of different shapes and angles. I could plainly see every different shade of each soul bone.

He was a thick slab of armor. From the bulging shards across his skull, the ridges of his cheeks, his jaw, to a manipulated breastplate that shielded his heart and ribs. The warrior was hardly himself at all.

"He has locked on the boy and on me. The lust for blood will hunt us."

"I will keep him," Skul Drek snapped.

"But you . . . you cannot kill him, can you?" I could make out the lashes across the bones, doubtless made by the shadows. They acted like knives against the trapped souls in the bones. But none reached the Berserkir's heart, his lungs, or his true skull.

I held my palms in front of me. The roar of the magic burned in my chest, the taste of ice and salt and smoke settled on my tongue.

"There is no time," Skul Drek warned, as though he already knew what I was considering.

I ignored him and pressed both palms against a thick, jagged shard of a soul bone melded to the Berserkir's ribs.

Through Tomas's unwarranted mercy, I knew to unravel melded bone ached and burned on my own body. Dozens of stinging jabs prickled along my skin until the bone shifted under the Berserkir's skin.

Narrow threads that had been fastened in place over the soul bones were still there, stitched by another melder's craft. Like a hem on a skirt, I tugged on the threads, unstitching each one.

Skul Drek grunted when the Berserkir's bright form shifted. He was fighting back.

"I can make him vulnerable."

The assassin snapped his teeth again. "You wish for pain."

"I know it is painful, but he is lost to the violence of corrupt bones. They are so armored we cannot even take his head. Tell me another way to kill him, or do you plan to battle him until the gods intervene?"

Skul Drek looked behind him into the nothingness. "Make haste."

I returned my palms to the gilded stitches across a soul bone shielding the Berserkir's neck. One by one, I unlaced the old melding. The bone snapped free and the warrior's form jerked. Skul Drek tightened his shadows, holding the man in place.

I cried out, doubling over when the agony of unbreaking craft burned in my stomach.

"*Melder.*" Skul Drek shifted, almost like he was torn on how to act—keep the Berserkir in his grasp? Or step beside me?

I held up a hand, bile on my tongue. "I'm fine. A little more."

The warrior thrashed. I didn't hear him scream, not in the mirror.

Chips and pieces of rune-marked bone flickered and fell away until the gold bone faded to the glowing ashes and drifted away on the icy wind.

Teeth clenched, I found a final piece that would open enough of a gap to sink a blade inside to his heart. Pain in my own body felt like falling into a bed of hot coals.

I cried out and stumbled.

A cold hand reached out, catching me under the arm. Skul Drek did not release me until the final thread snapped.

I bent over and heaved, retching from the pain.

"Go." Skul Drek spoke in more of a growl than a voice. "Do not be seen here."

"Pull back the ravagers," I said weakly. "They follow you. Pull them back."

He hesitated. "As you say."

His blazing eyes looked between us. The rope was as thick as the one that once held him bound to the distant shadows. There was nothing at his back, no chain fading into the mists. Now it seemed to have altered course and bound the assassin to me. I didn't understand it, but there was little time to fret over it.

Skul Drek took a step closer. "You brighten the night, and I will fight to keep it."

A gust of cold chased away the inky shadows of the mirror. I fell onto my side on the damp cobblestones.

The clatter of steel over the stones drew my attention. With the same stance as in the mirror, Skul Drek held the Berserkir in his inky tethers, only now the warrior was bloodied and misshapen. His skin was shredded like claws scraped over his skin.

All gods. I'd torn him apart. What appeared as unraveling gilded threads in the mirror was slaughter in reality.

Blood bubbled over the Stav's lips. "P-please." His foggy eyes looked at the blade in my hand.

I clutched the dagger against my heart, holding the Berserkir's gaze. "Dine in Salur tonight."

On the next heartbeat, I thrust the point through his heart.

The feeling of carving through flesh, bone, the shudder of his body, the wet gasps as he fell, all of it was sickening. It was merciful. It was a death I caused.

The dagger caught in his chest and took me forward when the Berserkir toppled to the side. Cold, harsh hands caught me again.

I looked to Skul Drek, pulse frenzied. He said nothing for a drawn-out moment, then all at once shoved me in the same direction Krisjan had fled. One foot caught on a raised cobblestone, flinging me forward onto my knees.

I whirled around, but by the time I looked back, Skul Drek was already gone.

LYRA

WHEN THE HORNS SOUNDED WITH THE RETREAT OF the ravagers, Mikkal—steadier from Hilda's bone tonic—insisted he escort me to the palace before anyone noticed my absence.

Once I was properly placed outside the doors of the healer's wing, I nudged him forward. "You should let them see to your wound."

"I am quite well," he said.

"Then return to your mother and father, before they fear the worst."

Mikkal hesitated. "Thank you." He clenched his teeth and stared at the woven rug under his boots. "Thank you, Lyra. I-I am filled with shame, for I do not even know if I was cruel or kind to you while you served in our household."

I scoffed, exhausted, terrified, hands still coated in blood. "I did not wish for anyone to notice me, Mikkal. If you ignored me, it was my desire."

"Because you knew, right? You knew you were a melder."

I nodded.

"So did my brother?" Mikkal winced when the bandage over his wounds caught. "I hope I am as honorable as Kael. I stand with you, Lyra. For how you have defended him, and now me, I will stand with you should you ever need it."

It was endearing. So young, hardly able to grow a damn whisker on his chin, but Mikkal puffed out his chest, declaring his fealty in such a way that he seemed merely a younger Kael.

With a squeeze to his arm, the boy finally abandoned the wing.

I shoved through the doors, disheartened by the chaos. So many wounded. Panic choked in my throat, fear of whom I might find among the dead being stacked against the far wall.

Long dark hair brushed past me. "Yrsa? Princess, I mean."

Yrsa spun around, still clad in a thin night shift, tears on her cheeks. Her shoulders slouched in a touch of relief, and in the next breath, the princess threw her arms around my neck.

"Lyra, gods. I was so frightened they'd found you when your room was empty."

I rubbed her back when she shuddered in a strained sob, one she fought mightily to keep buried.

"Everyone I love was out there," Yrsa whispered. "Damn Thane slipped out again. What is wrong with the man?"

"The prince was there?"

Yrsa's chin trembled. "It is like he cannot stand to sit back and not fight. The feckless, bold, stupid fool."

A smile wanted to crack through my own fears. I understood the feeling of being left behind, and I was beginning to understand how the prince earned his name of Thane the Bold.

"Have you seen any of them?"

The princess pulled away, using the heel of her hand to wipe her cheeks, and nodded. "I know my foolish future husband is alive. He's boarded up with the king's healer. The bastard had the audacity to smile and insist he only earned a few superficial wounds, as if that changes anything!" Yrsa's cheeks flushed. "Emi . . . Emi is alive, thank the gods. She was talking, but took a deep cut to the ribs, and I don't . . . I don't . . ." The princess didn't finish.

I hugged her again. "She will be all right. I will meld a soul bone over her heart if needed."

Yrsa's lips twitched in a small smile. "That helps, Lyra. Thank you. I saw your brother over there. He looked well."

I blew out a breath, burying the snap of guilt for not first searching out Kael. I'd been searching for someone else.

At the sight of Kael standing, gathering his weapon belt, I nearly knocked him to the ground with my embrace.

He grunted. "Good gods, Ly. It is a good thing nothing was at risk of being split open."

I tilted my head back. "You're well?"

"I'm fine."

"Mikkal is all right. He's a great deal like you, and I think you have become his hero."

Kael tried to keep stoic, but his smile couldn't be stopped.

"Have you seen Edvin?" I briefly shared how his boy had gone searching, but I did not say more. Nothing about the brief alliance with the assassin who'd brought the attack.

Kael assured me Edvin was home. He took a hit to the face, but had a great deal of confidence it would scar and Freydis would not be able to look away from her husband's new ruggedness.

His features fell after a moment. "You should never have been there."

"I know it was reckless—"

"It was stupid."

I frowned. "*Reckless* as it was, I couldn't stand doing nothing, not when my craft could've been useful."

I did not make choices for Skul Drek, but I spoke to him in secret. He came to me first. We had somehow fashioned an eerie connection, and it was risking lives I loved.

We fell into a thick silence as herb healers and Stonegate bone crafters worked with bone tonics and herb pastes and draughts for the wounded.

While a mousy woman worked on a gash across Kael's shoulder, I scanned the nearby nooks. There was a face I didn't see.

"Kael—"

"I know what you're going to ask." He frowned. "Last I saw of Sentry Ashwood, he refused a healer's touch and abandoned the hall. I doubt the king will allow him in with the prince, so since he is *your guard*, he very well might be searching for you."

There was an accusation in his tone, but I did not have the strength, nor desire, to give up any secrets tonight.

"I ought to inform him I'm alive before the palace is under siege with a new search."

Kael's mouth tightened. "Right. You'd better."

"Are you . . . will you be all right?"

"I'm fine." He pinched my cheek in the way he used to when we were young, all to irritate me. "Go."

I kissed the side of his head, but felt his gaze on my neck with each step from the healer's wing.

MY CHAMBER WAS FREE OF THE SENTRY, BUT MORE THAN ONE Stav Guard stood watch outside the door. I kept low, never giving up they guarded an empty room.

After searching the great hall, the gardens, and the sparring field, I found my first glimpse of Roark Ashwood on the balcony of his chamber. Moonlight kissed his bare shoulders, and he was inspecting something on his waist.

Without signaling I was there, I entered the Stav Wing.

Rooms were bare. Few guards were in their beds, most still under the care of healers or too much ale in other rooms of the fortress. I slipped into the stairwell, winding around the tower, until I reached the upper floors where officers and the Sentry kept their personal rooms.

Roark's door was unlocked. I snorted. For a man who was on the brink of drawing a blade at the slightest threat, he was rather unconcerned with his own security.

As the Sentry he had a small sitting room with a hearth, a table, and fur-covered benches. I paused at the table and looked at the scatter of books on the surface. Lore and myths and a few children's tales with painted pages. My lips curled. All his violence and Roark read tales of heroes and villains and quests of the gods.

One hand covered my mouth when I stepped into his bedchamber.

The bed was unkempt and smelled of the fresh rain and oakmoss of his skin. A wardrobe was opened, and inside his uniforms and tunics and cloaks were arranged neatly, but that was the extent of it. In one corner were pairs of sloughed-off boots and a few unsheathed blades.

Roark was collected and pulled taut in the face of everyone, but here, he could simply be; he was free to be messy and at ease.

He was a beautiful conundrum.

I leaned against the door of the balcony. He was tending to a wound on his side. A discolored gash that looked almost dead

around the edges, but if there had been a great deal of blood, it
had stopped flowing.

His hair was glistening and damp. His skin had more than one
bruise, but looked freshly scrubbed. His trousers were without a
belt, and hung seductively low on his hips, revealing the two
dimples on his lower back.

The man was a sight I never anticipated needing.

I knocked on the edge of the doorway. He spun around with a
start.

"Good to see you alive, Sentry." My voice was strained, heavy
with emotion.

Roark had my face trapped in his palms in a breath, and in the
next, his mouth was on mine.

Unexpected, but welcome. For a moment I forgot about battle,
blood, and assassins.

I dug my hand into his hair, and water from the wash slick-
ened my fingers when I tugged at the roots. A low moan rumbled
into his kiss. He parted my lips with his tongue, greedy and possessive. He claimed me, marking me with his mouth, his teeth,
his hands.

When he dipped his chin to break the kiss, he pressed his
forehead to mine, our breaths tangling.

Roark lifted a hand. *You were missing.*

"I was looking for you." I traced the edge of his lip. "*You* were
missing."

His eyes brightened with a new heat that was frightening and
intoxicating all at once.

You went to town, Lyra.

"You saw?"

I was told. Then I could not find you. Roark shook his head, letting his hand drop to his side.

Tears burned. I blinked them away. "I couldn't stay. Not . . . not after what happened. Watching you go, watching everyone go, I couldn't stay because . . ."

How was I to explain any of it? Would Roark think me mad? He was hateful at our first meet; to return to indifference and duty felt like a dreary feat I didn't want to risk.

He tilted my chin, forcing me to look at him. *Tears? What must I do to return them to your eyes?*

Emotion, fear, and unknowns I'd kept buried broke. My forehead dropped to his chest, against the even beat of his heart. Silent sobs shuddered down my spine. Roark tightened his embrace, holding me close to his body.

He did not try to speak. He let me stumble, and caught me in the end.

"I don't know how to explain any of it."

Roark slipped his fingers through mine, and led me into his disordered room. If he had any embarrassment he didn't let on, merely sat me on the edge of his bed, and lowered to a crouch in front of me. He opened his hand, signaling for me to speak.

A tear landed on my cheek. He wiped it away with his thumb. "There . . . was a reason Skul Drek was in my chamber. It was not our first interaction."

I chose my words carefully and described what happened whenever I melded, of the hunt for the Wanderer's bones. I told him how the assassin insisted there were four pieces to the armor buried across the lands. Perhaps one was here. Roark listened as I described the roar of craft, even while melding a fealty shard. I told him of the rotted mirror land, the cold and shadows, the moments when the phantom of Skul Drek appeared.

I used the heel of my hand to wipe another rogue tear away. "I don't know if he is man or illusion, but he has power. I cannot help but shoulder the blame of what happened tonight. I killed a man with Skul Drek, Roark. Gods, what you must think of me."

Roark shook his head, lifting my hand and pressing a kiss into the center of my palm, before he replied. *You survived. Nothing more.*

I scoffed. "Roark, I knew he could attack. Whenever there is a soul bone taken, he will take a soul in its place. He will kill. I should've taken the threat with more care."

Roark placed both his palms on my thighs, gently rubbing them, and I told of my part in the death of the Berserkir.

"I broke him apart." My voice trembled, but I bit back any more tears. "Instead of fighting Skul Drek, I helped him kill one of our own."

Roark rose to his feet and drove his fingers through his hair. He shook his head. *I despise soul bones.*

It wasn't the response I expected. Truth be told, I considered his devotion to his duty as Sentry might've overshadowed any feelings he'd developed for me. I wondered if he would drag me off to confess before the king.

I tangled my fingers in my lap. "Is that why you refuse to be melded?"

The power alters a living soul. Roark kicked at the leg of the wardrobe and kept pacing, his gestures frantic with anger. *They corrupt, Lyra. Sometimes they amplify goodness if the fallen soul had strong honor, but if the soul lived in darkness, the new soul grows hateful. They become King Damir's monsters.*

The Berserkir was prepared to slaughter a child. He'd practically beamed at the sight of little Krisjan, helpless and vulnerable.

"But Prince Thane isn't all that changed."

I tried to choose a bone that did not feel heavy with hate. But it was still a risk. Same with Darkwin. I selected carefully.

"You can sense a soul?"

He closed his eyes. *Must be the Draven in me. I've learned to listen to the power inside.* Roark knocked his fist against his wall, summoning my gaze. *You saved that boy.*

"But I am drawn to a killer, Roark." I covered my face with my palms. "I don't fear him like I should. There is something that's connected us. There is something I trust in him."

Gods, to speak the truth out loud was horrifying.

The rough heat of Roark's hands tugged my palms back, letting them fall, so he could speak. *Blame is not on your shoulders tonight.*

"No need to mollycoddle me—"

Roark cut me off by squeezing my hand twice. *The gates were unlocked from within.*

My heart stuttered. "What?"

Roark nodded and sat beside me on the bed. *Ravagers were welcomed inside to destroy the union of kingdoms, or take you. Likely both. We were betrayed. Another reason I want to rage at you for leaving your damn chamber.*

They were welcomed inside the gates. By the gods. There were traitors inside our walls. "Stonegate is no longer safe."

I won't let anyone touch you. He cupped the back of my neck, and his thumb ran over the front of my throat. Roark's gaze seared into me, branded me deeper than the burn in my chest. His fingers brushed against my cheek, speaking words I could understand now through touch alone. *Stay.*

Everything slowed, and my body went liquid with heat. "What if someone thinks I've gone missing when I don't return to my chamber?"

I'll tell them you are under my watch tonight.

"Full of lies, Sentry Ashwood."

His grin was a shade of wicked. *Stay.*

I dragged my tongue over the rim of my bottom lip. "All right."

He left the room for a moment, delivering word the melder was safe with the Sentry to one of the men under his command. When he returned, Roark closed the door to the front room, clicking the lock in place.

Nerves coiled in my belly when Roark's fingertips traced the sides of my arms. His body crowded me; I leaned into him, letting my head fall back against his shoulder.

With one hand, Roark unraveled the laces of my bodice. He pushed the shoulders of my gown aside, letting it fall indecently low until my breasts were nearly bared. I shuddered when his teeth scraped down the slope of my neck.

Over my heart, he gestured. *Do I stop?*

Slow swirls of his fingertips teased the swell of my breasts as his lips caressed my bare shoulder.

"No," I said, breathless and needy. I combed my fingers through his hair. "Don't stop. Don't ever stop."

Roark let out a rough breath when my hands trailed down the flat planes of his stomach, memorizing the divots, the curves of muscle.

I paused at the gash in his side. "Are you well or should *I* stop, Sentry?"

He gripped my chin, answering with a bruising kiss.

I whimpered when Roark frantically slid my gown down, so it settled around my hips.

He kissed over my heart, the side of one breast, my navel, until he settled on his knees, pushing my skirt over my knees where the top bodice was bunched around my middle. Roark dragged his teeth along my inner thigh, rolling his eyes up to meet mine.

You have me on my knees, what should we do about this?

My core ached. "Make good on that promise, Roark Ashwood, and kiss me."

With a beautifully vicious grin, Roark pressed a hand on my middle, guiding me to sit on the edge of the table. With one heated look, he draped my knees over his shoulders and ran his tongue over me between my thighs. I could not draw in a breath. The cautious life, the safety I'd always craved, shattered beneath his kiss, the rough grip of his hands on my thighs.

In this moment I did not want caution. I wanted passion and madness and desire that could be relieved only by his hands, his kiss. I let my knees fall open, my heels digging into his upper back. Roark followed his tongue with his fingers, drawing me to the jagged edge too soon.

I grasped at his hair, my head falling back. "Roark."

The sound of his name spurred him on. He gripped my hips, holding me steady as he deepened his kiss and nipped at the sensitive flesh of my core.

I sucked in a sharp gasp when Roark flattened his tongue, drawing deeper; my thighs trembled around his head. Unable to stop, I bucked against his mouth, lost in a delirious haze.

Tap, tap, tap. His gentle claim struck my thigh.

My hips writhed under his vicious kiss. Need and desire coiled low in my belly, spilling through my core with every shift of his face to reach a new angle, with every groan he breathed over my soaked core.

He added his fingers, curling them, pressing his thumb against the sensitive apex between my thighs.

"Don't stop." I let out a strangled rasp when Roark swirled his thumb in a new direction.

Sobs of his name came out in rough pants. Roark gripped my thighs, his fingertips digging into my flesh. By the gods, I never wanted him to let go.

My head snapped back when he sucked harder. Another sharp gasp, another shudder, and my body went rigid as the taut pressure snapped.

His name came out in a strangled cry from deep in my chest.

Roark kissed his way up my stomach, his mouth swollen and glistening when he found my lips. He hooked my legs around his waist and carried me to his bed. My skin felt overheated, my head a fog. He made quick work of peeling my dress off my hips and tossing it aside.

Next, Roark fumbled with his belt until he shucked off his trousers. His cock sprang free, thick and strained.

I couldn't breathe. The blaze of desire in his eyes left me wanting to bare everything, to never leave this bed until he'd claimed every piece of me. Roark reared over me, palms beside my head. Our noses grazed, lips parted, and for a moment we hovered close to each other, sharing breath.

"I-I've never . . ." Words ran dry, and I looked away.

Roark tilted my chin, nudging my gaze back to his. He shook his head, brow arched in a question.

I dragged my knuckles down his cheek. "But there is nowhere I want to be other than right here."

I don't want to hurt you.

"You won't."

One of his palms slid between the cleft of my breasts. Roark held my gaze and tapped his palm three times, then with care took my hand and placed it over his own chest.

Emotion knotted in my throat. His. Mine. He was claiming my heart and giving me his.

I stroked my fingers down his cheek. "I want you."

He swallowed, and I followed the motion of it down his throat. He held a hand over my face. *All of me?*

Vulnerability lined his face. For a moment the stoic Sentry was a man who'd cracked open his chest for acceptance or ruin.

I clasped his face and nodded. "All of you."

I drew his mouth to mine and kissed him, deeper, firmer. As though to prove how he'd somehow come to consume every piece of my heart.

Roark palmed one breast. I moaned into his mouth and arched against his touch. He pinched the hardened nipple, tugging and twisting. I clawed at his shoulders and let my knees part when he settled his hips between my legs.

Roark's tongue circled the peak. His teeth, his lips, his mouth dragged breathless pants from my throat and he'd yet to fill me. I slid my palms down the muscles of his back, down every divot of bone along his spine. I dug into the curves of his ass, yanking his hips against the throbbing heat between my legs.

His voice came in soft, breathy sounds, but there was a roughness to the grunt he breathed against my skin.

He lifted his head, eyes dark with desire. *You are making it hard to be gentle.*

I nipped at his bottom lip. "Then don't be."

True to his word, Roark crashed his mouth back to mine, rough, needy, desperate. The Sentry was intent to worship my mouth, his hands laid claim to my body, and the hard length of his cock rubbed against my slit.

Gods, I wanted him to devour me.

I slid my hand down his stomach and wrapped my palm around his length, hard and warm.

My thumb ran along the pulsing vein on the underside.

Roark's brow furrowed with pleasure. He dropped his head to my shoulder, kissing the curve of my neck as I touched him. Free of the title of Sentry, of rescued Draven, of Death Bringer. In this moment, he could be worshiped as a man, as a lover.

His hands trembled when he took hold of my wrist with one and spoke with the other. *I will come in your hand.*

"Then let go, Roark," I said in a breath.

He shook his head and pulled my hand away, a new beautifully dark grin on his lips. *Inside you.*

Gods. I did not hear his voice, but he still managed to speak the most sensual, commanding words I had ever known. He gave me no time to prepare before the tip of his cock eased into my core.

He held me close through the snap of pain, one palm curling around my head when I arched up. My fingers dug into his skin, deep enough they'd leave marks. Roark didn't move for a breath, then gently eased my knees farther open, until he was inside me from tip to hilt.

We moaned in unison, both in pleasure and with a sting of pain. For a long pause we stayed there, filling each other to the brink, then slowly he rocked his hips. The more he moved, the more the sting shifted to something else.

My body responded and matched his pace. He deepened his movements, rendering me breathless. Roark's mouth went to my throat. He laced one hand with mine, the other slid between us, finding that pulsing spot between my thighs with his thumb.

I moaned his name, unable to form a coherent thought.

My body tightened. A roll of blood and heat began in my toes and flowed upward until it filled my head with a delicious fog. I cried out as my release flooded my veins. It didn't stop.

"Roark . . ." All I could do was dig at his back, try to find purchase as my body burned for more of him.

He rolled his hips and hooked one of my legs around his waist, deepening his angle. In another breath, Roark stilled over me. His breaths were rapid and warm against my neck. His cock twitched and the heat of his release spilled into me, pulse after pulse.

When it ended, Roark pressed slow kisses down my throat. Sweat dampened his forehead. He lifted his hand, but didn't speak, tracing the lines of my nose, my lips. Each touch he followed with tender kisses.

After a moment, he stepped into the washroom, returning with a clean linen. Roark cared for me, sweetly kissing me while he washed and soothed between my legs.

When he finished, Roark rolled onto his back and pulled me close.

I draped a leg over his waist. Roark held my head to his chest, his slow fingertips drawing circles over my shoulders and back until my eyes grew heavy.

For the first time since arriving at Stonegate, I breathed in pure, unadulterated contentment. I let my lashes flutter closed. Roark pressed a kiss to my brow, and mouthed words I didn't catch before I fell into the peace of sleep.

ROARK

I CAUGHT LYRA RIFFLING THROUGH THE PILE OF OUR DIS-
carded clothes before the sun rose. Mists of gray morning
cast her bare skin in soft light. She was stunning and I could not
look away. I knocked my knuckles against the post of my bed,
halting her movements.

Hair draped wild over her brow, shielding the pretty flush to
her cheeks.

What are you doing?

Lyra hugged her discarded dress to her breasts and tucked a
lock of her hair behind one ear. "Protecting your upstanding reputation."

I snorted. *Let talk spread if it brings you back to my bed.*

Lyra let her dress fall back to the floor. She crept over the furs
and quilts, leveraging her naked thighs in a straddle over my
hips. On instinct, my palms went to her waist, as though not
touching her would bring physical pain.

Do you hurt at all?

She grinned. "A little. Very worth it, though."

I curled the end of her hair around one finger and spoke with the other hand. *You planned to leave without a word?*

Lyra's smile faded. "You were injured in battle. I wanted you to rest."

I slept better than I have in seasons. Rest can wait.

"This won't be accepted, Roark. You know it. Damir will consider it a distraction from your protection of the prince, and my duty as his melder."

A king's word will not stop me wanting you.

Her teeth tugged on her bottom lip, the corners tilted in a small grin. "Treasonous talk, Sentry Ashwood."

I kissed her, my fingers tangled in the hair at the base of her head. A dozen words I wanted to whisper against her lips danced in my mind—she brightened my heart, my damn soul. I wanted her to know now that I'd had her taste, no one would satisfy but her. Her touch was still burned on me like it had burrowed into my skin and would never leave.

I didn't want it to.

"I truly must go," Lyra whispered against my mouth. "But I truly want to stay."

It was a cruel reality. We had our duties, and I had strayed from my purpose here. There'd be no returning. From the moment I met the fiery gaze of Lyra in the jarl's house, what I thought I knew of my life, of my existence, had unraveled.

One thread at a time.

AFTER LYRA LEFT, ESCORTED BY A YOUNG STAV TO THE PALACE, I managed to slip on a clean tunic by the time a heavy-handed knock pounded on my door with a summons to the great hall.

A smaller crowd had gathered than expected. The prince without his bride. Edvin, his hands on the shoulders of a small mousy boy. I did not know why the bone crafter was in the hall; he mattered little to the king.

Damir and Ingir were both seated on the dais, and Hundur had taken his place, but Yrsa's mother was absent.

The Myrdan king kept rubbing his melded claws, a feral gleam in his gaze. Baldur stood in the center of the hall, reporting on his unit's actions last night. Tension was palpable and sour on the tongue.

No one knew who'd welcomed the ravagers into our gates. I felt the same, but for reasons different from the king's. He wanted his posterity and power protected. For me, I wanted to pluck out the bones of the traitor for the risk they put on Lyra's head.

"Good morning. Enjoyable evening?" Emi's voice came from behind.

I spun around. Emi and Darkwin, two wraiths in the corner, stood side by side. Both were pressed and clad in their Stav uniforms. Kael in his black tunic with the white wolf head, Emi in a crimson cloak she'd worn in Skalfirth.

My cousin wore a cunning sort of grin. Kael appeared to be made of stone; only his shadowed gaze followed me.

I settled next to Emi, unnoticed for a moment. *Were you injured?*

"Darkwin made it out with shallow cuts, but I nearly met Salur. It is good bone tonics favor crafter blood and worked swiftly."

Damn the gods. I was an ass. While she'd suffered last night, I'd hardly had a fear for her. I'd tangled myself up, thought of my wants, my heart, of Lyra, and no one else. *You are well?*

Emi smiled softly. "I'm all right." My cousin looked me up and down, settling her attention to the side of my neck. "And you?

You seemed to have had an . . . enjoyable night after ravagers were chased away."

Darkwin faced forward, the muscles in his neck pulsed.

The night was fine. I schooled my expression into something flat.

Emi clicked her tongue. "Disappointing. Sounds utterly adequate and dull. I expected more."

I pierced my cousin in a cutting glare, then faced the dais as Baldur stepped aside for Edvin and his son.

"Darkwin." King Damir waved his fingers, summoning Kael forward. "I understand you were in the market."

Kael dipped his chin. "A few scattered ravagers managed to slip past the line. They were set on breaching the palace. My fellow Stav, myself, and Mikkal Jakobson caught them."

"Yes. I heard the Jakobson heir was wounded." Damir rubbed his chin and looked to Edvin's son. "And you, boy. You are here since I understand you were present when my Berserkir was slaughtered."

With a gentle nudge, Edvin urged his boy forward. Next to Damir, the child looked thin and fragile. "There were monsters."

"Boy's first encounter with a true warrior." Damir chuckled and bent forward. "Sometimes, while in the throes of battle, a warrior may seem monstrous."

"He went for Súlka Bien and the other monster helped save her."

King Damir looked to Edvin for clarification.

"My son believes he saw the Draven assassin who leads the ravagers, sire."

"Skul Drek. The wraith of Dravenmoor." Damir's movements were stiff as he descended the steps of the dais. "And why, exactly, was my melder near a Draven assassin?"

"Bad seed, that one," King Hundur grumbled. "Talented, but bad seed, Damir."

I curled a fist around the hilt of my blade.

"Easy, cousin." Emi spoke from the corner of her mouth. "No need to have everyone question your loyalties."

"You consider my melder your kin, Darkwin." The king clasped his hands behind his back and squared his shoulders to Kael. "What do you know of it?"

"I spoke with Lyra in the healer's wing," Kael said. "She was unharmed, but from what I understand, Berserkir Ake had succumbed to the berserksgangur. However, instead of the strength of his melded bones guiding him toward ravagers, the bloodlust was aimed at the boy and the melder."

The king hummed, a cruel sneer on his mouth. "And why was my melder beyond the palace gates?"

Kael hesitated. "She admitted it was foolish. The Sentry saw her safely in her chamber, but she left shortly after. She told me the thought of . . . those she cared for being at risk spurred her to act, my king."

King Damir huffed. "Foolish indeed. What do you know of her interactions with the assassin?"

"Marvel that she came out alive," Queen Ingir muttered with a touch of disappointment.

Perhaps the queen lived for a good tale; perhaps she despised soul bones as much as the ravagers.

"I do not know much, sire," Kael said. "From what young Krisjan has said, it seems the Berserkir was entangled with the assassin, and both the boy and melder used it as an opportunity to escape."

"Father." Thane stepped beside Kael. He walked with a limp, but no visible wounds were on his skin. "This is not a council to question the melder's motives. Every soul she values was fighting, and she believed she could protect them. Simple as that. What we ought to be asking is, Who betrayed us and opened the gates for ravagers?"

"The Berserkir no longer had the melded bone," said Hundur. "You think such a thing could be done by anyone but a melder? She is not to be trusted."

Emi's touch was the only hint that I'd shifted at all. One step had been taken toward the dais. Gods, what was I planning to do? Attack a king?

"Keep your head," Emi said through her teeth.

"You are still angry over your dead seneschal's son, Hundur," Thane shot back to the Myrdan king. "But if we're going to continue leveling accusations, all right, let us make accusations. Strange how the gates opened after your arrival. Could it be you are displeased with your daughter's betrothal?"

"Enough." Damir held up a hand, stalling the arguments. "Myrda and Jorvandal will be united as bonded allies sooner rather than later. By tomorrow's moon you will wed the princess, Thane."

Thane shifted, uneasy, but gave a nod.

"But"—Damir's lip curled into something vicious—"to see the ceremony safely concluded, I am instating mandatory rank melding come morning. Every Stav."

My blood went cold. Baldur's eyes gleamed with delight, but Emi shrunk back.

King Damir lifted his gaze to me. "Including you, Sentry."

"Father. Ashwood answers to me."

"And *you* answer to me!" King Damir roared. "If he serves Jorvandal, then he serves me. My Stav Guard will be melded with every last soul bone. We will show the Dravens what becomes of fierce warriors when they are made fiercer. We will take the power of the gods until the ravines of Dravenmoor run with blood."

"You plan to empty your stores of soul bones?" Ingir said, a quiver to her voice.

Damir looked back at her. "All of our forages will be melded before the vows. Not a single Stav Guard will go without."

"That could kill Lyra," Thane shouted. "One meld nearly brings her to her knees."

"Then I will see to it she is well rested." Damir plucked a horn of honey ale off the table and sloppily drank before tossing it aside with a clatter.

"You believe her to be this strong?" Ingir asked.

"She has abilities not even Fadey could match."

The queen rubbed a green pearl in one of her rings. "Well, I stand by your choice, husband. The gods have provided us with a way to restore the kingdoms to what they once were."

With open arms, Damir spun around. "Blessings of the gods must truly be upon us, my wife and I see eye to eye."

Chuckles filtered through the hall. I heard nothing but the blood pounding in my skull.

The stores of soul bones were kept under guard, and not even I knew how many had been gathered over the years. Lyra wouldn't survive it. Craft would devour her, and every Stav, every good soul I knew, would be corrupted.

"Now, on the matter of who unlocked our gates," Damir went on. "Captain Baldur, you will investigate. Begin with any who might have a distaste for my son's upcoming vows or our new melder."

Baldur pressed a fist to the wolf emblem on his tunic.

"I will need the melder under vigilant watch." The king snapped at Kael, "Darkwin, an obvious choice as her brother, you will assist the Sentry in ensuring the woman is never alone. I don't care if you stand watch as she takes a piss, you are there."

The same as Baldur, Kael pounded his chest. We'd gotten on fine enough, me and Darkwin, but when he returned to my side, he said nothing. He did not even look my way.

When the king dismissed us, the three of us followed Thane. The prince asked Emi to be the one to inform his bride of the change to their vows, no one the wiser of his ulterior reasons. In truth, he was offering a final evening between two hearts before life changed for good.

Thane was a greater man than me. His selflessness held no bounds, he sacrificed for others, and did what was best for the kingdom.

I would burn the whole of this land to keep one heart beating.

"Sentry Ashwood." Kael kept his gaze trained on the floor. "A word."

There wasn't time. I needed to see to Lyra. I needed to find a way to keep her from the damn soul bones. No time, but I had the dignity to look the man in the eye.

Thane gestured he would return to the hall. Hopefully he'd be bold like his namesake and kill his father before the power-mad king killed Lyra.

Kael kept one hand on the hilt of his blade. "I need to know that Lyra is not a conquest to you. I live in the Stav Wing. I know what it is like."

Gods. I had no time for his misplaced speeches about Lyra's honor. A cruel sort of grin split my mouth. Kael understood some of my hand speak, but not enough. I pulled out a strip of parchment and wrote my reply.

Lyra is the one who lives through this. That is my only conquest. Keeping her alive.

When he looked at me again, his eyes were less hardened. "Do that, Ashwood," he said in a grit-rough rasp. "And there will be no troubles between us."

I could respect the man for his defensiveness toward Lyra. It would be needed now.

We took the staircase to the upper floors in silence that danced across the skin in a discomfiting tension.

Emi waited for us there, twisting her fingers nervously.

You should go to Yrsa, I gestured quickly.

"I will. But first, how do you plan to keep her from the bones?"

I shook my head. I'd think of something. There was no choice.

"What are you talking about?" Kael's face tightened again.

Emi glanced at me. I waved my hand, a lazy gesture to give her freedom to speak what she wished.

"You heard Thane. Lyra will not survive melding so many bones, Kael."

"But King Damir—"

"Is obsessed with power." Emi kept our pace of two stairs at a time. "He grows in might and viciousness the more bones he uses. This attack was an insult on his fortress, so he will prove his strength without considering what will happen to Lyra when he does."

I gestured wildly. *Soul bones always fuel the Dravens to act. They will come against Stonegate with their Dark Watch. Not only ravagers.*

"Why?" Kael quickened his steps to meet my pace. "Do they want to use the bones for their armies, like Damir?"

I shook my head. Lyra knew the king was searching for the Wanderer's bones. Lyra had only just learned the truth, but I had known it all my life.

The soul of the man who once commanded all craft was the prize of Jorvandal, and always had been, since Damir's grandfather melded his father's bone to his chest. It'd be wise to give up the truth to Darkwin. The more he knew of the risks, the more his own devotion for Lyra's safety would take hold.

I glanced at Emi. *Tell him.*

She gave a swift explanation of foraging the burial grounds of the Wanderer's armies. Fallen crafters of old. But Kael came to a halt when she told the rest.

"The Wanderer was . . . real?"

Emi shook her hands, as though sloughing off a swell of nerves. "We believe he was. Damir wants to meld the soul of the Wanderer to his own, but the bones are scattered. Soul bones don't merely strengthen a body, Kael, they bring a soul damn close to immortality. But they can also corrupt. That was why Ake could not escape the lust for death. He was a vicious man before, and his bones made him crueler."

"I don't feel a great change after taking the soul bone."

"You just nearly threatened the Sentry," Emi said, grinning. "The man I met during frost trainings would not have dared meet Roark's gaze out of turn."

"So I'm damned to become a brute?"

"No." Emi snickered softly. "I truly think that came from your love for Lyra. You would've been much crueler if the bone in your chest was one wrapped in darkness. Roark chose it carefully."

"You're plotting against the king." Kael raked his fingers through his hair. "Aren't you?"

What did I say? Damn them all if they threaten her, I told him without looking away.

"Lyra will not survive, Kael," Emi said. "But more than that, if Damir uses so many soul bones, Dravenmoor will be ready for war as much as Stonegate."

"Godsdammit. Then what do we do?" Kael finally asked the question for which I had no answer.

I shook my head and rounded the corner to the corridor that would lead to Lyra's chamber.

There was a frenzy in my blood, something desperate and chaotic. I'd been controlled and collected most of my life. Now I could scarcely form a thought beyond finding some way to get Lyra free of these walls.

Free of it all.

Emi went on in a tone laced with bitterness. "Someone let the ravagers in, and I would gamble on my life that it was for Lyra more than disrupting the vows."

"Then enemies are already here," Kael insisted.

"Closer than you think," another voice answered. Yrsa stepped from one of the alcove windows, head shrouded in a dark cloak.

Emi rushed to her side and took her hand. "I was coming for you. They've . . . your father and Damir have moved your vows to tomorrow."

Yrsa dropped her gaze to their entangled hands. "My mother told me it was a possibility."

I knew this night was trying for them, for Thane, for most in Stonegate, but I could not waste time.

I pounded a fist against the wall, drawing the princess's attention. *What have you learned?*

The princess knew of our familial bond. She cared for Emi and in turn, during the lonely months spent in her own kingdom, she'd practiced enough she was nearly fluent in my hand speak.

"I'm not certain. Just talk of enemies in the gates," Yrsa said, voice low. She took hold of my hand. "We ought to be wary, the lot of us."

When she stepped back, the princess returned my glare with a gentle smile.

Darkwin and Emi insisted the princess return to the protection of her guards. I turned and unraveled the crushed strip of parchment Yrsa had deftly placed in my hand.

I read the name she'd written in the center. A name of whom she believed to be responsible for opening the gates. It was an accusation she would not want to make openly, but knew if she told me, the Death Bringer would make good on such a reputation.

My blood burned in my veins. Darker edges of my soul sliced to the surface like jagged bits of stone. I was going to do horrid things.

Vicious things.

I could hardly stand the wait.

LYRA

CORRIDORS WERE QUIET, AND I COULD NOT SHAKE THE feeling that something had gone on since dawn came.

I'd expected a meet with the king. Perhaps an order of execution for my head.

Fears I hadn't shared with Roark. In his arms, for one peaceful night, I'd forgotten to be afraid.

I leaned over the basin in my washroom, studying my features in a gilded mirror.

Glass jars sealed with wooden lids were lined atop a shelf over the wide basin. One of the jars nearly slid from my hands when the golden edge bled with murky black, when sunlight burned in cold, blue skeins through the window.

I drew in a sharp gasp of air, readying to scream, when his dark, billowing reflection stood behind me.

Before I could utter a sound, Skul Drek twisted me against his body, a cold misty hand—or a bit of his darkness—muzzled over my mouth.

"Do not take the bones with the sunrise." The thick rasp of his voice was different, almost desperate. "Enemies stand on both sides. They will find you, hunt you." I shuddered against the frosted breath on my skin when he tilted his hooded head near my cheek. "Do not take the bones."

Ribbons of night slithered off my skin, phantom chills left in their wake, when he pulled away. "What . . . what bones?"

"Any of them. Every bone the Thief King has found."

"Damir's soul bones?"

Skul Drek stepped to the corner of the washroom. He was fading, drifting. Sunlight was returning to warmth.

Whatever craft kept him here, he was allowing it to pull him away.

I held out a hand to stop him. "What do you know? Why are you warning me?"

Darkness encircled me. Cold breathed over my skin, and I was drawn in deeper, like an embrace of shadows. Like the phantom had pulled me close. His burning gaze steadied me. "Your soul is mine. I won't lose it."

I didn't breathe. He believed I belonged to him?

When warmth returned, when darkness retreated, I slumped against the edge of the basin, hardly able to draw a breath. Skul Drek was gone.

A heavy knock sounded on the washroom door.

In a rush, I wiped at my eyes, reorienting myself to reality. The way I could fall into the mirror realm was horrifying and I didn't understand it.

When I opened the door, my eyes fell on the Sentry.

"Roark." Memories of his touch, his kiss, the rough, low gasps he'd breathed against my skin, collided when his sharp eyes found me.

Roark held up a hand, then went to the chamber door, turning a brass key until the lock clicked. In three long strides, he had me in his arms. I clung to his waist, biting down on my bottom lip to muffle the fear.

"What is happening out there?" I pressed my forehead against his chest.

Roark's palm cupped the back of my head, holding me to his heart for a long silence. He led me to the chaise and laced our fingers together before he spoke.

The wedding vows are now set for tomorrow evening.

I bit down on the inside of my cheek. "How are Thane and Yrsa?"

Prepared. Roark's knee started to bounce. *Lyra, for added protection, Damir has ordered you to meld every Stav, me included, with the lot of his soul bone store. Every bone.*

Do not take the bones. "He knew." I closed my eyes, my grip tightened on Roark's hand. "Skul Drek was here."

He looked at me, befuddled.

"He . . . he can't be a man. He was there and gone, like a damn haunt." I leaned onto my knees and buried my face in my palms. "He told me not to take the bones. He knows. That means ravagers know."

Roark used one knuckle to tilt my chin. *Ravagers are not the threat. It is the bones. That many will kill you.*

My blood chilled. Roark didn't spare my fears. It was frightening and refreshing to be trusted with the vicious truth rather than sweetened omissions. He admitted his fear for what melding would do, fear for the retaliation from Dravenmoor.

It won't happen, Lyra. One palm pressed against my cheek.

"There isn't an escape from it," I said, voice small. "Where am I to go?"

Roark's jaw worked in tension. He shook his head, his thumb tugging on my lip. *I don't know yet. But I will not let him touch you.*

His words lanced through me, sharp as a blade. The Sentry, fealty melded to the heir of Stonegate, was speaking of desertion, of treason. As a Draven, to commit such crimes against Stonegate would most assuredly mean a brutal death for Roark Ashwood.

I kissed him. I kissed him with a frenzy and passion that felt wild and out of control. Roark wasted no time in claiming me back. He tugged on my waist, pulling me over him so my thighs straddled his lap. The crescent moon of his Sentry sword dug into my skin. He made quick work of ridding himself of the bearded ax and seax with the clang of heavy metal against the wood floors.

I was frantic. He was desperate.

Hands tugged at clothes, at laces, and belts, until his length was deep inside me. I braced my hands on his shoulders, using him as a ballast as I lifted slightly, then sat back over his cock. Roark's gasp was hot against my neck. He guided my hips with his palms and rocked against me.

I pinned him to the chaise with my body, using my movements, touch, and kiss as a sort of command to the Sentry to give over his control, the worries crushing his spine. Brow strained, Roark let me.

His head fell against the back of the chaise, and his bleary eyes watched as I writhed and bucked over him.

I took my time, adjusting to the fullness of him.

Those molten eyes locked with mine. His callused palm glided up the curve of my waist, the divots of my ribs, until he palmed the whole of one breast.

I bowed my spine, pushing into his palm. Roark pinched and

tugged at my nipple, then adjusted on the sofa and took the other side between his lips, sucking and licking until the peak hardened.

I cried out his name when he rolled the tip between his teeth while his fingers worked the other. I rocked against him, gasping when he bucked, striking a new depth.

Heat pooled low in my belly.

My head fell back, his name cascading over my tongue again and again; my body shuddered through my release.

Roark gripped my chin, forcing me to look at him again. The heat of my pleasure still throbbed in my core, but when I followed his gaze down, looking at us joined together, watching as his length still moved in and out, I thought I might lose myself again.

My arms rested on his shoulders, but I gripped the back of the sofa, keeping my head down so I would not miss a moment.

Roark's breaths were hot against my neck. One hand gripped my waist, holding me in place as he deepened his thrusts. Each motion shifted the wooden legs of the sofa a little more, wood scraped over wood. We didn't stop, didn't slow.

Roark freed a rough groan and went taut. His cock twitched and the warmth of his release spilled into me.

Spent and breathless, Roark tucked a lock of hair behind my ear, meeting my gaze.

I dipped my head and kissed him gently. For a long while, I didn't move off his lap. We stayed there, joined for a time. Roark held my head to his heart, and sometimes his lips would press into my hair.

On my bare spine, his fingers moved in deliberate patterns, and it took me a moment to realize he was repeating the same thing over and again.

Yours, body and soul.

WHEN KAEL ARRIVED AT THE DOOR, ROARK WAS THE SENTRY again, steadfast and standing watch near the window.

Kael pressed a kiss to the top of my head and took a seat beside me. "I'm assuming you've been filled in on King Damir's plans."

"I'm to be his sacrifice."

Kael clenched a fist over my knee. "We're going to find a way to make sure that doesn't happen."

"Yes." I cut a glance at Roark. "So I've heard. Trouble is, I'm not sure how either of you can declare loyalty to me when you are bound to serve Damir."

"I serve Stonegate," Kael snapped. "I serve Jorvans. Not just a king. You are Jorvan, you are family, you are of Stonegate. I will serve and defend you."

Stupid, reckless, brave Kael. I took hold of his hand and squeezed.

Roark turned. He didn't address me; instead, he spoke to Kael. *Keep watch until I return.*

"Where are you going?" Both Kael and I asked in unison.

Roark paused at the door. *Darkwin. Fail her, and I tear out your spleen.*

Kael hardly seemed bothered by the threat.

"Wait, Roark. Where are you going?"

Roark looked at me. *I have a meet I cannot miss. I'll return soon.*

I had no time to press the Sentry before he slipped out the door without a glance behind. Bastard. It was intentional. One look, and Roark would know I would delay him, question him, tempt him to stay.

My pulse raced. Where would he go? "Why did he threaten you?"

Kael scoffed and kicked out his legs, crossing his ankles. "If I had to guess? Because he's completely in love with you. The man simply says it in odd ways."

ROARK

MOONLIGHT SPLIT THE BLACK SKY IN SILVER, BUT NEVER reached the corners of the old woodsheds in the far edges of the garden.

I waited, never moving, my head shrouded in a thick, woolen cowl. Stav patrols took their routes on the narrow garden paths, this way and that, muttering to their patrol partners about nothing of significance—trysts from the feasts, reprimands from their superiors, one found an odd boil on his cock that had him worried.

All the while, none knew I was crouched in the shadows by the shed.

Unseen until I wanted to be seen.

Footsteps came from one of the bowers at my back. I didn't turn around, not even when she crouched beside me. "Going to tell me what was so damn important you tore me from Yrsa on the last night before I am made a mistress?"

Thane would never mistreat Emi, but no matter the prince's

thoughts on the arrangement, it was true—Emi would always be a royal mistress.

We have a meet beyond the gates. I'll need your words. I paused at the door to the shed. The night was silent enough, misplaced sounds would be simple to hear, and the old door was the sort to screech on the hinges.

I managed to pry open a gap wide enough for us to slip through and close the door without more than a small groan. Emi didn't wait for my word and walked sideways through the maze of old root crates and stale casks until she reached the far corner.

Together we peeled back the thick woven mat and lifted the narrow hatch built into the floor.

The tunnel was simpler to take when we were lanky youth, but we managed to creep through on our bellies well enough. Dug when Emi sent her plea to me for rescue after my uncle nearly snapped her neck, we'd kept the tunnel open and hidden if ever there were a threat.

I never anticipated slinking about in secret, forbidden tunnels to protect a melder.

Then again, I never anticipated a melder to rob me of my heart.

I pulled myself free first, then clasped Emi's hand and tugged her out. The mouth opened beneath black willows. Silvery buds adorned the drooping limbs and leaves, causing the trees to keep the appearance of frosts throughout the seasons.

I ducked behind a rocky mound with a direct vantage to the path leading away from the fortress, toward the sea road.

"Roark." Emi pulled her crimson hood up. "What are we doing? Aren't you supposed to be protecting Lyra?"

I am.

No mistake, I was keen to get this part of the night finished.

Whatever I learned in these moments would help us plot our steps for how I'd get Lyra away from those damn soul bones.

No bells rang in warning. Drums and plucking strings were the only sounds from the palace. More revelry, more feasts. The celebrations leading to Thane's approaching vows had not ceased despite the attack. Damir would not want to allow anything to bring into question his abilities to protect his kingdom. In turn, the king behaved like nothing was ever amiss.

With Damir's new command for me to protect Lyra, no one would wonder where I'd gone. Thane would be unsettled, but hiding it behind a grin at his father's side. Through our fealty bond, he might sense my unease if he took the time to draw upon the bone shard.

Soon, I would need to admit hard truths to a man I considered my brother.

I hoped, someday, he might forgive me for what I needed to do.

"Who's coming, Roark?" Emi peered around the thick trunk, scanning the night road.

If we're right, Yrsa already sent a summons to the one who opened the gates.

Emi blew out a breath. "Under your name?"

Do you take your lover for a fool, cousin? She suspected a traitor and merely followed her instinct by sending an unsigned meeting place summons. If we're clever enough, we may find all our answers by asking the right questions.

I handed over Yrsa's note with the explanation and name she suspected. Emi scanned it in the dim light and murmured a quick "Bastard," but said nothing more until the crunch and click of hooves over stone came from the road.

I pulled the cowl farther over my brow and stepped out onto the forest path, Emi at my back.

Tomas Grisen reared back on the harness on one of the palace horses. My cousin hissed a curse under her breath.

"Come to deliver on your promise at long last." Tomas spoke with effort now that his jaw was still fused in some areas. His voice was strained and slurred.

Soon enough, it wouldn't matter.

I nudged Emi. *Speak for me, but do not let on the words come from me.*

She stepped forward, standing in a way that allowed her to watch my gestures in the dark and still speak to Tomas.

Emi chuckled. "What is it you think you deserve from us? And, truly, why would we do anything for you?"

Tomas's misshapen mouth worked side to side, grinding his jagged teeth. "You swore if I caused the distraction, you would fix what that whore did to me."

There it was—his motivation. Yrsa's note gave up her suspicion Tomas had something to do with the attack, but not why.

Emi grinned, shadows from her hood adding a formidable darkness to her features. "And you call what you did a distraction?"

Tomas kicked one leg over the horse, fists clenched in fury. "I risked my life summoning the Dark Watch."

Emi played the part as indifferent, giving her time to follow my questioning. "And yet I did not get what I wanted."

"It is no fault of mine if you didn't kill the woman."

"The melder?"

"Who else?" Tomas took a step back. Fear edged his voice.

I reached behind me and took hold of the ax handle, ready to pull it free of the sheath. Heat prickled along the scar on my neck.

With my other hand, I directed Emi. *Find out how long he's been aligned with Queen Elisabet.*

"You played your role. But I must ask. Ser Grisen, have you

always been a traitor to your king?" Emi tossed back her hood, revealing her features. "Aligning with Dravenmoor—"

"You?" Tomas stiffened. He looked into the trees, his face losing color. "You wrote the missive about the gates? But . . . you're Draven?"

He summoned the Dark Watch but . . . was he not working under the demands of the Draven queen? His unease at Emi's heritage was discomfiting and I didn't understand it. Who else would want to involve Dravenmoor in Lyra's slaughter save their queen?

Tomas swallowed thickly. "But you wanted her dead to take her bones and make room for your melder. Why would Draven folk keep a melder?"

I tapped the ground. Emi looked down with the slightest tilt of her head to read my hands. *It wasn't Dravens who wanted Lyra this time.*

My stomach cinched. Another melder?

Tomas's stun was sincere. He believed whoever conspired with him to open the gates had the craft of melding at their disposal to heal his jagged jaw. But his befuddlement hinted to us the missive came from a traitor *within* the fortress. Not from across the ravines.

The bastard was so desperate to be healed, he allowed the slaughter of innocents and he nearly caused Lyra's death.

I'd see to it he endured the same.

A slow rumble of a laugh built in my chest until the sound shifted in my throat.

I took hold of the ax and spun the head once, twice. My skin overheated, and rage and violence blurred out conscious thought. Before he had a moment to take note of my movements, the sharp beard of the ax rammed into the back of his shoulder.

He cried out and stumbled forward. The horse nickered and ran off down the road, back to its stables.

Stav would see the beast soon enough and alarms would be sounded. I had plans to be curled against Lyra's body before the first signal.

Tomas whimpered in the dirt. Fool tried to scramble away on his stomach, blood fountaining from his back. I took slow steps, deliberate, and intended for him to hear each stride. He cried out to the gods when I stepped between his shoulder blades, pinning him to the dirt, and wiggled the ax head free of his bones.

I lowered to one knee, gripped his hair, and wrenched his head back. The night darkened around us the more my disdain for the man boiled in my blood.

One hand gripped his manipulated chin. I tossed back my hood, taking a great deal of pleasure in his wide eyes, wet with fearful stun.

Gods, I'd waited for this from the moment he put his damn hands on Lyra Bien.

Another soft, muffled sound rolled from my chest. The sound shifted into something deeper, something heavier. Until it scrambled with Tomas's screams of terror and I lunged.

"FINISH YOUR MEET?" KAEL'S CHIN WAS PROPPED ON THE CLAW of his hand where he sat in front of the inglenook.

I locked Lyra's chamber door at my back and lowered my chin in a nod, not giving up anything else before striding into the washroom. I placed my bloody ax in the basin, hair lifting on my neck, the burn of eyes on the back of my head.

"Do I get to ask?" Kael filled the doorway.

I shook my head and tore off my tunic.

Darkwin seemed as though he might like to argue, but thought better of it. "She's been asleep for the better part of a bell toll."

I clapped him on the shoulder, gestured that I would be keeping watch inside her room, ignored the roll of his eyes, and slipped into the bedchamber.

Lyra hugged one side of the bed. Sleep had taken her with a worried brow. I kicked off my boots and slipped beneath the furs from the other side, careful not to wake her. She let out a sigh when I draped my arm over her waist and curled my body around hers.

I breathed in the sugared scent of her hair until her body sank against mine and her breaths were deep and steady, at peace.

For now.

LYRA

I WAS ALONE IN THE BED WHEN THE PALE MORNING LIGHT stirred me from sleep. Still, I knew Roark had slept beside me. The other half of the down mattress smelled of him. I hugged the second pillow, breathing in the dewy forest scent of him before I dared face the day.

I could not shake the unease that no matter what happened, my life after today would not be the same.

Foreboding never lifted, not during a somber morning meal with my two silent shadows. Kael had nothing boisterous to say, a few smiles, a few comments about my lazy braid. Roark hardly met my gaze until commotion in the corridors drew our curiosity.

"What is it?"

Roark held up a hand, inspected the chattering stampede of noble folk and courtiers rushing to the wide window at the end of the corridor. A few ladies covered their mouths, gasping in horror. Even a man or two wrinkled his nose, cursing to the gods.

Roark held out a hand, waiting for me to take hold, then led us to a narrower lancet, away from the crowds, and peered down to the courtyards below.

"Good gods." Kael's soft curse blew against my hair when he peered over my head.

Waves of sick churned in my stomach. Displayed over the gates that had been left open during the attack, Tomas Grisen's head was spiked at the top. Limbs were draped over the walls; ribs and what looked to be a spine were propped against the gate.

It was horrible and gruesome and filled with rage.

And my heart knew.

While others retched and gasped at the sight, there was one who grinned.

Roark's mouth was set in a look of satisfaction.

I glanced down at his freshly scrubbed palms, to his damp hair, noting the clean scent of his skin. A shudder danced down my arms when he stepped against me from behind. On the small of my back, his fingers moved slowly, giving me time to *feel* his words, heart-deep.

He lived once after touching you. He opened the gates, believing the Dark Watch would come for you. I could not ignore the insult a second time. Do I frighten you?

Roark's body crowded mine. I couldn't breathe, couldn't look away from the slaughter below. I ought to be afraid, fear the true nature of the Death Bringer. I wasn't afraid, and I did not know what sort of woman that made me.

I shook my head and squeezed his palm three times. He drew in a sharp breath and covered my heart, gently patting my skin, once, twice, three times.

He was mine.

And I was his.

"WE ARE NO CLOSER TO A WAY TO KEEP LYRA FREE OF THE SOUL bones." Kael paced the length of the sitting chamber. "Though I applaud your . . . creativity, Sentry, you've admitted Tomas did not give up those who made the deal. I think it's time we get Lyra out of the gates."

I could not shake the image of Tomas's mangled form.

I always imagined love meant being willing to die for someone. I supposed it was true. But what no one told young, girlish hearts was sometimes they fell for a man who *killed* for them instead.

"Kael, the gates are lined with Stav and Myrdan guards. If we try to leave, we'll need to fight our way out."

An option, Roark offered.

"No." I shot him a narrow look. "It isn't."

Roark leaned against the wall near the inglenook. *I should speak to Thane. He'd distract guards, lie, anything. He does not want this any more than we do.*

"He is preoccupied today."

Then he can speak to the king on your behalf.

I tilted my head. "You believe King Damir will bend on this? He is waging war, not entertaining guests."

Roark closed his eyes for a breath, then spoke in hurried gestures. *He might get him to delay, use the wedding as a reason. At least we would have more time.*

Kael squinted, clearly doing his best to follow, and in the end he nodded. "If there's a chance the prince can help us create a delay, then I agree we should tell him. Even one night could help, Ly."

Roark made a move for the door.

"Wait." I shot to my feet. "That's the decision? No other options? What if Prince Thane can't meet with the king, or what if Damir doesn't listen? What then? We have no other plans, and if we have no other plans, what do we do if it all goes awry?"

Words tumbled free in a rush of breath. Roark altered his course and took my face in his palms, soothing the panic with a few strokes of his thumbs over my cheeks.

For a moment we were alone, and Kael was not a silent observer. It was only us.

Roark pulled his hand away to speak. *We have no time for other plans. If it does not work, I will take to blades if needed to get you free of these walls.*

I gripped his wrists. "That's what worries me. You cannot take on an entire unit of Stav and live."

Roark pressed a kiss to the side of my head before gently moving his fingers near my face. *No faith in me.*

"Bastard." I pinched his waist. "That's not what I'm saying."

My skin was colder when he stepped back, returning to the door. *One bell toll. Give me that. If it does not work, we run. By any means.*

"I could try to meld. It might not be so taxing. Didn't Damir say I had more connection to the bones than even Fadey?"

"No," Kael insisted at the same time Roark shook his head. "Not even worth the risk."

Roark pointed at Kael, agreeing, then looked back to me. *One bell.*

My chest tightened with nerves when the door clicked at his back.

"I believe him," Kael said, studying the door. "After seeing what he did to Tomas, he'd burn Stonegate to the ground if it meant you were safe."

"I'd like to avoid bloodshed." I went to the window, unable to keep still.

Outside, folk traipsed the inner gates for the wedding feast, dressed in fine fur cloaks, jerkins, and gold-trimmed gowns.

King Hundur and his queen walked among them, condescending to their jarls and nobles. He still preened over his new melded claws, hardly concerned over the death of Ser Grisen. Hundur never cared Tomas's jaw had been manipulated; he only cared about being made a fool by the young melder. Today was a time of glory and power for him as his folk and Jorvan's offered boons to their house with well-wishes that his daughter's marriage would carry on his glorious line.

Tomas Grisen was nothing but a forgotten name to the Myrdan king now.

I had yet to catch a glimpse of Damir and Ingir.

"I should've run with you." Kael rested a hand on his seax pommel. "I was selfish, Ly."

"Selfish? Kael, you are not selfish."

He shook his head. "I wanted to prove Jakobson wrong for dismissing me. Gods, I wanted to rise in the ranks of the Stav so desperately. I never should've gone to training."

"It's required for every son."

"I don't give a damn." Kael rubbed the back of his neck. "Lyra, I lost my family, but found you. You are my sister and I . . . I should've run with you. Hidden you."

My face pinched. I flung my arms around his waist. "It isn't on you, fool."

Kael hugged me against him. "I still take the blame, pest."

"Perhaps it is best to face my fate. In here or out there, I will always find those who despise me or use me."

"Don't," Kael warned. "Giving your life for a king's lust for power is not why the gods blessed you with their magic, Ly."

I didn't know how long we stood there, but a rough knock

split us. Kael held up a hand, demanding I stay back, and cautiously opened the door.

"Captain Baldur." He straightened as Baldur shoved into the room.

Six Stav remained in the corridor, dressed in dark blue, the finer threads of their uniform reserved for grand festivals like a royal wedding.

"Stand down, Stav Darkwin." Baldur did not even glance at Kael. With a bit of reluctance, he dipped his head in a greeting to me. "Melder Bien. I've been sent to escort you."

"She is under the charge of the Sentry." Kael stepped between us. "We both were tasked by the king, as you heard yesterday, Captain."

Baldur's eyes darkened. "And my men and I have been sent as additions, Darkwin. I am not here to steal your duty. Which, speaking of, where is the Sentry?"

Kael hesitated. "He was called away by the prince."

Baldur chuckled. "Clear to see which duty matters most to Ashwood. Melder Bien, if you would." The captain opened an arm for the door, frowning when I didn't move. "What is it?"

"I'm not . . . certain I'm prepared to meld such a great number of bones. I've been feeling rather ill all morning."

Baldur's lip twitched. "Much like the king."

"What?"

"The king has been rather unwell. I have no knowledge if he is delaying the melding. I am not here to bring you to the king. The inner noble houses—which our queen and future queen consider you part of—are gathering in her wing. They would have you join them."

The queen and her damn luncheons. "The princess is in attendance?"

Baldur nodded. "For a time. To dress for the vows, I believe."

I cracked one knuckle. "The Sentry will need to be informed of where we've gone when he returns."

With a grunt of frustration, Baldur gestured at one of his men to seek out the Sentry. "May we leave now?"

I did not know how else to stall. Tension eased some knowing Yrsa would be there, knowing the gods might've taken pity on us and Damir's health might delay his rank melds.

Kael drew close to my side, never wavering, and we followed Baldur and his men into the gardens that were built off the queen's wing.

Most of the windows in Stonegate were placed in Queen Ingir's wing to let in the sunlight. To counter the dull shades of rugs and tapestries, the queen had small tables evenly spaced down her corridors topped in glass bowls with floating flowers to add a touch of color.

Bright as it was, I did not care to venture to this side of the palace. In the mirror world, the darkness was always thickest here.

Baldur led us into an open room near the back of the wing. Humid air brushed my cheeks—scents of silken blooms, damp soil, and rain filled each breath. Glass doors took up the whole of one wall and towering indoor vines with dewy blossoms and herbs crawled up the walls from painted pots. Delicate wooden tables were positioned to host numerous guests.

All the tables were empty.

Queen Ingir bent over one of her herb pots and poured a trickle of water from a small ewer.

"Ah. Melder Bien. You're safe. How glad I am to see it."

My heart bruised my ribs. "Is there any reason I wouldn't be, Highness?"

Ingir's red-stained lips curled. She said nothing, but Baldur spun on Kael, a narrow dagger leveled under his chin.

"What are you—" Kael's words cut off when Baldur nudged the point of the blade deeper, drawing blood.

"Stav Darkwin, you are to be tried for the murder of Ser Tomas Grisen, a nobleman of Myrda."

"What!" I tried to reach for Kael, but another of Baldur's guards pulled me back. "He didn't. No, stop. He had nothing to do with Tomas's death."

Gods, where was Roark?

Ingir's gentle hands curled around my shoulders, drawing me close. "I know, my girl. It is troubling to hear, no doubt."

"No!" I tried to shirk her hands, but the queen only tightened her grip. "He did not do it. He was with me the whole night. Stop." My voice grew shrill and desperate when a Stav kicked at the back of Kael's leg, knocking him to his knees.

They rid him of his blade and weapons in the next breath.

"I did not kill him," Kael gritted out.

Baldur chuckled. "You are a known liar, a man who ought to have been tried for treason for hiding the melder. Why would I believe you?" The captain turned toward me, a cruel grin on his face. "Keep him in chains until we see if someone else might give him a chance for a different fate."

The five remaining Stav surrounded Kael. One clamped a set of manacles around his wrists. He shoved. "Lyra! Go. Get to him. Get to him."

He was telling me to run, to find Roark. Something was horridly wrong here.

I screamed Kael's name when the guards dragged him away under the command of their captain. I writhed and tugged and clawed.

Queen Ingir hissed when one of my fingernails scratched over her hand. She shoved me aside, but Baldur was there to catch me.

The grin was wicked, ruthless. Every bit as cunning as his namesake of fox.

My eyes narrowed. "He did nothing."

"I'm sure he didn't." Baldur curled a hand around my jaw, squeezing. "But the queen is the authority of Stonegate, and whether he lives or dies now rests on your shoulders."

I trembled. "Where is the king?"

"We'll get to that." Baldur lowered his hand, but kept a firm hold on my arm. "I've wanted to *truly* meet you for some time, Súlka Bien. We're long overdue for a discussion. Listen closely now, lives may depend on it."

Queen Ingir's eyes had grown hateful and hard. When Baldur dragged me deeper into her room, toward one of the far tables, she looked more like a feral cat ready to lash out at the slightest movement.

Crates were stacked beside him. One lid was cracked, and inside were soul bones. Marked and prepared to be melded, bones by the hundreds were in piles inside each box.

Baldur took me around a tall beam coated in tangled ivy. A scream cut from my chest. My knees weakened.

I could not take my eyes off his mutilated face. King Damir was sprawled on the stone floor, unmoving, clad in his finest clothes. Fingers were melded as one, his skull was flattened so his chin was soldered to his breastbone. Open wounds bled through gashes in his gambeson, like he'd been pricked and scratched dozens of times.

My blood grew cold enough my body shivered.

The king was dead.

LYRA

MY FACE WAS WET WITH TEARS, BUT I FELT COLD, numb. I did not try to stop the tears; I couldn't even feel them fall.

Across the table, Baldur had taken one of the chairs, Queen Ingir at his side, a few seidr runes, dried black leaves, and a small paring knife in front of her.

"I'm sure you're confused." Baldur reeked of smugness. "Allow me to explain. It is no secret that the queen had a strong distaste for the king, but I, gods, I dreamed of the day I might finally watch the light leave his eyes. All those years on my knees, my body not my own, all for a prize he did not deserve."

Baldur's voice was sharp and rolled off his tongue like every word was rotten.

I lifted my chin, fists curled tightly in my lap. "What prize?"

"Don't play the fool. The Wanderer. You're searching for the bones."

I didn't deny it. What would be the point?

Baldur drummed his fingers on the table. "All that trouble in staging my own death, only to be drawn back by a simple woman who does not understand the true power of her craft."

I swiped my tongue over my lips, tasting salt and blood. "Who are you?"

He opened a hand, gesturing at King Damir's body. "I thought by the state of him, it would be quite obvious? No? All right, you know me as Baldur the Fox, but the name I was given was Fadey."

Panic rose in my chest. "Fadey."

Baldur—Fadey—opened his arms wide, chuckling. "Mesmerizing, isn't it?"

"But how . . . the prince, he has known Baldur's face since childhood."

"Oh yes. Baldur was practically raised here."

"But Prince Thane would know if you were not him."

"Not if I were to become someone new, Melder Bien." Fadey paused for a breath, as though considering how to continue. "Now, studying his mannerisms from the shadows, that took some doing. With Ashwood's keen eye always watching, I had to learn with great care how the Fox shifted his tone to how he scratched his cock."

I couldn't draw in enough air to fill my lungs. Only short, haggard breaths. He'd stalked, studied, then slaughtered the real Captain Baldur.

"Bone crafters are a lesser magic, but can be rather brilliant when given the chance," Fadey said. "With Baldur's true bones after his death, it wasn't so difficult for Stav Uther to rebuild his likeness on me. Body and face. Painful, but rather impressive."

"Stupid boy." Ingir shook her head and aligned the rune chips in front of her.

Fadey nodded. "Uther was a Stav Guard who was found dead right before you arrived. He was quite talented with his craft."

"Until the boy got greedy." Ingir frowned.

"Pity." Fadey rubbed his chin. "Once he began feeling like the allowance he was paid was not enough, he began his baseless threats. Talk like he would tell the king of our betrayal. Such a waste of good craft, but he had to be removed."

I could not stop shaking. "But Fadey's body was . . . it was found. He was tortured."

"Baldur's body." Fadey waved a hand around his face. "I thought I just explained what a talented bone crafter can do. Painful process, but a few pieces of my old features made up poor Baldur's new, tortured face."

"The king buried him right outside of my wing," Queen Ingir said. "He thought I despised Fadey, so it was meant as a slight. Little did that fool know."

I had felt the darkness of her quarters in the mirror land and beyond it. Baldur's body was in unrest, no mistake. It billowed pitch-black shadows from his angry soul.

"I was never truly convinced the melder child was dead. I tended to believe the rumors that she'd been smuggled from the raids." Fadey's eyes darkened. "For seasons, I worked with zealots, Unfettered Folk, even a few greedy ravagers to hunt down any rumor of a melder. I desperately desired freedom, and you were my way out. Replace me with a younger melder, and Damir would hardly mourn my unfortunate demise."

I blew out a rough breath. "Then why are you still here?"

Fadey smiled, but there was nothing bright to it. "After seasons of never sensing a single drop of his power, I believed the Wanderer's bones to be lost to myths and lore. Then the blood crafter we assigned to your little village sent word of silver scars in a simple servant girl."

Gods. Fadey was the man behind Vella's betrayal; the missives she'd written were to him.

"What did it matter if I was here?"

Fadey scoffed. "You truly know nothing about yourself. Why the very existence of you ended in bloodshed between kingdoms, all to find you?"

I curled my hands into fists. "I have a feeling you're about to tell me."

"In *Tales of the Wanderer*, who was it who taught the first craft king how to meld?"

My teeth ground together. I did not wish to speak a word, but Ingir dug a small knife into the side of my ribs, piercing the skin. I glared at Fadey. "The god-queen. From desperation to stop the greed of her own husband!"

Fadey laughed with bitterness. "Right you are, Lyra. The god-queen had the talent for the crafts through her high-born blood. There would not be a soul with her strength, her power, for centuries. Old sagas and poems from scholars translated prophecies and vows of the gods, and most believed the god-queen's power would be reborn in another." Fadey leaned onto his palms over the table. "You are the first female melder in centuries, Lyra Bien. What do you think everyone was to believe?"

Breath caught in my chest. No. This was madness. "I am not the god-queen."

"Of course you're not," Fadey sneered. "It is not a reincarnated soul, it is her strength the kingdoms desired. I thought it all shit before, then I saw you meld. What a find you are. One touch and you connected to a soul bone deep enough you fell into the melder's trance. That is when more bones are sensed and found.

It took me five winters of melding before the trance overtook me, and it was never as strong as yours."

Fadey rubbed at his own eyes. Blue tears spilled onto his cheeks, and beneath a thin sheen of color was a bolt of silver that distorted the black center.

I lifted my chin. "Why stage your death if you wanted me here anyway?"

Fadey ignored the question and asked his own. "What do you know about blood craft, Melder Bien?"

I cast a quick glance at the queen. "It heals, summons, wards."

"That is some, yes." Fadey paced along the edge of the table. "Most consider blood craft to be the weakest, but did you know it can create a blood tether between two people?"

My pulse quickened. I said nothing.

"Blood crafters often tethered each other during marital vows to show devotion." Fadey tugged a wooden talisman in the shape of two coiled serpents from beneath his tunic. "It isn't to be taken lightly, for a blood tether allows one to step inside the thoughts and mind of another, even borrow strength through the bond for a time."

I went still. "What are you saying?"

"Once you were found, it truly was not so difficult to get some of your blood." Fadey shared a wicked sort of grin with the queen. "You should not have been so reckless with that blade against your own throat in Skalfirth."

He draped the talisman in front of my face. Crimson stained the grains of the wood.

"With this," he went on, "the queen provided a way for me to follow you into your trance." His teeth flashed. "I know you are completely drawn to the souls of the fallen, and there, my, what secrets you keep."

Queen Ingir rose from her seat. "How long have you been bonded to Dravenmoor? To their assassin? You tried to slaughter my son!"

Her palm struck my face before I had time to dodge. I staggered in the chair, clutching my face. "No. I never sent any of the attacks."

"When I finally saw into your thoughts, I saw the soul bond between you," Fadey snapped.

"Soul . . . soul bond?" Did he mean the gilded rope between Skul Drek and me? "If you saw everything, you would know I did not understand what was happening, nor did he."

Fadey rubbed his chin, as though considering my words. "I couldn't see everything, more pieces of your time there. But it was enough to sense the bones. You have done something that no melder was able to do before. You've found a way to walk among the fallen, to sense their resting places like I never could. You will be able to see what I cannot see."

"The bones?"

Fadey sneered. "I have thought of nothing else but the Wanderer since I learned what Damir was after. I know the bones are scattered, but we've found one, and your strange bond with the assassin will be the key to taking it." He glanced back at Ingir. "We cannot get through the wards, and I cannot see them, merely sense a power unmatched. But with you, now all that will change."

"You want the Wanderer for yourself?" My voice came out in a dry rasp.

"I do."

"We do." Ingir paused in organizing her herbs, her tone abrupt.

Fadey pressed a hand to his chest. "We do. When Ingir's spell cast sensed a new power, a strong power, we wondered. When I tried to fall into a melder's trance, but was warded against the burial site by a new kind of magic, I knew we'd found something with unmatched craft."

I lifted my chin, terrified and furious all at once. "I will never meld them for you."

Fadey barked a laugh. "Oh, I already knew after this you'd feel betrayed enough you would never help us. But your strength and craft will do well enough."

"You can't have it."

"You won't have a choice over what bones I take. You'll be dead, Melder Bien."

I froze. My bones.

Fadey tilted his head. "You understand, don't you? I know it is unnatural and you are no warrior, but to meld your bones to mine will give me the power of your soul. I won't need your help to see and find the Wanderer's bones, for I will be strong enough to sense them myself. Maybe I'll even be able to keep your assassin pet."

"You cannot murder, or it corrupts the soul."

"Worth the risk to win the power of all crafts and kingdoms, my dear."

Ingir hummed while she made a circle with rune stones.

Gods, they were going to cut me to pieces.

"I know it is frightening," Fadey said, almost gently. "But when I gather the Wanderer, no crafter will ever fear cruel treaties. They will live under one king, one voice, as they once did. Your sacrifice will protect our folk for generations, Lyra."

"You're mad." I sat back as far as I could possibly move away from the man.

"No." Fadey chuckled. "Not mad. Determined."

"You might think you can run," Ingir said, adjusting the final rune piece, "but remember we have your brother. We'll corrupt him."

Fresh tears burned in my eyes. I would give my life for those I loved. To my soul I knew it.

"You killed your bone crafter," I said, reaching for anything to stall. "You will not be able to mark my bones with the soul cast."

Ingir pointed to her rune circle. "There are ways to be convincing, even to bone crafters. Perhaps we'll pay a visit to the pretty crafter you brought with you. Or her brother. Either will do."

Tears of hate stung. They'd compel and threaten Edvin or Hilda, keeping them imprisoned when they were only beginning to start anew with their families.

"I will give you painless herbs." Ingir stood and strode across the chamber to a row of potted plants. She looked over her shoulder. "You won't feel the blade."

My heart ached at the thought, the pain Kael would feel when he learned the truth.

The pain Roark might feel.

My lips trembled. Roark, who risked treason now, all to see me safe. Would he mourn the loss of me? Would he return to the stoic Sentry folk feared or resented?

I glanced at the knife Ingir left on the table beside her rune chips. The woman was a fool. There was a lesson Roark had taught me only this morning—to die for the ones we loved was honorable, but to kill for them was beautifully terrifying.

Without thought, I gripped the hilt of her knife and lunged to the other side of the table as Fadey scrambled to his feet. Ingir spun around, taken aback. She gathered her skirt and raced from her herbs, shouting at me to stop.

She would be too late.

Fadey wore the face of a Stav, but he was no warrior. Slow to react, allowing his stun to dull his instincts. I had time to ram the point of the knife through the top of his hand.

A weak strike. He cried out in pain all the same. The blade tore through his flesh. That was all I needed.

My palm covered the open flesh. Craft surged in my nose, my lungs, my tongue, a storm on the sea.

Fadey's shouts cracked in new fear when he realized what I was doing. Bone snapped, heated.

He tried to wrench his hand away from the table.

Already too many of the small bones in his fingers, his palm, had shifted to molten material, spilling out over the wood. I made quick work of opening another wound on his leg. Fadey cursed me, hissing and spitting, but weakened by the pain of his twisted hand.

I yanked his wrist enough to touch the golden threads of craft flailing off his palm to the open wound of his thigh, where new strands of gold bled off his bones beneath the flesh.

One stitch, two, was all I managed before his opposite fist slammed against my skull, knocking me back.

Still, slivers of bone from Fadey's hand were melded to the place above his knee, forcing him to hunch.

His skin flushed red with hatred. His eyes flashed like the burn of the molten hell when he tried to remove his hand and stand straight.

"You *bitch*." Spittle flung over his lips. "Kill her. Ingir, kill her!"

I ran toward the glass doors that opened to the knolls near the back gates of the fortress. Ingir shrieked and raced after me. I didn't stop, didn't look back.

Outside, the sun burned my eyes. I kept running, dodging some wandering guests and curious gazes.

"Stop her!" Ingir's voice was a broken sob. "S-stop the melder! She . . . she *murdered* the king."

I thought I might retch. Horns blared the longer the queen cried out my crimes. She sank to her knees for good measure. All sides of the sprawling lawns were edged in Stav Guard answering their lady's commands.

I spun back and forth. No direction was free from the glare of the white wolf symbol.

I was trapped.

ROARK

Something wasn't right.

I looked over my shoulder, expecting to see something dreadful. There was nothing but an open door and my cousin softly whispering to Yrsa as she helped pin the last of her braids in place.

My blood began to simmer, like some deeper piece of me could not shake the cloud of unease. It continued to gather like smoke from a doused fire.

"All I'm saying is I would've appreciated a word of warning." Thane fastened a silver arm ring around his wrist, two wolf heads snarled at each other on either end. "Might've even gone with you to slaughter the bastard."

Tomas doesn't matter now. I followed Thane to the end of his bed, speaking as we went, until the prince sat on the foot and tugged on polished black boots. *Lyra cannot meld, not so many. We need to delay, or rid Damir of the idea altogether.*

"Roark." He held up a hand. "I haven't heard from my father all morning. My mother sent word he is unwell. We have a delay." The prince stood and clapped a hand on my shoulder. "After the wedding, I will insist war is rather improper after such a celebration. If I am cunning enough, I might be able to earn us an additional week."

I won't leave her here to die, Thane.

The prince tilted his head, one brow arched. "What are you saying?"

My jaw tightened. *I think you know.*

Thane the Bold spoke a great deal, taunted and jested, but he was somber and silent for a long moment. "How long have you loved her?"

How would I ever explain the truths unraveling in my head the more I was near Lyra? I shook my head. *It doesn't matter. I won't watch her die.*

Duty above it all was the law in Stonegate. Thane had a duty to his kingdom to wed, to breed, to rule as his ancestors had always done. Good-hearted as he was, I did not anticipate he'd give up his honor for the desire of my heart.

No matter how close we were, to Stonegate and the royal house, I was still the Draven boy here to serve them. They were not here to serve me.

"They wouldn't take you in Dravenmoor."

I looked at the prince, a little stunned.

He paced, rubbing his chin. "We could hide her again in a small village, she's accustomed to that. But my father would never quit the search to find her again. There is nowhere else unless you plan to smuggle her over the Night Ledges and abandon her with Unfettered Folk. Maybe they won't eat her."

I frowned.

"What?" Thane tossed one hand up. "What would you have me do? I am not king here, and you cannot..." The prince paused. "Roark, you realize your presence would be a risk to her. If we take Lyra somewhere else, you cannot go with her. It will only draw too much attention, a Jorvan woman with a Draven."

This does not mean you can keep her. Sometimes you must give them up if it's what's best.

I'd been told I couldn't keep Lyra Bien once before. It was true then, and likely true now. I lowered my gaze. If it kept her alive, perhaps I could walk away from her again. The thought of it churned my insides in sick waves.

Thane dropped a hand to my shoulder. "We have time, my friend. I'll do all I can to give us at least a week to keep her safe. You're not the only one who cares for her now."

A week was time we needed to think of some other way to get her free.

A throat cleared. In the doorway was a young Stav. "Forgive me, my prince. I was sent to inform the Sentry that Stav Darkwin and Melder Bien were meeting the . . ." His gaze fell on Yrsa. "Well, they were meeting with the queen and the princess, but I can see the princess is here."

Lyra had not met with Yrsa.

Kael wouldn't take Lyra out of her chambers without reason, without a higher command.

There wasn't anyone who would command it but me, Thane, or perhaps the king.

"I never summoned Melder Bien," Yrsa whispered, her gaze falling to me.

"Roark—" Thane tried to take hold of my arm.

I shirked him away and took hold of the Stav swift enough the guard stumbled. I didn't know what I was saying, but my gestures were too frantic, and the younger guard gave Thane an imploring look.

"Who came to retrieve Melder Bien?" Thane's palm patted my chest, nudging me out of the doorway.

"Captain Baldur, Highness."

"And he was told she would meet with my mother and my bride?"

"Yes, Highness."

My body seized for a breath, then spurred into action. I shoved past the Stav Guard, storming into the corridor.

Thane's shuffled steps hurried to keep up. "Roark, keep your damn head, you stubborn bastard."

More steps ran after us, lighter than Thane's. Emi, no doubt. I didn't look back. A hand gripped my shoulder, spinning me around. I shoved Thane back, something dark, something cruel clawing to the surface.

I drew in a deep breath through my nose until the prickle of heat in my blood soothed. *Do not stop me again.*

"Think." Thane tapped the side of his head. "Baldur is pompous, but he has no reason to harm my father's precious melder. My mother might've summoned her—"

And your father might force her to meld. I waved my hands in a frenzy.

Thane sighed. "All right. We'll find her. If Baldur took her to meet with the queen, then we go to my mother's wing."

Emi placed a hand on my arm and squeezed. "Thane's right. We go there. All is going to be well."

Yrsa followed, a look of worry shadowed in her eyes.

I drew my seax, used my head to point toward the outer lawns, and did not wait for any farewells to be had to the princess before taking the staircase to the lower floor two steps at a time.

Something was not right.

The taste of smoke and brine burned like bile on my tongue. I felt the urge to lash out, to succumb to smoky shadows until I fell into nothing but the sharpest edges of my soul, hate and rage and avarice.

Wind whipped across the lawns. I shoved through mounting crowds strolling the outer courtyards, ignoring their gasps and declarations; some men had boorish manners.

Emi and the prince caught up, Thane still securing his short blade to his belt.

Instead of taking the paths through the gardens, I carved through one of the archways and down another set of steps, which would spit us out near the back of the queen's corner of the fortress.

I'd only stepped off the final stair when the bellow of ram's horns broke through the still morning. Boots stomped over mossy cobbles, and Stav captains shouted down from the watchtowers, bellowing commands.

"Go." Thane shoved me between my shoulders. "You're right, you're always right. Go."

We sprinted around the corner. The gentle slope looked down on the queen's private garden planted beside the wall of glass doors. Open lawns spread out to the knolls and final walls.

There, scrambling toward the edges of Stonegate, was Lyra.

From all sides, Stav Guard hunted her. Queen Ingir screamed on her knees, wailing over something I could not hear. Most sound was muffled anyway. The roar of craft filled my ears. For so long it was untamed, not mine to command. No longer. The power in my blood was mine to summon—to terrify, to kill.

"Roark?" Thane's voice was distant though he stood next to me. "What's on your scar? Is it bleeding?"

"Thane." Emi's voice trembled. "Step back."

The division of two pieces had never been mine to control until recent weeks. Until Lyra.

Little by little, the chains keeping the power out of my control had returned. My soul was tethered to hers and I would slaughter anyone who tried to break it.

Lyra stumbled. A Stav Guard grabbed hold of her ankle before she could run again.

Darkness, so cold it burned, ripped through every pore. Fear bled from her soul. I was consumed by it and it snapped the final strand tethering my will to keep control.

I freed the lash of darkness with a rough, chilling cry of her name.

LYRA

I RAN STRAIGHT AHEAD. I WOULD KNOW THE TRUTH, BUT TO anyone else, it appeared as though I'd wrongly attacked a Stav captain and slaughtered the Jorvan king.

The wall was my last resort. It took me too far from Roark, from Kael. It took me to open trade routes and ravagers in the wood.

I kept running.

Horns sounded again. The vibration of them rattled my marrow. I tightened the hold on my skirt and quickened my pace, only to snag my toe in a divot of earth.

My cheek struck the soil, grass coated my tongue. I scrambled to my knees, desperate to get back on my feet.

A strong, gloved hand curled around my ankle. "Melder Bien, stop. What has come over you?"

I screamed when the Stav Guard yanked me back. I kicked and thrashed. One arm was pinned behind me as the guard climbed over my back. Too strong, too tall. My sob cracked against the soil.

He reached for my hair. My elbow knocked into his jaw.

"Damn you." The Stav gave up any attempts to be gentle.

I rolled onto my hip, facing the courtyard, and my heart skipped. Sword in hand, his dark hair like the gloss of a crow, Roark stood, flanked by Thane and Emi.

"Roark!" I cried his name, the sound of it cracked. "It's Fadey!"

I wasn't certain if he could even hear. But there was strange relief knowing he was there. Hands still pawed at me, I was still in danger, but the sight of him was a lull in a storm. The Sentry saw me, and I'd been witness to what his rage could do.

Roark bent forward, like he'd been struck. His shoulders heaved for a few heartbeats. When I thought he might fall, Roark straightened.

"*Lyra!*" My name cut from his mouth, but it was stretched and prolonged, like an echo.

The jagged sound pulled away from Roark at the same time something dark, like black blood, spilled from the side of his neck, his shoulders, his ribs. A gruesome, coiled shadow billowed until it took shape with wide, broadened shoulders, long, strong legs wrapped in misty shadows. A phantom with a blade that gleamed like real steel had been the one to shout my name.

Wind and breath slowed to nothing. The guard gripping my body went still.

By the gods. Roark, my safety, my calm . . . he was Skul Drek.

Or he was part of the assassin in the shadows.

I didn't understand it and foolishly gaped, as though frozen, as Roark straightened again. He rolled his sword in one hand, then raced down the slope, darkness and misty shadows at his side.

Skul Drek lashed through a few Stav nearest to the queen's wing. Never drawing blood, merely overtaking their minds, their damn souls, until the guards fumbled on their feet, disoriented.

In the next breath, frigid coils of the inky filaments of the assassin wrapped around me and the Stav Guard. The warrior tried to flee, but the moment he turned over his shoulder, he aligned with Skul Drek's hooded face. Colorless flesh, copper-flame eyes, the sneer that could slice through the heart.

The Stav Guard had no time to move before daggers of shadows pierced through his chest, spilling through his veins like pulpy, swollen branches over his flesh. Inky black dripped from the Stav's eyes, robbing him of whatever lived in the marrow of his bones, whatever lived in the man's heart.

It was more harrowing than slicing through flesh.

When the darkness pulled back, the Stav Guard slumped forward, eyes dull. As though the man had lost any desire to thrive, he slumped onto the grass, almost lifeless.

By the gods, was that what Skul Drek did? He was a phantom connected to souls—did his shadows rob the very life from a heart? Not dead, but hardly alive.

Somewhere in the tumult of darkness, I thought I might've screamed. Only at my fear did Skul Drek cease his attack. Almost like he'd gotten lost in his own viciousness, forgetting why he'd come at all.

Palms on the damp grass, I lifted my chin. The assassin held my gaze, fire and starlight. Roark. If I peeled away the darkness, the cruelty, the fear, I could almost make out the face of the man who'd stolen my heart.

"How—" Words cut off when hands hooked under my arms.

Roark—my Roark, solid and warm—tugged me to my feet. I shoved him away, but he encircled my waist.

"No. No." Thoughts were spinning. I could not grapple with

all I was seeing. More Stav approached, but Skul Drek seemed to be all places at once. Darkness blinded the guards, then his shadows struck their hearts, never drawing blood, only taking their essence, the soul that burned unique within.

Roark held me close. He was home, warm and solid, but my mind whirled with the truth, desperate to reconcile what I now knew.

All this time, Roark Ashwood had been the demon at the gates. He'd manipulated me, attacked me, he was made of darkness.

I tried to break his hold. He pinned me to his chest and shook his head, his eyes wild. Blood soaked his neck, and his breaths were heavy.

"Lyra." Emi sprinted for us. She shoved at my back. "Not now. Go. They're coming for you!"

Drums and the bellow of horns sounded an attack.

"Hurry. We can take a horse," Emi cried. "Distract them until we reach the stables. Hold the connection, cousin. Hold it a little longer."

Roark's face contorted into a wash of pain, but he took my hand and sprinted after Emi, drawing us across the lawns toward one of the fenced yards for royal chargers to graze. Stav nearer to the outer gates bustled about, uncertain what was happening on the lawns.

Whatever pestilence came with Skul Drek dimmed the palace lawns in gloomy mists, as though a storm had descended around the royal house. It was difficult to see through the haze.

Roark stumbled. On instinct, I reached out to steady him.

Our eyes locked. There, buried in the wild gold, was pain, fear. He looked at me with a desperation I'd never seen before.

I pulled my hands away, stepping back, hurt and betrayal like venom in my blood.

"Attack at the palace," Emi cried to three fellow Stav who patrolled the outer edges of the grounds. "Sentry Ashwood was wounded. We're to evacuate the melder."

She kicked at the horrified guards. Roark's neck was sopping in blood, and his breaths came heavy. With effort, he gestured at the men to follow Emi's command, to defend the royal house.

They were taking me. No. I couldn't leave. "Wait, no!"

"Lyra, get on the damn horse." Emi shoved between my shoulders, nudging me toward a tall, black gelding. "You are the melder and must be protected. King's orders."

Good gods, she was playing such a role. Shouting loud enough any Stav would hear and ignore my frenzy, while heeding hers.

Betrayal stung.

"They have Kael," I sobbed when Roark hooked an arm around my waist, heaving me toward the horse. "They have Kael!"

A rough gasp sounded in Roark's throat, like he was choking on the blood coating his neck, or angry to think Kael was taken from me. His shoulders heaved with heavy breaths.

"Roark. Make your choice," Emi snapped. "We are out of time."

He faced the walls, then turned to the mists that looked too reminiscent of the mirror world. Sweat dampened his brow. His skin was pale. When his arms tightened around my body, my heart sank.

"No." I shook my head, fists curling around his tunic.

You above everything. His words moved against my face. *Burn it all if it means you still live.*

Roark was not gentle when he bent me across the flanks of the horse. Emi moved even swifter. She reeled around, forcing me upright in a position on the back of the horse.

"Emi, gods, stop!" I tried to shove her back as tears bled down my cheeks.

"Open your eyes, Lyra! There is no place for you here, not a place where you survive long enough to tell whatever it is you know."

Roark kicked a leg over the horse, settling behind me. I was half wrapped in his arms, half clinging to the mane of the horse.

"Go." Emi smacked the flank of the beast. "I'll meet you at the willow!"

Without a word, Roark fled toward the gates. Stav Guard were frantic, most rushing toward the palace, others preparing to seal the gates.

He sat stiff and powerful. To those watching the Sentry race away with the melder, no mistake, it would appear like a sanctioned escape to protect the king's prize. To me, I heard the rattle of his breaths, felt the heat of blood on his skin, absorbed the tremble of his hand pressed possessively on my middle.

Tears burned in my eyes, catching flecks of dust and dirt as we rode until it was difficult to see much of anything.

Ten paces from the gates and a broken, venomous shout shattered through my heart.

"Roark."

It was the only voice capable of bringing Roark to pause. The horse snorted and Roark twisted around, peering through the wisps of mists the shadow of Skul Drek kept stirring.

Thane, sweat-soaked and weary, let his sword fall from his grip.

Roark winced, and pressed a hand to his chest, a simple gesture, a plea for forgiveness.

The prince's face twisted with pain, and Roark Ashwood turned his back on Stonegate, racing us into the wood beyond the gates.

50

LYRA

SUNLIGHT PARTED THE CANOPY OF BRANCHES OVERHEAD when Roark slowed the gelding.

He shuddered and doubled over, knocking me forward across the withers.

"Roark." My throat was rough and dry from shouting. I scrambled to catch him before he toppled off the side, but merely managed to fall with him.

The horse whinnied and plodded off in a start, circling the copse until it settled for a bit of long grass. My ribs ached from where I'd struck something hard. Roark had landed on his shoulder and his body shuddered.

Darkness peeled off the trunks of trees, gathering from the edges of the wood, from every corner. Thick and cold, a shape was tangled in the billows of pitch—Skul Drek. The shade of his vibrant eyes was undeniable, and there for a mere moment before the darkness shrouded Roark.

His muscles clenched and pulsed, but as soon as the robe of shadows took him, it faded like morning mists.

Roark's teeth clacked as his body convulsed, his muscles locked. He cracked his eyes and waved one hand, trying to speak.

"What?" I rested a hand on his chest, watching his fingers.

Over and over again, he repeated one word. *Fealty*. Then lifted his opposing finger.

The fealty bond with Thane. The prince could find me through Roark.

A tap found my wrist. Roark's warm, shocking eyes locked with mine. He moved his fingers against my palm. *Take it*.

I shook my head. "No. You're . . . you're a traitor."

Roark shuddered, his jaw tensed. *Not to you*.

"It will destroy him, Lyra."

I jolted and spun toward the trees. Emi, disheveled and coated in smudges of ash and dirt, stepped between two trees. She blinked, a tear falling to her cheek. When she swiped it away, a streak of mud smeared over her face.

Emi took out a knife from a sheath on her thigh. "The place where the fealty shard was taken must be removed or the craft binding the vow will kill him. If you care for him at all, even if it is only that you want answers, sever it."

"You do it." The thought of cutting through Roark's bones was nauseating.

"Thane's connection will overpower any forced severance unless it is a person to whom Roark holds more loyalty. You are where his loyalty lies."

My pulse would not cease racing. Emi held out the knife. Roark's body was damp and flushed. He gritted his teeth, watching my every move. No mistake, he was in a great deal more pain than he let on.

If what she said was true, the loyalty he'd vowed to Thane was stronger for me. He'd said as much on the lawns—burn it all if I kept breathing.

A furrow dug between my brows when I positioned the knife against the tip of Roark's finger. Emi slid a damp twig between his teeth and drizzled the flesh and blade with ale.

She capped her skin with a shrug. "Best I can do right now."

I glanced down at Roark. His eyes burned in the golden fire I loved. The man stole his way into my heart, and now his truth tore it in two.

I swallowed, hand trembling. "I want answers."

He hesitated, but after a moment gave a quick nod.

I pressed down on the handle of the blade.

Roark's neck arched, threaded in tension, his jaw so tight I thought he might bite through the twig. Emi made quick work of wrapping the bloodied tip.

"Dammit." Emi faced her cousin, pressing her hands along his scar. Roark's face had gone pallid and more blood spilled from the wound and down his chest. "Lyra, in my pack, I have bone tonics. Get them. Now!"

My fingers were locked in spasms of nerves, but I dug through Emi's satchel until one hand curled around the cold glass of a jar. I crept to her side, unsealed the lid. Cedarwood and dust struck my nose.

"I was afraid of this. Dammit." Emi wasted no time and dipped her fingers into the slate paste. "Roark, keep breathing. Don't you dare stop."

"What's happening?"

"Someone is trying to regain control of the dark half. If they succeed and force the split when Roark is trying to hold his own control, it could kill him. We need to soothe the wound and calm the cruel edge."

I didn't understand much of anything, other than Emi thought this would kill Roark. His eyes were shut, his jaw taut, but his body wasn't thrashing so violently.

Emi coated the bloodied gash with the paste, cursing when more blood poured through. "Gods. He's moving too much; it keeps splitting the skin."

I didn't know what to do. I couldn't even think long on what had been done to cause his wound. All I could think was how I didn't want him to die. My fingers curled around his sweaty palm, and my other hand rested over his heart.

Roark's shoulder twitched, but his hand tightened around mine, almost controlled and calm.

Emi's hands stalled. She blinked to my touch, then grinned. "Keep doing that. Maybe talk to him."

I looked down at his face. Beneath the blood and sweat, Roark was there. I combed my fingers through his hair.

"I don't know what to say. Wake up, Roark Ashwood." I let my brow fall to his chest. Blood on his tunic heated my skin. I didn't pull back. "Wake up, so I can see your eyes when I kill you for all this."

At least then I will know you're alive.

ROARK'S BODY STOPPED THRASHING, AND HE LOOKED MORE LIKE he was sleeping. Emi leaned over him, checking his pastes. I finished securing torn bits of my dress around branches. We'd fashioned a makeshift bower to keep us concealed from nearby roads.

Emi placed her cloak over Roark's shoulders, then came to sit by my side. I hugged my knees against my chest and looked to the few glimmers of stars overhead.

"Lyra."

"Don't." I closed my eyes.

"Be angry if you wish, but at least allow me to explain something."

I didn't encourage her to speak, but neither did I tell her to stop. Emi's eyes glistened. She used the back of her hand to wipe away tears. "First, we will find a way to get back to Darkwin."

I pressed a fist against my mouth. With the threats Fadey and Ingir leveled at him, I could not stomach to think of what they would do.

"We love people in those gates too," Emi said, voice soft. "People who will feel utterly betrayed—"

"Because you *did* betray them." I tilted my head so my cheek rested on top of my knees. "You have kept this from everyone, from me. I told him I was being tormented by Skul Drek and all this time it was *him*."

"Tormented." Emi scoffed and looked to the sky. "You would know if you were tormented by Roark's soul."

"His . . . soul?" Soul craft.

"He should tell you his tale, for it is his. Not mine." Emi hesitated. "You are angry, and I am sorry if you feel betrayed, but what you do not know is Roark has had very little control over his existence."

"Meaning?"

"Meaning Skul Drek—even as a piece of my cousin's soul—has not answered to him. Beyond his control, blood has spilled for a duty he could never escape."

"He seemed to command it fine enough against the Stav."

"Because of you." Emi shook her head, calming her tone. "Roark is a split soul. Divided between his darkest desires and the man he is in his heart. Skul Drek is a glimpse of his most brutal, cruelest, most inhumane attributes. A damn weapon to be summoned by the one who split his soul. And he was, for years. Until you."

"I don't understand."

Emi folded her legs underneath her and held her hands, palm facing palm. "Imagine being divided in two and one side can reason and act on your own accord. The other is tethered to another mind and purpose. Half a prisoner."

With slow movements Emi began drawing her palms closer together. "Now imagine new, stronger ropes begin pulling the two halves back together. One by one the old tethers begin to snap and the divide between the sides shrinks. They start to align and move as one again. Soon, this new rope entwines with both halves and the old bonds are broken. Two halves are restored and can work as one again."

The gilded ropes in the mirror. Each time I spoke with Skul Drek one rope frayed more, and another strengthened.

I picked at a blade of tall grass at my side. "Are you saying he has drawn the two pieces of his soul back together?"

"I am saying your soul is the new rope, Lyra. You are entwined with him—both sides of him—and you fractured the craft curse that keeps him half a prisoner." Emi played with the ends of her hair. "Roark is not the first Skul Drek. It is a curse that has been burdened on an unfortunate Draven soul since the first Jorvan king realized he could steal the souls of the fallen through bone. But he is the first Skul Drek I know of to restore his two sides because he fell in love with a melder."

"Did Roark . . . know it was happening?" I lifted my gaze. "He fought Skul Drek in my chamber."

"Not at first," Emi said. "He could always sense a shift, but he wasn't connected enough to know the actions or thoughts of his dark soul. He only knew when a soul was taken, Skul Drek would be summoned to slaughter any Jorvan or Myrdan to replace the stolen soul. But the more he was near you, the more control he gained. He struck Skul Drek that night, didn't he?"

I nodded. "He threw his knife."

"I don't think either expected a wound to form. It was the first hint they were closer to converging than they were separate. The wound that should've appeared on the soul, appeared on Roark."

"Why do it if it would bring him harm?"

Emi smiled. "You still don't understand? Roark had no trust for his own divided soul since they had little connection. He took a strike to protect you."

My eyes went wide. I thought he'd been cut by Skul Drek, but Roark had injured himself . . . defending me from the darkest piece of himself.

My head was spinning. I did not know what to think. Any thought that formed faded into the next just as swiftly, all to keep the chaos spiraling in my mind.

"He was bound through his own curse and had no choice but to retaliate for every soul bone." Emi tapped my knee and stood. "I don't know much about entwined souls, but I believe you are his sjeleven. I've thought it since you admitted you can feel his words."

My breath caught. Lore on sjeleven was a romantic myth, the notion of two lovers so connected it was as though they shared one soul.

"To what depth, I can't say," Emi went on. "But I know you have brightened the darkness that has consumed him more than anyone before."

Emi left me to find a place to sleep. I looked at Roark's sleeping form and all I heard was Skul Drek's cold rasp. *You brighten the night.*

LYRA

I WOKE TO THE SNAP OF TWIGS UNDERFOOT. MISTS CURLED through the small bower hut and the surrounding wood like serpents. On the edge of the camp, Roark stood, facing the darkness of the trees. He was still dressed in his Sentry black, but his weapons were shed and his tunic was half-untucked.

For a moment I could see him as before, the Sentry, handsome and mysterious, silent and passionate.

Those hands touched gently and killed brutally.

Then on the second look, I saw the eerie eyes of a darker soul, the cold touch, the hiss of a rasp. He was Skul Drek, the assassin who'd slaughtered many, an enemy living within the walls of Stonegate.

But if he didn't realize . . .

I eased off the ground and rubbed the chill from my skin. Arms wrapped around my middle, I went to him.

One pace away, Roark turned his head, but he looked at me

only when I came to his side. For a breathless moment, we studied each other as if we'd forgotten how to speak.

When he made no move to form a gesture, I spoke first.

"I never saw the glow of your form."

A groove formed between his brows.

One corner of my lips curved into a weak smile. "When I would meld, anyone in the room glowed while I was in the trance. But not you. I didn't realize it until now."

Roark squared to me. The pastes had dried and chipped off his scar. It looked as it always did now. Raised, red skin from jaw to the opposite side of his chest.

"Whenever I went into the mirror," I repeated, "I didn't see the light of your soul because you were there with me."

He held out a hand, but recoiled when I flinched.

Roark dropped his chin. *You did not see the light because it does not exist within me and you were never meant to see my darker pieces.*

"So you would've gone on lying to me, letting me love you?" My voice croaked. Roark's head snapped up, but the words would not stop. "I told you about how I feared the shadows, how I feared him, how I was *drawn* to him, and you said nothing.

It should never have meant anything. Roark took a step closer. *I was supposed to despise you, hunt you. Instead, you've brought me to my knees, begging for more of you.*

He towered over me, our chests touched, and I didn't step back. We faced each other, a challenge, a desire.

Roark's eyes softened, and he spoke close to my face. *Break me, I no longer care, as long as it is you who wields the destruction.*

"I don't know what to think. Emi told me you could not control it, but now you can." I closed my eyes for a heartbeat, trying to slow the noise in my thoughts. "After all that has happened, all the lies from everyone, I only want a bit of truth."

Roark swallowed, and when I sat on a fallen log, he sat beside me.

Yesterday was the first time I commanded the divide within me. His gestures were slow and deliberate. He did not want me to misunderstand a word. *I think that is why it erupted with such violence.*

Roark gestured at his scar.

I lifted a hand and ran my trembling fingertips along the jagged scar over his throat. "You told me this was done to you."

He nodded. *It was done as punishment, cursing me to be the one forced to find you.*

I blinked. "But why?"

Roark looked at me, eyes shadowed. *I remember the raids now. Everything.*

"You remember that night?" I swallowed. "You were the one who took me away . . . to the sea, weren't you? I was placed on a longship."

I was there.

I pressed my fists to my forehead, moments spinning, some felt like a dream, others real enough I could smell the sweat, the spray of the sea. "A tide wanderer brought me to Gammal. I . . . I think we met in a market and she took me to the young house."

Roark nodded. *The woman was from across the Night Ledges from one of the Unfettered clans and cared little about craft. She would not give you up.*

"Why were you there, Roark?"

He bent his knees and let his forearms drape over the tops. *I wanted to be one of the Dark Watch. I followed the prince's raiders, got turned around in the wood, and stumbled down a knoll into the goat pen of a small house.*

I closed my eyes. "I remember. My mother sent me to lock the goat pens. We didn't know what was coming." I blinked my gaze back to him. "Why didn't you kill me when you saw the scars?"

Roark pressed a hand to his chest, then with a bit of hesitation, reached across and touched the place over my heart. *You brightened my soul and I knew.*

Blood thudded between my ears. "Knew what?"

He held my stare for a long pause. *You were mine.*

Mine. Skul Drek said my soul was his; Roark claimed the rest.

With the heel of my hand I swiped away a stray tear. "How could you know?"

Soul craft is in my veins, Lyra. Because of it, soul bonds are felt so fiercely it is undeniable. They are sacred in Dravenmoor. I felt it the moment you touched me that night.

"But you hated me in Skalfirth."

Roark dropped his chin and traced the long trail of his scar. *The bond was shadowed. For a moment. That first damn star plum you threw at my head cracked the shields against you. I could not take my eyes off you. If I hated you, it was because I could not understand why I wanted you.*

It had been much the same for me, from the way Roark had pinned me to him in the great hall in Skalfirth, to moments on the longship. I'd yearned to detest him, but found a calm around him in the same breath.

"I lied to you," I said slowly. "About learning your words. I felt them from the beginning."

Roark's jaw worked for a breath before he looked to the soil, as though he didn't know what to say.

I cleared my throat. "You say you were punished because you got the prince killed. Is that the truth?"

His palm rubbed the side of his neck. *Prince Nivek saw me speaking to you. When he cornered me in the wood, I told him the truth. The melder was supposed to be a monster, a brute we should delight in killing. Not a girl who burned through me. Once the prince believed me, he agreed to help hide you.*

"The arms in my dreams," I whispered more to myself than Roark. "Why don't I remember?"

The prince was called the soul shadower. Roark's eyes burned with regret. *His craft helped him darken experiences a soul has endured.*

"And doing so takes the memory?"

Shadows it.

I coiled a lock of hair around my finger. "Until you. The memories returned the more I was around you."

Perhaps I was not the only one who brightened a soul.

"The prince took me to the sea. He saved me." I didn't want to ask the question. "How did he die?"

Roark raked his fingers through his hair. *My uncle discovered what we had done. Our people determined the prince was a traitor, and . . . slit his throat before he could even get a trial.*

All gods. Bile burned on my tongue. An enemy prince saved me, then lost his life for it. "And you? They did this to you?"

My fingers gingerly touched the cursed scar.

My mother pled with the council to punish me another way. Used my youth as the bargaining chip. They agreed to split my soul, forced me to kill, until the lost melder was found again. They knew you were still alive. I wasn't welcome to wait with my clan and was left at the gates of enemies. If I survived, if I proved myself, then I would earn a place in the clan again.

"And how were you supposed to prove yourself? I've seen you kill many Dravens."

Roark let out a breath. *I was to kill the lost melder when she was found.*

It was as though a fist struck my throat, robbing me of breath. For a moment we were still, silent.

"But you didn't."

Roark shook his head. *Before you ever reached Stonegate, I was planning to kill you, but I was already drawn to you. When the fara wolf was sent, I couldn't let you die.*

"Sent?" My voice cracked. "The wolf was *sent* to kill me?"

Yes. Roark studied his palms. *The attacks came to the walls because I betrayed my folk again.*

Because he didn't kill me. The same as he'd done as a boy.

"Why were you not supposed to kill Fadey?" I asked. Roark's soul had been divided while Fadey still served as the melder.

I had to learn to fight. The more blood I spilled as a Stav, the darker the soul became. Fadey was allowed to meld, so attacks would be leveled at Stonegate, to give me a chance for bloodshed.

"But you killed your own people."

Roark's face was twisted in bitterness. *Ravagers are expendable. Thieves, rapists, traitors. To fight against the Stav is their trial. Survive, and they can return. Die, and their penance is paid. I didn't mind killing them.*

"I don't know what to think," I said, voice soft. "Did you know the darker soul spoke to me in the melder's trance?"

No. Only a sense, at first. The more time went on, the more I recalled and was drawn to you.

"Did you truly have no control over the attacks after soul bones were taken?"

His fingers moved slowly. *Control belonged to another. I gained more as time went on, but there was always a divide until this.*

He waved a hand around at the trees.

Fate or something crueler had always been there, weaving my path with Roark Ashwood.

"How does"—I struggled to speak the name—"Skul Drek kill if it is a dark piece of a soul?"

Roark studied me, remorse in his eyes. *By killing a soul.*

By the gods. "How?"

I can attack piece by piece until a soul's light flickers out and nothing but a husk is left behind for blades to finish.

"The soul bones shield against it, though, don't they?" I thought back to the endless battle with the Berserkir. Only after the shield of soul bones split was it possible to destroy him.

Roark gave a stiff nod.

My head spun in endless questions. "Will those who controlled your darker soul retaliate, knowing they've lost you?"

Roark looked over his shoulder toward the cliffs in the North. *We should make our way to the Night Ledges before we find out.*

"I cannot leave Kael at Stonegate, not with Fadey and Ingir. They will hurt him. They could hurt everyone."

Roark's fist curled over his knee. He spoke briskly with the other hand. *We need to plan before we return.*

"You'll . . . you'll go back for him?"

Roark's gaze burned when he met mine, the same familiar viciousness of the Sentry written in his features. *I swear it.*

The declaration was simple, but each gestured word cut to my marrow, a vow deeper than blood.

I did not know what to make of him. A liar? A protector? A lover? I looked down at my hands, tangling my fingers in a patch of long grass. "Thane didn't know about Skul Drek, did he?"

Anger faded from Roark's features and they filled with pain. He shook his head.

"And you weren't pretending to care for him?"

He narrowed his gaze. *Thane was the brother I did not expect. I betrayed him and will deserve his hatred. My folk wanted my loyalty after tearing out my voice to split my soul, but my fealty to Thane was not a lie. I simply had more loyalty to you in the end.*

I rested a tentative palm on his leg. "How is it Skul Drek can speak?"

He shook his head. With a bit of hesitation, Roark touched the place over my heart with one hand, and spoke with the other. *Soul to soul.*

My breath caught. The more I thought on it, the more it was true. Skul Drek spoke to me with only his rough, strained voice when we were in the mirror land. "The soul was speaking to mine?"

I didn't know such a thing was possible. The slightest grin tugged at the corners of his mouth. He looked at his bandaged fingertip. *We will need to find a way to warn the prince about his mother. If he will even listen to me.*

"Thane will understand."

Do you?

I wasn't certain how to answer.

When I took too long, Roark looked away. *My duty was to destroy melders, even if it meant harming Thane. And I did, remember?*

"I remember the prince was attacked by Skul Drek." My voice was steady, gentle. "And I recall the despondent Sentry who sat by his bedside until he was healed. A man who, I now realize, was likely blaming himself for something beyond his control."

Roark looked at me like he hadn't truly seen me before. *I never lied about what I feel for you, Lyra. Do you know that?*

Perhaps it was true, but he'd been the man fated to capture me, destroy me. Then again, he'd saved me as a girl and loved me as a woman.

Both Roark and Skul Drek had become a united force to keep me alive.

Roark rubbed his thumb over the back of my hand. *There is something else you must know about me—*

"We're not alone." Emi shoved through the bower, blade in hand. Her pale hair was wild and tangled, and her stormy eyes were red and swollen. Did she cry for Yrsa? For Thane? For her cousin? Likely all of it. But there was the warrior gleam in her eyes now as she scanned the treetops. "We're being watched."

Roark stood, one hand on my arm. He urged me behind him. Emi tossed him his bearded ax. He caught the handle and rotated it once in his palm.

I saw nothing, heard nothing, until a twig snapped. Until dark figures split the mists. Shoulders, broadened with furs and cloaks, stepped into our hideaway. Some held blades with black-leather-wrapped hilts. Others kept arrows made of wood with raven-feather fletching trained on our hearts.

My heart stilled when half a dozen fara wolves entered the clearing, heads lowered, jagged teeth bared. Each wolf had runes painted on their fur and leather bands around their neck, as though they were common hounds.

"Saw you in the trees." A man tossed back his hood, revealing similarly inked runes across his brow and a tight ridge of dark hair braided in a long plait, the sides of his hair shorn close to his scalp. "Been some time since I laid eyes on you. Finally saw it done, then?"

Roark stiffened, and nausea rose in my stomach. They were not Stav, but they did not dress as tattered as ravagers.

Emi let out a sharp gasp when two archers parted and a woman stepped between them.

She was beautifully frightening. Sharp features, dark lips, and amber hair wrapped in tight braids around her head. Blue eyes took in each of us as they swirled and thrashed like a cerulean tide. She laced her fingers together, the bloodred paint on her sharp fingernails a contrast to her dark gown and bear fur mantle across her shoulders.

Atop her head was a circlet in the shape of black ivy.

I did not need to see the warriors nearest to her genuflect to know her—Elisabet. The queen of Dravenmoor.

"I have awaited this day for so long," the queen said, her grin pinned on Roark. "This is the melder, I presume?"

Roark stepped in front of me, his grip tightening on the ax handle.

Elisabet's features hardened. "You still protect her? After all I did to keep you alive."

She tried to keep Roark alive?

He spun the ax in his hand again as a reply.

The queen rolled her shoulders back. With a glance at her men, she waved her hand toward me. "Seize her."

The instant the shrubs moved with Elisabet's Dark Watch, shadows surrounded me and Roark's hand took hold of my wrist, but there was more.

The Draven warriors reeled back when Skul Drek's menacing presence enveloped me—a dark shield between me and them.

I leaned into Roark, holding steady, ready to reach for the dagger sheathed to my thigh if it came to that.

Another sigh, and the queen waved off her guard. "Enough."

Little by little the darkness of his divided soul faded, but the ferocity of Skul Drek remained written on Roark's face as he made swift, threatening gestures to the queen.

"We do not stand down if the melder is not given safe passage with your men," Emi translated, a slight quiver to her tone. She feared the queen.

Rightfully so. When Elisabet looked her way, a snarl curled

her painted lips. "Your father will be looking forward to seeing you, niece."

Niece? My insides tightened.

Roark cast a look my way. *I was trying to tell you.*

He didn't have time to go on before Elisabet lifted her hand. "Lower your blades. We are kin. If safe passage home is what you require for the woman, then you shall have it."

Swear it, Roark demanded.

Emi's voice was not so sharp when she relayed the command.

The queen's peaceful facade cracked for only a moment before she snapped her fingers at the man who'd first spoken. "Fillip, tell the others in the trees the melder will reach our gates unharmed."

A man with golden hoops pierced along the curves of both ears dipped his chin, and barked orders at the others. They wasted no time raiding our camp.

Elisabet looked back to Roark. "We're not here to battle, after all. We only have cause for celebration. My second son, our prince, has finally returned home."

GLOSSARY

Berserkir (bare-ser-kerr): Elite warriors of Stonegate.

berserksgangur (bur-serks-gahn-gr): Untamed rage and bloodlust of Berserkirs.

blood craft: The magical ability to cast spells with runes and blood.

bone craft: The magical ability to manipulate, weaken, and break bones.

craft: Magic.

Divisive Wars: The battles that divided the realms into the three kingdoms.

Dravenmoor: The kingdom of Queen Elisabet. Home of soul crafters.

elskan: An endearment like "darling" or "my dear."

fara wolf: Trained and bonded wolves used by Dravenmoor.

florin: Currency.

fossegrim: A water spirit from Norse folklore that uses a fiddle/violin to lure humans.

god-queen, the: The Wanderer King's wife.

jarl/jarldom: Similar to a lord, the jarl leads and hails over his/her own territory within a kingdom.

Jorvandal: The kingdom of King Damir. Typically the home of bone crafters.

Jul: A winter holiday.

melder: A rare magical person born once a generation with the power to meld dead bone to bone to summon the strength of a fallen soul into the living.

Myrda: The kingdom of King Hundur. Holds an alliance with Jorvandal and is typically the home of blood crafters.

Night Ledges: Mountain range dividing the realms of Stìgandr from open territory.

realms of Stìgandr (stee-gander): The continent of the three kingdoms.

Salur: Otherworld, like Valhalla.

seasons: Term to signify years or passing time.

seax: A type of sword.

ser: Sir, mister.

soul bones: Marked bones of the dead used to create Berserkir warriors.

soul craft: The magical ability to manipulate, sever, and control souls of the living and dead.

Stav Guard: The warriors of Stonegate.

Stonegate: Royal keep of King Damir.

súlka: Miss, ma'am.

tagelharpa: A stringed instrument.

thorn blossoms: Used to create dyes to hide silver scars in the eyes.

Unfettered Folk: Clan living over the Night Ledges that serves no kingdom.

Wanderer King: Believed to be the first king of the realms, the father of magical craft.

ACKNOWLEDGMENTS

I've written many of these acknowledgments, but this one is special. It is my first with a wonderful publisher who stepped onto this journey with me.

First, as always, I must thank my husband, Derek, and our four kids. You have walked through the mud and late nights and Viking metal music with me from the beginning. You all are literally in the author name of this book. I love you all so, so much.

To Katie Shea Boutillier, my agent—I will never forget the first time we connected. I will never be able to thank you enough for the place you've helped me to rise to in my author career. I will die on the hill of you being a unicorn agent. There's no changing my mind on this.

To my family—both blood and found—I could not do this without you. My parents, for supporting me through it all and instilling my love of storytelling. You both never let a good story go by, whether it was the sagebrush (which was really troll hair) or reading books to us at night. To my sisters—Katie, Aubrey, and

Shalee. How lucky am I to have you bouncing around the country with me to book signings and our random "staff" meetings where we ramble more than anything. I couldn't do this without any of you. To Sara, for always reading every word I write and helping me see things in a different light.

To Kaylee and Jasmine—gosh I love you both. I am so grateful for your guidance in my stories and your help when I feel like I can't see my own plot. Here's to many more books.

To my editor, Kristine Swartz—thank you for helping me realize I can't just say something epic happened, I actually need to explain how it was even a possibility. With your insight, this book turned into something not even I could see when we first started developing this idea. I have learned so much from you and can't wait to learn even more. Thank you for helping find Roark and Lyra and giving them the story they deserve.

Thank you to my beautiful readers. I get emotional just thinking of you, Wicked Darlings. You have cheered me on, helped me realize how strong the book community can truly be, and have become some of my favorite humans. I owe so much to you and you will always be my "folk."

Thank you to my father in heaven for leading me on this journey. It has been life-changing.

And last of all, I'd like to thank the LJ from nearly ten years ago. I'd like to thank her for never giving up on the stories in her head even when it seemed like no one would ever read them. Here's to us for pushing through it all and finding our voice. And, of course, here's to more wickedly romantic tales.

Thank you,

LJ

Keep reading for a preview of the first book
in the Ever Seas series by LJ Andrews

THE
EVER
KING

That Night

THE ENDING NEEDED TO BE ALTERED.

The girl spent the whole of the afternoon crossing out lines with her raven-feather quill, then adding new, better words to read to the boy in the dark. A tale of a serpent who befriended a songbird. A tale where they lived happily ever after, for in the girl's version, the snake never devoured the bird.

Long after the moon found its highest perch in the night sky, the girl slipped from the loft in the battle fort near the shore. Crouched low, she used the tall snake grass as a shield until she found her way to the old stone tower. The top had caved in, and it wasn't much of a tower anymore, but the walls were thick as two men standing side by side.

Along the foundation, iron bars covered a few openings. In her head, the girl counted six barred windows before she crouched at the final cell.

"Bloodsinger," she whispered. Since the end of the battle, she'd practiced the breathy pitch to be loud enough so the boy inside would hear, but the guards stomping along the borders would think it nothing more than the hiss of a forest creature.

Five breaths, ten, then red eyes like a stormy sunset appeared from the shadows.

He was a frightening boy. A few turns older than her, but he'd fought in the war. He'd raised a sword against her people's warriors. A boy who still had dried blood on his skin.

Her heart squeezed with a strange dread she didn't understand. This was the last night she might see the boy; she needed to make it count.

"Trials come with the sun," the boy said, his voice dry as brittle straw. "Better leave, little princess."

"But I have something for you, and I've got to finish the story." From the pouch slung over her shoulder, the girl took out a small book, bound in tattered leather. Inked over the cover was a black silhouette of a bird and a coiled snake. "Want to hear the end?"

The boy didn't blink for a long pause. Then, slowly, he sat on the damp earth and crossed his legs under his lanky body.

The girl read the final pages marked in her new, palatable ending. The songbird and serpent grew to be friends despite their differences. No lies, no cunning, no tricks. Each word drew her closer to the bars until her head rested against the cold iron and one hand drooped between the gaps, as though reaching for the boy inside.

"'They played from sunup to sundown,'" she read, squinting at her messy writing. "'And lived happily ever after.'"

A smile crossed her features when she closed the bindings and glanced at the boy.

He'd reclined back onto his palms now, legs out, bare ankles crossed. "Is that what we are, princess? A serpent and a songbird?"

Her smile widened. He understood the whole point. "I think so, and they were still friends. That's why tomorrow at the trials you can, well, you can say we won't fight no more. My folk will let you stay."

No more blood. No more nightmares. The girl couldn't stomach any more blood from hate and war.

When the boy kept quiet, she dug back into her pouch and took out the twine. On the end was a silver charm she'd used her last copper to buy. A silver charm of a swallow in flight.

"Here." She held out the handmade necklace through the bars and let it fall. "I thought it could remind you of the story."

All at once the distance between them was a blessing. Any closer and the boy might see the flush of pink in her cheeks. He might see that her hope in the charm was less about recalling the tale and more about remembering *her.*

With slow movements the boy took hold of the charm. His dirty thumb brushed over the wings. "Tomorrow I'll see the gods or be sent away, Songbird."

Her stomach dipped and something warm, like spilled tea, flooded her insides. Songbird. She liked the name.

"That's what happens when you lose a war." The boy's lips twitched when he placed the twine around his neck. "There's no stopping it."

The race of her heart dimmed. She dropped her chin. Hopeful as she was, the girl wasn't a fool. She knew the only thing saving the boy's neck was that he *was* a boy. Should he be a man, he'd lose his head. He had fought against her people; he hated them.

Like the serpent from the story hated the birds in the trees for their freedom in the skies.

She didn't care. A feeling, deep in her bones, drew her to the boy. She'd hoped he might be drawn to her too.

Hope failed. While he was young, he'd always be marked as an enemy. Banished and forbidden.

She blinked and reached once more into the fur-lined pouch. "I know this is important to your folk. Thought maybe you'd want to see it once more."

The girl cupped the gold talisman, shaped like a thin disk, with care. It was weathered and aged and delicate. A faint hum of strange remnants of magic lived in the gritty edges. If her father ever learned she'd snatched the piece from the lockbox, he'd probably keep her locked in her room for a week.

Overhead, the moonlight gleamed over the strange rune in the center of the coin. The boy in the shadows let out a gasp. She didn't think he'd meant to do it.

For the first time since she'd started reading to him, the boy climbed up the stone wall and curled his hands around the bars. The red in his eyes deepened like blood. His smile was different. Wide enough she could see the slight point to his side tooth, almost like the fang of a wolf, only not as long.

This smile sent a shiver up her arms.

"Will you do something for me, Songbird?"

"What?"

The boy nodded at the disk. "That was a gift from my father. Watch over it for me, will you? I'll come back to get it one day, and you can tell me more stories. Promise?"

The girl ignored the wave of gooseflesh up her arms and whispered, "Promise."

When the sound of heavy boots scraped over the dirt nearby, the girl gave one final look at the boy in the darkness. He held up the silver bird charm and grinned that wolfish grin once more before she sprinted into the grass.

The speed of her pulse ached as she hurried back to the longhouse. Her gaze was locked on the disk in her hands; she never saw the root bursting from the soil. The thick arch snagged hold of her toe and sprawled the girl facedown in the soil.

She coughed and scrambled back to her knees. When she looked down, her insides twisted up like knotted ropes.

"Oh, no."

The disk she'd promised to protect mere moments before had fallen beneath her body. Now the shimmer of gold lay in three jagged pieces in the soil. Tears blurred her vision as she gathered the pieces, sobbing promises to the night that she'd fix it, she'd repair what was broken.

Perhaps it was the despair that kept her from noticing the strange rune, once marked on the surface of the disk, now branded the smooth skin below the crook of her elbow.

In time, the more she learned of the viciousness of the sea fae who attacked her people, the more the girl looked back on that night like a shameful secret. She made up tales about the scar on her arm, a clumsy stumble down the cobbled steps in the gardens. She'd forget the boy's promise to come for her.

The girl would start to think of him as everyone else—the enemy.

If only the girl had kept away from those cells that night, perhaps she would not have unraveled her entire world.

LJ ANDREWS is a *USA Today* bestselling author of fantasy romance. She mystically creates worlds of dark Nordic and Viking myths bound by conflicts that bring together impassioned heroes and heroines. In her non-author moments, she is courageously corralling her four children to the myriad of activities that life involves, along with spending time with her favorite hero, her husband. Add two high-maintenance dogs and a sassy conure to the mix and that sums it up. LJ Andrews thrives spending time in the Rocky Mountains in Utah, where she lives.